Praise for

THE SHIKSA SYNDROME

"Saturating this fluffy romantic comedy of errors is a more subtle commentary about religion and identity that raises the question: How much of yourself do you have to give up in order to be with someone else?"

—*San Francisco Chronicle*

"Aimee's stumbling journey to self-discovery . . . provides funny moments."
—*USA Today*

"Readers will enjoy Aimee's chance to rediscover herself and to recognize what she truly values."
—*Library Journal*

"A witty read with the satisfying crunch of crusty rye and the sting of hot mustard, no matter what you put between the slices."
—*Jewish News of Greater Phoenix*

"At first, Laurie Graff's novel made me wish that I was a shiksa. Then I was glad that I wasn't. Now I'm more confused than ever."
—Alan Zweibel, Thurber Prize–winning author of
The Other Shulman and *Clothing Optional*

"If you've got a funny bone, Graff will latch on and refuse to let go."
—*LibraryJournal.com*

"Hilarity ensues."
—*Glamour.com*

"On a scale from one to ten this gets ten stars . . . of David."
—Beyond Her Book, *Publishers Weekly* blog

"A light, fun read . . . amid the dead-on descriptions of Jewish life in New York [the author] slips in many profound observations."
—*Jerusalem Post*

"Navigating the cyber pond with Karrie Kline while *Looking for Mr. Goodfrog* leaves one laughing on the outside while your heart is breaking on the inside! I found it ribbiting."   —Jamie Gertz, actress

"Graff . . . offers a fun tour of New York, and readers will welcome the return of her smart narrator."   —*Publishers Weekly*

"Sweet and satisfying."   —*Chicago Sun-Times*

"Readers will be happy . . . and will eagerly turn the pages."   —*Booklist*

ALSO BY LAURIE GRAFF

You Have to Kiss a Lot of Frogs
Looking for Mr. Goodfrog

The
Shiksa Syndrome

LAURIE GRAFF

Broadway Books
New York

For my mom, Lonnie, with love

This is a work of fiction. Names, characters, places, and incidents either are the product of the author's imagination or are used fictitiously. Any resemblance to actual persons, living or dead, events, or locales is entirely coincidental.

Copyright © 2008 by Laurie Graff

Published in the United States by Broadway Books,
an imprint of the Crown Publishing Group,
a division of Random House, Inc., New York.
www.crownpublishing.com

BROADWAY BOOKS and the Broadway Books colophon
are trademarks of Random House, Inc.

Originally published in hardcover in the United States by Broadway Books,
New York, in 2008.

Library of Congress Cataloging-in-Publication Data
Graff, Laurie.
  The Shiksa syndrome / Laurie Graff.
      p.   cm.
  1. Jewish women—Fiction. 2. Dating (Social customs)—Fiction.
3. Jewish fiction. I. Title.

  PR9199.4.G69S55 2008
  813'.6—dc22

                                                2008001539

ISBN 978-0-7679-2762-8

Printed in the United States of America

BOOK DESIGN BY AMANDA DEWEY
ILLUSTRATION BY PENNY CARTER

10 9 8 7 6 5 4 3 2 1

First Paperback Edition

ACKNOWLEDGMENTS

My agent, Irene Goodman, knew this would be a novel before I did, and with her persistence and encouragement I finally had no choice but to write it. Especially after she sold it! Irene's been my rock, and without doubt if you are reading this now it is because of her.

How fortunate I am to work with the talented team at Doubleday Broadway! Led by my editor, Stacy Creamer, it includes Anne Watters, Lindsay Gordon, Laura Swerdloff, Jean Traina, Elizabeth Rendfleisch, Vicki Haire, Sean Mills, Julie Sills, Caroline Sill, and Judy Jacoby.

Extraspecial thanks to Deb Futter; also to Dianne Choie, Abby Weintraub, Barbara Poelle, and Miriam Kriss.

My gratitude extends to Jamie Callan, my go-to person for everything; brainstorm buddy Sean Hanley; photographer Eric Liebowitz; sounding board Stew Zuckerbrod; and my brother, Steve Levine. Nancy Kellogg-Gray, Marian Sabat, and Yitzhak Buxbaum answered questions along with Karen Rice and Pastor Ken Gorsuch of the West End Collegiate Church. Janet Widzbell and the Hilton Scranton were most helpful on a research trip to Pennsylvania made with Buck Wolf. I had great support from many friends, my entire extended family, colleagues at TheLadders.com, J. Roderick, Inc., and the WorkShop Theater Company, and my own Congregation B'nai Jeshurun.

Ramy Cosmetic's pink perfection of *Shiksa Goddess!*, a lipstick created just for this book, is a thrill (www.ramy.com).

All was shared with my uncle, Jerry Graff. A musician, he thrived on the creative process. Even on his worst day of chemo, he championed both me and this book. Sadly, he won't get to read it. I like to think that somehow a copy has found its way into his hands.

shik·sa (shĭk'sə)*

n. Yiddish

1. A non-Jewish woman. 2. A quintessential blonde
beauty. 3. The polar opposite of the quintessential
Jewish mother. 4. A type of woman who instills deep
longing in short, dark, swarthy Jewish men. 5. A Jewish
boy's dream. 6. A Jewish girl's nightmare.

* Yiddish/Hebrew glossary appears at the back of the book.

Boy Vey

I T WOULD BE ONE THING if I didn't love being Jewish. If I
were more like my cousin Marni, who boasts about exchanging Hanukkah gifts on Christmas because she's such a bad Jew.
Perhaps I'd understand if I grew up in some small remote town,
in the only Jewish family for miles on end, total assimilation the
key to survival. But I didn't. Raised on New York's Upper West
Side, I never even rebelled. Shiksa wannabee nowhere on my
wish list. So standing next to my gorgeous goyishe boyfriend, à
la *American Gothic,* I'm way beyond bah, humbug.

I watch Peter carve the ham as expressionless as the girl in
that portrait. Knowing I don't want to be here cohosting this
party. Guiltily wanting to leave now and go back to work. Wishing I could just celebrate Christmas the Jewish way, with Chinese food and a movie.

"Hey, everyone," Peter calls out to the room of hungry or-
phans, half of them tangled up in a game of Twister. Oh. Not
what you think. It's an orphan Christmas party, for people who
can't make it home. "Listen up. Dinner is served."

"And," I chime in, "after Christmas dinner we're going to play *dreidel, dreidel, dreidel* and then have latkes and sour cream for dessert."

Baxter, Peter's lovable mutt, barks in approval. But his master only shakes his head. "Aimee Albert."

"What?" Like I don't know.

"It's enough you brought bagels," says Peter, looking at the mixed dozen strategically placed between the green bean casserole, marshmallow sweet potatoes, and his grandmother's pumpkin pie.

"Well, you told me to bring bread." A publicist, I always know a good spin.

"Hey, great party, McKnight," interrupts Jax, Peter's new best bud from the LaughTrack. He grabs an everything bagel and with a fork smears the insides with mustard. "Making myself here a big ole ham sandwich. And then point me to those latkes. Christmas was never like this in Scranton."

"See, P. What've you got to say to that?"

Peter doesn't answer. For a stand-up, he's not so fast with the comebacks.

"You made it," he says, instead, greeting the couple who just walked in. A couple who happen to be my parents.

"Will you look at all this," says Maddie, unzipping her black down coat before handing it to my dad. "Peter, you did all this yourself?"

Running her red manicured fingers through her touched-up brown hair, my mother's sure to catch my eye when she speaks. We had a big to-do this morning when she found out I was going into work instead of coming straight to Peter's.

"You're not going early to help him?" she shrieked into my cell phone. "You're just going to show up? Like a guest?"

The working-on-Christmas tradition began almost a decade

ago with my then boyfriend. Sam's gone more than six years, but it's continued. My tradition's harder to break than my fast on Yom Kippur. Besides, Peter managed just fine.

"Everything like my mom," he answers, I think a little sad. The first Christmas he's not spent at home. Last year, we'd only known each other a few months, and he went without me. This is his first with me, and a first for me.

"Hey, can you heat up more of those latkes?"

"Mom, Dad, this is Jax," I introduce. "Peter's friend. A comedian from the club."

"Sid Albert," my father says, extending his hand. "So how's the comedy business, Jax? I'll be honest with you. I always wonder how anyone makes a living at that."

So do Jax and Peter, I think, grateful at least one of them is out of earshot.

"What do you do, sir?" Jax responds, appropriately ignoring the question.

"Advertising. Consumer. Like Aimee here," Sid eagerly explains, seventy-two, retirement nowhere in sight. He talks over his shoulder as he goes to the food table to make himself a plate.

"Actually I'm in consumer PR, and it's a totally different thing," I tell Jax before I head to the kitchen. I hear the voice of my father, who's found a captive audience, trail behind me.

"Aimee says PR creates news you can use, but all that's the spin. You're really just talking about a product. I'm telling you, Jax, if you have good advertising . . ."

". . . you don't need PR," I mouth, finishing the sentence along with my father and suddenly my mother, who followed me into the kitchen. We shake our heads and laugh while I pick up a potholder to open the oven door.

"This party is so lovely," says Maddie. She pulls a small ice-cream chair out from under the small, round table and sits. "Daddy and I just dropped by for a bit. We're making a matinee. I thought we'd all go, but I'm glad you're here with Peter. You should celebrate with him. After all, it is his holiday."

She's so observant.

"How's Daph?" I ask. My sister and her husband, Rich, fled the New Jersey burbs of West Orange to spend the holiday at their time-share in Aruba. The luxury of being married to a part-ner in a law firm. Ever since Sam, this is a subject my mother and I no longer discuss.

"She sent an e-mail to say they landed. Your father got it out of the computer. I'm still not sure how to work that *farkakte* printer."

Maddie's Hanukkah gift from Sid. Or maybe Sid's Hanukkah gift to Sid.

"Hannah and Holdenn are having a ball," she says. Grandchil-dren courtesy of my younger sibling. The middle, I now think of my older.

"Jon still in Italy?" I ask, removing the hot dish from the oven and placing it on top of the stove.

"You want me to put the latkes on this tray?" Maddie stands, eager to help.

"He's on location. And I can tell by what he doesn't say my son's got a new one." She blows on a potato pancake before tak-ing it into her mouth.

"He e-mailed something vague about an Italian *Vogue* model." The humdrum life of a Soho photographer. "So. Another lasting *shidduch*, huh, Ma?"

"Jonathan doesn't have to marry right away. He has more time. He's a boy."

"Hello. He just turned forty-four," I say, annoyed with the double standard, biology, and my mother's quick defense of the

Jewish Prince, rightful pedigree of her firstborn son. "Speaking of, guess who I ran into today? Remember Michael Cohen?" He was all I talked about as a teen; how could she not? "He's in finance now, married, two kids. They're moving back to the city."

"Really!" Though my mother's quite fond of Peter, I swear she's disappointed I'll never reconnect with my old Hebrew school flame. "Jewish?" she asks, I know, of the wife.

"Converted." Finding more eggnog in the fridge, I begin to pour several containers into a big mixing bowl.

"Makes sense to me. Girls will do anything for a good Jewish husband. And why not?"

"*That* was really unkind," I bite, as the comment does. Though my mother *has* mellowed. If ten years ago I brought home a non-Jewish out-of-work comedian, Maddie would have gone through the roof. But that was *before*. Now having hurt her, my mother barks back.

"What's going on in here?" My father's gray curly head pops through the kitchen door. The damage control detector heard above the noise of the party.

"We're coming. Can you grab that, Ma?" I say of the hot tray, eager to escape the heat of the kitchen.

"Oh, Aimee, I forgot to tell you," Maddie chatters behind me. "I ran into Rosie and Bill in the elevator, and guess what? Stefani Carter's getting remarried."

Only I don't quite make it out unscathed. "Why are you so provocative, Ma?"

"Who's Stefani?" intercepts Jax, rushing to take a few latkes from the tray before Maddie even makes it to the table.

"Neighbors in our building. She grew up with Aimee," my father says, beaming at the mention of the buxom blonde.

I still shudder when I remember rehearsing our number

from *The Sound of Music* for her church's Christmas pageant. As Maria, little Stefani danced barefoot across her living room, her hills alive. Meanwhile, I practically sweat to death as Mother Superior. My head clad in scarves, itching in my mom's black wool dress. A habit I wanted to break.

"Says the guy's crazy about Stef," my mother proceeds to tell Jax. "He's a director on that soap she's on," she continues, rearranging the food. "And this one's Jewish."

"And why not? Makes total sense to me," says Sid.

"How so?" asks Jax, reaching past him for the sour cream. Sid's new sidekick.

"She's what they call a Shiksa Goddess," says Sid, cleaning his wire-rim glasses with his shirttail. "Jewish men are very attracted to that," he explains to the clueless comic.

"So she's as cute as Aimee?" asks Jax.

"No one's as cute as Aimee," rescues Peter, putting his arm around me. "Hey, come on. We're ready to play Thieving Secret Santa. You guys in?" he asks my parents.

My mother looks at her watch. "We're going to have to leave," she announces. Not a moment too soon. "Thank you for everything, Peter. Sid, get the coats. And Aimee, come here for a second. I want to talk to you."

I signal Peter to go on without me. My first mistake. Then I turn to talk to my mother, about to make my second.

"If I tell you something about other people, it has nothing to do with you, you understand?" she says. "So I don't know why you make everything so personal. I'm just talking."

"Good. Are you done?"

About to say more, she is interrupted by my father.

"Mad, come on." At the front door with Peter, Sid calls to my mother, her coat draped over his arm.

Maddie's eyes shift up, and with a quick glance I see her check the clock. Knowing her routines by heart, I expect she'll now remind me mine is ticking . . . and loudly. "If we waste time, we'll miss out," we both hear my father interject. Her point exactly, and so conveniently made, she just gives me a kiss good-bye and brushes past, leaving me to rejoin the party.

My mother is gone, but her words stay behind, sticking around for the rest of the day. By the end, they attach themselves to all the dirty dishes, glomming on to each piece of silverware, every glass and tray. Later, at Peter's kitchen sink, I clean up the mess. But despite many squirts of Joy, it will not be washed away.

Stefani marrying this Jewish director really bugs me. Everything does. In this round my mother and I did not go as far as usual. Thankfully, I did not have to hear *At least she's making a life for herself.* But it's as if I had.

From behind I feel Peter, lifting my long dark curls and kissing my neck. His right hand reaches past me to the faucet. He turns the water off. Leading me into the living room, he seats me under the tree. Let the gift giving begin.

"Ruff! Ruff!" Baxter nuzzles his way in, so he gets his presents first. He tears through the wrappings with vigor. His bulky, black body presses on a stuffed elf that squeaks "Merry Christmas" as he chews on a brand-new pig's ear.

"He's easy to please," I say. But so is Peter, who's already wrapped the gray cashmere Barney's scarf around his neck and tossed the matching hat on his head.

"Extravagant," he says, kissing me before he reaches behind the tree and hands me a very small box. "Here, Aimee. Merry Christmas."

I look at Peter taking the very small—jewelry-box-small—gift into my hands. Oh, no. He couldn't have. He shouldn't have.

He's going to propose. And on Christmas! In all my fantasies of getting engaged, there was nary a one that ever took place under a tree on Christmas.

My heart thumps; my French-manicured nails slide across the package and carefully undo the red foil wrap. The rim of the little black box is lined with gold. I lift off the top, but instead of a dazzling diamond there's a square piece of paper.

Good for One Super-Duper Massage . . . PLUS!!!
Love, Peter

I instantly burst into tears.

"Now what?" asks Peter, immediately removing his presents, placing them back in their gift box. "Not enough?"

Sad to be disappointed and sadder to note I also feel relieved, I find it easy to embrace my guilt. And a lot still lingers from Hanukkah.

"I love this," I wail, clutching the homemade coupon. "And you so already outdid yourself."

I gave Peter a Gap sweater, and he gave me a Jewish cookbook. Then, in front of the entire Albert clan, he gave me another gift: a state-of-the art thirteen-inch flat-screen TV. Peter worked like a dog, pulling in extra bartending shifts just to make the holiday a really big deal. A Jewish guy would have known Hanukkah's only a big deal for the kids. Not to mention a Jewish guy would never have paid retail.

"So what is it?" Peter grabs a beer from the cooler, twists off the cap, and takes a slug. He sits facing me on the club chair we found on the street and, not counting the stoop, schlepped up four flights of stairs. "Aim, just tell me what you want."

"I want," I begin, or try to. How can I describe what's going on to Peter when it is only now being revealed to myself.

"A guy who makes more money?"

We are off to a very bad start. Although not quite as bad as it would have been if Peter had actually given me a ring. Be careful of what you want. That it's time to admit we're not ready to marry is obvious. That we can no longer continue this way is not.

"It's not money. It's . . . ummm . . . direction," I finally say, practically whisper, my words still at the starting gate. Words I now feel are mine, not my mom's. "And . . ." I take a breath. "I don't see where this can go," I finish, letting them out as they race away.

"Just give me another year," Peter says, right away. "In another year I'm sure the work can turn around."

He said the same thing last year.

Has it really been a year and a half since that day of my firm's annual summer outing? When I asked for a Perrier, and the bartender surprised me with a Sea Breeze? The bartender in the white T-shirt, sunglasses perched on top of his dark blond head. With a happy smile and eyes two pools of blue. The one I instantly knew would turn out to be somebody.

"Or maybe we should move in for a while and see . . ." Peter trails off.

Every New Yorker's nightmare, it's a hot topic. Tenants for thirty-five years, my lucky parents live in a rent-stabilized nest on West Ninety-sixth Street. They pay less for their Classic Six than I do for an L-shaped studio in a doorman building on the Upper East Side.

"You want to look in Brooklyn?" he asks.

A queen bed just fits into the L, converting my big high-rise studio into a small one-bedroom that's larger than Peter's Hell's

Kitchen one-bedroom walk-up. But ultimately it's still a studio, and still too small for two people. Plus there is the dog.

"More space," he says. "It's still the city."

"To you it's the city because you're from Minnesota. But it's one of the outer boroughs to me." Everyone's all about Brooklyn these days. My goal is to someday buy in Manhattan, not rent in Brooklyn. "Besides, it's too far to ever walk or take the bus. You'd have to spend your life on the subway."

"In Brooklyn we could probably afford parking. We could get a car."

"Peter—"

"You're the only adult I know who doesn't drive."

"I can't," I say. Well, I sort of can, but I can't because I don't have a license. Living in Manhattan, I don't need one.

"I always offer to rent a car and take you out driving, but you never go. It's limiting, Aimee." He pauses. "You should drive."

"You know why I don't," I say. Superstition and terror closely related, my automatic reflex has me spit twice between my two forefingers. Making sure I don't give myself a *kaynahorah*. Fearful of the evil eye. "And what if I did? What difference would that make?"

"Well," says Peter, quietly. Too familiar with this subject, he treads on thin ice. "If you drove, we could live in L.A."

"*L.A.?*" Now and again Peter will talk about the *other* coast and his desire to check it out. "You don't want to live in L.A."

"*You* don't want to live in L.A. I don't know what I want 'cause I never tried it."

"Are you saying you want to?" I ask. "Or . . . ? I mean, I know you just had that talk with your dad . . . you don't think?"

"No, Aimee. I don't think I want to open the New York branch of St. Paul's Happy Home Insurance. I have to pursue this comedy. Maybe a few more years. I think my forties can be lucky," says Peter, who hit the decade in August. "Okay?"

"Yes. Of course. Of course you should follow your dreams." Peter looks relieved. So relieved, his face relaxes. "Only . . . what about mine?"

"You've got a great job," he says. "You're set."

"What?" I can't believe he can be so lame. "I want a family, Peter. And I'm . . . I'm . . . I'm running out of time," I say, hoping the admission has not set off an alarm that will recall my biological clock.

"And one day I hope to give you what you want." He comes over and kneels next to me. "So can you hang in there? Can you?"

Surprisingly, I don't even think. "I'm sorry, P, but I can't," I have the guts to declare. When I finally got together with Peter, I felt great. I never thought I'd see it. I actually got my life back, except . . .

"I'm a woman. I come with an expiration date on having a family."

Though we never really discussed it, I always assumed Peter and I were on the same track. It looked different than the one I ran with Sam, but I was okay with that. "So just tell me now, because if you don't think it can be a Je . . ."

I catch myself. Stop. Well. I *thought* I was okay with that. But averting Peter's eyes, I see the elephant in the room. And he's wearing a yarmulke.

"Don't think it can be a what?"

"Forget it."

"Aimee, just say it, okay? Whatever it is, just spill."

I breathe deep before I do. "Would you raise children Jewish?" I pause. "Could you ever . . . ? Would you ever consider"—I pause longer—"giving this up?"

Peter looks about the room to see what *this* is.

"Christmas," I answer, sure to make Ebenezer proud.

Look, I'm not against Christmas. But the season, itself, is festive enough. By the time you get to the actual day, it seems like a lot of work for a holiday that just doesn't resonate emotionally with me. Christmas doesn't evoke childhood memories; it has no real significance for me, spiritual or religious.

"Man." Peter looks straight into my eyes. "I'm not"—he hesitates to say it, but he does—"I'm not up to any of this, Aimee."

"Which part aren't you up to? The Jewish part? The giving up Christmas? The kids?"

Talking about this with Peter, whom I love, not only feels horribly awkward but is really difficult to explain because when it comes right down to it, I'm not what you'd call religious. But I have a very strong Jewish identity. *Yiddishkeit* is my blood. I love the traditions and the culture. I want a Jewish home, to pass that on to my children. And I need a man who will share that vision as ours.

"Funny you bring this up," Peter says, stroking Baxter's belly, all of us under this tree a very unmerry threesome. "Because I was just thinking today how you never ask me anything about my religion."

My forehead gets hot; beads of embarrassment trickle down my face.

Peter rolls up a piece of discarded wrapping paper and talks into it like a microphone. "Seriously, folks, does his girlfriend really know how he feels about being Presbyterian?"

"Okay. I know it's totally unfair," I say, "but I guess I always feel that my holidays are . . . well, dominant," I finish, kind of ashamed of how I feel. "It's probably because everything's here. My family. Synagogue. New York. For me it's all the same things like always. Only it's better because now you're here too. Though—"

"What?"

"I wonder. Are you ever homesick?" I went home with Peter only once. A weekend. His cousin's engagement party. No more than a glimpse into his life, unlike his up-close-and-personal view of mine. "Do you ever want your stuff back?"

"Sometimes. I know I'll never move back, but sometimes I really miss Minnesota. The snowstorms. *My* family. Sunday dinners. All of us going to church. I never told you this, but I sang in the choir as a kid."

I always picture Peter not Jewish, but I never actually picture him going to church.

"But it never really did it for me," he says. "When I first got to New York, I tried a few places. Felt like I was missing something. But all that changed when I met you. I really enjoy your family. I can totally get into all your traditions."

Liking what I hear, I breathe again, which only shows me how tightly I hold on to what's mine. Too tight? I wonder.

"Committing to you feels like having to commit to your world. Not just New York, also about how you're Jewish." He pauses. "I mean your Jewish identity."

I never realized Peter gave this so much thought, but I feel assured knowing he has. Because I see he gets it. He gets me. Now that we're actually talking, we can figure this out. We can deal with each issue and make each one work. We can—

"But, Aim, I can't. I'm sorry."

What?

"I can't even think about it until I'm in a different place with work. Till I'm earning real money. And I'm . . ."

Uh-oh. My whole body tenses. Where'd this come from? Oh

no. This is not good. Please, Peter, stop. Stop talking. God, why did I even start?

". . . just not ready . . . not yet . . . ," he says. "I can't make *any* of these decisions now. And I won't make any promises. I still want to be with you, but it has to stay like this until . . ."

"Until when?" My body jerks when I suddenly stand, and my head knocks up against a branch. An angel ornament breaks a wing; pieces of tinsel fall on my head. But pieces of me are already missing. I feel them spilling out, slipping away. I fall to my knees to find them, to fix them, but they are nowhere to be found. *"When?"*

"I feel like I'm just too young—"

"To what? Grow up? I don't get as many choices, Peter. I'm a woman. Turning *thirty-nine.*" Said aloud, the number is like a villain, its sharp edges cutting into my options. "A guy in his forties these days is like twenty-five. I don't get the same free pass. And if, ultimately, we won't be compatible with . . . with . . . a religion . . ."

It had been the pea under the mattress. Although it was always there, our frolicking, our laughter and love were so much weightier, we'd sleep like babies through the night. But the pea was never removed. And now it will keep us awake.

"You know"—Peter leans over and tilts his head in—"it's not like I'm a Republican."

"There is that," I say. Quite seriously.

"Look, I'm so not close to being there. But you are," he says, running his fingers gently down my cheek, using them to wipe the silent flood of tears. "You're ready. So maybe it's best. I don't want to be wasting your time. I love you."

"I love you, too," I say, because I do.

It's so quiet and undramatic, I can't believe it's real. I only pushed because I never thought anything bad would happen. We love each other. But it does not conquer much; who says it conquers all? I want to rewind, but suddenly everything's moving fast and forward. I don't move, as if to make it stop. I wait for Peter to tell me something that will make things change. He doesn't. He just leans in to kiss me. So I kiss him back.

Peter carries me to his bed. His window faces front. A streetlight shines through the blinds, and we hear the sound of a siren. The panic of the sound fuels our passion.

I kiss. Touch. The emotion drives me. Rolling into a release that sets me ablaze, rocking my world, and wishing it could set it straight. Peter stays close. When it's over, we both cry. It feels like make-up sex. Except this time we both know it's break-up sex.

Going Down

A HHHHHH!" I SCREAM. So excited, I accidentally knock off my glasses and hit myself in the nose. I put them back on and reread. Is there a better way to start the New Year? Given my hellish holidays, the answer is yes. But, as always, the Work Gods smile down on me. And from my corner office on the thirty-second floor, I'm already close to heaven.

To: a.albert@prwap.com
From: ellen_dunn@ramy.com
Subject: Re: KISS COPIER LAUNCH CAMPAIGN

Hi, Aimee,
Spoke with Ramy. He does remember you from that GLAMOUR event. So long as proceeds can go to CancerCare, Ramy is open to a tie-in with your copier launch.
And yes, we can supply lipsticks for the kissing contest. That in mind, we think the product names of the line are right up your alley: All His Fault! Chutzpah! Next!
Catch up soon. Cheers to the New Year!
Ellen

I dial Jay's extension to cash in on the kudos. When the senior VP has you spearhead a major initiative on a new product launch, it's no small thing. And the KISS launch is big.

"...and will return from vacation on Monday, January eighth..." His outgoing message reminds me Jay's on a white, sandy beach in Cancún with his new lover. I imagine Enzo rubbing sunblock into Jay's pale skin while he sips a frozen daiquiri out of a coconut.

"Ahhhhhh! Ahhhhhh!"

What the? Okay, I'm still excited, but those screams are not from me. Yet I hear another and another and—ohmygod. A terrorist attack! Oh, *no*. Not today. Not on the day I get Ramy.

I race down the hall, following the noise. The terror leads to the kitchen; the entire consumer marketing practice is crammed together. Instantly, I'm swept inside the frenzy, latched onto the giant clump. Seventeen women and three gay men move as one.

"Ahhhhhh!" Cut off, suddenly, I detach. I free-fall forward into a blaze of light so bright it's blinding. No. Oh no. I scream again, fearful to open my eyes. When slowly I do, I discover the brilliant blaze, in fact, comes from Heather Thomson's big, beautiful rock of a ring. It knocks me backward.

"Terrorist attack...or engagement?" Both Krista and her conspiratorial comment serve as a cushion. I turn and see my best friend and colleague feeding money into the vending machine. Exchanging quarters for salvation.

"It's a little early in the day for that, Ms. Dowd." Her usually modelesque blonde mane hangs like hat hair, and the dark circles under her teal eyes indicate a definite lack of sleep. But believe me, I'm not one to talk.

"Used to be funny, but it's getting kind of old," she says, ripping into a green Gummi bear as well as our running joke. It's what we say whenever someone from PR With A Point gets engaged, which seems to be every other week.

You'd think it a good thing that *Newsweek* retracted its twenty-year-old prediction that a single, forty-year-old woman had a better chance of being killed by a terrorist than getting married. Granted, *Newsweek* only meant to be glib. And who could have ever predicted 9/11? But using the words *Doomed Spinsters Marrying* in the new headline did nothing to make you feel safer. Especially if, like Krista, you were turning forty-one.

"Have a nosh on Nancy!"

Swinging her head so her silky black hair flips to the side, Nancy Cheng circulates with a big heart-shaped tray. We each take a few celebratory hors d'oeuvres: red caviar piled onto bite-size matzo crackers. Nancy has obviously been influenced by her new relationship with Heather's fiancé's newly divorced brother.

"So things are going well?" asks Krista, while I jealously hope they're not. Though far from over Peter, I'm already worried about who (if anyone) is next. If this is any indication, there's hardly a ton of available Jewish guys.

"Oh, my Jordan is such a manch."

"He's a mensch," I correct.

"Of course he is," agrees Nancy. "He's Jewish."

We hush now to hear. In a southern accent saccharine sweet, Heather tells the story of her New Year's Eve proposal. ". . . and she tucked it in her bra and never let those mean Nazis get it," she drawls of the heirloom passed down from Danny's Grandma Gussie.

"That ring is so big, she should have used it as a weapon," Krista whispers under her breath. Meanwhile, behind us with the gay men—two Jewish and one Italian—we overhear Nikka

Pearlstein, Lianne Levinson, and Jamie Birnbaum complain of the dates they meet on JDate.

"Well, since the site's gone gay, *I've* been doing great," brags Sean Borrelli, who tried unsuccessfully for years to get into Jay's pants.

With that, Krista gives me the signal to exit the kitchen. "Do you see what I see?" she asks once we're safely down the corridor.

"That office romance is limiting to a straight single woman in PR?"

"That Jewish men are the ticket," says Krista, just back from Providence and fresh off a bad breakup. Reunited two years ago at a high-school reunion, Krista was forced to have a long-distance relationship with Tommy as he was tied to Rhode Island because of his son.

"But his son was *not* the one texting him all New Year's," she commiserated over the phone when I told her about Peter. "Tommy's cell was faceup on the table while he was at the bar. When it went off, I looked over, expecting to see the name Tim. Instead I saw Pam."

Tommy confirmed the affair, providing the additional bad news that it was going on, *ahem*, almost nine months.

"And you don't think a Jewish guy would ever do that?" I ask. We are stopped at the fax machine for Krista to check on one. Both at the same level, we started at PR With A Point at the exact same time.

"No, I don't," she says. "And now that it's over with Tommy, I'm choosing one of the Chosen. I've actually been thinking about it for a pretty long time."

"You're kidding? Really?" I want to be supportive of Krista, but something about all these shiksas with my potential Jewish men feels slightly unkosher. Thinking back on that yuletide talk with my mom doesn't help. I wonder now if Stefani will convert. For all I know, my brother already found a *mikvah* on a ski slope for the model in Milan.

"Yes," Krista answers with brevity as we switch into back-to-work mode. Picking up our stride, we hurry down the hall. "I've already checked it out, and this Saturday night there's a fabulous Jewish singles event," she says, parked outside her office door.

"I hate to break it to you, Kris, but there's no such thing as a fabulous Jewish singles event."

"And you're coming with me."

"I'm not going anywhere, and neither are you. You want to date a great Jewish guy. Stay right here. I know just where to find one."

I march through reception, out the doors, and past the elevator bank to Layton Real Estate, the firm that moved into the empty office on our floor eight months ago. Andrew Zeman, commercial real-estate developer, and I met in the elevator right after Thanksgiving. He'd just broken up with the "JAPped out Lindsay Kasow" and had sworn off Jewish women. "Never again!" he said. He might be perfect for Krista.

Approaching the wide glass door, I see him turn the bend into reception with some blonde. I guess a client. Smiling, Andrew practically glows. He looks tanned. He doesn't look like he spent his holidays pining over Lindsay. In fact, he looks pretty good. Pretty, pretty good!

He's tall, like Krista, successful, Jewish, and funny; she will definitely like him. Andrew's a catch, I think, placing my hand on the steel hardware to open the door.

Wait a second. Successful, Jewish, and funny Andrew is a

catch. Forget Krista. *I* like him. And now that I'm available, he might like me. I may be Jewish, but I sure ain't no JAP.

I dart off to the side to fix myself up. My boots bring me up two and a half inches; that's good. I pull the scrunchie out of my hair before pulling the bottom of my purple turtleneck down to cover my tummy. Happily it seems a little flatter than usual. Usually I'm busting out of these pants, a six, but come to think of it, they did feel a little roomy this morning.

"Hey, you," I shout when I enter, Andrew and the client walking toward the door. "How was your New Year's?"

"Cool. Hey, glad you popped in. Aimee, meet Selina. She just moved in with me. Wild, huh? Happened so fast," he says, winking at the goddess. "She dropped by the office because she misplaced her keys."

"Wow. That's uh . . . mazing," I manage to say. "How'd you meet?"

"JDate," says Selina, flashing Andrew a white, toothy smile.

"I know what you're thinking," says Andrew, reading my mind. "But there's an option in the 'how religious are you' category, and Selina checked—"

"Willing to convert," she says, finishing the sentence and closing the deal.

Huh? I daresay that's got me a little *fermished*. JDate, the biggest in online Jewish networking, actually encourages Jewish men to do that search? Man, there are plenty of online dating sites that are secular. Jewish people supposedly join JDate in order to meet other *Jewish* people. It feels a wee bit competitive to be up against non-Jewish women on the Jewish Web site. Of course, it also enables a Jewish woman to search out a gentile man who is willing to convert. It's just that I have yet to meet one.

"Lots of SHIZkas go on that site looking for great Jewish guys," Selina explains. "Aimee, maybe you should try it."

"Me?"

Andrew cracks up. "Aimee's practically a walking Yentl."

"You like to gossip?" Selina asks, to Andrew's delight.

"She knows *yenta*!" He kisses the top of her head like a puppy he is training. "Where'd you learn that, honey?"

"Oh come on, Andrew. I doubt she grew up under a rock—"

"Denver," says Selina. "You're a smart yenta," she tells me. "I learned it when I was in a community theater production of *Fiddler on the Roof.*"

"She wrote that into her profile," says Andrew.

"Well, that's nice, but he didn't say *yenta*; he said *Yentl*," I point out. "It was a movie where Barbra Streisand plays a Jewish girl who poses as a boy so she can be allowed to study Torah."

"Why can't she study as a girl?"

"See, in Judaism men are considered superior," Andrew says proudly, no doubt setting up the dynamic for this relationship.

"In Judaism," I tell Selina, "women and men have different responsibilities; with more religious people, women are separate but still equal. Things are different, though, with modern Jews." I look at Andrew. "Maybe not."

"Well, on the *one* hand . . ." Andrew says, imitating Tevye, the pious milkman in the ever popular *Fiddler*. "And on the *other* hand . . ." Selina practically guffaws. Tickled pink, she matches her angora scarf.

"Hey, *I* played one of Tevye's daughters once at some talent show when I was at camp. Maybe I should write that into *my* profile," Krista tells me Saturday night while the two of us, freezing, wait on line to get into the fabulous Jewish singles event. Finally our turn, she hands me thirty dollars so I can buy her ticket.

"You think they ask to check your purse and your lineage at the door?"

I should have known when she told me the club's in the meatpacking district. It's wall-to-wall people and music so loud it's lodged itself in the hollow cavity of my chest. Each thump fuels my uneasiness, for when I look around DOWN I get its conception. Along the perimeter of the huge room are big down pillows, big wide chairs, and enormously big *beds*. I'm sure I'd be much happier being miserable at a mixer in the Temple Shalom basement than down here amid these fabulous beds.

"Ready to roll?" shouts Krista. Her vodka tonic clinks against my merlot.

Not exactly a wallflower, I confess I'm better one-on-one. But my friend's in her element, and far be it from me to hold her back. However, she's already taken off. Alone at the bar, I try to check out the room, but without my contacts I can't see. I fish inside my purse and find my glasses, when I feel a tap on my shoulder.

"So d'ya have a happy?" I turn and face a guy my height with a hairline that's receded; a satin flower fastened to his lapel. He pulls down on a little red string so the words *Happy New Year* are revealed. Reaching into his left pocket, he produces two cardboard party blowers. NewYearsGuy positions the gold one in his mouth, handing the silver one over to me.

"Ya ready? Okay. Blow."

I don't.

"What's the matter? Never mind, forget it," he answers himself, his hands deep into his pants pockets before making two fists. "Pick one."

NewYearsGuy's hooked nose bobs over his fists to indicate that I choose. I take my party blower and tap his right hand, but it's empty. Like a magic wand, he waves his party blower over his left, slowly opening his hand to reveal three silver Hershey's chocolates in his palm. "How about a kiss?"

"Thanks, but I'm allergic." I'm quick to take my drink and my cue to walk away.

I drift in and out of unwelcoming hubs; conversations zip through the air like bullets. My eyes bounce about the eight hundred people, hoping to run into someone nice. Unaware of where I'm walking, I bump up against the stomach of a mustached man who looks like the Jolly Jew Giant.

"Call me SixFour," he hollers down, hovering exactly a foot above me. "That's my username. Want to dance?"

I can never say no to a dance. Four years of my childhood were spent doing the five positions in a West Side ballet studio with six-foot-tall windows. In third grade I got to be in *The Nutcracker Suite* at Lincoln Center. A Russian doll, I got carried offstage by mice. SixFour gyrates up and down, with each of his jerks forward I do a pirouette and spin away.

The song now ended, so has the dance. "You're nice," says Six-Four, pulling me off the floor. "I'm visiting. I'm in sales. I live in Miami. You want to lie down?" He points to a free spot on a bed.

"Sorry," I say. "I'm not sleepy."

I cross the dance floor to search for Krista. The ball is over, and I'm ready to go home. On my right, I notice a small group of men are gathered. All good looking, they catch my eye. When I get nearer, I see Krista, dead center, poised on the arm of a big, wide, white chair.

"Hey," she yells, and leaps up to greet me. "Guys, meet my friend Aimee. She's why I'm here."

Two men on the outer limits of the Krista circle zero in on

me. One is supercute, a *GQ* banker type, and the other looks like a nice, normal guy. I compare this to my recent encounters.

"Any friend of Krista's is a friend of mine," says GQ.

This is more like it. I give Krista an okay sign with my eyes, but she doesn't notice. Her dance card full, she divides her attention among three men I wish would pay attention to me. Normal walks away, but GQ remains. About to talk, I look straight at him, but something else catches my eye. A few feet behind GQ I see Someone. And he looks like someone I want to meet.

I walk past GQ, whose head does a nod I'm sure says *Come back when you're done.* It gives me confidence. So I inch forward, but only far enough to note that Someone is finishing a conversation. Believe it or not, I can actually hear.

"Here's my card if you want to call me," says a pretty-average-looking girl to Someone's handsome stranger.

He takes it. I know he won't call. He didn't ask for her card. Besides, his eyes connect with mine. I smile.

"Talk soon, Josh," the girl finishes with Someone. Then, yes, the girl walks away.

Josh. Nice name. Nice eyes. Nice smile.

I take a big breath before my next big step. Josh's eyes are on me, but then a female hand is on his shoulder and . . . he turns. He turns? *What?* I see their banter begin.

A shark only at work, I cannot stand here and wait to go in for the kill. I'm not good at this. If it's *bashert*, we'll catch up later. That thought extreme, I feel disappointed Josh doesn't break away to approach me. Forget it. I head back to Krista's clique. Fortunately, GQ is still there. When I grow close, he makes a space to invite me in. Not wanting the night to be a total bust, I regroup.

"So did you go away for the holidays?" I ask him.

"Four days in Jamaica, nothing big," he says. "What did Krista do?"

"What do you mean?"

"She's totally my type, but I can't get near her. I've been hanging out waiting for you. Can you put in a good word for me?" GQ hands over his business card. Too mortified to look up, I look down. Merrill Lynch. Investment Banker.

Eyes glued to the floor, my head does not move. As if an egg's been cracked on top of it, I feel it slowly drip and cover me in gunk. Coming down here tonight, I was concerned Krista might feel awkward. However, I feel like the interloper.

Once certain GQ is gone, I force my eyes up. They see Krista. She looks like an actress in a film. Her hair cascades over her bare shoulders. Her head falls back as she laughs. Are any of those guys even that funny? I watch her hand a card over to one admirer while she catches the eye of another. Krista can take care of herself just fine.

I wave my hand to get her attention. This time I do. Like a performer in a silent movie, I mime to show I am suffering from a headache. I stretch my hand so my forefinger points into my ear, my pinky down toward my mouth. Then I point my thumb back to show I'm soon gone. The moment Krista winks, I am.

Stonewalled

"YIT-GA-DAL ve-yit-kadash she-mei ra-ba."

Maddie holds a card with the Mourner's Kaddish printed on it and reads the transliteration aloud. I bring my own siddur to read in Hebrew. She sounds the words out slowly, stopping whenever she has trouble. It is often. I step to the side of my mother so I can honor my grandpa Jack my own way.

"Ye-hei she-mei ra-ba me-va-rach, le-a-lam u-le-al-mei-al-ma-ya," I recite. I read Hebrew well. It rolls off my tongue, and I like the feel of the words.

Today marks ten years my grandpa is gone. Still alive, he'd be a hundred. He died the day after my twenty-ninth birthday, if it's not bad enough having a birthday on Groundhog Day. For the longest time, it cast a dark shadow on my day. I got past it. But not this year. I don't want to come out of hibernation.

It's been weeks, but I'm still far from up after going to DOWN. Krista, however, is having the time of her life. She gets at least one great date out of every awful event. I'm not sure if there's a front-runner yet. It's hard to keep track. Tonight's a Jewish singles wine tasting, and she wants me to go. I don't think so. Krista can't wait. For Krista, a kosher wine tasting can become cooler than one of those beer commercials where all the beautiful people cavort on the beach.

My parents took me out last night, a birthday dinner and a show. I slept at their apartment with the plan to come to New Montefiore today. Way out on Long Island, the cemetery's a big ride from Manhattan. One my mother never wants to do alone.

"O-seh sha-lom bim-ro-mav, hu ya-a-seh sha-lom alei-nu, Ve-al kol Yis-ra-eil, ve-i-me-ru: a-mein."

Finished, I search the lawn for a nice stone to put on his grave. I get one for my grandma Frieda's too. I wish I'd had her longer.

"YE-HEI ... SHA-SHI-SHE-LA ... M ... MA-RA-BA."

My mom struggles but remains intent on saying this prayer for her dad. He lived with my parents the last five years. When I sleep in my old room, I still occasionally come across a hankie, a comb, or some little knickknack that belonged to him. I put them in a box labeled *Grandpa Jack—Keepsakes to Remember.* The same purpose as these stones, I think, and remember when I place them on the graves.

"How's my little *rebbetzin*?" my grandfather always asked when I was a girl and we'd visit my grandparents' in the Bronx on Shabbat. Selectively religious, Grandpa Jack would avoid riding on the Sabbath whenever he could.

"Yech! Stop," I'd scream.

I know he only said it because he was proud I went to Hebrew school. At ten or eleven, the idea of marrying a rabbi was horrific. A rabbi's ancient, isn't he? However, calmed down by the assurance I could marry anyone I like—so long as he was Jewish—I'd sit with my grandfather on the couch and read to him in Hebrew. He would *cvell.* Then he'd give me a dollar.

I was his pride and joy. My mom's an only child, and, in her day, women were not sent to Hebrew school. Daphne quit after a year for ballet and Girl Scouts. And Jon, well, I think he quit at his bar mitzvah ceremony the second he sang the last note on his haftarah.

From afar, I watch my mother place stones on her parents' graves. She has my father and her children. Grandchildren. But her parents. To lose your parents and no longer be somebody's daughter. My mother turns to look at me. I do my best to smile.

"I'm finished," she says, walking toward me. "Come on. Grandpa Jack would want us to go eat. And you can use it."

It is apparent that since Christmas I dropped down a size, the Depression Diet. My mother walks to the car. The Honda is parked on the road nearby. I walk behind her but stop before getting in.

"Give me a few minutes, okay?" I ask. Already in the driver's seat, my mother presses the button for the window on the passenger's side. It slides down, and she can hear. "You know where to meet me, all right?"

Maddie's look changes. "Aimee, sweetheart, please. Let go. And just get in the car."

"No." I quickly turn and run in the all-too-familiar direction. I run as fast as my high-heeled boots will allow.

I hear the ignition turn on. My mother follows with the car. She catches up and slowly drives alongside me.

"You're not helping yourself, you know," Maddie shouts through the open window. "This always upsets you, and it serves no purpose."

As fast as I can run, I know my mother can outdrive me. But I pick up speed to show I'm not changing my mind.

"Aimee."

"Leave me alone!"

I run down the paved road until I reach the place where I can cut across the grass. I run past Joe Fleischman, Loving Son, Husband, Father, and Grandfather (1898–1981), make a right two down from Lily Moskowitz, Loving Daughter, Sister, and Wife (1912–1995), and reach my left turn at the tragic and untimely Eve Blumenthal, Beautiful Daughter and Sister (1955–1971). Fifteen seconds more. I stop short, hold my breath. I always expect to see him. Except, of course, I don't.

SAM FEINSTEIN

A Special Son, Brother, Uncle, and Friend

October 22, 1965–September 11, 2001

"Aimee, you're not at your desk. Wanted to hear your voice. Hey, good thing we woke up so early. Got into work, and that new service didn't pick up the documents for the financial company's nine o'clock, so guess who's down at the Trade Center playing messenger? Anyway, just waiting for the elevator. Before I head back, think I'll pop over to Chinatown and pick up a salmon to cook for dinner. Cool? Call me. Love ya."

Message received Tuesday, September 11, 8:42 AM.

Those first months were atrocious. I was at my parents' almost every day. The following year I moved. It helped, though memories tend to follow. I always worked. I started going out. People said I seemed much better. No matter what the perception, there are always scars. But the heart must be our most resilient organ for, over time, though it never forgets, it heals.

The whole time I dated Peter, I didn't visit Sam.

"I had a boyfriend, but we broke up," I tell him now. "He's not ready." The loss of both men feels overwhelming. "He's not

steadily employed. He's not Jewish. And . . . and . . ." No longer
able to stop the tears, I don't even try.

It feels good to let it all out. It takes up so much space, and
there's really no place to put it. I feel I'm a groundhog who sees its
shadow and wants to retreat to her burrow. I look out. My mother's caught up, and parks a safe distance from the gravesite.

I say the Kaddish, then place three stones on Sam's head-
stone. One for his past. Another for the present we had. And
the last for the future; one we did not share, and one I am left to
discover on my own. I kiss two of my fingers and place them on
his name. Sam.

Honk! Honk!

"I'm hungry, Aimee," Maddie screams from the car. "Come
on, already."

Sentimental indulgence not my mother's strong suit, it
makes her nervous to indulge mine. I walk to the car and think
of Grandpa Jack and Sam. They missed meeting each other here
by six months. I wonder if they have Starbucks in heaven. I hope
they meet for coffee. And I hope the refills are free.

"I see you've been crying. So what do you accomplish by visiting him?" Maddie, I see, has been crying too. I can't protect her
tears, what makes her think she can protect mine?

"Ma, you're so warm and fuzzy, I just don't know how to contain myself."

This gives us both a chuckle.

"You're a good navigator, so get me out of here, okay?" Maddie hands over a map of the cemetery grounds. I direct her to
make a left when we reach the first juncture. For someone who
doesn't drive, I have a pretty good sense of direction.

We find a good diner off the Southern State Parkway. Two orders of pancakes with Canadian bacon and eggs later, we drive on three more parkways until we reach the Triborough Bridge. My parents always have a car in the city. It's something Sid will never be without. But when it comes to parking, don't ask.

My mother was the one who got stuck spending *hours* all those mornings sitting in the car. Waiting for the time she could move it and park across the street. They were counting on me for some relief, but that never happened.

A good driver's ed student in high school, I was confident behind the wheel and scheduled for my road test. But just as my mom and I were headed out the door, the phone rang. Grandma Frieda had had a heart attack. First I thought it was a joke, for whatever reason she was afraid for me to drive. But when she passed away, I became incredibly spooked and let it go for years.

Back up to speed—new learner's permit, driving course, the works—I made an appointment, again, to take the test the week of my birthday, right after I turned twenty-nine. Yes. And Grandpa Jack died. I couldn't have possibly passed the test then. Sam finally got me back on track. But believe it or not, it was on my calendar to call and schedule a road test on September 11.

The alternate-side-of-the-street parking hell paled in comparison to that one. Even now, as my mother talks, I quietly turn to the open window and spit into my forefingers. Pooh-poohing away the fear the memories stir. But all the drama did get Sid to agree to a garage. Back in the city, it's always heaven to pull right in.

My mom's cell rings when we are out on the street. The weather not too cold, I interrupt to say, "I'm walking home through the park," and give her a kiss before I go.

"Wait a sec." She closes the phone. "Come up for a bit." Maddie's eyes shine. "We have a surprise."

I love the word *surprise.* So even if it's just to show me she learned how to work that *farkakte* printer, I'm game. But turns out it's much bigger than a bread box.

Jon greets us at the door. I jump up to give him a hug. We may spar, but I love him dearly. My brother's been away since Christmas.

"So you're the surprise. Look at you." He's got a little wind-burn from skiing and, as always, looks great. Jon is tall, dark, and handsome. Not quite *GQ*, more like urban cool. Chocolate brown eyes, a great haircut, and clothes always the epitome of casual perfection. "How was it?"

"The shots are awesome. Definite cover. And no complaints about working in Italy!" He pats his stomach. WORK HARD, PLAY HARD is the motto Jon lives by.

"You never gain an ounce." I wish I took after the Rosen side instead of the Alberts. Unzipping my jacket, I take a hanger from the front closet in the small foyer and put my coat away.

"Well, look at *you*. Turn around." I don't, so he spins me. "Whoa! Isn't this like the thinnest you've ever been?" You can count on Jon, a fashion photographer, to notice these things. "New diet?"

"Of sorts," I say. "You must have heard."

"Exactly!" Jon waves his hand to follow. Excited, I realize somewhere in the apartment is yet another surprise. Maddie trails behind as we go down the hall to my old room. I shared this room with Daphne. Jon slept off the kitchen in what was once the maid's quarters. Way before Sid Albert's time as head of house.

My father, in the middle of the room, leans against the bu-reau talking up a storm to a hip, dark-haired woman with a ring on every finger, plus another in her nose. A snack table is set with makeup, a scissors, hairbrush, blow dryer, and an assort-ment of beauty products. A full-length mirror is propped against a wall, and in front of it sits a small wooden folding chair.

"Hi, Aimee," she says, and breaks away from Sid, forcing Sid to take a break. "I'm Jackie. Happy birthday!"

If she popped out of a cake, I couldn't be more confused. I look at my brother.

"Jackie's a top hair and makeup artist in the city. I use her on a ton of shoots. So for your birthday I thought I'd surprise you with a little makeover."

"Jonathan." The word *makeover* plugs me in. "Why? What's the matter with me?" But the second the words are out, I know they are the wrong ones. Honesty not always the best policy, in a surprise situation it has the tendency to be the gut reaction.

"Nothing!" Jon and Jackie confirm at the same time.

"I'm sorry, sweetie," says my brother. He sits down on one of the twin beds. It's covered in a mauve quilt my mother bought in the eighties. "You don't have to do this if you don't want. I just thought it would be fun for you to be pampered."

I instantly feel horrible. Not to mention I can probably use it. "It would be. Don't mind me," I say. "*I'm* sorry." My cell phone rings. "Excuse me."

I walk over to the closet to better hear. This gives everyone in the room the golden opportunity to talk about my outburst. And conveniently behind my back. I chat, then turn my head quickly. As if playing Red Light, Green Light, I catch the group in the act and make them freeze.

"Okay, you're on," I say when I finish my conversation. Closing my phone, I stick it in my pocket and face them. "That was Krista begging me to go out with her tonight. I said yes. So you know what, Jackie? Knock yourself out. Reinvent me."

Jackie gets busy, and Sid gets displaced. But I get to be in someone else's hands. For the moment I think that's just fine.

A Shiksa by Any Other Name

WAITING ON THE CORNER of Eighty-eighth Street and West End Avenue, I watch my friend walk past me. I'd like to tell you I'm unrecognizable because I'm all bundled up. But I'm not. Because it's not that cold. I'm just unrecognizable.

"Krista, over here."

She hears her name and stops. Looks. And as if she has seen no one, turns and walks away.

"*KRISTA.*"

"Huh?" She looks again but doesn't see.

"It's me. Aimee."

"Aimee? Is that *you*?"

"No, it's someone else with my voice," I say, and see she finally does. "Come here."

Krista walks back, circling slowly and taking me in.

"What—in—the—world—happened—to—you?"

"It's that drastic? I know it's drastic, but it's not *that*. I mean, we're not talking one of those extreme makeovers." I pause. No answer. "Are we?"

"We're talking one of those *supreme* makeovers," she says, causing me to take note of two things. How naturally beautiful Krista is, especially when she smiles. And how gracious she is to spin the spin.

"So. Is it okay?" I ask because at this point I don't even know. Back on Ninety-sixth Street everyone cheered when I sashayed into the living room like I was on a reality show doing my reveal. The response gladdening, then saddening. After all, I didn't really need a makeover. Did I? Don't answer.

Krista studies me before she asks, "How'd you get green eyes?" I can't believe she's that observant.

"If I still had my dark curly hair, I could look like Vivien Leigh."

Jackie shrieked when she finally washed out my hair. I would have too . . . if I was able to see. To be fair, it wasn't entirely her fault. She kept telling me it was time to wash my hair. Saying I needed to get into that bathroom pronto. Insisting I'd be sorry if we left the henna on too long.

But once I felt it begin to drip down my forehead, I removed my contact lenses. One dropped. And, yes. I should have been rinsing out the henna instead of looking for the lens . . . which, by the way, I never found.

"Well, you sure can pass for a *Scarlett* O'Hara," says Krista.

My hair turned orange. Or red. Or something very, very bright.

"The henna was just supposed to add some warmth. Depth," cried Jackie, apologizing. "I can make this work. Trust me."

So when she offered to cut layers into my shoulder-length hair, I agreed. And when after the blow-dry she suggested a flat iron to make it straight, there was little to no point to keeping it curly.

Without contacts and with my glasses in my apartment on the East Side, I was lucky I still had my same optometrist on the West. Thank God for New York, where everyone's open on Sundays. Eye Guys had my prescription on file and sold me a box of contacts. There was one left in stock. The contacts came in green.

I was meeting Krista just blocks from my parents'. Late, there was no time to go home to change clothes. Not that anything in my closet even fits. After I picked up the lenses, I stepped into a boutique on Columbus and walked out with the perfect quintessential, overpriced, sexy little black dress.

When I returned, Jackie did my makeup using colors to match the thin, pale, green-eyed redhead who was suddenly me.

"And that's what happened," I tell Krista. "How do I look?"

"Like my long lost sister." She grabs my hand, happy to have found me, and leads me into the synagogue sponsoring the event.

Our twenty-five dollars gives each of us admission and a wine goblet. We enter the big sanctuary that's now set up for a party, and head straight to the bartender to fill our glasses and taste some kosher wines.

"What would you lovely ladies like?" asks Zev, whose moniker is printed in all caps on his name tag. Tall with glasses, wearing a black suede yarmulke, Zev points to a dozen bottles set out on the table. "Red?" he asks, and points to my head. "Or white?" he says, and points to Krista's. We laugh, so he laughs. However, knowing we are laughing at different things, we know we get the last one.

"Red," I say. "Whatcha got?" I smile. I suddenly feel much better.

"Well, these are 2007 vintages of reds and whites from a winery in Australia that made its U.S. debut this past Hanukkah." He seems pleased to relay the info. "The name of the wine company is L'Chayim." Zev looks from Krista to me. "That means 'To life!' It's used like a toast," he tells me in an overexplanatory way.

"I know," I say.

"Oh, you do?" He sure gets a kick out of something. "And do you?" he asks Krista.

"I do now," she says. "I'll try the cabernet."

"Me too."

He pours a taste of the wine into our glasses, pouring off a drop into a glass for himself. He lifts his glass and motions for us to do the same.

"L'chayim!" he says as we click our goblets together. The sound resonates in a quick, light ping. The wine tastes surprisingly good.

"Want to circulate?" Krista asks.

Zev looks at me before we leave. "Come back later," he says. "I'll tell you all about the origin of kosher wine."

"Good deal," I say, and we're off.

Unlike the mob scene of DOWN, the lights are on, and you can see everyone in the room. This is not necessarily a good thing. Services are also held in here. On occasion I've attended; they are lively and musical. Upstairs are pews, but down here are freestanding chairs, now pushed against the walls. Rich red carpet covers the spacious room, regal with stained-glass windows, the high ceiling exposing thick metal beams.

"Look to your right," says Krista. We walk the periphery of

the room, classical music playing in the background. Two guys, standing and drinking wine, have been looking at Krista and me. One wears a yarmulke. "Come on," she says, leading me over.

"Krista . . ."

I know she wants to date someone Jewish, but I don't think she's actually up for someone JEWISH. For all my conflicts about religion with Peter, I know the extent to which I want to be *religious*. But I feel the beauty of the Jewish religion is that it *is* so vast; so open to interpretation and individuation, there is room for all. Krista approaches and claims her space.

"Hi," she says. With a white silk camisole under a black cashmere shrug, she looks, as always, like she stepped off a page of *InStyle*. "I'm Krista Dowd, and this is—"

"Wait, let me guess," says the guy with the yarmulke. "You two are *Friends*, right? So you're like the blonde one," he says to Krista. "And you . . ." He studies me. "You're kind of like Monica. The one that's supposed to be Jewish on that show. Gimme a break. Okay. So you're Dowd, and you're—?"

Wait. He thinks I look like *her*? If only. Her hair's dark. And I'm hardly that thin. But I'm flattered.

"I'm Aimee. Aimee Albert," I say, and emphasize Albert. "But I spell *Aimee* the French way," I explain, as I always do, liking the added cachet the spelling gives my otherwise ordinary name.

"Of course you do," says the guy who's yarmulkeless. We sit with the awkward moment until he says, "Dave and Stew," pointing to himself before his friend. "It's nice to have you here. We don't usually see women like you at these events."

Krista continues to chat, finding out what the men do, and hearing all about the merits of kosher wine. Interested in neither the grapes nor the guys, I observe. My observations propel me to make my excuses to the group. As I walk through the room, I feel eyes all over me. Not just men, but women. Seeing a small group of three, I decide to introduce myself.

"I've come to these events to meet men, but I probably miss out on meeting lots of nice women," I say. "Did you all come together?"

"We always do," says the one in the middle. Pretty and plump, short dark hair, and what is referred to as a Jewish nose, reminiscent of the one I had.

"Safety in numbers," I respond.

"Well, I doubt you and your friend will need much protection," she says, referencing Krista, who joins us. But as soon as she does, two other men come to the outskirts of the circle. I hang back, assuming they are here for Krista, but together they zoom in. One on Krista, and the other on me.

"How'd you both find out about this party?" the better looking of the two asks Krista.

"JDate," answers my friend, loud enough to be overheard by the three women we've left behind. Krista has now posted a profile. Her username is Shiksallure. As she talks, I sneak a peak at the women's reactions. They are less than overjoyed to be at this party with someone who, no doubt, is "willing to convert." I can't say I blame them. My thought is interrupted when the other guy asks, "Are you on it?"

He waits for an answer. He beams. He almost turns red. It's hard not to make snap judgments in these situations but it seems you have to. Very neat, a little overweight, the guy doesn't grab me, but he does look like a solid citizen.

"Sort of," I tell him. "I filled most of it out and put up a picture, but I haven't really used the site." Four people have already written me, but I've yet to become a paid member so I can't write back even if I wanted to. I point to Krista, who, regardless of her interest level, is always social and chats up a storm. "I'm with her."

"I can see you are! So tell me your username. So I can look you up."

"What do you want to know? You're talking to me now." What a world. Would people really prefer to live in cyberspace?

"Come on, just tell me. What's your username? I bet I can guess. Shiksappeal?" he says, quoting a famous episode from TV's totally famous *Seinfeld*.

"Huh? That would be her." I point to my friend. Boy, in this Jewish singles climate Krista really sticks out. "*Not* me."

He looks so disappointed.

"What's the matter?"

"Nothing. I was just going to ask if we could e-mail so I could tell you why you're right about wanting to date Jewish men."

"I'm here. If you want to tell me, you can tell me right now," I say, feeling very right about not dating him, but very wrong about meeting Jewish men at these events. I motion to Krista, moving us on our way. She follows me into the lobby, and we take the stairwell one flight down. After a powwow in the bathroom, we check the time to see if it's not too late to still catch a movie. This event is pretty much a bust.

Our coats are on two of the chairs in the main sanctuary. We leave the bathroom and climb the first flight of stairs, stopping on the landing when Krista says "wait" to rummage through her purse.

The door to the men's room opens, then closes. A man bounds up the stairs. He pauses on the landing and gives us a quick smile before he continues up.

"I left it in the ladies' room," Krista says of her lipstick, and turns to go back. "And I have to make a quick call."

"I'll meet you by the coats," I say. "Take your time."

Climbing the stairs, I follow the back of the handsome stranger. Peering from outside the main doors, I watch. He gets a refill of wine, stands by himself, and surveys the room. I wait. When he looks in my direction, I come through the door. He sees me and smiles. This one confirms it. *Bashert*, I think, when I walk over to meet him, because I'm sure this man is Josh.

"Hi, there," he says. He's wearing a black jacket over a black button-down shirt, his dark hair is short, and his demeanor is bright. Unlike so many others, he seems comfortable in his own skin.

"Having fun?" I ask.

"Better since I saw you and your friend on the stairs. We met, you know."

"I think we *almost* met," I say.

"Oh, not us," he says. "Your friend and I. We met. For a second. At DOWN." He gives me a sexy, lopsided grin. "How come you weren't there?"

"I was. I thought that we . . ."

"Were destined to meet," he says. "I'm Josh."

"I'm Aimee," I say, happy to forget about DOWN.

"Aimee," he repeats. But I'm sure he's thinking Amy, so I say, "The French spelling, though. *A-I-M-E-E.*"

"Mais oui," Josh says, and takes a sip of wine. "Josh Hirsch."

"Aimee Albert."

"Albert. That's a nice solid American name."

"I guess," I say. "Believe it or not, my grandfather actually came from Glasgow. In Scotland."

"I believe it." Josh grins, again, before he gulps his wine.

"Hey—not bad for kosher stuff. Not that I am." He looks at me. "I'd bet neither are you."

"Nope," I say. "Never was."

"I'd think *not*," says Josh, as if the thought were most absurd.

"Would miss out on too many great foods," I say, thinking of my penchant for shellfish, especially lobster.

"And too many great restaurants," says Josh. "I'm something of a foodie."

"I like that," I say. "So what brings you here?"

"Before I saw you, I was wondering the same thing. These Jewish things . . . What can I say? It's really not my scene."

"I can see why," I say, and really do because after just two of these events, it's not mine either.

"But I do like wine," says Josh. "And I work nearby. Family business. We manufacture bread. Ever hear of LoveLoaves?"

"Yes," I say. Excited. "I *love* bread. I always buy your sourdough and the fourteen grain."

"Seven grain," says Josh.

"It's so good, I doubled it."

"You're *so* cute."

"Oh?" So is he. And his confidence makes him cuter.

"Factory's out in Jersey, office here on the West Side. Plus a ton of our clients. We sell to Zabar's, Fairway, Artie's Deli, Barney Greengrass . . . actually do all the challahs for this synagogue whenever they have a *kiddish*."

Hearing the word *kiddish* from Josh is music to my ears. I feel elated. I like him. My world's just turned. On a dime. Giddy, I giggle.

"I'm sorry," he says.

"Excuse me?"

"Of course you wouldn't know. You girls are so polite," says Josh as we both notice Krista making her return. "A challah's a Jewish bread, and a *kiddish* is a kind of meal they have sometimes after a service."

"She knows that," says Krista, patting her purse to show me she found the lipstick. "I'm Krista," she says. "You look sort of familiar."

"DOWN. We sort of kind of met. I'm Josh," he says. "So . . ." he pauses. "How do you two know each other?"

"Work," says Krista. "Consumer PR."

"Cool," he says. "We once hired a small firm, but my father thought we'd be better off just advertising."

"He should meet my dad," I say, amazed Josh gets it.

"Maybe he will." He winks. "What made you ladies decide to pitch to the other team?"

On second thought, maybe he doesn't.

"You mean get into PR instead of advertising?" I ask.

Josh and Krista laugh.

"You're sweet," says Josh of me. "So naive."

I look up because I know there's a joke hovering over my head. I glance at Krista. What am I missing?

"Well, first I thought it'd just be fun, then I really wondered, but I can tell the fit is working for me," Krista tells Josh. "Also, living in New York, I've been more exposed to Judaism than in Rhode Island, so . . . I'm not there yet, but . . . I really like it."

"Guess you can always appreciate something more from the outside, huh?" Josh says to me.

"Well, Aimee's family is partially responsible for—"

"Encouraging Krista to be open to new things," I finish for her. Uh-oh. I think I get the joke. And I hope it's not on me. "We had a big discussion about Judaism last year around Easter," I say, remembering we talked about this when Krista came to my family's seder.

"Passover," Krista tries to correct.

"Oh, yes. The two holidays are closely connected," I quickly counter.

"So your family has a big Easter dinner," says Josh. His comment justifies my suspicion. "That sounds supernice."

"*My* family always does a nice Easter," says Krista. "Aimee's family—"

"I think Josh was talking to *me.*"

"Whatever." Josh doesn't want to ruffle anybody's feathers. "Figure you both have nice holidays. Easter and Christmas. All of that."

It all comes together; it's been unspoken all night. When I catch Krista's eye, the look between us says it all. But it's so wild, I have to say it. Josh thinks I'm a shiksa. Like her. I give him my best winning smile, because in a moment he'll find out I'm not. And for the first time in my life, I'm afraid what knowing that will do.

"I grew up in Hewlett. Long Giland." Josh mispronounces *Long Island* on purpose, choosing to say it in that very New Yawk way. "You're Rhode Island?"

"Providence," says Krista. "But Aimee here has really traveled far. From the Upper We—"

"Western part," I cut Krista off, "of . . . Pennsylvania," I say. "Ummm . . . Scranton," I finish. Scranton, the first shiksa-sounding city that comes to mind.

"Isn't that northeast?" asks Josh.

"It is. It's upper east. No. Upper north. East. Did I say west? I mean east." So nervous, I giggle again. "I get so confused."

"God, you're cute." Josh keeps those grins coming. "Nice country out there," he says. "You look like a country girl."

If I could turn to Krista and stick out my tongue, I would. So there. She's not the only shiksa who can get dates with decent Jewish guys. There's also me!

What???

"Ai-mee." Krista looks at me in disbelief. "You mean you're not going to tell Josh—"

"That I was head cheerleader at my high school in Scranton?"

Hah! You just mind your P's and Q's, I think, when I look at my friend and smile like the cute, polite shiksa I'm mistaken for. Krista should consider herself lucky because what I really want to do is puff up with my New Yawkese chutzpah and scream, "Hey. Yo. Butt out."

"I always wanted to date a cheerleader," says Josh.

I bat my eyes. "I was a ballerina too."

Krista makes an excuse and bails. "Meet you in front in five."

"What's with her?" asks Josh.

"Oh nothing," I purr. "I think she has her friend," I whisper.

Yikes. What am I doing? Krista is right. I need to stop. I am handing Josh my business card and giving my home number. It's not too late. I can tell him now. He checks his BlackBerry. He's free next weekend. I can tell him then.

Michael Cohen's wife darts through my mind. I can tell him the week after. I think of Heather. Of Nancy. Or maybe the week after that.

"Can't wait," he says when the date is in the bag. "I'm so glad we met."

Josh goes to shake my hand but pulls me forward and gives me the softest, sweetest kiss on my cheek. I think of Stefi, Selina. And then I think of *Yentl.* I think it's best I wait until the week just after never.

With Six You
Get Eggroll

"THE LAMB RIBS ARE INCREDIBLE," says Josh. He looks great, wearing a gray V-neck sweater under that same black jacket. "Let's get one of those. And . . ." He practically devours the menu. "You like shrimp? Crab? The lobster pancakes are excellent."

I've never been here before, but menupages.com rates it $$$$$. Each dish is about twenty dollars, except for the lobster pancakes, which, at market price, are even more. And these are just the appetizers. China Grill is one coveted reservation. A hot place to be and a hard place to get into. Especially on a Saturday night.

Josh called early in the day to confirm: "Aimee Albert. How's the cutest little redhead this side of the Hudson? Made a reservation for tonight. China Grill, 8:45. Thought I'd swing by and get you before. Call me on my cell: 917–555–2639. Josh."

That turned out to be a good thing because when I got his message, a couple of things became clear. First, my hair. The color is still good. I'm told I will soon find out just how much it takes to maintain red, but I'm already finding out what it takes to maintain straight over curly. My local salon was booked solid, so I had to wait forever as a walk-in for a wash, blow-dry, and flat iron. Though if I can do it every three days, I think I'll be okay.

Next I had to go back to Eye Guys and order more green lenses. If Josh and I fall in love, I may remain a shiksa but skip the contacts and just go back to glasses. Then I met up with Krista back in my hood for a manicure/pedicure. Our conversation over toes painted *Chocolate Kisses* made it apparent my closet does not reflect the sweet, petite I am pretending to be.

"They all sound great," I tell Josh of the appetizers. Knowing there will also be entrées, I worry now about eating so much food. "You choose. Whatever you want works for me."

"Let's go for the lobster," he says.

"Perfect." I smile. "I love lobster anything."

"See, I bet you *other* women would have just wanted that one because it's the most expensive," he says. "But you're really considerate. I appreciate that."

I smile to show how considerate I am, considering my more than acquaintanceship with the *other* (I'm guessing Jewish) women. I know, for a fact, that this *other* would have also encouraged Josh to get whatever he wanted. Yet from her it would not have been appreciated.

What I can appreciate is the power of brand building. Don't let anyone ever tell you first impressions aren't everything. See, your brand stands for something to your customers. They can relate to who you are because somehow you've created a connection with their soul. And you can control that perception.

"A bottle of wine?" asks Josh. "Or . . . I know. I bet you want a mixed drink. Vodka tonic, maybe?"

Why did he have to mention Krista's drink? Oy. I feel like there's a shiksa code and I haven't read the handbook. With nothing to wear, Krista took me shopping. She, too, was more than impressed with China Grill, only wanting to know if Josh was able to get the reservation for tonight today.

"Try this." Her pink manicured hand slipped through the door of the fitting room to hand me a pale green cashmere cardigan.

I looked at the label. "What's P/S?"

"Petite/Small. And over that cream-colored cami," she called behind, as her heels click-clicked back to the sales floor at Ann Taylor LOFT. I often pass it, just blocks from my apartment on Eighty-seventh Street, but never go in. Being there with Krista was like having my own personal shopper.

Unbuttoning the little cardigan, I slipped my arms through the soft three-quarter-length sleeves. Petite/Small. I'm withering away. I was so nervous about being a fake, I'd eaten less all week feeling happy about my upcoming date with Josh than when I was just legitimately sad about the breakup with Peter.

"Do you have pearls? And a headband?" she asked later, back at my apartment when I tried on Spring Shiksa to model. We looked at all the same racks, but Krista pulled items I didn't see. It's not that I don't buy nice clothes. Because I do. And it's not that I don't spend enough because, believe me, I do. But something's always off. Only I never know just what.

"I really look different. And I do look like a shiksa," I stated for reassurance, for prancing across my living room, I confess, I felt different . . . and beautiful. "I don't look Jewish, do I? I mean I do look gentile, don't I?"

"You may look like a shiksa, but you sound like a neurotic Jewish girl who grew up on the Upper West Side. Stop with all the moosh-e-gas."

"Moose gas? *What?*"

"Craziness," explains my gentile friend who's obviously cramming with my handbook.

"Oh. *Mishegas*," I tell her, and it sure is. Only I don't know what's crazier: my pretending to be a shiksa or Krista acting like a Jew.

"So, Aimee," Josh's voice snaps me back. "The drink. What's your fancy?"

Oy vey. He doesn't want to know about my fancy. One glass of wine, and I'm out.

"Ummm, wine is nice for me," I say. "Unless . . . uh, you want a cocktail?" Cocktail. Bonus points. Way to go, Aimee!

"Does your family do cocktail hour?" he asks, the question putting the kibosh on my standard story about my family's drink of choice being the water from New York City taps.

"My father's been known to dip into the martinis," I say, not lying.

"Oh, really?" For some reason Josh likes this. "Hey—you want one? This place is known for their Purple French martini. You'd like that, wouldn't you?"

"Of course," I say. "Like father, like daughter." Except I don't want a martini, purple, pink, Italian, or French. I want a glass of merlot. *One* glass. And I should have said that because it's not a Jewish/not-Jewish thing; it's just my thing.

"Cool. My last girlfriend would never have anything but a glass of red wine, if she would even drink at all. Jewish girls." Josh shakes his head. "Uptight. Glad you're open," he says. "It's way more fun."

Two Purple French martinis arrive. Josh lifts his glass for a toast. "To way more fun."

"Oh, yes." I take a gulp of mine. "Way more." I feel the first gulp land. *Whoa!* And suddenly it's not quite as important, but tell me again what a light drinker has to do with being uptight?

But I'm not. Color me purple. Besides that, I feel like I haven't eaten for a year, and the food is amazing. We've gone through those appetizers. Josh is on his second French Fuchsia Fancy; I'm still flying from my first. He likes to talk about himself, and since I can't, with complete authenticity, talk about me, I'm quite happy to listen. And laugh. He's funny. Actually everything is.

"So when did you move to the city?" asks Josh. He leans across the table, fork-feeding me the pasta while I rip apart a dish called Drunken Chicken and am I ever.

"Feels like I've been here all my life," I say, or maybe slur. "You?"

"Bought my apartment on East Twenty-second almost two years ago. When I started with LoveLoaves, I stayed on the island. Then I rented a studio uptown. But most of the time I stayed with that girlfriend in her place. We were involved, in and out, a really long time. But it didn't work out."

"What happened?"

"We originally met in law school, years ago. Hooked up much later. Oh yeah, I had bigger aspirations than the family business." Josh gives me a wink. "But I quit. Hated the grind."

"I can understand," I say, remembering Sam. Hmmm, another Jewish lawyer. Sort of.

"So she was on the partner track. Total workaholic. And in the end really disappointed I wasn't quite the Jewish professional she hoped me to be." Josh pauses and takes a swig of his martini right here. "She wanted what she wanted, and, I have to tell you, it kind of made me rethink Jewish women."

"Well, all Jewish women aren't the same." Though in some

ways I feel Josh has just described me. I wonder if Peter's out on a date now telling that same story to some real non-Jewish woman.

"Well, none of them are like you," he says. He's got that right. "How come no one has snatched you up? When was your last big boyfriend?"

"Oh, pretty recent. But we also had, uh . . . well, we had lifestyle differences too."

"Like?"

"Like career stuff," I say, "and you know, direction-type stuff and stuff with re"—I catch myself before it's too late.

"What?"

"Re . . . recreation. We, ummm, we liked to recreate very differently." Relieved with the ease I got out of that, I smile.

"Are you adorable or what?"

Happy to take the compliment, I smile again.

"Hmmm . . . I have a hunch you like to ski, do you?" he asks. "Because Alpine, in New Jersey, has a pretty good cross-country trail, and I'm going with a few friends soon, and I'd love if you'd come."

"Wow."

"Great. You have your own skis?"

"I do. I did. But now I don't. I mean they're . . . I left them at my parents' house. In Pennsylvania."

"You want to take a ride to—"

"No! Definitely no. My mother's using them." I say. "To lose weight." *Oy vey*, I think at the thought of my mom. On skis, yet. And in *Scranton*? *Oy gevalt.* "But she did, so she sold them. And then they sold the house. Now I just rent." I pause. "So do they."

"No problem there," says Josh. "We can get you some skis."

I don't know what we are talking about. But looking at my

half-drunk glass, I figure it's not anything that can't be worked out with another gulp of that martini. I'm such a cheap date, I can nurse this all night. Anyway, Peter took me out skiing a few times. He glided through the snow like an angel. I think I can manage cross-country okay.

"But don't expect me to be any good," I disclaim. "It wasn't my main sport of course. I spent so much time learning cheers."

"Did I hear cheers?"

I turn around and see Krista with the totally cute Matt Goldman she told me about earlier today standing next to our table holding drinks.

"What are you doing he—?"

"Hi, everybody," Krista announces as if she were invited. "Matt, this is Aimee, best friend and best coworker, and her date, Josh."

"Hey," says Matt. "How's the food here?"

"Everything you hear about and and more," Josh tells him.

"Hope you don't mind us crashing," Krista says. "Weren't sure you'd still even be here, but we were in the theater district and wanted to go somewhere cool for a drink. Just wanted to say hi, and we're headed back to the bar."

The place is fairly big. In fact, it's sprawling. We're way in the back, so it's not exactly like they'd be honing in on us from the bar. Still, I can't believe Krista showed up. I think she's afraid for me. If I wasn't so tipsy, I might be too.

"Join us," says Josh, with an ease I immediately admire. "We're just about to have dessert." He looks at me patting my bulging tummy. "Come on, Aimee. Let me feed you. How can you say no?"

"What'd you see?" I ask, giving the okay to Josh and sneaking a peak at the *Playbill*.

"Spring Awakening," says Matt. "It was awesome. About adolescents' sexuality. A client of mine got the tickets."

"What do you do?" asks Josh.

"CPA. Entertainment folk. You?"

"LoveLoaves. Family business. We're into bread. Edible and non."

"Cool."

Krista gave me the lowdown this afternoon.

"His name is Matt. Matt Goldman," she said with reverence. "He's two years older than me. A CPA. Works midtown, near us. Grew up in the Bronx. Riverdale. Lives on East Fourth Street. Practically walking distance."

"Or a very cheap cab," I said, commuting Krista from her Morton Street apartment in the West Village over to Matt's.

"He IM'd. JDate. Went back and forth, but we had that KISS meeting and I had to stop. So we decided to just meet after work for a drink."

That was a few nights ago.

"I loved the show," Krista says now. "You two should go." Krista's not big on Broadway, but the big Saturday night date is a showstopper.

"I'm game," says Josh. "And maybe you two would like to join us skiing."

My friend looks at me and bursts out laughing. "Aimee on skis, *oy VOY.*"

The guys both chuckle. I turn my head as it's unexpected and incorrect: her assessment of me on skis *and* her pronunciation of the Jewish word. Still, it comes out pretty cute. Like a shiksa speaking Yiddish. I couldn't affect that if I were Meryl Streep. It's annoying that Krista can use these words now and I can't. Of late, she incorporates Jewish words into her vocabulary whenever possible.

"What's so funny, Krista?" I overenunciate, my annoyance signaling the cat's still in the bag. *"I ski!"*

"Well, I don't. Not really," says Matt.

"Oh, honey, you can pick up anything." She faces the table. "Matt's totally athletic. And he golfs and plays tennis. Like me."

"We're already talking about a permit," says Matt.

"For tennis," adds Krista, glowing.

It all seems very romantic, so Josh reaches across the table to squeeze his sweet shiksa's hand. I promised Krista I'd tell Josh the truth tonight. I know she popped by to see if I'm okay, which I am because I haven't told. And though Krista's shiksa is honest, her success only encourages mine. I squeeze his hand back.

"Can't believe you two know each other less than a week," says Josh after ordering dessert.

"Felt *bashert*," says Matt. "I taught Krista that word."

"That means 'meant to be,' " Josh explains.

"I know what it means," I say automatically.

"*I* told her," Krista quickly covers for me. "I hope you don't mind, honey," she says to Matt. "It was just so nice, I needed to share."

The waiter puts down plates of all things creamy, drizzled, and chocolate. I watch as Matt kisses Krista's forehead. It's been three dates in four days, and they do look happy.

"Funny how life happens, isn't it?" remarks Josh as he looks across to me. I see he wants to kiss me. He wants a taste of his Jewish-boy-finds-shiksa-girl piece of the pie.

"Sure is," I say, eager for the same treat. Meanwhile, the sweets before us are scrumptious.

"You know, you look familiar," Matt says to me.

"What do you mean?" I'm suddenly panicked that maybe he, too, went to U of P and knows me from my year in Hillel. But even worse, Matt says, "I'm sure I saw you on JDate some weeks ago. It was before you posted your profile, Kris."

"You're both on JDate?" Josh asks. "Why?"

"For a man like Matt," coos Krista, leaning over to kiss him on the cheek.

"Who wrote who?" asks Josh.

"I checked for girls 'willing to convert' in my search," says Matt, "and there she was. But I do think I remember your profile, Aimee. Time2Share or something—I always remember things with numbers."

"Believe me, that wasn't Aimee," insists Josh. "She's not even Jewish."

"Could have fooled me," Matt says, and makes my heart stop. When Josh looks at me, I know Krista's stops too. Thank God she's here. For if I was tipsy, I have just sobered up. This is it. I will now be revealed. Shamed. Tarred and then feathered.

I look back at Josh. He searches my eyes. And in that moment I see. Josh wants to be fooled. He buys my brand. Consumers can relate to who you are because somehow you've created a connection with their soul. And it allows you to broaden the product because they trust you.

"Busted. Okay. Maybe *I'm* 'willing to convert,' " I say, nervous laughter aiding, abetting, and deflecting the moment.

"Uh, let's not even go there, okay?" says Josh, putting his arm around me.

Tension dissolved, Krista and I burst out with the giggles. Josh is relieved, so he laughs. Matt is embarrassed, so he laughs.

I vow to log on to the site and deactivate my stupid unfinished never-paid-for profile as soon as I get home.

"Me convert," I say, and laugh, this time for real. "*That's* funny."

"That's really *craziness*," says Krista.

"Sure is," I say. "Total—"

"Moosh-e-gas!" We happen to say together, and crack up again.

"Moose gas?" asks Josh, totally amused.

"Mishegas," explains Matt. "How do you two know that?"

"We have a Jewish boss," says Krista. Under the table, she locks her pinkie firmly inside mine—that old schoolyard custom—and before we let go, we each make a wish. I smile at Josh and hope mine will come true.

Not-So-Gay Paree

"Ahhhhhggghhh," I scream in the ladies' room. "Could you believe that? I thought I'd die."

"Matt's sharp, isn't he?" says Krista. She unsnaps her black beaded purse and takes out her lipstick.

"What do they call that color?" I say, concentrating on the smaller, less obvious problem that I need new makeup to match my new hair and eyes.

She turns over the silver cylinder and reads the name on the label on the bottom. *"Moxy!"* says Krista, applying Ramy's creamy matte to her lips.

"Let me see that." I grab the lipstick and turn it over to confirm the name. Just yesterday, Ellen from Ramy messengered over some samples. I apply it to my lips, and it looks so good. "This is definitely my color."

"In more ways than one," says Krista, taking back the lipstick and tucking it inside her purse. "That would have been way embarrassing."

"I know," I say, and run my fingers underneath my hair to give it a bit of a lift. I'm really liking my new hair, new eyes, new weight, new guy. "I decided. I'm not telling."

"Aimee!" Krista leans up against the marble vanity sink shocked, not awed. "You of all people. I can't believe you would go on with this sham. Especially after everything you've been through. How can you do something like that to Josh?"

"I don't feel I'm doing anything to Josh he doesn't want done," I answer, but don't want to face her so I go into the bathroom stall, close the door, and pee.

"You should have heard him at dinner," I continue, talking from behind the locked door. "He has so many preconceived ideas about Jewish women. Get this: he thinks I'm really different from those *other* girls. We see what we want to see, huh?"

Feeling on stronger ground, I reemerge. "I'm actually helping him to break his stereotypes."

"And create a set of new ones," she says. Now Krista goes into the stall. Once she moves, I use the sink.

"Look, by the time he gets to really know me, it won't matter. I mean, I'll still be me and—"

"If all else fails, you can always convert," she shouts over the flush of the toilet. "Seriously, Aimee. I'm worried about you. I mean, I know you. Are you even ready to date? I doubt you're over Peter, do you think maybe you're—?"

"Us both being Jewish can make having a family a lot easier," I go on, oblivious, speaking over the running water. Krista now stands behind me. I see her reflection in the mirror. "But I'm going to need your help," I talk to her image, unable to actually face her. "Can I count on you?"

She doesn't readily answer.

"Krista?"

"I don't want to start my relationship with Matt off on a lie," she says.

"Wow. You're like already serious. Did you—"

"No. Not yet, and it's not going to happen tonight," Krista quickly responds. "I don't want to go that fast."

"By the way, how fast does a shiksa go?"

"Depends on the shiksa!"

We laugh.

"Well, let's say . . . the shiksa is me," I say, and, for the time being, we are off the other topic. Whatever happens, I'm grateful that at least circumcision won't blow my cover.

"Well," she says, studying me. "What are you?"

I look at her and draw a blank.

"It depends what kind of shiksa you are. Just like you Jewish girls, we're not all the same, you know. Sex is different for every denomination."

"Really?" True or false, Krista scares the panties off me.

"Didn't you do your homework?" she asks.

"I hadn't thought of it, but—"

"Well, think about it. Are you a lapsed Catholic, practicing Protestant, a Baptist?"

"Okay, definitely not a Bap—"

"Lutheran, Presbyterian, Methodist . . . ?" Krista waves the white paper towel she's just used to wipe her hands in the air as if it were my flag of surrender. "I'm surprised at you, Aimee. You're usually so detail-oriented."

"Okay, I see your point." I confess to being more than just a little bit out of my league. "I'll do some research, I'll figure something out . . . you know, in case he asks. But I think he already knows." This last comment pops out of my mouth only for protection but inspires a comforting idea.

"How can he know what you don't?"

"Because, Krista," I say, educating my friend as I suspect she may soon opt to become a member of my original tribe, "you're either Jewish or you're Not. To Josh, my religion is Not. And I betcha anything Not'll be enough."

Suddenly I miss being Jewish. Although I'm not quite sure what I'm missing because nothing has been taken from me. Well, perhaps a little of my humor . . . some of my disclosure . . . parts of my vocabulary . . . and a lot of my Jewish know-it-all because now I don't. But I am enjoying Josh and love feeling like a sweet, adorable, pampered girl.

Krista and Matt catch a cab downtown while Josh and I walk for a bit. The chill in the air feels refreshing. Josh holds my hand and leads me to Fifth Avenue. We stroll uptown passing fancy storefronts displaying shoes, dresses, jewelry, and leather. Each one outdoes the next with its high-end wares.

The city is such a fantastic backdrop. Whatever's going on in your life, it feels as if with the proper underscoring you could be playing a scene, the star of your movie. If ever I felt that way, it's more so now.

"You're a quiet girl," says Josh, breaking the silence.

"Oh?"

The bathroom chat with Krista replays in my mind and creates two new tapes. Telling and Not Telling. Mentally, I try to play each one out. I don't see why I need to spill the beans just yet. I mean—*quiet girl!??!* Uh-oh. No one's ever accused me of that before. But it's easier and less dangerous, so I stay that way.

"I have to say I was a little alarmed when Matt said he saw you on JDate," says Josh when I don't respond. "I know you two are friends and that's how he met Krista. But I also know what he meant."

Be brave, I think. "And why would that be alarming?" I ask because I need to find out.

"Because with you I feel like I'm finally dating the right

kind of woman. I mean, man . . . I know JDate well. I've been through . . . don't ask because I won't tell."

"Okay," I say, aware Josh has not answered my question. "But let's say Matt was right."

"But he's not," Josh says, and pushes me up against the store-front window of Bergdorf Goodman. It's late. The street is empty. The glimmer of a new moon shines above.

"But what if—"

"Sssssshhh," he says, and presses his finger to my lips. "I was just thinking out loud. You don't have to be alarmed about anything, Aimee." He pronounces it "eMay," the French way. It sounds exotic. It makes me feel new.

It is still winter, but the mannequins behind us are decked out for spring. Tote bags, Audrey Hepburn sunglasses, and color-ful cinch belts accessorize white-cuffed button-down shirts and capri pants, pleated floral skirts, and patent leather sandals. For the first time in my life, I feel like I can look like a woman in the Bergdorf window. I want to move in. I want to be there. With Josh by my side, I feel I can go places. And oh, I so want to travel. I want to fly.

Josh holds me and is very gentle. I am a China doll that can easily break. He moves his full mouth over mine; his lips touch, circling above and below, over my lips. An interlude. The pause before the surrender. To a kiss. The first kiss. It is lovely. And I hope the first of many.

Closer, we continue uptown. His arm around me, he tucks me into his frame and we walk. We walk past Bergdorf's, past the Plaza Hotel, past the gold-leaf statue at the beginning of Central Park. Along the cobblestones we go. Past green-painted benches and the entrance that takes you to the zoo. I know exactly where we are, but I feel transported. Not just from New York. From Sam. Peter. From Aimee to eMay. When Josh hails a cab and holds open the door, it is eMay who hops in. We ride through the streets of Paris, and all the world is gay.

Until we reach my building on Second Avenue.

The doorman glances through the wide glass window to see who I'm with. Tova Steinman, my neighbor in 15F, is back from a late supper after the Philharmonic. She exits her cab in the circular driveway seconds after we step out of ours.

"Good evening, Aimala."

A shopping bag, undoubtedly containing leftovers, hangs on Tova's wrist, the concert program held in her hand. She smiles approvingly, giving Josh the once-over before the doorman, who's just rushed out, will usher her in.

"Hi, Tova," I say to the dynamo of an older redhead. She wears a beautiful mink. The top unbuttoned, her artsy pewter-and-turquoise necklace peeks through.

"I just heard the most marvelous Rachmaninoff," she tells us in her animated Israeli accent. "Lorin Maazel. What a conductor. What a talent." Willie, our doorman, looks on with pride as if she was speaking of him. "So who is this? Introduce me."

"Tova Steinman, meet Josh Hirsch."

Josh extends his hand. "Nice to meet you, Tova. You can teach me a thing or two about classical music."

"Ahhhh!" She laughs out loud. "Wonderful. This is a sweetheart," she exclaims. "What did you say your name was? Hirsch?"

"Yes."

"Aimala . . . it's about time," she says, and gives my arm a not-so-subtle squeeze before Willie escorts her through the doors.

I look at Josh and hope he didn't catch the remark. Tova always liked Peter. A great deal in fact. A singer herself, she encouraged me to encourage him, supporting all artists and all art. But I always knew she'd prefer I'd be with someone Jewish.

"It's about time what?" Josh asks. "What's up with Hirsch?"

"She thinks it's about time she sees with me with someone so handsome, and she wants to remember your name. That's all," I say. Sweetly.

"Oh yeah?" This makes Josh feel good. "That other dude wasn't as handsome as me?"

I don't want to say anything negative about Peter. Especially something untrue, so again I simply smile. Josh feels great and pulls me out of Willie's eyesight so he can give me another kiss. I can't believe how easy this smiling is. I mean, you can use it as an answer for anything. No one knows what you're really thinking, but no one really cares because you're smiling. When I think of all the words I've needlessly dispelled. But I stop thinking because Josh is kissing me again, and it is so soft, so warm, so sweet, so . . .

"Can I come up?" he asks.

"Mmmmm." Okay, as noncommittal goes, you have to admit that *mmmmm* is a good match with the smiling.

"Is that a yes?"

"Mmmmm," I say, again. But I'm already imagining Josh in my apartment.

Kissing me again in the elevator as we ride to the fifteenth floor. Walking down the burgundy carpeted hallway to 15J. Pushing me up against the door frame as I fumble for my keys. His head hovering over mine, eyes gazing. Seeing my mezuzah nailed inside my doorpost.

Carrying me across the threshold into my living room. Ravaging me on the sofa with *Stars of David*, my newest coffee table book, staring straight up for all to see.

Thank God he won't be hungry after that meal. The kitchen will be off-limits. Did I finish the Golden cheese blintzes? I know I ate the last of the lox. Tova gave me the other half of her challah. And you can bet donuts to dollars my freezer's full of bagels.

But Josh is hungry for ambience. He will search for candlesticks and find my grandma Frieda's ceramic pair—Hebrew letters hand-painted on each—atop the bookcase. Set on the shelf below my bat mitzvah album, right next to my menorah.

Interested to know what kind of books I read, he will skim titles. *Remember My Soul: A Journey Through Shiva and Jewish Mourning, The Committed Life*, by Rebbetzin Esther Jungreis, and *The Haggadah with Answers*. (I'm sure he'll want a few.) All bookended by the siddur presented to me when I was a bat mitzvah. AIMEE ALBERT and the date, embossed on the cover in gold.

And should he want to share a romantic glass of wine, he will not have to look much further. Because beside the books is a silver kiddush cup. The front engraved with AYAH, my Hebrew name. Translated, it means "vulture." Its meaning is not lost on me.

"eMay?"

I stare at him. I can't do this. I just can't.

"You look terrified," he says. "What? Tell me. It's okay."

"Josh"—I take a deep breath—"I really like you. I had a wonderful time tonight. It's just that . . ." Oh God.

Josh holds me tighter. His eyes coax me to continue.

"It's that I'm not . . . I'm not . . ." Aimee, you can do it. "I'm not—"

"That kind of girl," he finishes for me. "Of course you're not. I didn't mean to upset you by asking if I can come up. No. Whenever you're ready. No rush."

Josh kisses me on the nose, then nods to the arriving cab he's going to take it.

"You get a good night's sleep, Princess, and I'll talk to you in the morning."

He steps into the cab and is whisked away.

Princess. I guess not the same as JAP. Mmmmm.

Love in the Fast Lane

MEDIA ALERT   *****MEDIA ALERT*****

Contact

Aimee Albert—PR With A Point

a.albert@prwap.com / 212-555-1910

KISS Announces Newest High-Speed Color Copier
"KISS in Color" Technology Transforms
Traditional Copier Market

WHO: KISS KIC725 Copier

WHAT: Introduction to KISS "Kiss in Color" 725 copier and latest innovative imaging and printing capabilities

WHERE: XXX—NYC (speak w/Jay)

WHEN: Late May X? / Early June X? (speak w/Jay)

WHY: XXX—Tie-in Ramy w/KISS and contest (sched brainstorm)

A head start is always a good thing. Especially in PR. We won't need a media alert until "week of." But I like to know all Five Ws early on. Once they are set, I know how to proceed. But not today. The Ws not the only things out of place, I am distracted beyond distraction. Besides which, it smells like a funeral parlor in here. Seems as if everyone in the office has received flowers.

The reception area of PR With A Point faces front, in front of a U-shaped hallway along three sides. I step into reception and take my copy of the alert out of the printer. Then, paper and latte in hand, I walk the perimeter looking for Jay, peeking into offices and cubicles to see who got what for Valentine's Day.

Jay's corner office has a round table visible near the open door. The entire top is taken up with an arrangement of lilies of the valley, presumably from Enzo. Do I hear wedding bells?

A dozen pink roses bloom in a tall glass vase on Nancy Cheng's desk. Across the hall in Heather Thomson's office are a dozen white. Krista is elated with an orchid plant, and Sean Borrelli distributes chocolates, dropping handfuls of small dark cocoa squares onto everyone's desks.

"A.A." Jay calls to my back as he races down the hallway. His pace couldn't be faster if he was running a marathon, and his speech pattern's just the same. "Been meaning to tell you, honey, that you look *fabulous*. Oh my. And even from the front." Caught up, Jay says that to my face, though he continues to talk and walk.

"Thanks. I think." I wish he'd slow down. "Look, can we schedule a—?"

"Information. KISS approved a celeb."

"Yes?" My antennae are up.

"They want a celebrity to judge the kissing contest."

"So they like it?" Everyone internally was all over my idea at our last meeting.

"They love it. You PR Star."

"Fantastic," I say, thinking ahead. "So they must have a good budget then, right? Like what? Like seventy-five, a hundred grand? Plus travel expenses?"

Jay feigns a faint. With his hand, he pretends to slice the number in half. And then slice it again.

"You're kidding! What *name* is going to give four hours to judge a contest and talk to the press for just twenty-five thousand dollars?" This news is awful.

"Work your magic," Jay says, quickly dashing past. I see he's looking good.

"If it's an L.A. celeb, the event's still in New York, right?" I call behind him.

"Don't worry, if it goes L.A., we'll rent you a nice convertible," Jay shouts from inside his office. "Maybe something red."

I immediately grind to a halt and do an about-face to where JAY SPIEGEL, EXECUTIVE V.P. is engraved on a thin metal plaque on his office door. I barge in.

"Jay!" At his desk and back online, his time for our conversation has ended.

"Fast, fast," he says, acknowledging me though his eyes stay on his e-mail.

"The launch has to be in New York because you know I don't drive," I blurt out. Fast.

"Still?" His trim body collapses into his black leather chair. "Are you saying you have yet to handle this?"

"Yes. And I don't want any surprises."

"Aimee, Aimee, Aimee." Jay looks at me. Disappointed.

"What?"

"We go through this every time we plan an event," he says. "You may even be worth it, but car service for the PR firm is not a given in a client's budget. And don't make me remember Utah."

The coup of KISS and its new line of digital cameras as a corporate sponsor at the Sundance Film Festival was short-lived. After days of a media blitz and no sleep, not to mention frigid weather, the second it was over everyone packed up and took off in order to make the flight. No one realized there could be ramifications to my driving both me and the superexpensive signage to the airport in the rental car.

"Is that what you're saying? Are you first telling me now that *you don't drive*?" Jay shouted repeatedly into his cell until some mountain made him lose his signal. I lost face, sleep, my flight . . . don't ask about the rigmarole to fix it.

I had been able to conceal my driving phobia from PR With A Point for several years, but the more we travel, the more it comes up and the more problems it potentially creates. Of late, we've been traveling a lot. And everyone's just about had it.

"Here's a tip: when creating the event, create why it's New York based," Jay now advises. "And alongside that, consider how to get over your problem. Don't tell me how, but by the time of the launch I'll expect you have. Understood?"

"Understood." As if I had just signed someone's death sentence, I almost cry.

"Please don't." Jay wipes away a fake tear. "This is important. I'm taking you at your word, okay?" He extends his hand to shake on it. "I do have the number of a great phobic shrink if you want."

"Really?" I ask, as I shake. Literally and figuratively. "What freaks you out?"

"An account supervisor on the cusp of becoming a VP who still can't drive at forty."

"Excuse me. Who you callin' forty?".

"Gotcha." Jay winks. "Now get out." His hand shoos me as if I were a fly, the aroma of the flowers following me into the hall.

I'm dizzy when I leave. But determined to figure this out. I'll come up with the perfect celebrity-based New York City KISS event. Sans cars. And after, when this goes down as a big success, *maybe* I'll consider . . . Oy, I hope I won't have to explain to Josh how I grew up in northeastern Pennsylvania without a driver's license.

At the end of the corridor, I press the button that opens the door to exit into the main hallway. Past the elevator bank, I turn left to the ladies' room and use my key to enter. Next to the row of sinks is a full-length mirror. I feel pleased when I catch my reflection on the way to the loo. Even though I have never looked more together, I have never felt less. But one thing's for certain. I must protect my job. Whatever may happen, work remains my constant. The place I at least imagine I maintain control. Now Jay is saying there can be a stop sign. A time I won't get to go unless I drive there.

"Zeman," I shout when I exit the bathroom, seeing Andrew waiting for the elevator. "Happy V-Day!"

"Same to you," he says. Not wearing a coat, he's just running downstairs to Starbucks for his morning fix. He mimes holding a cup and taking a drink. "Want?"

"Have. Thanks." Walking by him, I wave, pausing in front of PR With A Point's front doors to swipe my ID to get in.

"Hey. How's Bread Guy?"

"Cool," I answer, holding the door open with my back in order to face him.

"Cool. Want to double?" he asks. "Selina wants tips on being a Jewess. What do I know?" Andrew steps into the elevator, typing on an imaginary keyboard to indicate we will e-mail to discuss. But once the elevator doors close, so does that discussion. That double-date among the last things I need.

"There was a delivery for you, Aimee," says Tanisha, our receptionist, when I walk back in.

"Oh thanks, but I got it."

Bright and early, first thing, Office Services delivered a dozen red roses from Josh to my office. The card read, "A Valentine Tasting Menu Awaits! 7:30 tonight. Pick you up in front of your office building." Josh may not know the real me, but even this version doesn't leave the office at six. I called him immediately to thank him. And I will give him my gift, Godiva heart-shaped dark chocolates, in person tonight.

"No," says Tanisha. "Not that gift. Another one."

"You sure?" I bet anything Josh sent another dozen roses. He strikes me as the type that can go over the top.

"Oh, I'm sure," she says. "This one wasn't through a messenger service. The guy hand-delivered it himself. The Messenger Center called for you to go downstairs and pick it up. But the guy didn't want me to call you. Office Services went and got it. They probably brought it by your office."

Peter? Ohmygod. Peter came here? What if I had just gone with Andrew and ran into him? What if he'd come up here and seen my red roses? What if he'd seen my red hair? No. He wouldn't do that. He's not thinking of me. It's not for me. It must be one of the other girls. Maybe Tanisha is wrong.

But, alas, Tanisha is right. Next to the roses, front and center on my desk, is a package from Peter. I recognize his handwriting, my name written on the envelope of the card. I open it. It simply has a picture of a heart sketched on the front, one word printed inside: *Happiness.*

> *Aim,*
> *It's not the same without you. But I see, now, it couldn't stay the same. Trying to make changes. Hope you're doing well.*
> *Happy Valentine's Day!*
> *Peter & BAXTER*

I open the package—wrapped in the front page of today's *New York Times* and tied with a red ribbon—and find a square wood frame. The words *Bow Wow* are engraved in four different fonts along each of its sides. Inside is a photo of Baxter, wearing a red bandana around his neck, a pumpernickel bagel sticking out of his mouth. It is so dear, I'm moved to call Peter. Except my cell rings and it's Josh.

"Hi, there," he says with the confidence of a man who feels he has done well. And he has. The roses come from an exclusive Madison Avenue florist nearby. Not to compare, but the arrangement outdoes all the other dozens I have seen today. Still, my eyes shift back to the photo of Baxter. The note from Peter.

"Aimee, you there?" asks Josh.

"Yes," I say. "I am."

"Good. Me, too."

And suddenly it becomes clear.

MEDIA ALERT   *****MEDIA ALERT*****

Contact

Aimee Albert—PR With A Point

a.albert@prwap.com / 212-555-1910

Aimee Albert Announces Newest High-Speed
Dating Technology
Shiksa Imposter Transforms Traditional Dating Market

WHO: Aimee Albert: NYC Jewish, single, 39-year-old PR gal

WHAT: Introduction to latest innovative imaging methods used to secure love, marriage, and the traditional Jewish family faster

WHERE: NYC and wherever else

WHEN: Now

WHY: Because to catch a Jewish boy, a Jewish girl may pretend to be a goy.

Out of the Box

"I T'S ALL YOURS," I say. I release the carton, strapped to one of those luggage carts, and dump it in the middle of Krista's living room. "Josh is picking me up back uptown. I don't have much time. So let's do the exchange. And quick."

"Good morning to you too," says Krista, drinking coffee out of her PR With A Point black mug, tousled hair pulled up in a scrunchie. Padding around barefoot in blue plaid pajama pants. "Now why did you wake me?"

"You did it."

Krista only grins. Ear to ear, I observe.

"Valentine's Day," she says. "And every day since!" The sunlight pours into her living room, illuminating her smile and sections of the original hardwood floor.

"Ohmygod." I cover my eyes with my hands as if any second Matt will walk out naked through the bedroom door. Or worse, ask what's in the box.

"Tennis. Don't worry. He's gone," she says.

"Good." I crouch down and unfold the flaps, also unfolding the words written across them: *Jewish Things: To Be Opened When I'm Safe and Married.*

"How fabulous," says Krista, rummaging through the box before taking out my siddur and the pair of ceramic candlesticks. "Ooooh, I like these. And I need something pretty for ShaBOAT."

"ShaBOT," I correct. "And since when did you start lighting *Shabbas* candles?" I say *SHAbus*, using the eastern European pronunciation to purposely get her confused.

"I thought it was ShaBOAT."

"ShaBOT."

"Yes, that too."

"Well, that's the modern Hebrew way of saying it," I explain. "After lighting candles, my grandparents would say, 'Good SHAbus,' but I grew up saying 'ShaBOT Shalom.' "

"Then that's the one I'm going to learn when I go to my conversion class," Krista tells me.

"It's not even a month. Are you kidding me?" That Krista openly gets to be Jewish upsets me no end. Especially as I hand over my most beloved possessions.

"They say when it's right, you know," she tells me. "Only I never did before." Krista sees the look on my face. "Look, it's only in my head. We obviously haven't discussed it yet, but it feels . . ." She pauses so this word comes out right. *"Bashert."*

"I think it is," I say, doing my best to separate my own fears from my happiness for my friend.

"Oh, don't worry, Aimee, I'm going to share everything with you. And before you know it, Josh'll want you to go to Jewish school too. Then you can get it all back." Krista's my friend, so she tries. But she doesn't believe it for a second. And after Valentine's Day, perhaps, neither do I.

We had a wonderful evening at Blue Hill on Valentine's Day. I've been to my share of great restaurants, but a three-star place has never been my norm. The poached duck was a delicious surprise, but not bigger than when Josh said his mother makes that every year for Christmas dinner. I was just slightly aghast to discover Josh's family always celebrates Christmas. With a tree!

"We work so superhard in December, it's just the logical day off," he explained.

Logistically it makes sense to me, but not emotionally. Still, it doesn't necessarily seem like a problem because Josh *is* Jewish. And from the Five Towns on Long Island. It doesn't get more authentic than that. So Christmas with the grandparents. Hanukkah at our house with the kids. But first you have to have them. If you built it, they will come. I even think bearing gifts.

"Okay, so you'll hold this box for me until I'm ready to take it back? You can use whatever you want. Just don't tell Matt where it came from." Krista has agreed to a don't-ask-don't-tell policy that, so far, seems to be working. "And can I have your stuff now?" I point to my watch. "I've got to get out of here. We're going to Alpine in less than an hour. And I spent the better part of the morning getting my hair washed and ironed dry."

"I told you I'd bring it to the office," she says, dashing into her room to get it.

"He picked me up every night after work," I yell after her. "I know he'd have looked in the bag. Besides . . ."

Krista reenters the living room with a big J. Crew shopping bag that, among other things, I know includes the brand-new ski outfit she got for Christmas.

"He *has* to come up to my place tonight. I've put him off half a dozen times, and with all the KISS work I didn't even have time till first thing today to de-Jewify my apartment."

"All right, calm down, don't worry. Look"—she holds up the

pale blue soft-shell jacket—"this will look great on you. Feel how light."

"Gee." Pulling the jacket over my head, I run to the mirror and observe myself as I pull the black zipper up under my neck to the top.

"I gave you two boxes of Christmas cards, leftover Christmas wrap, green grass and plastic Easter eggs, a bread basket, a butter dish . . ."

"What's that for?" I ask.

"We'll get to it. There's a few slices left of white bread, two bananas . . . I emptied out my fridge for you."

"What about the vodka?"

Krista pulls open a small cabinet door on her wall unit, revealing a makeshift built-in bar. "Here ya go," she says, adding tonic water and an almost empty bottle of Absolut to the bag.

"Absolut Shiksa," I brand out loud.

"There's half a head of iceberg lettuce," she continues, "Kraft mayonnaise, almost a full quart of whole milk, and my prized *Betty Crocker's Quick & Easy Cookbook*." Krista takes a breath. "Make sure you don't spill anything on that, okay?"

"Okay."

"I also made you a list. You want to see?"

"Can you just read it to me?" I ask. I can't tear myself away from the mirror. I love how I look in my new gear.

"Are his friends Jewish?" asks Krista as she unfolds the printed list.

"I wouldn't ask. Only a Jewish person would ask that," I explain, both as information and advice. "And *only* to another Jewish person. But I do know it's a couple."

"Well, unless it's two gay guys, you better be on guard."

Krista's questions and responses are sounding more and more like me. *Before.* "Now pay attention," she says, and reads aloud.

SHIKSA DOS & DON'TS

1. Refrigeration
DON'T. Bread, bananas, and butter are always out on the table.
"But I always refrigerate ev—"
"And now you don't."
"Gross," I say.

2. Shopping
DO always buy retail. Forget a good bargain.

"What if she asks where I got this?" I say of the blue jacket, hoping she will. I never bought such cool athletic stuff before, and this is a whole new world.

"If someone asks where you got anything, just say Bloomingdale's. The words *Filene's* and *Loehmann's* are never to leave your lips."

"But you shop—"

"I learned from you. Who'd you learn from? Next."

3. Dinner conversation
DO speak *only* speak when spoken to. Cross conversation is not allowed.

"That's easy," I say. "Now," I confess. "I can't talk as much as I used to."

"Try to keep it that way. Okay, we sort of went over this . . ."

4. Cooking

DON'T run to Zabar's. Betty Crocker does it best.

"So let's say I have Josh over for dinner. I couldn't go there to maybe pick up a chicken because I know he'd like it?"

"Let him ask for it. For now, you always have a casserole in the oven."

5. Decorating

DO learn to abandon solids. Flowers, patterns, and clashing colors always work best.

"But my apartment's so tasteful," I cry. "All muted earth tones."

"A woman would catch that faster than a man, but take these." Krista gets one striped throw pillow and one flowered one from her sofa and tosses them into the bag. "And a few fake flowers wouldn't hurt anything either."

Fake flowers. Like the silky ones they always string across windows. Over curtains. I have wood blinds. But curtains? On second thought, I like that. I'll have to be on the lookout.

"You said you were going to give me some of those saint guys," I say. "Did you?"

"In the bottom of the bag is the prayer to St. Anthony. He helps you find things. And I'm afraid you've lost your mind." She looks at me and laughs.

"Krista!"

"Hey—it's not like I gave you St. Jude."

"What does he do?" I ask as I gather up the shopping bag.

"He's the patron saint of lost causes."

"Thanks a lot," I confess to getting the joke. But boy, I sure love all my new toys. Plus my new outfits and accessories. "Shiksa Barbie," I say, sure to blow Krista a kiss before I'm out the door.

I hold on to the feeling, because when I get into Josh's black BMW, it's JAP Barbie sitting in the back. And I'm sure I've met my Midge.

"Hi! I'm Stacy. This is Adam. Josh has told us *so* much about you."

Josh has not told me so much about them. In a glance, however, I see. Her diamond ring, large enough to knock my eye out, and matching diamond wedding band indicate they are married. And Stacy's large belly, protruding through her maternity-cut sweater, is proof positive she is busting with child.

"So nice to meet you," I say, turning to face them from the beige leather heated seat in the front. Josh carefully closes the passenger door before making his way to the driver's side.

"Everything you said," declares Adam when Josh gets behind the wheel.

"She's a peach," Josh agrees, and leans across his seat to give me a very sweet kiss.

"Whoa, Josh," says Adam.

"Adam, really," Stacy says somewhat sharply. I not only feel tension in the adjustment they make seeing Josh with someone new, but imagine it's fueled by their history. Could Stacy be one of Josh's exes? Already losing my bearings, I'm not quite ready to know.

Josh heads up First Avenue, getting over to the right to go north on FDR Drive. We practically glide. I don't know much about cars, but I sure like this one. The ride is so smooth, and the seat is toasty.

"Before we blow town, does anyone want to stop to pick up coffee or bagels?" asks Adam.

"Not for me, thanks," I instantly say. It's closer to lunch, but you can always eat a bagel. But to keep my new weight, I need to be a lot more careful. And as much as a bagel is a New York thing more than a Jewish one, I am quick to detach from my association with one of my favorite foods.

"She eats like a bird," explains Josh. "I'm up for it."

"Me, too," says Adam. "Pull over here. I'll pop in. Girls, anything?"

"Bottled water," says Stacy.

"Me too, please," I say.

Adam flashes a very sweet smile as he gets out of the car.

"So how do you all know each other?" I ask. Ready or not.

"Stacy was my office mate at my first job out of law school," says Josh. He gives her a look and shakes his head. It's obvious he and the law were not made for each other.

"And Lauren was my roommate at Cornell," says Stacy. "So it was pretty funny when they had the blind date I arranged and realized they had already met in law school at Cardoza."

"Lauren?" I sweetly ask, though I know exactly whom she means. So that's what I feel. Stacy's loyalty to Lauren. Still.

"Josh's ex," says Stacy, shooting Josh a look that says, *You mean you didn't tell her?* "She's a lawyer like me. Lauren made partner, Josh. Did you know that?"

"Aimee's in PR," he responds. "Consumer. An account supervisor." Josh looks proud. "And soon to be a VP."

"Josh." I giggle. It's sweet, and I feel pleased he toots my horn. I turn to Stacy. "We have a big product launch coming up that will be a determining factor."

"Bet you work really long hours," she says.

"Ohmygod," I say. "You can't believe it. Well, you're a lawyer. You totally can."

"So you're ambitious," says Stacy. "And you work *a lot.* That's *interesting. Isn't it,* Josh?"

"And Adam's an architect," he says, ignoring Stacy's question. "And one of my best friends," Josh tells me by way of explaining why he puts up with her. "So don't worry about being stuck on a trail with a bunch of stuffy lawyers." He doesn't appear rattled. I have a hunch he's been through this before.

"Thanks a heap, Joshy. But I'll be inside drinking hot chocolate. You wear a size seven shoe, right?"

I nod.

"Did he tell you you're borrowing my skis?" Stacy asks.

"Not yet," Josh answers for me.

"I had to come, anyway," she says, and pats her pregnant belly. "I just had to get out of that apartment."

And see Josh's new girl so you can report back to Lauren.

"When are you due?" I ask, knowing it's safe.

At my first job out of college I rode the elevator with a co-worker I was certain was pregnant.

"When are you due?" I asked. "Just the short time I've been here you've gotten *so* big." I beamed at the woman awaiting her response.

She stared a moment before answering, "I'm not pregnant." The next seconds of the elevator ride were an eternity.

I ran to my desk and called my mother, crying from embarrassment. I thought she would tell me not to worry, that it was okay. Instead she asked what I learned from this and told me never again, under any circumstances, assume a woman is pregnant until she says so.

"May baby," says Stacy, who happily pats her oversized tummy. "Give or take."

"Cool," says Josh. "Boy or girl? Did you ever find out?"

"We're waiting," she replies. "But you'll have to save a date. There'll be a bris or a baby naming either way."

A bris or a baby naming. It sure would be fun to go with Josh to a bris or a baby naming.

"Yeah," says Josh. "I've got my cousin's son's bar mitzvah coming up somewhere around then also. Gonna be one Jewish spring."

"You'll manage, Joshy," says Stacy. "He always makes such a big deal about any Jewish stuff and holidays."

"Hey, I barely know how to pronounce them." Josh turns to me. "You know about that stuff, honey? Aimee's not Jewish," he seems to boast.

"So I heard," says Stacy. "And you met at a kosher wine tasting after seeing each other at some other Jewish event? That's *really* interesting."

I smile at Stacy to corroborate her story. Then I turn to Josh.

"Of course I know about that stuff," I answer, slowly. Be brave, buy time. Stacy is a lawyer, and I have to derail her before she begins to depose me. What did I tell Andrew? Selina didn't grow up under a rock. Well, neither did eMay. "After all, I do live in Manhattan."

"But she comes from Scranton," says Josh.

"How quaint."

Stacy doesn't trust me. I don't know if she sniffs my Jewish blood or if she's just bitter about Lauren.

"It's quite a celebration," Stacy continues. "In New York a bris is getting to be as big as a bar mitzvah." She laughs. "Bet there's not much opportunity for something like that in Scranton."

I've been to many a bris, and they're not all some big extravaganza. And I note she doesn't say one thing about the spiritual significance. She thinks I don't know anything, so she's trying to impress me. Stacy sounds like such a snob. Not to mention condescending to me and to Scranton.

I begin to feel like I used to in Hebrew High. It's reminiscent of the JAP-Sticks! All those skinny, JAPpy girls who had big blowout Sweet Sixteens. They always made sure to compare theirs to my afternoon party catered at our apartment. Those girls made me miserable. I tried to compete with them, but I couldn't. I only wanted to feel accepted. To prove we were the same. But I never thought to embrace the differences.

"Actually Muffy Plunkett, my neighbor in Scranton, married a Jewish fellow from Philadelphia," I tell Stacy. "And my family was invited to Muffy Steinberg's—that's her married name—son's bris. Muffy agreed to have the bris ceremony when her son was born. Well. It was *quite* an experience." I pause for dramatic effect. Thinking of a bris, I'm not even acting.

"They had a *very* nice party. At one of the finest restaurants in town. We thought it was fancy," I say. "But my mother said Jewish people often do things very, uh . . . big. And they like to have *a lot* of food. She says it sure is nice if you can afford to do all that. Even Mrs. Plunkett, herself, said if it was up to her, she'd have just had a garden party in her backyard and served tuna casserole and deviled eggs." (Thanks to Krista, I just read those recipes in that Betty Crocker cookbook going home in the cab.)

"But Muffy would do anything that Marty wanted. The most important thing to Muffy was being a good mother and a good wife to her Jewish husband."

"Hey, I say more girls should be like this Muffy Steinberg," says Josh. Stacy now quiet, I resume breathing.

"Who's Muffy Steinberg?" asks Adam, climbing into the car. Stacy appears sullen when he hands us the bottled waters.

"Thank you, Adam." I smile. "Josh. You have *such* nice friends."

I smile at Stacy, then turn and face front. I reach across and graze Josh's hand. The open road lies ahead. I am ready.

Over the River and Through the Woods

"Wait, how's this?"

Josh stands behind me. Taller, he places his chin on top of my head. My ski poles dig straight down into the snow. Josh's seem like extensions of his arms, which wrap around me.

"Say cheese," Adam says, and clicks on Josh's phone to create a memory.

"Our first photo," he says, and kisses me on the nose. "Let me see that." Adam hands Josh the phone to look. "Cool. Might just make this my main wallpaper," Josh says, and shows me the picture.

"That's so romantic."

Stacy, standing slightly on the sidelines, spent her time in the lodge sipping hot cocoa as promised. She met us outside upon our return. "He's so sweet," I say.

"A peach," she responds.

Back from an hour of cross-country skiing, I feel the most comfortable with Josh yet. The three of us on the mountain was the most fun. Totally harmless, Adam was vying for my attention and giving Josh his approval every step of the way. And I managed most of them. Well, yes. I fell. A few times. But that was the very best part. Josh would pick me up. Then plant a kiss in each new place he thought it might hurt. Adam teased. Josh was cool. I was coy. Big bumps were easily avoided, both on and off the trail.

I am most impressed with how beautiful it is here in New Jersey. Alpine could be Aspen, as far as I'm concerned. Fresh air, scenic mountains, country beauty. And to think, all this just nine minutes from Manhattan. Go figure.

"I can't believe I've never been here before."

When I was in high school, I remember a big TV campaign urging you to Discover the Beauty: New Jersey. Why? I would always wonder. If I walked down to Riverside Park, I could see it across the Hudson. And that was as close as I wanted to get.

"So you like?" says Josh. "If you're into this, there's a ton of good stuff to do in the summer."

"Really?" I light up. The good stuff, to me, is that Josh thinks ahead to summer.

"Oh yeah," Adam joins in. "There's a water park, an apple orchard . . ."

"An apple orchard." I am delighted. I may say I'm a country girl rediscovering her roots, but I am a city girl discovering her country.

"A winery," says Josh. "That's for me. And some real sweet little B&Bs." Josh's eyes narrow, and he looks into mine. "It may not be Napa, but it's near."

I love this. He is so much fun. I haven't been doing things like this since somewhere between a long time ago and never.

"It sounds divine," I say, hardly sounding like me at all.

"You live right across the river, Aimee," says Stacy. "You never took a drive? How many years are you living in New York?"

"Most people who move to Manhattan from out-of-state have the tendency to just spend all their time in the city." Through the girls at work, I even know this to be true. More or less.

"Well, now you guys can not only visit Joisey"—Adam pronounces it in that faux mafioso way—"you've also got a place to stay."

"Oh yeah . . . ," says Josh. "So you're really makin' the leap, man."

Josh gives him one of those macho hugs accompanied by a few punches, the kind that always looks less like congratulations and more like the beginning of a brawl. By this time we are in the parking lot and back at the car. Josh opens the car doors and turns on the heat before the three of them head to the back. They all talk while the men load the equipment into the trunk.

I climb right into the car and practically dissolve into my heated seat. It's luxury. And I am ready to collapse. Containing the lie has me more tired than anything else. On the trail, the guys suggested an early dinner at a local steakhouse in town. Closing my eyes, I imagine a fireplace burning behind us, easy talk over a good meal, and a nice glass of red wine.

"We're this far already," says Stacy. Her door closes with a bang when she enters the car. "What's the difference?"

"It's like the opposite direction," says Adam. "It could take forty-five minutes to an hour. If we can even find it."

Adam's door bangs in the back, followed by Josh's in the front.

"Doesn't Josh have one of those talking navigator thingys?"

Josh looks at me like he's stuck in the middle. Of what, I have no idea.

"Do you have that?" I ask.

He points to the dashboard.

"You know, I read an article that said many women are actually jealous of their spouse's relationship with the voice." Only Josh and Adam laugh. I continue anyway. "Seriously. They say it's smart and a little sexy, but it doesn't talk back. It always fulfills your needs, and it gets you wherever you want to go."

Josh leans over and gives me another kiss.

"Well, if you two can stop necking for a minute, how about programming in Lenox Terrace in West Orange, and let's get on our way before it gets dark."

West Orange? In New Jersey? Oh, no. Not *that* West Orange, New Jersey. I pray there are two.

"Okeydoke," Josh says, talking and tapping and feeding the information in. "You don't mind, eMay, do you? They just closed on a house in West Orange, and Stacy wants to check in and take a look. Be fun, okay?"

"Sure," I say. Loud. Too loud. "Ummmm, what's that address again?"

"Lenox Terrace is the street," Adam says from the back.

"Lenox Terrace?" I shout.

"You want to take the wheel of this baby and drive?" asks Josh.

"Oh, no!" I involuntarily cry as it computes. Daphne and Rich live on Beaumont Terrace.

"Why not?"

I have no idea about suburban planning, but I figure the two houses are not that far from each other. And what did Josh just ask?

"Why not what?"

"Why don't you want to drive?" he asks.

"Oh." It takes a few seconds for me to catch up. "Because I don't."

"You've got to be kidding!" Stacy's cackle overrides both guys' questions of incredulity. "Now *this* is really *interesting*."

"Really, eMay?" asks Josh. "I don't think I ever met anyone who can't drive."

"Me either," says Adam.

"I just, uh . . . well, I learned. A few times. But I never, uh, took the test."

"So how *interesting* is this?" chortles Stacy. "A girl from a rural area can't even drive a car? Give me a break. How'd you get to school?"

"Scranton's not exactly rural, Stace," says Adam.

"There was a school bus."

"In high school?" Stacy practically bullies.

"Maybe she got a ride," offers Josh. "With a friend."

"In fact, I did." I take the bait. "Muffy used to take me," I turn to tell Stacy in the back. "Muffy Steinberg had her own car."

"Well, don't worry. Because it's now my mission to make sure you get your license, eMay," says Josh. "Sound good?"

"Sounds . . . *interesting*." Turning my head, I lift my fingers in the smallest gesture to spit-spit pooh-pooh away the evil eye. One problem down, another to begin.

Do I even hear a word anyone says during the whole rest of the ride in the car? Known now for quiet, I stay that way. I try to close my eyes, but they open soon after. Is sleep actually required for something to qualify as a nightmare?

"There it is," says Stacy when we pull up to a nice white house. A nice white house that looks, to me, a lot like Daphne's nice gray one. I won't get out of the car. What can happen to me if I don't get out of the car?

"E, you coming?" asks Josh.

"Of course," I say, getting out of the car.

I need an ally quickly. I immediately rush over to Stacy.

"This is *so* nice. Lovely. My, my my. I love this house. It reminds me of houses in my neighborhood growing up in Scranton," I say.

Stacy practically glares. Ooops!

"But nicer," I recoup. "*Much* nicer. Much more ... *upscale.*" That word makes her smile.

"We love it," says Stacy, and without much prompting she proceeds to tell me about the house. "It's got three bedrooms, two baths—we'll probably build more—a brick fireplace, central air, a stone patio, and listen to this ... It's a split level, but the laundry room is on the first floor with the family room, which will be so totally great. I'll be able to watch the kid *and* throw in another load."

"How soon will you be going back to work?" I ask, wondering how this high-powered lawyer can get that excited over doing laundry.

"I don't know you well, Aimee, but I swear. If you had dark curly hair, you'd almost be the spitting image of Lauren. Plus when I told her we were moving, that was like the first thing she asked me too."

The guys, behind us in the driveway, now catch up. Stacy takes the lead and rings the bell.

"If they're home, I'm sure they won't mind." But they aren't.

"So who's hungry?" I ask, anxious to get back in the car and out of here as soon as possible.

"Well, as long as we're here, don't you want to see the neighborhood?" asks Stacy.

Josh defers to me. Stacy shows there'll be no deferring. Adam tells us he grew up a few towns away, so he is the tour guide. We follow him down Lenox Terrace, and he shows us the sights. Josh holds my hand as we pass house after house, driveway after driveway, SUV after SUV. Following one leafless tree after another, Adam regales us with tales of his childhood. Riding home from school on his bike, something he hopes in a neighborhood like this his kids will also get to do.

At that exact moment, as if to prove his point, a bunch of children burst through a front door, running to greet parents who have gathered on the lawn to pick them up. We near a corner I am hopeful does not say Beaumont Terrace, but it no longer matters as my hopes are dashed when someone calls, "Aunt Aimee," and, though a common name, this Aunt Aimee is me.

"I didn't know you were coming today."

In her denim skirt and pink cowboy boots, a purple ski jacket on her little body, my niece is so delicious you could eat her up. I crouch to give her a hug as I certainly won't ignore her, my heart frantically beating as I wonder what will happen now.

"Aimee?" I look up and see a startled Daphne staring down at me and Hannah. Fortunately, Daphne and I never looked alike. "It is you. When Hannah said it's Aunt Aimee . . . well, it doesn't even look like you. *Your hair.*"

"Daphne! Hello!" I say, and jump right up. "I thought maybe you lived near here when we talked of West Orange, but I wasn't quite certain. Meet my friends." I say each word with deliberation, hopeful my sister will infer deeper meaning. "Daphne and her husband, Rich, live . . . nearby," I tell the group.

"I'm Stacy," she says, and extends her hand. "We're moving into the Gordon house on Lenox next month. What happened to Aimee's hair?"

"Nothing," I pipe in. "Daphne and I haven't seen each other in so long and . . . mine used to be . . . short. Like hers. *Remember, Daphne?*"

"Sure. I remember."

Good. Daph will help me out.

"I don't remember your hair short at Hanukkah, Aunt Aimee."

"It was. It only seems longer now. Because your mom just cut her hair a lot, lot shorter. Right, Daphne?"

"Hanukkah?" asks Josh. "This past Hanukkah?"

"Daphne, this is Josh," I say, making important eye contact with my sister when I say his name. "We met a few weeks ago."

"Is this your sister?" Josh seems confused. I can't blame him.

"Yes," answers Daphne. "Aimee and I are—"

"Very close. Like real sisters. We're from a *special* sorority," I explain. "We're so close, at one point we even shared a room."

"Cool," says Adam. "Where'd you girls go to school?"

"Yeah," asks Stacy. "Where'd you two go? We're Binghamton, Syracuse, Cornell," she says, pointing to Adam, Josh, and herself.

Not a clue what's going on, Daphne waits for me to answer. In the longest two-second pause in history, a million things go through my mind. Of course I told Josh U of P, but I'm afraid Daphne will announce her school. I don't know what to say, and I know I have to answer. But uncomfortable that I haven't, my sister figures that maybe she should.

"Brown," I stupidly say, at the exact same time "U of P" comes from Daphne.

Crap! We automatically both try to fix it.

"U of P," I say, as my sister says, "Brown."

"She transferred!" I say. *"From* U of P. We met there first. At our sorority. And became sisters."

"Phi Beta Phi," I say while Daphne says, "Alpha Beta Alpha."

"Alpha?" / "Phi?"

"Phi?" / "Alpha?"

"Beta, beta beta!" I throw my hands up in the air and move them right, left, right with the words as if I was doing a cheer.

Josh lets out a big laugh that gives me a sigh of relief. "I only wish I could've seen you in that little uniform."

Adam, too, is delighted, which annoys Stacy no end. Totally confused, Daphne and Hannah clap.

"Daphne and I have always stayed in touch," I say. "Her children are like my own niece and nephew. And when I moved to the city from Scranton, we got even closer. Like Hannah said, I spend many holidays with Daphne's family. At her parents'."

"Grandma and Grandpa are visiting today," Hannah tells me.

"Really?" I smile. In case I decide to kill myself, I think it would be nice if that was everyone's last memory of me.

"They came to see me and Holdenn."

"Your parents are actually *here,* Daphne? That's *incredible.*" I put my arm around her waist to illustrate the closeness of our bond. Then I dig my thumb deep into her back to let her know she better keep her trap shut.

"You want to walk over?" asks Josh. "You're close by, right?" he asks my sister.

"We're going to have to get back to the city," says Stacy. "Sorry."

"No problem," I say. "I see them. Often enough," I add.

"We saw Aunt Aimee on New Year's and for Hanukkah with her boyfriend Peter. But they broke up," says Hannah. "Mommy says he's not Jewish."

No one knows where this is coming from. But Daphne is now potentially accused of antigentile comments behind my back. My sister is so stunned, she simply looks embarrassed. As is everyone. Except Josh. For he's just been crowned king. More handsome than the other dude and Jewish to boot, he has officially dethroned my former ex.

"Well, Hannah," begins Josh, squatting down to the five-year-old's height, using a talking-to-kids voice. "Not *everybody*'s Jewish. And that's really okay. Just look at your aunt Aimee."

I grind my knuckles into my sister's back, giving her one more noogie just to make sure.

"Owww!" Daphne shouts, and in the same moment quickly picks up Hannah. She fusses with the chocolate ice cream left on Hannah's mouth. *Owww* appears to only reference a messy daughter. Fussing with her chocolate mouth helps keep Hannah quiet.

Josh stands up and puts his arm around me, pulling me closer to protect me from the small-minded Jewish people. Stacy and Adam look at their new neighbor with understanding. They feel simpatico, certain she didn't intend to make some slur. Poor Daphne, unsure whether she's coming or going, a good guy or a bad, finally composes herself, takes Hannah's hand, and is ready to mosey on home.

"Oh. Aimee. By the way." Daphne stops right after she has said her good-byes. "This may sound weird after all this time, but I just never can remember."

"Excuse me?"

There is a glint in my sister's eye. She is setting me up for something.

"Of course you're not Jewish," says Daphne, and I know I am

the only one able to see her tongue stuck in her cheek. "But I always forget your denomination. Just what exactly are you?"

"Protestant," I say without any hesitation. "But middle-of-the-road kind of Protestant. Congregational." This PR girl did her homework. "Plymouth Congregational Church. That's us."

"Interesting," says Daphne.

"*Very* interesting," says Stacy.

"Cool," says Josh. Adam nods in agreement.

"Aimee," says Stacy, catching up to me after we walk away. "I can't believe she just asked you that."

"Why?" In this moment I am nothing but totally grateful to Krista. "She didn't hurt my feelings."

"Well, of course she didn't," says Stacy. "It's just like, no offense, but who even thinks about that? Daphne seems nice, but really. So you're not Jewish. End of story. Isn't that enough?"

I turn and face Stacy. Appalled. Does this girl even know how to censor anything?

"Oh, sorry," she says. "You'd have to be Jewish to get it."

Of Meat and Men

"WHAT'S WITH YOU? You're so nervous."

I'm usually quick to counter, but my mother is right, so I refrain.

"We haven't seen you in a month, Aimee. And I can see you're very tense. You haven't even put back any of the weight. Sid, don't you think she's a little too thin?"

Too thin, two words not in my father's vocabulary, he ignores my mother.

"I'm just busy at work," I jump in. "I told you, we have the KISS launch coming up. And the budget's bad for a good celebrity. And it's doubly tough because it's better if they live in New York than Los Angeles."

"Why's it better to live in Los Angeles?" asks the voice behind the paper.

My mother grabs the *Times* out from under my father and hands it to me to put on the empty chair next to mine.

"It's not polite," she says. "We're not home. We're in a steak-house."

I laugh.

"What's so funny?"

"I barely think of Fairway as a restaurant, Ma, let alone a steakhouse."

"Well, it sure is," defends Sid, showing me the front of the menu that reads Fairway Café and Steakhouse. "It's just one of the city's best-kept secrets."

Sawdust sprinkled all over its big selling floor, Fairway is a gourmet food market that has everything you could ever want. Especially in the world of fresh produce. There are rows of fruits and vegetables outside the store on Broadway, and even more inside. But keep track of where you buy what. When you send that bag of apples down the conveyor belt, it'll be up to you to holler "inside" or "outside" to the checkout person. The prices are different. So if you don't catch on right away, I guarantee you will learn.

With such popularity, Fairway opened a café upstairs. It started with bagels and coffee. Now it's progressed to steak.

"Let's get a couple of the specials," says my dad.

"I'd like the strip steak," says Maddie. "Who wants to share with me? Aimee?"

"The portions are huge," confirms Sid. "And let's get a rib eye. If there's leftover we'll take it home."

"No you won't."

I look up and see my brother, kissing my parents hello before removing the newspaper to slip into the window seat next to me.

"You made it," says my dad. "I knew you'd be done in time for dinner. Good."

"I thought I could get Daphne and Hannah up here, but they ran back to New Jersey," says Jon, opening and closing the menu, agreeing to share the rib eye with my dad.

"Daphne and Hannah?" I ask. "Where'd you see *Daphne and Hannah*?"

"She says to say hi," he says.

Is it my imagination, or is there some deeper meaning to that hi?

"And?" I practically demand.

"And what? She said to say hi. Boy, A, what are you so nervous about?"

"That's what I said, but your father doesn't listen to me. So where'd you see Daph?"

"We're doing a shoot for Lacoste and need a few kids. Hold-enn's too young, but I had her bring Hannah to the casting."

"Can't you just give her the job?" asks Maddie. "You're the photographer. She's so adorable."

"Maddie, you know the client has final say," informs my father. "But she is adorable, all right. And precocious."

"*I'll* say," and I sure do.

Everyone turns to look at me. Or rather turns to turn on me. Protective of our Hannah. What unadorable precocious thing could little Hannah ever do? The question looms through their glares. And though I am with my own *mishpacha*, I have now learned a new way to answer. I smile.

"Well, I'm putting her on my list of recommendations," says Jon.

After that encounter with Daphne and Hannah in New Jersey, I was too afraid to speak with my sister. Besides which, when we got back to the city I was just a little preoccupied. Josh, still feeling like my protector, said and did all the right things. He dropped off Adam and Stacy, then drove to my building, where, conveniently, there was a parking spot right on my block. He finally came up to my apartment.

In my frantic rush, I had left the shopping bag Krista gave me half unpacked in the front entry hall. We tripped on it coming in, Christmas cards and wrap spilling out.

"Glad to see you're normal," Josh said of the small mess all over the floor, in the hall and beyond. "I like stuff hanging around. My ex was so compulsively neat, it always drove me crazy."

The de-Jewifying left my apartment in a less-than-finished state. Books on the coffee table, newspapers and magazines on the carpet. I was mortified to leave it like that, but the doorman announced Josh downstairs and I was just glad I made it back in time to not be late. I put Krista's white bread and a stick of butter on the kitchen counter and was out the door in a flash. And wouldn't you know? That was another of the things Josh noticed after we came in.

"Hey, E . . ." He came up behind me kissing my neck after he'd gone into the kitchen to get some water. "I thought you were into LoveLoaves?"

I turned and faced him, beet red.

"No big deal. I'm going to get you into the good stuff. Next time I'll bring you some kick-ass bread. But I don't know about putting that melted goop on it." He made a face to show that although undesirable, it was, indeed, adorable. "Would you keep a thing of Breakstone's whipped in the fridge for me?"

"Of course," I said. Relieved.

After buying the sticks, I gave away my brand-new unopened container of Breakstone's whipped butter to Tova. I wondered if Josh meant the regular or the—

"Salted," he added, unbeknownst to him the perfect answer to my unspoken question.

And talk about perfect. After he weans me off the goop, I can get my refrigerated butter back. Bagels aside, I will also have a legitimate reason to keep away from the more fat, more calories, less fiber, and less desirable white bread.

When Josh went into the bathroom, I muted the volume on the answering machine, shut the ringer on my landline, and powered down my cell. Momentarily safe from being called on my escapade. With the technology turned off, I thought I could get turned on.

We were on my couch. Me rushing in, recoiling back. It felt so good, until I thought about what I was doing to Josh. Then I felt so bad.

"Princess." His hands were under my shirt. "So sweet," he murmured, searching front and then back to open my bra.

"Josh!" I called out when I felt him locate the hook, hardly a call of the wild.

It's not that I wasn't desirous. Quite the opposite. I hadn't been intimate since Christmas. My body was willing. As was my heart. But my brain. So *fermished* was this shiksa, I knew the night would hardly feel intimate if I chose to go that way.

Josh's fingers fished around the back strap, figuring how it unhooked. I felt so free when the bra fell open. I lunged. Then quickly stopped. If only I could. I lunged again. I felt tempted to just do it anyway, but my body language must have read differently.

"I'm sorry," said Josh, reaching around to rehook the bra before sitting up on the couch. He pulled me toward him, resting my head in his lap. "It's okay, eMay," he said. "I get it."

My heart skipped a few beats. He gets it? Oh, no. *He got it.* Just from making out with me! *Omygod.* But how? It must be my passionate Jewish blood. Jewish women are known to be great in bed.

"I know all about you Waspy girls," he seductively whispered into my ear, nuzzling his nose up against it. "Not to get into it, but you're not my first."

Incredulous, I looked at Josh.

"Oh, don't worry, my little ice princess." He lifted my chin and gave me a tender kiss. "I'll thaw you out."

He'll thaw *me* out? Just who does he think he's talking to? Oh. Well, yeah. I guess there is that.

"Oh, Josh," I cooed in character. "You're just *so* sensitive. But are we really that different from Jewish girls?"

Josh cleared his throat and used a Catskills comic voice. "How do you know when a Jewish wife reaches orgasm?"

I just shook my head; and not because I didn't know the punchline.

"She drops her emery board!"

"Ha. Ha. Ha." I wanted to slug him, but as my brother would say, "You started it."

With everything going on, plus work, it took a while for me to return Daphne's calls: ten messages on my home phone and six on my cell, not to mention how many deleted e-mails. Finally she sent a text.

r u crazy?

To which I replied:

pls keep secret! call soon. shiksa sis xx

I look at my family seated around this table. So far so good. So I think. Daphne and I have since caught up. And while she constantly threatens, as far as I know she's remained mum. I haven't told my parents I'm even dating. Each day is for me and for Josh. And I'm trying to make sure each one's not our last.

"So you kept the hair," says my brother, I think with approval. "I'll have to tell Jackie. You like?"

"Changed my life."

"I like it," says my dad. His eyes shine bright, and it makes me feel good.

"It's a nice change if you're in the mood for one," says my mother. "But I like you better with your real hair. That's my Aimee. This is pretty, though. Makes you look like a shiksa."

I practically spit out my water, but their reactions confirm everything. There's something about shiksas Jewish men find exotic, but for a woman—even if she's my mom—I always sense some potential threat. I don't quite understand it, but for my purposes in my current circumstance, I am totally pleased.

"I told Krista to meet us here," I say, changing the subject. "She's going shopping downstairs."

"What's with her since she broke up with the Rhode Island boy?" asks my mother.

"We're always talking about boys," says my father. "Tell me about this product launch," he says, and I see he has hurt my mother's feelings. But I will gratefully discuss the launch to avoid talking about boys.

Out of all the configurations of our nuclear family, I think this one, my father, Jon, and I—Albert Media—is my mother's worst. When I see her puttering in the kitchen with Daphne, kids underfoot, she glows in her rightful matriarchal status. For selfish reasons, I don't come to her aid as often as I should, so when I see her like that I always feel especially good.

"So it's the launch of KISS's newest, greatest, best ever yet color copier."

"Wow," says Jon. Unimpressed.

I give him a look. "At the event we're going to have a kissing contest. And I'm pretty sure that Ramy, that great cosmetics company, will be a corporate sponsor."

"Haven't you shot with them?" Sid asks Jon.

He nods in agreement. There is a momentary silence, but only to start our appetizers.

"So. You get it?" I ask.

"I don't see the *tie-in*," says my mother, digging into her Caesar salad and into my father, letting him know she is a part of this loop.

"Go on," says my dad, chomping on his salad. Oblivious.

"People will donate a dollar a kiss—the proceeds will go to CancerCare, okay—and plant the kiss on a blank piece of paper. We'll color-copy them and post all the kisses on a big board or something. Then the other half of the couple will have to choose whose lips belong to their partner."

"And they can do that because . . . ?" half-asks Jon.

"See, the idea is the digital imaging is so authentic, so exact, how could anyone not recognize the lips of the one they love?"

I take a sip of water and pull a long strand of cheese out of my French onion soup. It feels so good to not have to think first, and just be able to eat and talk.

"Let's say fifty couples guess right," says Jon. "How does a couple win?"

"KISS has budgeted for a celebrity judge. All the couples that are close will have to have a real kiss. And the judge will pick who wins. And they'll get a prize. They'll win a fabulous prize."

"Like an office-sized color copier that won't fit in their apartment?"

"Very funny. And I almost have a great celebrity lined up."

"Who?" asks Maddie. "I love celebrities."

"Laura Bell Bundy!"

"Who?"

"Who's Laura Blue Buns?"

"Never heard of her."

Oy. This only confirms what I fear. KISS will feel the same way. But what can the company expect for such a small amount of money?

"Well, she's fantastic," I say, and this is true. "She's the star of that Broadway musical *Legally Blonde.* And there's talk of a Tony Award."

"Why do they keep turning movies into musicals?" asks my mother. "Why can't anyone write for the theater anymore?"

"KISS thinks she's high enough profile?" asks my dad, done with his salad and anxiously awaiting the steak.

"How's she going to attract the attention of the press?" asks Jon. "And what does anything about her or her show have to do with kisses?"

All right. She's all wrong. "It doesn't matter," I lie, already dreading our staff meeting in the morning.

"Wait a sec." Rather than look at me, Jon puts down his knife and fork and peers into his prosciutto and melon. "What if a gay couple enters? A male gay couple?"

"Your point?"

"One of the guys has to wear lipstick."

My parents laugh. But I can't say the same for me. My brother continues to look for a glitch to get into. The food is on the table, and I prefer to get into that.

"It's just to do the picture," I diffuse, and put a big helping of creamed spinach on my plate. "That's all." I take the piece of steak my mother's cut off for me. "What, Jon?" I can see he's not done. And I don't mean with the meal.

"It's just that the initiatives your firm tends to do are all so white-bread," he taunts, before he munches away.

White-bread? *White-bread!* He knows. Jon definitely knows. Daphne has told him. Yes, and he is trying to get my goat. He sure as heck got my dander.

"This from a guy who spends his day airbrushing away any ounce of character that could possibly appear in his work," I attack back.

"That was uncalled for, Aimee," says Sid.

"What did I do?" I look from Jon back to my father. "Daddy, make him apologize."

"For what? Having a conversation? What is it with you? What are you so nervous about?" asks my father.

"You finally noticed," says my mother.

"I'm not trying to be difficult," says Jon. Feeling in the right, he is now able to come to my rescue. "I think you're gangbusters at your job. It's just that I think sometimes your work has the tendency to create—"

Here we go.

"Okay, that's enough," says Maddie, catching my eye. "We're eating. We're done talking about work. Stop it now. The both of you." My mother is hardly annoyed as her place in the family structure, once again clear, makes her happy.

Jon and I look at each other and go back to our steaks. He knocks his knee against mine under the table. I chew a bit, then use my knee and knock his back.

"Ma-a," he sing-songs like a ten-year-old. "Tell Aimee to stop knocking my knee."

"He started it," I say, and look at Jon. This is our way of making up. Sometimes I think we bring on our regressions just to feel young. The outburst, however, also helps me to let off a little steam.

"You know," my brother says under his breath, "I really didn't do anything, except maybe point out the obvious."

"Well, if you want to know the truth, the budget sucks so a big celeb is tough. Besides, I wanted someone based here because I need the launch to be in the city. L.A. means rental cars. And Jay is leaning on me again."

My family exchanges knowing looks.

"Aimee. There is no evil eye," my brother explains. "Let go. It's time to move on."

"That's what I always say," says Maddie.

I look to my father for support, but he's cheering the other team.

"Go online," says Jon, "and download the manual to study and take the test for a learner's permit. You're going to have to get an eye test and stuff too. When you get the permit, you can practice or take real driving lessons."

"If you want, we can practice on Sunday," says my dad.

"I thought you liked staying alive," Jon tells him.

"What's this I hear about Sunday?"

Everyone looks up from the table and happily shouts Krista's name. At this moment she couldn't be more welcome if she were the Messiah.

"Join us," says my dad. "What do you want? Order something."

A passing waiter adds a chair to the head of the table. Comfortable with my family, Krista sits.

"Thank you, Sid, but I'm meeting my boyfriend later for dinner," she says, her eyes wide as she not only lets the cat out of the bag but makes sure the opening's large enough for him to jump. "He plays tennis some nights after work."

And the conversation turns back to boys. But it's Krista's boy, and all the Alberts are excited to hear.

"Aimee didn't tell me about this," says Maddie. "You look happy. Good for you."

"He's a dream," says Krista. "And guess what? He's Jewish!"

My parents practically applaud. It's always been a phenomenon to observe. When I told them Peter was Not, it wasn't a problem, but it also was not a reason to raise your glass in merriment. Conversely, however . . .

"Whoa," says Jon. "Go, Kris."

"What does that mean?" I ask. But I already know. It means Jon thinks her guy is cool. Hunting outside his tribe, he brings back the coveted prey. Even without having met, Jon has more kudos for Matt dating Krista than if he was dating me.

"Well, it's really because of all of you I was even interested in dating a Jewish man," she says.

"You mean the neurotic Jewish family is a turn-on?" asks Jon, making my father laugh.

"I think it's lovely," says Maddie. "Isn't it?"

"Whatever," says my brother.

"You know, her boyfriend's kind of into it, Jon," I tell him. "He's pretty knowledgeable. Observes traditions. Krista goes with him some Friday nights to services. Matt's not like you."

"Oh," says Jon, and I see he makes a slight adjustment. Perhaps the guy's not that cool, after all. "Well, just don't go all Jewish on us now, Krista. You know how sometimes when non-Jewish women convert they get superreligious," he says, the idea not at all appealing.

"And what if she did?" I ask, both of us jumping Krista's conversion gun, talking about her as if she isn't there. "Why would that be so bad?"

Krista blushes. It brings up things she is mulling over but not ready to discuss in public. Things personal. And things private.

"All right, I see where this is going," says Maddie. "I'm a referee tonight," she confides in Krista. "Everything is an argument."

"So"—Sid turns to my friend—"welcome to the Jewish family."

Inside and Out

J ON HAS HIS CAR in a garage nearby and offers to drive everyone home. My parents jump on it, but Krista has not done
her food shopping and I have yet to do mine.

"I'll take them now and come back for both of you. How's
that?"

After I get my license, I wonder if I'll get a car and drive
around the city like the characters in *Seinfeld*. Even though it
takes place in Manhattan, they drive everywhere as if they live
in the burbs. Most people in the city don't do that. Although
Jon, now, does. Living downtown, he often teases that he has to
renew his visa in order to come uptown and visit.

"He knows," I tell Krista, pushing our carts down the meat
aisle. "I can see it in his eyes. Jon knows." Krista immediately
heads to the kosher section. Something I never do.

"I want to cook Matt a Shabbat meal," she says, I note cor-
rectly. She picks up an uncooked kosher chicken and throws it
into her cart. "What makes you think he knows?"

We continue on as I pick up a package of pork sausages. Both
bypassing the blintzes and heading straight to the soups.

"He was awfully testy with me tonight," I say, putting two cans of Campbell's New England clam chowder into my cart.

"Isn't that just the way you guys are?" Krista asks, and takes a can of Manischewitz chicken soup off the shelf.

"So you know," I tell her, "it also comes with matzo balls."

"It's okay," she says. "I'm going to make my own."

"Impressive. Look, tonight was different. I'm really worried about him talking with Daphne," I say, and watch Krista reach upward for a package of matzo meal. "You're learning so fast?"

"Well, Matt told me his grandmother used to make the best knoodles." She glows when she says this.

"You mean *knaidlach*?" I ask, never having made them myself. After the kugel, it was the next recipe I was going to try in the cookbook I got from Peter.

"No, this time I mean knoodles. That's what Matt and his younger sister used to call them when they were kids."

"Sweet."

"I don't think he knows," she tells me. "I just think you're paranoid. Oh!" Krista reaches across the aisle and drops a box of Minute Rice into my cart. "You'll need this."

"Huh?"

"For your hearty sausage-and-rice casserole," she explains, pointing to the contents in my cart. "Perfect for after work. Recipe should be on the can of the soup. Takes only fifteen minutes to prepare. And you can fool around for the hour it takes to bake."

This from a shiksa. Ice princess, my ass. What does Josh think he's talking about?

Krista and I both check out and then go outside to wait in front of the store. Jon has phoned and is on his way down from Ninety-sixth Street to pick us up.

"So that part's good between you guys?" I ask. Fishing for more.

Krista, usually an open book, is unusually quiet about Matt. This is the first time she has really been discreet. I respect that, but I miss her stories. My favorite was about the guy who was lying with her in bed, hands at his sides, and was leaning over to kiss her. The whole thing not going anywhere and not quite knowing what to do, Krista took his hands and began moving them across her body. "Oh," he finally said, perking up. "You mean you want me to touch you?"

"God yes," she exclaims now, referring of course to Matt. "It's definitely good." She checks her watch. Counting the hours until he's back from tennis and they have dinner. "Believe it or not, Matt was my very first Jew," Krista confides.

"Really?" This tidbit is juicy enough to make up for all that privacy. "But what about Scott Solomon, and Kenny Something-berg—oh, you know who I mean."

"Nope. Never. They were only one or two dates." Krista giggles and reflects. "Are they all that good?"

"I usually don't have any complaints," I tell her. I quickly think through my past boyfriends and see I am right. As great as it was with Sam, in a completely different way it was incredibly wonderful with Peter. I don't think of sex exactly as a religious or cultural activity. It's really just the personal chemistry. But chemistry does start in the brain, and I'm seeing the potency of the power of belief.

"Matt says that Jewish women are uptight, but us Catholic girls are really wild."

"Oh he does, does he? Well, can't say I've ever been with one, but I've always heard Catholic girls are repressed. And I can tell you, firsthand, Jewish women are wild."

So put that in your hat!

"Oooooh," says Krista. "Sounds like you guys are having fun."

"Not yet. I've been a *bisel* uptight." I look at Krista, pleased to not have to state the obvious as to why. "Now Josh thinks I'm a Waspy ice princess."

Honk! Honk!

"A *bisel*?" she asks.

"A little," I translate.

"A *bisel*. I'll remember that. Icy or not, is a Waspy princess hotter than a Jewish one?" asks my friend.

We look up and see Jon illegally double-park his new navy blue Maxima in front of Fairway. He gets out of the car to help us with our bags, lined up on the ground near the curb.

"I don't know. But I think we're on the way to finding out."

Jon steps onto the sidewalk to help carry our bags to the car. Between us, we have five. Krista did more shopping than me. Not terribly interested in cooking, I'm more of a binge chef. I hope Jon doesn't think anything of the sudden stock-up.

"Okay, whatcha got here?" he says, and takes three bags at once. Krista and I follow behind and watch as he opens the trunk. Our remaining bags rest on the street. "I'll separate them so you don't get them mixed up when I drop you off."

Even though he's a creative, I always appreciate my brother's organizational skills.

"Okay," says Krista. "I'll show you which ones are mi—"

"It's okay, Kris. I can see for myself," Jon says, and laughs. He peeks inside a few of the bags, overflowing with Jewish food.

Manischewitz mixes, matzo meal, and matzo ball soup—backup in case the homemade ones don't turn out well. A jar of gefilte fish, another of horseradish. A round challah, a dozen chocolate *rugelach* cookies, a separate bag for the uncooked chicken . . . and that's just for starters. Potato pierogi, sour cream, a bottle of borscht; even I can't believe she bought that.

"Now really, whose would these be?" Jon says, and winks at me.

"Actually"—Krista actually gets the word out before I jab her with my elbow.

"We'll put these on the left," says my brother, "and I'll grab them when we get to Aimee's."

"You don't have to do that," I tell him. "Willie will get them for me."

"And risk having you tell Dad I made you carry?" says Jon. "No way." He picks up the remaining bags to put in the trunk. "Boy, you two can shop. The women I date wouldn't even eat if not for me," he continues, but first looks into the bags.

He's now into mine. I look at Krista. She waves her hand in such a way that tells me not to worry about it. But I don't know what's going to happen when we get to my apartment and he goes to get them. And I don't want to wait till we're there to find out.

"This is more interesting than going through a woman's purse," says Jon.

He is baiting me. Boy, is he ever. I appeal to Krista while a nosy Jonathan makes his way through food bags filled with the American dream, complete with a package of ham, Kraft macaroni and cheese, Pillsbury buttermilk biscuits, Ronzoni spaghetti, Mrs. Paul's fish sticks, and a quart of homogenized whole milk.

"Krista. I think the Shake 'n Bake era is over," he says, and presses down to close the trunk.

My good friend good-naturedly laughs. With her eyes she urges me to do the same. I chortle.

"Okay, everybody. Get in."

Krista moves forward. Walking a few steps, she opens the door to the backseat. I don't move at all. I've got to figure out how to get me and my food away from this car and into a cab.

"A, get in," Jon calls from the driver's side of the car.

"You know what?" I call back. "I just remembered I forgot something. Or maybe it got mixed up in Krista's bag. Can you pop the trunk?"

Jon pops open the trunk, and I see our bags neatly placed on opposite sides. Opposite sides. If that's not a metaphor for my life. Okay, I can take my bags out and make an excuse to not take the ride, but then when he gets to Krista's he'll realize those American dream ones were mine. I should have just said they were. We grew up eating ham and macaroni and cheese. For God's sake, we drank milk. What is my problem?

"Aimee, come on," calls Jon. "I don't have all day."

I hear the back door open and close. Krista now stands beside me. She looks at me with exasperation. She does not like having to constantly cover for me.

"Just take yours into the backseat, okay?" I urge. "And I'll take mine. We'll say we were afraid that things would break in the trunk."

"And when he goes to help me?" Krista asks.

"Put the eggs or something on the top to cover that other stuff. Look, he's not going to look in there anymore. This is all Daphne's fault. I know she told. Maybe not the whole thing, but enough to make him suspi—*Aaaaaah!*"

I jump, as suddenly Jon is behind us, a policeman standing next to him.

"See, Officer, we're leaving *now*. Aren't we?" He brushes past me and Krista, slams down hard on the trunk, and practically pushes the two of us into the car. "That was close," he says when we pull away. There's a red light so we don't get too far.

"Makes you appreciate the suburbs," says Krista from the back. I instantly turn my head. Knowing everything, how dare she talk about the suburbs?

"Well, I wouldn't go that far," says my brother. "But Daph loves it in Jersey. She said she ran into you the other day, A. Mum's the word? Or is it Mom?" He laughs.

I knew it. I'm going to kill her. If I could drive, I'd be flying across the George Washington Bridge, ready to do it now.

"Pull over," I say to Jon as the light changes. "I'm getting my stuff out, and I'm getting a cab home." Not paying any attention, I open the passenger door just as he starts driving. Quickly making a sharp right, Jon instantly veers the car over to a space near a hydrant. He slams hard on the brakes, and we hear a horrible sound. Like an accident in the making, except it doesn't happen.

"Are you crazy?" he screams.

What!!??

Are you crazy? Are you crazy? *r u crazy?* I knew it. I KNEW IT.

"How could my own sister betray me like that? So I'm pretending to be a shiksa. So kill me."

"You think I'm going to take you out driving? Opening the door when the car's in motion? What's up with you tonight?" Jon hollers. My head is down; I have to get away. "All Daphne said was that you had a new guy. No one said anything about pretending to be a—"

Silence. There is silence in the car. I can feel the thought absorb itself into Jon's brain faster than the borscht can get into your bloodstream. He looks at me. First in disbelief. And then delight.

"This is priceless." My brother laughs. He laughs harder. He laughs so hard, he has to hold the side of his stomach as his head falls down over the dashboard.

"Jonathan," I cry. And I do mean cry.

"Aimee, this is better," says Krista. Consolingly, she thinks.

"You know about this?" Jon turns to her. "Of course you do! You two are in cahoots. You have a Jewish guy, and you have . . ." He turns and faces me. "What *do* you have?"

"A Jewish guy," I answer. "Not one like Sam, though. A guy with shiksa syndrome. Like you," I say accusingly. If it weren't for men like Jonathan, I wouldn't have to go through this charade, now would I?

"Shiksa syndrome?" My brother laughs even harder. "Wow, I never realized just how creative you PR girls really are. Now there's a spin for ya."

"Fuck you!"

"Hey—watch your mouth, Aimee."

"I'm sorry, Jonathan," I instantly say. Embarrassed I cursed. Sorry I'm not calm. Or composed. And really sorry I lost it. Lately I am losing it so much, I begin to wonder if I will ever find it all again. "I'm so on edge," I try to explain. "Forgive me. But he's a supernice guy, and it's working. So . . . do me a favor and just don't tell. ANYBODY. Okay?"

Jon looks at me as if we never met. "It's weird because I obviously know you *very* well. But"—he studies me before he finishes—"you can sort of pass."

"Really?" I lighten up. These words give me so much confidence, this whole car thing was almost worth it. "Well, it is in part thanks to you," I credit my brother. "It started the night Jackie gave me the makeover. Standing next to Krista at this Jewish singles event, I was mistaken. For Not."

Jon nods his head. He gets it. Then he turns to Krista. "Wait, does the guy you're dating think you're Jewish?" he asks.

"No. My guy knows I'm Catholic. But I might become Jewish."

"Ah yes," he says, remembering the grocery bag with the kosher chicken and all its Hebraic trimmings. "And your plan, A? To become Catholic?"

"Very funny. First of all, I'm a Protestant. Just so you know. And I'm waiting for Josh, that's his name, to start introducing me to becoming Jewish. Which I imagine will happen very soon."

"I see," says my brother. Highly amused. "Well, then . . . don't let him take you driving until you convert. You don't know what Yiddish expletive might pop out of your mouth when you're behind the wheel."

More time having passed than planned, I suggest Jon go ahead and drive Krista downtown so she is not late to meet Matt. I take my two grocery bags and decide to walk on Broadway a few blocks to chill before I hail a cab. Passing Fairway, I see a few dancer girls exit from Steps, the dance school whose door is practically hidden between Fairway's outside stands of berries and grape tomatoes. I duck inside and take the stairway upstairs.

The moment I walk inside, a sense of calm overtakes me. The sight of dancers transports me. Beautiful bodies in colored leotards walk by. Capezio shoes, footless tights, bare feet, ballet slippers. I walk through the reception area, noting the night's classes written in red on the big white magnetic marker board. In the studio to my right I can look through the glass window. I put down my grocery bags and watch the class called Advanced Beginner Ballet.

About fifteen students line up in rows in the center of the floor. Practicing the steps after seeing them done by the teacher. Learning tonight's combination. The teacher claps her hands, and they disperse into a corner of the room. The pianist begins to play. Sprightly and gay, classical music seeps through the door.

"Pirouette, pirouette, pirouette," calls out the instructor. "Jeté right, left, jeté right, left, right." They dance. In groups of three across the studio they glide. Light and lifted. "Now grand jeté!" Starting from one leg and landing on the other, in a series of long horizontal jumps, the students travel across the floor.

I want to dance. As if no one is looking. To feel that abandon. To travel. To fly. Just like the first night with Josh in front of Bergdorf's. I feel that desire now.

"Josh!" He answers his cell on the first ring. "Where are you? It's me, eMay."

"Thought you were having dinner with Krista," he says. I hear an ambulance trail off in the background.

"We're done. Where are you?" I ask.

"In a cab," he says. "Just left work. Heading down Broadway. Just passed Eighty-sixth."

"I went shopping after. I'm in front of Fairway," I say, picking up the bags with my left hand and bolting back through reception. He'll be here in a few seconds. Fairway's on Seventy-fifth. "Pick me up in front and let me take you home."

Tonight. Tonight I will leap. My grand jeté. I open the door to leave Steps and practically dance on down the stairs.

Shifting Gears

"So you think you would have liked me if we had met in college?" Josh asks as we drive off the Syracuse University campus. We came up yesterday from the city for his college reunion.

As reunions go, this was a small one. A Saturday night dinner on campus honored his class of economics majors. Josh is still uncertain who began the e-mail trail that hunted down and successfully brought together a large enough percentage of alumni. He only knew he wanted to be there.

That he wanted to be there with me blows me away. Since becoming lovers he's most attentive. (Though possibly more out of bed than in.) Josh always has a plan—theater tickets, dinner reservations. He must see every movie and has season tickets for the Mets, the Yankees, and the Knicks. I'd never been to a basketball game. To educate me, yesterday, we went to a game at the Carrier Dome. Josh says the Syracuse stadium ranks up there with Madison Square Garden. The Orangemen played Notre Dame. My favorite thing, the twenty-four-second clock.

You probably already know this, but I didn't. Seems the clock starts when a player gets possession of the ball. Not only must it leave the player's hand before the twenty-four seconds are up, but it also has to make contact with the basket rim. Everything has to happen fast. Josh explained that on the college level the guys get thirty-five seconds. Still, it gives new meaning to the words *the ball's in your court.*

I think singles events—a situation only for pros—should employ the twenty-four-second clock. Though based on the two I attended, as seconds go I'm not sure you need the whole twenty-four.

We drive down the road, and I feel a sense of peace. It is great being out of the city with Josh. My neck of the woods, he calls it. Upstate New York, not far from Pennsylvania. Whenever he says that, I just giggle. Far from out of the woods, it is sheer relief to be on neutral turf.

People don't pay all that much attention to people's dates or spouses at reunions. The agenda, mainly, is to reminisce. Relay the stories of life back in the day. All I needed to do was lots of listening, nodding, and smiling.

"Hey, Hirsch," said Alan Resnick. His wife, Judy, home on Long Island with their three kids, he felt like a man about town. "Remember the night before that big midterm? Junior year? There was that bitch of a blizzard. And we had to sleep in the library and then go straight from there to take the test."

"Yeah, dude. Your feet wound up in my face in the corner of Women's Fiction."

You get a lot of information by observing. What I mainly observe about Josh is that he's not very observant. He's got a hand in everything when it comes to the big picture, but he's not into the details. Unobservant, he doesn't pick up on the small stuff, so he doesn't pick up that I do. I'm the total opposite.

We checked out of the motel before our time was up. Something I rarely do unless I have to catch a plane. I like to linger in bed, especially in the morning. But Josh seems to have a restless soul. Always on the go. I feel it takes away from our alone time. The intimacy of lying together and sharing. Outlooks, stories. Feelings, childhood tales.

I miss that time but also feel responsible for not helping make it happen. It's easy to blame what's missing on Josh, but I know a lot of it's because of me. I'm not exactly an open book; real sharing is something I rarely do. On the other hand, I don't feel I'm withholding because Josh doesn't ask me many questions. I often wonder why.

"Penny for your thoughts," he asks now, this moment potentially a crossroad if I would allow it. We are literally at a fork in the road and veer left, passing a gas station, a church, a post office, and a convenience store.

"Just content," I answer.

"It's amazing," says Josh, picking up speed, taking us onto the open country road. It is still winter, but it's now lighter. Spring about to leap forward.

"What is?"

"How easygoing you are," he says, driving over to the side of the empty road. Stopping the car. "You're so low-maintenance."

"Low-maintenance?"

He means this as a compliment, but I don't hear it that way. Low or high, it's one of those terms I do not like. What does it really mean? Everyone requires maintenance. So does everything. If the maintenance feels too high, it's probably more a reflection on the other person. He or she feeling that something or someone isn't really worth that level of their energy or attention. My brother once dated a wardrobe stylist he originally thought was the cat's meow. Unlike Jewish women, this girl was not high-maintenance.

Drinking at an outdoor café, I became so enraged when Jon said that, I poured my pinot grigio over his head before bolting from the table and heading straight into a cab. For Jon it remains a funny story. Aimee, insulted he called Jewish women high-maintenance, disproves his point by dousing him with her drink. *Not!* But several months later, he and the girl broke up, Jon saying his life was her life, and she didn't have one of her own. In the end she was boring. Perhaps too low-maintenance?

"What do you mean?" I ask Josh, anxious to hear him explain.

"Like now. I'm always in these relationships where those silences mean the woman wants to know where it's going. Always all this analysis. Man, it gives me a headache. But with you—"

Me? Oh yes, little ole low-maintenance me.

See, to be with someone, to be with anyone is to make accommodations. But if you really want to be with that person, you don't feel you are making them. Doesn't Josh see how he accommodates me by simply filling in the blanks? To prove this point to myself, I don't answer. I look at him. Questioningly. And then I smile.

"You just roll with it. You don't ask for anything. It makes me want to give that much more."

"Oh, Josh, don't—" I turn away.

"Don't what?"

Think so highly of me but "Flatter me so much" is what I say before leaning over to give him a kiss. It's so nice, I lean in further, kissing him more, but he stops me.

"Hey, a cow will see us, and I'll get embarrassed. Besides, I pulled over to give you something. Important."

"Really?"

Ohmygod. *Really?* This all worked faster than even I thought.

Josh shuts off the ignition and turns off the radio. "I want the conditions to be perfect. What happens today will set the precedent. And I want you to be able to remember it always."

It seems totally improbable, but it's happening. Okay, if he proposes now, can I just say yes and tell him the truth later? Would that wreck our lives?

Plan B. We can be secretly engaged. Say it's all too fast and it should be our secret for a while. Then I can tell him I'm Jewish before we announce to the world we've united as one.

"So . . . ?" I sweetly begin, and toss my long, straight red hair over my shoulder. Picture-perfect hair for which I slave away every three days (not to mention drop a bundle) to maintain, so I have what to toss for moments like these. "Just what do you want to give me?"

"A driving lesson," Josh announces, and abruptly unlocks both doors so we can get out and switch sides. "I've got the driver's manual right here, and we can do practice tests on the car ride home. And Monday I'll meet you at the DMV in the meatpacking district. After you get your learner's permit, we'll celebrate at Spice Market."

A learner's permit is good for five years, but when I do the math I realize that my last one has also expired. I'll now be getting my fourth. Is that a record? Monday afternoon we have an off-site meeting to look at venues for the KISS launch. For this cause Jay will allow me to meet up with Josh, but I'll have to go back to the office after.

However, I don't share any of this. Instead, I just thank Josh, feeling gratitude that he is taking charge. Relief that he did not question my living in Pennsylvania and relying on car pools. Trying hard to relax, I sit behind the wheel of Josh's perfect BMW. Hoping when we're done with this lesson the car will still be that way.

"Let's start at the very beginning," he insists, and though I've been behind a few wheels in my day I've never been behind his. So I let him show me the accelerator and the brakes, how to adjust the mirrors, how to lock and unlock the doors.

We turn on the lights and the brights, and signal to the left then the right. Water splatters across the window when I switch on the windshield wipers in the front and the back. Hot and cold air blows with the heat and the air conditioner. The dashboard, with its indicators, dials, and displays, is like a control panel in a spaceship. Josh places his hand over mine and shows me how to shift. Then he places the key in my hand.

"There's the ignition. Put it in and start the engine."

If ever I feel close to Josh, it is now. He is trusting. And trusting me. I turn the car on. The engine roars. My palms sweat. A tingle starts at my temples and trickles its way down.

"I . . ." I look at Josh. I have not done this in years, and I'm nervous. In fact, I'm downright scared.

"Face front," he instructs. "Don't look at me, look at the road."

The empty road lies ahead. I am now the one to get this car on it.

"Can you help me?" I say, gripping the steering wheel hard in both hands. "Can you please help me steer?"

"eMay, we're not going anywhere if you don't press your foot down on the gas."

Hesitant, halting, and halfhearted, I tentatively press my foot on the accelerator. The car lurches forward.

"AAAAAAAH!"

"Don't freak," says Josh, his right hand on top of mind on the wheel. "You don't have to give it so much gas. Lighten up."

First I go too light, and then I brake too hard.

"You just have to get the rhythm," he says, and when he does it becomes a dance. The rhythm. When we both feel it, Josh takes his hand off the wheel. And while I wouldn't be eligible for NASCAR, suddenly we are moving and I'm driving.

"Oh, God!" I scream as we effortlessly glide down the smoothly paved road. "I can't believe this. And now? What do I do now?"

"Just keep going," says Josh. I feel him in a ready position to slam on the brakes or grab the wheel if necessary, but he only encourages me to go. Praising me as we go along. "Look, you're up to forty miles an hour"—he points to the dashboard—"but don't look down."

After a straight run for what the odometer claims to be almost six miles, Josh helps me signal to the right and brake at the side of the road. I'm breathing heavy when the car stops. My heart almost does, too, except for the fact I did it.

"I drove!" I scream, raising my hands in victory before throwing them around Josh's neck and kissing him. "My first BMW." Talk about luxury. I feel exhilarated. A sense of power. Maybe I'm finally on my way.

"And all thanks to you, Josh." I give him the biggest and best kiss. "My God, I actually drove. Let's celebrate."

"You're on." Josh gives me a quick kiss. "But first . . ." Opening the glove compartment, he hands over the driver's manual. Back in the passenger seat we ride side by side, doing the questions out loud.

Minimum speed signs are designed to:

a. Keep traffic flowing smoothly.

b. Show current local road conditions.

c. Test future traffic signal needs.

d. Assure pedestrian safety.

You may pass another vehicle on the right if it is waiting to:

a. Turn right.

b. Turn left.

c. Park at the curb.

d. Turn into a driveway on the right.

And though I see out the same windows as before, everything now looks different. Especially Josh.

Control—Home

KNOWING HIS WAY AROUND, Josh turns in and out of streets, until we pull into a strip mall. The parking area is big and extends beyond the small handful of stores. For behind them is an old-fashioned diner . . . and a motel.

What a day this is turning out to be.

I look to Josh and grin. In terms of a celebration, we are on the exact same page. Or driving the same highway to heaven, I almost say, but fear I will sound less like a romantic and more like a nerd.

"Let's go," he says, giving me a quick kiss across the seats before turning everything off. "Need anything from the trunk?"

"Ummm . . ." He probably has some in his wallet. "I'm good," I say and get out of the car, walking in the direction of the motel. SYRACUSE ECONO LODGE AND BANQUET CENTER: HAVE YOUR NEXT AFFAIR HERE. I laugh.

"Yep, it's cute," he says of the sign and grabs the back of my jacket, turning me in the direction of the Round the Clock Diner. "You're going to love their cinnamon buns."

I instantly feel ridiculous. And worse than ridiculous, I feel rejected.

"Cool," I say, careful to walk behind Josh as the waitress takes us to a booth in the back. Josh offers to hang up my jacket, and I slide in. We face each other across the Formica table, each on our side of the booth, sitting on aqua green upholstered seats, silver gaffer's tape covering a hole.

"What's the matter?" Josh asks. As good an imposter I've been as a shiksa, I don't have quite the same ability when it comes to just being a girl.

"Nothing," I answer. Why do people do that?

"Okay," he says, and opens the menu. Not coaxing me to tell him what's really going on. As he drops it, so do I.

My stomach suddenly very queasy, I order only cold cereal and fruit, eyeing Josh's All Day Special of two eggs, pancakes, bacon, home fries, and coffee.

"See, this is exactly what I mean," he says when we finish a rather nice breakfast. "*Other* women (when he says this now, I know it's code for Jewish but think, sadly, for Josh Jewish means JAP) will say 'nothing,' which really means *some*thing . . . and that's true even of you," he acknowledges. "But after they say 'nothing,' they keep needling you. But you let it go. It's great."

With so much invested in my pretense, when I am confronted with an aspect of our relationship that is only about a guy and girl I am instantly overwhelmed. I am embarrassed to tell Josh I wanted to celebrate at the motel. And that I thought he did as well. That kind of spontaneity was the breath of my relationship with Peter, and though different, it was intrinsically sewn into the fabric of what I shared with Sam. But Josh?

The relationship fairly new, the jury is still out. But Josh doesn't seem to have the same propensity toward sex as I do. I mean it's nice. Really nice. It hits all the right marks. However, it does not feel integrated into the relationship. It feels compartmentalized. A nighttime-only activity to be experienced only in a bed, and only in the most traditional way.

"I let go because everything isn't worth making into something," I say, angry at myself. Quite sure that my boundaries are responsible for what must cause his.

"So there was something?" he fishes, picking up a package of toothpicks at the cash register, asking with his eyes if I want one of the mints.

"Only this," I say, and grab his hand. Against the hood of his car, outside, I give Josh a huge hug. "Thank you so much for this trip. For the driving lesson. For being able to"—I feel a catch in my throat—"trust me."

"Of course," he says, and kisses me.

I allow the kiss to grow. Then pull away and look over to the motel.

"Really?" asks Josh.

Sheepishly, I nod.

"Right after breakfast? In daylight? Wow, you are *so* melted," he says, or rather gloats, giving himself an invisible pat on the back. He clicks the remote to unlock the car doors. "I can tell you I never met a Jewish girl with your libido," he says before walking to his side to get in and drive away.

If Josh feels I am good at letting go, the time to prove him right is definitely now.

"We have tonight, eMay," he says, actually picking up on my thoughts. Josh is right, I think, as I buckle my seat belt and touch his hand, not saying another word. "Besides, we can do that anytime, and if we hung out here it would ruin my surprise."

Oh, no. Please, not another surprise. But Josh squeezes my hand back, and it feels warm. It is all good. I focus on that, allowing our warmth and the heat of the seat to send rays of comfort through my body. We drive for a long while; we talk. At some point, unaware, I drift off.

Peter stands on an empty road. He holds a stop sign. I drive past him and merge into a brand-new lane. Josh rides by in a flashy convertible. It has fancy seats with electronic arms that reach into my car and pull me in. Suddenly I am behind the wheel, driving that car. Josh is next to me, and we laugh while we ride, until I see Peter. Now he's on this road waving the stop sign. Only I can't. I step on the brakes, but they do not work. I cannot stop. I try and try, but I can't find the brakes.

"Look familiar?" asks Josh, nudging me with his elbow, jolting me back to reality.

My head darts up, and I realize I was asleep. Having a dream, or more of a nightmare. But unbeknownst to me, the real one is only about to begin. I look up and, larger than life, the sign looms before me: US-6 W EXIT 191B—SCRANTON EXPWY.

"Ohmygod!" I shriek when Josh exits.

"Surprised?" asks Josh.

"You can't imagine!" From now on, I will only be fearful of what once was a favorite word. I silently pray as Josh exits and drives toward downtown.

It's a Sunday, and downtown Scranton is quiet. The absence of any modern jargon or garb makes the place appear as a look back in time. HAPPY BIRTHDAY LIZ, written across a big banner, hangs in front of Rocky's, where I expect the Fonz and his gang to drive up any second. Sole proprietors hang out their shingles on a realty business, a law office, an optometrist's, and fashions for hair. We ride through town; so far so good. Until we turn onto Spruce Street.

"Can't wait for you to show me around," Josh says, and parks in an empty spot across the street from a post office.

"Not much to show," I say, not unbuckling my seat belt. "What you see is what you get."

"I put it together this morning," he boasts, ignoring me and putting on his jacket before getting out of the car. "Syracuse isn't far, so it wasn't really *that* out of the way. And you know how I love *The Office.* It made me curious . . . especially now with you."

I can't believe I gave in and watched that TV show over *Grey's Anatomy.* That I passed up sex and intrigue in a hospital in favor of a bunch of quirky people working in some fictitious Scranton paper company. Yes, it's funny. But every time we watch, Josh says one day we have to go there. I never dreamed it'd be this one.

"Come on," he says. "You can show me the sights."

I zip up my jacket slowly, anxious to buy time. Breathe. In. Out. What will I do now? Think. Can I say everything has changed since I lived here? That nothing is recognizable anymore?

But when I look straight ahead, it still seems like the eighties. And of the nineteenth century . . . not the twentieth. In front of railroad tracks is a block of row houses that, if their doors were to open, I'd expect women in bustle dresses holding parasols to exit. It looks like a charming town, one I'd like to explore for real. Perhaps some other time, I think, my hand unconsciously rubbing my tummy. Gosh, my stomach hurts.

"eMay, you coming?" Josh knocks on the window, waiting for me to get out of the car.

"In a sec," I say, putting on my new L.L. Bean Mad Bomber hat. Mad, indeed. I try to get some bearings and calculate all my lies.

I said my parents sold the house and moved to Florida. Planta-tion Island, I said. Having just read about the place in the Travel

Section, it was fresh in my mind and didn't sound Jewish. Not like Miami or Boca. He does know I have a brother in New York. But I told him I don't have any family left here, so thankfully a visit home will be out.

Good. We'll just walk around, and hopefully everything I see will look new and can therefore be new to me. Gee, how far away, I wonder, is that Plymouth Congregational Church I googled? It must be near *my house.* Is that close to here? Hmmm . . . Maybe my family hardly came downtown. Who says I need to know downtown Scranton like the back of my hand?

"Hey," I say, catching up to Josh in front of a comic book store. "See anything good?"

"How long has this been around?" he says. "Looks very cool."

"This place?" I look into the dusty window. "Oh, let's see. This has been around for, well, as long as I can remember. My brother and I used to get to come here for our birthdays. As a treat. He was all *Spiderman,* but I always loved *Archie.*"

The lie rolls off my tongue so easily, it even feels good, but I can't say the same for my tummy. Still we keep going. We walk. I chat away.

"Growing up was when we were just on the cusp of America turning into one gigantic mall," I pontificate, inspired when I see a sign indicating the Mall at Steamtown is a few blocks away. "But I totally love the little personalized shops." I point when we pass a shoemaker and a jewelry store. "When I was a kid there were so many, many more than what you see here now."

I flail my arms to prove my point, except when I actually look, I see these streets are filled with tons of personalized shops. Clothing stores, an ice cream parlor, the mom-and-pop drug-store, you name it. But no matter what comes out of my mouth, Josh is in agreement, so I carry on.

"Corporate America," I say, and point ahead to the mall. "Now you go to any city in the whole country and wind up shopping in all the same stores as if you never left home. Such a lack of individuation. Such loss. It's really such a pity."

Forget Scranton. I'm venting feelings about the very thing that's happened where I did grow up. I cried at Columbus Circle, a few years back, when the Time Warner Center mall opened. *A mall in Manhattan?* I always think New York City's different from the rest of America. But it keeps becoming more and more the same.

Josh and I turn the corner and spot a Hilton. A sign announces a new coffee bar in the lobby that now, proudly, brews Starbucks. The two corporations pretty much prove my point.

"I need the ladies' room," I tell Josh when we get inside. Oh, my stomach. Was there something wrong with the fruit at breakfast? Could the milk in the cereal have been sour?

"Okay, but hurry up. Because I can't wait for you to show me the house where you grew up."

The house where I grew up? *Oh my goodness.* THE HOUSE WHERE I GREW UP?

"Wow." I feel woozy. "Uh. Yeah. I'll be right back, okay?"

Josh takes a newspaper and settles into a big cozy chair, while I scoot across the marble lobby, pick up a brochure from the concierge, and run to the safety of the bathroom. Sweat pours down my forehead. I pull off the hat and wet some hand towels, creating a compress to place across my forehead. Then I take out my cell phone, lock myself inside a stall, and pray.

"You've reached Jonathan Albert Photography. No one can take your call right . . . ."

Oh, no. He's my only hope.

". . . name and number after the—"

Beep!

"Jonathan! Jon, are you there? Pick up. It's me. I'm in *big* trouble."

"Where are you?" (I squeal with joy when I hear him live.) "I'm coming right now," he says, while a female voice in the background asks questions.

"*No.* No, not that kind of trouble," I quickly say, happy to know my brother would drop everything if, God forbid, I was ever in need. "Just go to your computer and tell me when you get to Mapquest. And do it fast. Okay?"

There is silence on Jon's end.

"Did you hear me? I don't have a lot of time. Will you help?" I pause. *"Please?"*

His silence informs me that he is angry, not to mention I believe I interrupted him at a very inopportune time.

"Say something!"

The click-clicking tap-tapping of the keyboard comes through the phone and puts me more at ease.

"Okay. Good. Go to Directions and at Start type in *Hilton Hotel.*" I pick up the brochure so I can read, "100 Adams Avenue in Scranton, Pennsylvania, and then do *Plymouth Congregational Church in Scranton* for End."

"You're pretty adept at directions for someone who doesn't drive."

"Yeah, well . . . You doing it or not?"

"You're out of your mind," says my brother. "You're in Scranton now, right? With the Jewish guy?"

"I'm in the bathroom at the Scranton Hilton," I say as fast as I have ever spoken. "We were in Syracuse at his college reunion, and he surprised me with a hometown visit."

"I never could have imagined you had this in you," says Jon.

"Spell *Plymouth*. And why Scranton? How the hell did you come up with that?"

"It shouldn't take this long," I say. Spelling, clicking, more waiting, more tapping.

"Anyone in your family still live there?" he asks. Facetiously.

"Nobody. Mom and Dad sold the house and moved down to Plantation Island."

Jon cracks up.

"Aside from that, all I have is a brother in New York. You're not a lie. Except for the not being Jewish part, which half the time you try to act like you're not anyway."

"I never deny my heritage, Aimee. It's my identity, so don't go there, okay? Even if I don't follow tradition like you doesn't mean—"

"Look, you never want to talk to me about this stuff, so don't start now. Did you get it?"

"Got it. You're in luck," he says, and gives me the address of the church. "And it's just three miles from the hotel."

"I can't thank you enough," I say, actually happy to discover I grew up close to downtown Scranton. My cosmopolitan flair. "I owe you."

"Just make sure you call me when you get back to th—"

I close the phone and stuff the paper with the info into my pocket without saying good-bye. Josh will wonder what took me so long. I should really tell him I feel sick, at this point the only thing that's not a lie.

"Which way?" he asks, once we're back in the car.

"You know, it's not all that interesting," I tell him. "So if you just want to head back—"

"No way," says Josh. "I wouldn't hear of it." Definitive. Waiting. Ready to go.

"Okay," I say. I know when I'm stuck. "But before we go to my house, let me show you my church."

Because I tell him how much I love it, we feed the address for the church into the talking road navigator. The calm and assuring voice directs us the 2.7 miles from the Hilton. I praise the Lord when we find the Plymouth Congregational Church still standing. A parking lot is filled with cars of Sunday churchgoers; my fellow neighbors, my friends.

"That's it." I point. "The minister used to come by our house for eggnog every Christmas."

God, please forgive me for I have sinned. That'll be ten Hail Marys. Oh, wait—that's not my religion.

"You want to get out?"

"No, definitely no. We don't want to . . . interrupt anything. Besides"—I look at him with pleading eyes—"I really just want to go home."

"Just point the way," he says, misunderstanding, assuming I mean my long-forgotten Scranton home.

If I could think of any legitimate reason we should get right back on the road, I would. Instead, I look at the map on the navigator screen. All the blocks surrounding the church seem good. Oak Street. Maple. Golden Avenue. Wayne. They all sound residential. I make a decision and hope we'll find my childhood house on Oak.

"Um"—I keep my eyes glued to the computerized map—"go to the corner and take a right."

I study the neighborhood. Absorbing whatever I can. These streets define me. They are my roots. An industrial town, Scranton is known for coal mining and establishing railroads. Traditional. Middle-class. Blue-collar. I identify. I did grow up in Manhattan, but I wasn't a rich kid. Public schooled over private, rental over co-op. Summer jobs instead of sleepaway camps. My father instilled the importance of education and hard work.

Looking around, I see I have not chosen a background of wealthy WASPs, country clubs, and the cocktail hour. And I couldn't have planned it better if I had planned it.

We make a right at the traffic light and drive up Oak.

"This block?" asks Josh, not sure whether or not to slow down.

"Uh . . . we're close."

I need to find *my house.* And it's really important I find the right house because it will inform Josh's impressions of my childhood.

"Go slow so we don't miss it," I say, but as we continue to drive I don't see any place on Oak Street where I feel I could have grown up.

On my right we pass a place so run-down it almost looks like a shack. I look over to see Josh's reaction. Perfectly content, he keeps driving. Until we get to the end of all the residences and the beginning of a little town.

"Do I keep going?"

"Uh . . ." I look back to the screen with the map. I won't be able to navigate us much farther. "It's been so long I . . . I think we may have passed it. Turn around and let's go back."

"You sure you grew up here?" He laughs.

We drive back down Oak as I peer out the window to the side streets. I feel pressure now to pick a house. Any house. I'm afraid we are nearing the end of the street when I scream, "Here! Make a right."

To my great relief, McDonough Avenue's perfect. Some kids are outside. Families appear to fill conventional wood frame houses painted yellow, tan, or gray. Fairly close together, the houses each have a front yard and a back. Stacks of wood in winter, swing sets in the summer. Spring must be so pretty. Gardens will bloom, and leaves will cover the trees.

"This is my block," I say with pride. "McDonough Ave." My eye takes me to a scooter in the middle of a driveway. I assume a young family has moved in. Young enough so this family will not remember mine. "1764," I point to the address on a gray house with a white picket fence and white shutters. Around the back we see the side of an above-ground swimming pool and, though still winter, the place where there's a garden.

"We planted herbs back there," I say, hopeful now this whole house thing is over. But Josh parks across the street and jumps out of the car.

"Maybe they'll let us in." The thought gets him excited.

Uh-oh. Don't look now, e-May, but I think it's curtains. I look at Josh like he's crazy.

"Why not?" he asks. "I think they're home."

Eager, Josh opens the car door and grabs my hand to escort me. He jabbers about little Aimee. Wide-eyed, pretty red hair, home from church frolicking down this path. His words paint a montage of me. The me nobody knows.

A child runs out from the back as we head up the stairs to the front porch. Josh looks at her and waves. Perhaps it is her bicycle on this porch, parked under the big wreath that hangs next to the front door. Yellow, with a cross in the middle, the family appears to have a head start on Easter.

The family. Oh, no. *THE FAMILY.* I can't go in. Please, please don't be home. Please don't be in the house. But they are, and I'm afraid in a minute so will I.

"Ring the bell," instructs Josh.

What if I'm right? What if this house does belong to a young family? Will I be asked about its history? Will I have to give a tour? Where is my room? What if they renovated and I'm supposed to tell how everything was before?

But what if the person behind the door has lived here for forty years? What then? What if Josh asks them about the Plunketts? *What if he wants to meet Muffy?*

"Can I help you?"

Josh tells me later she was blonde and pretty and said she was a nurse, but I don't remember. For after I ring the bell, I run back to the car and throw up on the walk. His curiosity satisfied, Josh listens when I insist we leave. We drive back to the Hilton and I clean up in the bathroom. Now, finally, at long last, Josh takes me home.

House Calls

"AIMALA." Tova's strong, spry voice carries through my apartment door. "I want to see you. Can I come in?"

I saw her early today in the hallway, after putting my garbage in the trash room. Shaking my head, I indicated I was not able to talk. Though by the looks of me, I'd say it was obvious. Sleep deprived, dressed in sweats, dirty hair piled on top of my head, and all on a Monday. Reaching the end of my twenty-four-hour stomach flu, I took the day off from work and stayed home.

Josh was appeased yesterday; fascinated to see where I actually come from. He wasn't the only one. And while I'm not sure if it was the milk or my *mishegas* that turned my stomach, the timing worked out just right. Still, that homecoming cut close enough to make me reevaluate just what the fuck I think I am doing.

"I've been sick," I tell Tova, opening the door. Said aloud, I believe this to be true in more ways than one.

"Yes," she readily agrees, showing a small shopping bag before brushing past me into the kitchen. "I saw you this morning, and I thought you didn't look like Aimee." Tova speaks from the other room. "I brought you chicken soup. You can keep the container. Maybe you'll want to heat up some soup for dinner?" I see it is now that hour. Apparently, I slept the day away.

I do feel better, and it feels good to see her. My connection with Tova is somewhat maternal. As of late, I am so estranged from my own mother. I can tell when we speak that she knows I am hiding something. Certainly she could never guess what.

"You want to sit down?" I ask, leading Tova into the living area, taking a seat on the brown leather club chair to face her on the beige chenille couch.

"All right," she says, moving a needlepoint throw pillow to make herself a space. "I'm going to a book review at the 92nd Street Y so I cannot stay too long."

"Who's speaking?"

"It should prove to be a very interesting lecture," she tells me, rearranging the colorful bangles on her wrist. Tova always does interesting things accompanied by interesting people and very interesting clothes.

"A female psychiatrist," she continues, "who wrote a book called *I'm Jewish, You're Not.*" She lets out a big laugh. "And it's a guidebook to interfaith relationships."

"*Very* interesting," I say, definitely agreeing. "But why are you going?"

"Well, it happens my nephew, Ari, from Israel was visiting, as you know, a few months ago. He brings with him to New York a portable computer . . . a . . . a . . ." She moves her hands to approximate the shape of a box. "He calls it a top—"

"A laptop. Yeah."

"That's right. A laptop. So-o"—she says the word as if it is two syllables—"he is here three weeks for business, he wants a little company, and he tells me one night he is going on a date. On the computer!" This makes her laugh again. "Wait. I can tell you exactly from where." Tova pauses to think. "Something latch, snatch, catch . . . ?"

"Match.com. Go on." I want to hear the interfaith story already so I can assess if she is talking about Ari, or somehow she found out and is really talking about me.

"So-o." Tova pauses. "He meets a girl, very nice. Christina Murray. A divorcee, his age, no children, a teacher. They meet. They go out every day. Then they stay in touch with the e-mail and the fast messages. He tells me how, I don't even know what he's talking about. But finally she takes a trip to Israel, and they fall in love. Now she's moving there and wants to convert. Tonight I'm going to have the author sign for her a book. A present."

"How about that," I say. "And so fast."

"Oh, *very* fast. Like a whirlwind," says Tova, her bracelets clanging together as she demonstrates, waving her hand in the air.

I can't believe this. God, this is so not fair. Every single shiksa who dates a Jewish guy is instantly swept onto the J-Bandwagon except for me. What am I doing wrong? How is it that I'm at a roadside diner on my way to church, when everyone else is learning how to baste a brisket before they even get to the second date?

The whole way home in the car, all Josh talked about was Scranton. Scranton this, Scranton that. Home and hearth, holidays and holy days. Question after question about growing up in picture-perfect Pennsylvania. Whenever I countered with a question for him, Josh pooh-poohed it, insisting mine was the much more colorful background. No argument there.

"Excuse me," I say when I hear a buzz. I cross to the front door, next to it the intercom. A glance takes in Tova looking at the now sparse bookcase. Unlike my mother, she probably won't notice what's missing. "What, Willie?" I talk into the handset. "You're kidding?"

"What happened?" Tova walks over to the door.

The doorman tells me I have a visitor. He is supposed to be a surprise (Josh is literally killing me with them), but knowing I am sick, Willie wants to give me an alert. He says Josh is on his way up in the elevator and should be ringing my bell about—

Buzzzz!

"Are you expecting someone?" asks Tova.

"Uh, not exactly. I think it's—"

Buzzzz! Buzzzz!

"Aren't you going to answer?"

"Yes. Yes, of course," I say, and open the door to see Josh standing there with a shopping bag from Zabar's and a big bouquet of roses.

"Surprise!"

"Ah." I feign happiness. "Josh." And getting really good at this one, I feign surprise.

"Wanted to see how the patient was doing." He marches in, giving me a quick kiss before he stops in his tracks upon seeing Tova.

"Well, hello," she says, extending her hand. "We met downstairs—"

"Of course," says Josh. "Tova. The Philharmonic. I remember."

"Mr. Hirsch," she announces. "And look what he brought you, Aimala. Go sit with him in the living room," she says, taking the shopping bag and the flowers from his hands. "I'll put everything in the kitchen. I think I know where there is a vase. These are so beautiful, uh . . ." She searches for his first name.

"Josh," he fills in.

"Josh. Josh Hirsch," Tova practically *cvells* as she goes inside the kitchen.

I head straight for the couch and cover myself up with a dark green fleece throw. Is there anywhere left I can run and hide?

"Feeling better?" Josh sits at my feet, places them on his lap, and rubs them.

"I was," I say. "Until just a little while ago."

"Ohhhhhh." He sounds so sad. "I'm sorry."

Tova bustles out of the kitchen, holding a big crystal vase she found in the cabinet. The yellow roses splendidly arranged, she places them in the center of the square wood-and-glass coffee table.

"Look how beautiful," she says, and takes a seat on the club chair. "Aimala, look how nice."

"They are truly lovely. Thank you, Josh. Thanks, Tova."

There is a momentary silence. Tova looks from the chair and smiles. She approves. Now that she is actually sitting here with *Hirsch*, I know she will want to stay a few more minutes. In and of itself that's potentially harmless. On the other hand . . .

"Aimee got sick yesterday just as she was showing me where she grew up."

"So that was good," Tova says to Josh. "You weren't far."

Oh, boy. I thought they would talk about the weather. Snow so late in March. Talk of next year's election. But no, they have to get right to this and talk about that.

"It was fine," I declare.

"Well, you were just west," says Tova.

"Exactly."

"No, we were northeast," states Josh.

"Ninety-sixth Street is north, yes," says Tova. "But from her parents, you are west and come east."

Josh looks at me and shakes his head, no use trying to explain, right?

"How is your mother?" asks Tova. "I haven't seen her in a long time."

"She's in Florida," Josh answers for me. "On Plantation Island."

"Plantation Island?" Tova purses her lips together as if she is considering. "Miami, I know. Delray Beach. Boca. Who do they have on Plantation Island?"

"Tons of people," I say. "You know Boca; they know Plantation Island. You have a lecture, yes?" I say, standing, ready to escort Tova to the door. "You don't want to be late."

Josh, the polite guy he is, stands and asks, "What's the lecture?"

Of course he has to ask. He has to know. And now Tova has to tell.

"But our Aimee doesn't need *that* book anymore!" Tova winks after she has explained.

"I'll say," says Josh. "After yesterday I would never ask her to give up her religion or her church."

"Her religion?" asks a more than baffled Tova. "Her *church*?" She looks at me, but I avert her glance. I will definitely be sick all over again.

"Her church in Scranton. Where she grew up." Josh looks at me to say the unspoken. Either Tova doesn't know me well, or else she is losing her marbles.

"You know." I hurry over to my neighbor, take her arm, and walk her to the door. "I've told you all about my church many times, and we can talk about it more *tomorrow*."

I flash Josh a look over my back to let him know it's the latter. Yes, she is losing her marbles.

"Josh," I say. "Would you be so kind as to unpack the shopping bag and show me what you got?"

He nods and heads to the kitchen.

"So long," he waves when I open the door for Tova to leave, but she doesn't go. Not that fast.

"I am a smart woman," she says, standing outside the door, speaking quietly in the hallway. Her eyes peer into the apartment to be certain Josh is out of earshot. "You know I feel close and so I can always talk to you. So I will tell you, Aimee, something is not right. Not just today, because I can see. You've lost weight; you dress different; you have this red hair." She tucks a loose strand behind my left ear. "And always, you are nervous."

"I'm fine, Tova. Really." I step out into the hallway. Not wanting Josh to hear, I must be strong and end this conversation now. "Let's just say goodnight, and we'll catch up later."

I should just turn around and shut the door. I need to deal with my own business. After all, it is mine. But Tova does not move, and neither do I. I cannot be that rude. Besides, I'm just too exhausted.

"Does your mother know what's going on?"

I don't answer.

"This talk now with the church and what was that? Scranton? You're like somebody else. What? Did you tell him you're a shiksa?"

People say things, outlandish things, because once said it makes way for the truth. The real story is probably much less fantastic, therefore, much easier to confide. No one expects the outlandish story to be true. Why would they? It's outlandish. The accusation, now, from Tova is *so* outlandish I just have to laugh.

Don't I?

"A *shiksa? Me?*" I cackle. I cluck. I crow. "That's absurd. What in the world gave you the idea that I would ever say I was a *shiksa?*"

Tova looks me in the eye. She ain't buyin', but I ain't sellin' anything else. Josh comes to the door to get me.

"Come on, the soup will get cold. I'm giving Aimee Jewish penicillin," he tells Tova. "Do you know what that is?" he asks me.

"Uh? Chicken soup, right?"

"She knows, Josh," says Tova.

"Of course. Everybody who lives in New York knows," I say, looking at Tova, knowing now that *she* knows. Okay. So Tova knows. So does Krista, so does Daphne, and so does Jon. So what?

"Well, I'm off to my lecture. Good night, Josh. Aimee, I hope you are soon better and wake up tomorrow feeling like your old self," she says before she is off and down the hall.

Bolting the two locks, I quickly close the door. Whew. At least she kept quiet. I take one of the two seats at my square table, on the wall nearest the kitchen, to eat the soup. Josh got the good kind with the carrots and the noodles, the chicken chunks and the *knaidlach.*

"You like?" he asks as he sits and joins me.

"It's delicious," I tell him, my appetite for my soul food suddenly voracious. "Does your family have a special recipe for this passed down from generations?"

"My mother buys it ready-made," says Josh, blowing on the soup before dipping in his spoon. "It's a ton of work."

"I wouldn't mind giving it a whirl," I suggest. This is a good excuse to get my Jewish cookbook back from Krista. It would help get a few Jewish words back into my vocabulary too. "You know, for you."

"That's sweet," he says. "But don't waste your time. It's not important."

But, oh, how I wish it were. If only he'd let his Jewish traits out, they could rub off on me. I could get some of my personality back. What's up with him and being Jewish?

Krista was all aglow when she told me about Makor, the Jewish cultural club, where she's begun to study. She is very excited to prepare Shabbat meals for Matt. Telling me how they will go to Friday night services first and then have dinner after.

"You know, Krista's kind of involved now," I tell Josh, who has also put out a delicious LoveLoaves challah. My stomach stronger, I break a piece off, silently saying the *beracha* and blessing the bread. Ironically, in private, it's not something I've ever done before.

"She signed up yet to convert?" he asks, sounding a lot like my brother.

"Well." I seize this opportunity as my opening. "She's taking a class," I say. "Judaism 101: Or, I Know Nothing."

"Funny." He laughs. "*I* know nothing. Maybe I should go."

Now I laugh. Slightly encouraged.

"Except I don't really care," says Josh. It stings when I hear this, especially as I feel it's said with a hint of pride.

What I love about Judaism is that it is so accommodating, making room for the different kinds of Jews among Jewish people. It's already your culture and blood; you can observe any way you like and to the extent that you choose. So . . . why not?

There is comfort in tradition, strength in passing a torch from one generation to the next. But among a certain type of modern American Jew, there seems to be no room for anything unless it is secular. An attitude I all too often encounter, it would have hardly pardoned anyone Jewish during World War II.

A worrier by nature, I often worry how I'd have gotten through the Holocaust had I been born in that place at that time. Sometimes after reading a book, seeing a film about the war, being at synagogue and hearing a talk from a survivor, I internalize the emotions and bring them all home.

My parents and I once visited the Holocaust Museum in Washington, D.C. With Sam. When you begin the tour, you are given a card with the name of an actual person who was in the camps. You must wait until the tour ends before opening the card, learning whether or not your person survived.

We started with an exhibit replicating a typical home in Europe before the Nazi invasion. Room to room, you observed a comfortable family. The father cozy in the living room reading, the child playing in his room upstairs, the mother in the kitchen cooking. Suddenly, a knock on the door. Screams. Bang! The entry swift and, just as quickly, life as they knew it ends.

Chilling as that was, what chilled me to the bone were the shoes. Exhibited behind a wall of glass were all the recovered shoes. One pair piled on top of the next, high enough to create a small mountain. A mountain of hope destroyed in the soles of those shoes. Destroying the souls of those shoes.

At night, still, I lie awake and think of Sam. Like the Holocaust family, he felt safe. What harm could possibly come to him waiting for the elevator in the North Tower? I relive Sam's last moments as if I were with him. It is a movie. One I see again and again. Desperately rewriting the ending, but to no avail. Always the same, innocent people always destroyed. And for what?

In the world, not only is it more interesting and respectful to embrace and allow our differences, it is essential. But tolerance does not exist, so assimilation takes the lead. The safety of sameness. And not just with religion.

Scranton now has all the same stores as New York. When I watch television, I can barely tell one actor from the next; one look, one style, is dominant. In the attempt to unite, we are doing away with individuality. Compromising the individual spirit.

How relieved I was when, after the tour, I opened my card and discovered my person had survived. But the survivors are dying off, making it too easy to forget. The point, now, of the Holocaust is to remember. Still so near, 9/11 already feels too far. My foothold in Judaism is to continue the story. To always remember.

"But when Krista talks about things Jewish, it all sounds so nice," I tell Josh, eager to convert him in order to save myself. "In fact"—I take a breath, knowing just how far out on a limb I am about to travel—"she told me this Saturday night it's some holiday too. She says it's like Halloween?"

"That's a stretch, but okay." Josh laughs. "Purim."

Josh knows his stuff. If asked, he will claim it's only for work, being a distributor to many Jewish businesses. "Know your customer," he'll say.

"Yeah, Pooreem," I say. "And after dinner, she and Matt are going to some big service and a costume party. They're dressing as Bonnie and Clyde. Krista asked if we want to join them." I look at Josh through hopeful eyes. "Can we?"

"Look, it's sweet of her and you too, but believe me, it's pretty boring," he says of the *megillah* reading that is one of my favorites. Beautiful Esther and the villain Haman followed by hamentaschen cookies, colorful costumes, and carnival-like celebrations.

"No problem," I quickly say, remembering last year when I dressed as a flapper and Peter came as a cop. A joyful participant, he booed and hissed along with everyone during the service whenever we heard the name Haman.

"Don't look so disappointed, eMay." Josh reaches across the table and rubs my arm. "Just get better because this weekend I made way better plans."

The night of Erev Purim—all Jewish holidays begin at sundown—though Krista's with Matt at the nighttime service, I, too, find myself someplace new. At the communal table of the stunningly trendy Asia De Cuba, Josh and I drink Absolut and eat lobster mashed potatoes. A bacchanal befitting a queen. Still high the following afternoon, I fly higher when Josh takes me to a matinee on Broadway to see *Spring Awakening*. And is it ever. The feasts. The festivities. I feel my own awakening and privately own this Purim celebration while remembering the Book of Esther.

King Ahasuerus picks out Esther in a beauty pageant, and makes her his queen. But considering the negative political climate, she takes her cousin's advice and does not tell him she's a Jew. When Haman wants to annihilate the Jewish people, Esther appeals to her husband. She uses her feminine wiles but in an ordinary, girl-next-door way. Choosing the right moment, she reveals her identity to the king. Because he has fallen in love with her by then, she wins his favor, enabling the Jews of Persia to be saved.

In a beautiful art deco building I lay with Josh. Safe in his bed, tucked away in this co-cop, his one-bedroom castle. Though naked, I still wear my costume. Shiksa. One day I will take it off. One day when the time is right, I will choose to show my hand.

Meanwhile I encourage Josh to use his and to touch. Allowing myself to feel all I can. It is Purim, and we are commanded to eat, drink, and be merry.

Something Fishy

"Hey, you okay standing here?" asks Josh. After last night, I assumed this morning we'd linger, but he had us up and out. Showered and dressed, hailing a cab to take me for, you got it, a surprise. "They should have a table any minute."

"Oh, good," I say. "It is a little cold."

Last night was wonderful. *Much* better, we took a very sensual leap. The romantic I am thought we'd stay at his apartment, where we'd spend the day in bed with Sunday's *New York Times*. Cooking omelets and drinking Bloody Marys. So when the cab drove uptown through the park over to the West Side, I had no idea where we'd be going. But I sure am sorry it turned out to be here.

"It's worth the wait," he says of the line that's so far out the door it practically reaches the corner. "Barney Greengrass is my total favorite for Sunday morning Jew food. They're also one of our best customers. You know this place?"

"Mmmmm," I say, instead of mentioning I spent my entire childhood here splitting the lox platter. Exactly nine and a half blocks from my parents' apartment, I can only pray they really are in Plantation Island or maybe slept in New Jersey.

"You know what," says Josh. "Let me see if Gary's around. If he is, maybe he can help get us in."

"Great." I flash Josh a smile before putting my head down, not wanting to run into anyone from the hood.

"We're in luck," he says a few minutes later. Finding me on the line and extending his hand to take me off. "Over the holidays we did Gary a really big favor with two dozen seeded ryes, so the next table is ours. Follow me."

VIP treatment. And from a guy in bread. Who'd have thought? It's nice and warm when we get inside, and not just the temperature. The aroma of Jewish appetizing permeates straight to my bloodstream. Nova and salmon and sturgeon and sable. Tuna fish, whitefish . . . the smells so comforting, even the gefilte fish seems appealing.

"You ever see anything like this?" asks Josh, indicating the meat counter as we wait in the front while the busboy cleans our table.

"It's like I see everything with you through new eyes."

Josh beams. "Some other time I'll take you here for lunch," he says. "Their sandwiches are big enough for four. You like corned beef, pastrami? Bet you never had tongue."

"Tongue?" I ask because I think I should. I happen to love tongue. Most people don't. I don't think it's a dislike for the taste of the tongue as much as that it was once someone's. "Do you like tongue?"

"I'm pretty open-minded when it comes to food," says Josh. "But you can't get me there."

The host brings us over to our table. Josh walks close behind me, his hand guiding my back as he whispers into my ear: "Though after last night, I can think of a few things I'd like to do now with mine."

Before we sit, I kiss him in front of the table, totally oblivious to anyone but Josh. Unzipping my jacket, I pull off that bomber hat (this from a girl who only wore bowl-shaped suede ones with faux-fur trim) and feel quite *It* when my silky straight hair tumbles down. Menus now in front of us, we don't even look. Josh and I only have eyes for each other.

We must be giving off the vibes because I can feel all eyes upon us. Well, certainly the couple at the next table. We get the Stare. Josh doesn't notice, but I can feel it. Enough to try to sneak a peek and break it. Very gradually, I peel my eyes off Josh, casually dropping them down to the menu. I tilt my head to the right to do that thing with my hair. The top of my left hand brushes under it as I throw my head back, allowing it to slowly turn to the left. Coming face-to-face with the guy at the next table who's been staring.

"Peter?!"

"Well, if it isn't Aimee Albert. Fancy seeing you here." Peter pauses to take me in. "If that is you."

"H-h-h-hi." I exhale in staccato sounds that would make more sense if I were about to sneeze.

Now what? Oh. I need to introduce him. To Josh. And he has to—

"Aimee, this is Courtney. Court," he says, and I instantly have to wonder how long they're dating that he has already shortened her name, "this is Aimee."

"The Aimee?" asks Courtney. Courtney, I notice, with the real red hair. "I heard about you."

"Really?" This makes me extranervous. "How'd you two meet?"

"She's a waitress at the club," says Peter.

"Don't they serve liquor there?" I ask. She hardly looks old enough to be out of college, let alone a waitress at the club.

"I'm almost twenty-five," boasts Courtney, catching my drift. "But my agents say I look really, really young. They keep sending me out to play high school and college kids, but I haven't booked anything yet."

I look at Peter with nothing but disappointment. He is trying to make changes? This is how he plans to grow up? Seems to me he has only regressed in the three months since we—

"Aimee?"

"Huh?"

I look from Peter to Josh—ohmygod, it's a living hell to look from Peter to Josh—and have no clue as to whatever it was that was just said.

"Aren't you?" asks Josh. He motions to himself and then to Peter.

"Of course," I say, and now catch up. "Josh Hirsch"—I must say his last name—"meet Peter McNight."

"Hey there," says Josh. "Nice to meet you. So how do you know Aimee? We met like almost two months ago."

"Sweet," says Peter. "We know each other longer than that. I'm her ex—"

"Trainer!" I suddenly chime in. Having a whole new respect for actors who improvise, observing how, with everything, practice make perfect.

"Excuse me?" challenges Peter.

I turn to Josh. "Yeah, I had training sessions at the gym for a while. Like a year and a half. But I stopped around Christmas. So now he's my ex." My smile to Peter confirms it. "My ex-trainer."

"I never knew y—," begins Courtney.

"Ready to order?" breaks in Norm, our waiter.

"Not yet," says Josh. "But coffees all around?"

"Definitely," says Courtney. "Not that I want to really wake up after last night." She flashes Peter a young, dreamy smile.

"O-kay." Peter almost blushes. "Bring on that coffee. In fact"—he looks across to Josh and talks confidentially—"how 'bout we push these two tables together and share. Fun? What do you say?"

"I'm game," says Josh.

The two men stand and make the move, while Courtney and I wait to adjust our chairs.

"That's much better," says Peter, who now sits close, way too close for comfort, to me.

"So." Josh makes the attempt to start a conversation. "You did a great job training Aimee."

"I sure don't know about that." Peter practically smirks when he looks at me. And while I know he doesn't know what's up, I can see he's up to playing along.

"Modest. What club do you two work at?"

"The LaughTrack," says Courtney.

"Isn't that a comedy club?" asks Josh.

"Uh-huh."

"They have a gym?"

Oh boy, here we go.

"No, silly," replies Courtney. "Why would a comedy club have a gym? Duh."

"But you're a trainer?" he asks Peter.

"I never knew you were a trainer." Courtney now gets out the words. Anxious for confirmation, she reaches across the table and taps Peter's hand.

I give Peter a look. He is not pleased. On the other hand, he can see the possible discomfort if Josh knew of our relationship, so he complies.

"Peter is a stand-up comic," I explain for him, "who only moonlights as a personal trainer."

"I know you're also a bartender, but I never knew you were a trainer," says Courtney.

"Well, I am now," says Peter, eyeballing me. "A trainer. In training."

"Wow," says Courtney. "That's awesome. You're so many things, Pete."

"Sounds kind of like that boyfriend," Josh says to me. "Aimee told me her ex was a stand-up," he says. "Tough gig. Hard to make a living. Unless you can really hit—"

And though Peter is not a violent man, I see he would like to. Instead, he moves the exchange forward.

"What do you do?" he asks Josh.

"LoveLoaves. Bread. Family business," answers Josh.

"What do you do?" Courtney asks me.

"I'm in PR."

"Pete, isn't that just like—?"

"So what are we all having?" I interrupt nice and loud, the waiter gratefully arriving with waters and coffees.

"Trust me," says Josh, helping the waiter pass the hot coffees from his tray. "Everything here is great. And if you're into chubs, this is really the place."

Courtney squints her eyes in confusion and looks across to Peter. "Can I get some pancakes and bacon?"

"No," says Peter. "Not here. But I guarantee you'll like this stuff once you know what to order. Aimee's the one who turned me on to this food, and I'm hap—"

"You?" Josh interrupts. Incredulous. "Never would have guessed that."

Though I see he caught it, Peter lets the comment pass and continues, "I'm happy to see you found one of your tribe."

"What tribe?" asks Courtney.

"The food tribe, Court," I practically spit. "I'm a foodie. So is Josh. Isn't that right?" and I see the explanation has him satiated. "It's always good to try new things."

"Sure is," says Peter. "Hey, what was the name of that great crunchy thing you made? Kagel?"

"You mean kugel?" Josh looks beyond curious.

"The head trainer at the place where we worked out was Jewish," I say.

"Oh, you mean that place on *Ninety-sixth Street*?" Peter grins, also pleased with his improvisational skills. "She ran a tight ship."

"Uh. Yeah," I agree. "And I used to make little treats for everybody every time I reached another goal. Treats from every culture. Treats from around the world."

"eMay, how cool you know how to make a kugel," Josh practically *cvells*.

"*eMay*," Peter says, ripe with sarcasm, "makes one mean kugel."

"That sounds really good," says Courtney. "I'll have the kegel."

"I bet you will." Josh winks at Peter. "Bet you can get some good pointers in that area from your trainer here too."

"Josh!"

"Court," Peter speaks with patience as if talking to a child. "I'll tell you about that *later*." He puts emphasis on the word *later* for my benefit. "Kugel is a noodle pudding," explains Peter.

"I want to order the kagel."

"I'm not sure you'd really be happy with that for breakfast," Josh tells Courtney. "You all mind if I order? We can do lox, deli meat, a batch of eggs, bagels, cream cheese . . . something for everyone. What do you say?"

The table quiet, we all listen as Josh gives the waiter the order—except for Courtney, who repeats each item after he says it, checking with Josh she pronounced everything right.

"In case I ever audition to be a waitress in a Jewish restaurant, I should know," she says. "We never had food like this in Lake Wallenpaupack. It was so beat. I'm so glad I left Pennsylvania."

PENNSYLVANIA?

Ohmygod.

"So you and Aimee have something in common," says Josh. "How about that. She's from Pennsylvania too."

"Really?" says Courtney.

"Really!" says Peter.

"Whereabouts?" asks Courtney.

"Yes, *exactly* whereabouts?" Peter turns and asks the same.

"Scranton."

Don't ask. I got the word out, and let's leave it at that.

"Scranton!" Peter roars. "That's a scream."

"It is not," I defend. "It's a very sweet place."

"Totally," chimes in Josh. "We were just there last weekend. Aimee showed me the house where she grew up. And her church," he adds.

"Her church!" shouts Peter. "In Scranton!"

"Just like Jax," exclaims Courtney. (With her reference to Peter's comedian friend at the club, I get how I chose Scranton in the first place.) "Lake Wallenpaupack's not that far," she tells us. "Less than an hour east. But the Poconos are BOR-ING," she sings. "Did you like it better growing up in Scranton?"

"Um. Yes," I say. "It was actually an idyllic American child-hood."

"Isn't it really funny being here in New York and everything?" Courtney now says to me, girl-to-girl. "I mean not just the whole *Sex and the City* life. But take this. Like there was no Jewish food in Lake Wallenpaupack. I didn't even know any Jewish people. The comedy club was my first time."

"Well, growing up in Scranton was different."

I aimlessly pick up a knife from the table, noticing my reflection. If I don't use it on myself first, I bet I will soon see my old nose growing back. Getting longer by the second.

"I'd guess it's pretty different," says Josh. "Plus Aimee had a neighbor who married Jewish. Muffy Steinberg."

"Muffy Steinberg!?" Peter is about to burst. "I'd like to hear about Muffy Steinberg," he tells Josh. "Please. Fill me in. I'm all ears."

"Well, it was just a little story about how she introduced Aimee and her family to Judaism, kind of. When Muffy married a Jewish guy and they had a bris."

"Wait," says Peter. "Go back. Muffy *introduced* Aimee's family to Jud—?"

"Do you have to have a bris if you marry a Jewish guy?" jumps in Courtney.

"If I'm right about what's going on here, Aimee might."

"Peter!"

Josh, too, feels offended, only he has no idea why.

"You don't have to be so mean to me just because I stopped training with you."

"Well, you know, you train someone for a year and a half, and you think you know them. Then one day you run into them at breakfast and—*SHIT.*"

"SHOOT."

Peter's right hand holds the handle of his coffee cup; my water glass is in my left. Afraid of what he might say and unwilling to find out, I kick him under the table, hard. So hard, his right hand jerks into my left, causing the coffee and the water to spill on the table and drip down onto our laps.

A momentary quiet takes over, allowing the dust, or in this case the dribble, to settle. Coffee is all over my brand-new designer jeans. Though, all things considered, this is the least of my problems.

"Ooops," I say. "Guess we were just having too much fun." I stand. "Excuse me, Josh. I'm just going to the ladies' room to wash it off."

"Want me to get you some club soda?" he asks.

"That's okay," I say, giving Josh a kiss on his head as I pass him.

"I'm kind of a mess too," Peter says behind me. "Be right back."

Hearing that, I speed to get to the bathrooms before he does. Unoccupied, I turn the knob to the ladies' room and step right in. But before I get to slide the latch, someone stronger pushes through. Peter locks the door behind us, then turns and makes me face him.

The Smear

SCRANTON? THIS IS RICH," he says, his back up against the door. I notice for the first time Peter wears the gray cashmere scarf wrapped around his neck, falling down onto that black Gap sweater.

"Looks nice," I say, pointing to the clothes.

"Why, thanks," he says, coming forward.

"So if you can just move." I try to step past Peter as he blocks the sink in the tiny bathroom.

"Aimee, knock it off." Peter pauses. "I'm sorry. I mean eMay"—he cracks up—"knock it off."

"It's not funny," I say, turning on the hot water, reaching into the stall, ripping off a big piece of toilet paper, and then soaping it up. "And look what you did to my new pants."

"Look what I did to your—?" Peter turns me by my shoulders to face him. "Okay. Let me get a look. A good one."

He studies me. And in that moment I feel it. The penetration of those intense blue eyes. Piercing into me, as if he can see inside and out.

"You look different."

"Thanks," I say, turning from him to try to deal with the coffee stain.

"Wait a sec." Peter gently grabs my wrist, not letting me near the sink. "What makes you think that was a compliment?"

"Excuse me?" In the last weeks, and for the first time in my life I might add, I have gotten nothing but. "Everyone thinks I look terrific," I find the gumption to say.

"You're slimmer, it's cool. But you were always sexy. Voluptuous."

I try, but can't move. It's like he's casting a spell on me.

"The hair." Peter shakes his head. "Now you look like every other woman in the city. Like every woman in New York who's trying to look like someone in a magazine. It's pretty, Aim. Don't get me wrong. But I'd be afraid to touch it, you know. To mess it up. But *your* hair," Peter recalls. "That long dark beautiful curly mane . . . Now I could get lost in that."

He did. I remember that he did. And I remember how.

"Everyone's allowed a new look once in a while."

"A new look," says Peter. His voice brings me back; his fingers push the ends of my hair behind my shoulders. "A new birthplace. What happened since we broke up? You went undercover for the CIA?"

Guilty of some things, I don't want to admit to anything. I push past Peter to the sink to get the stain out of my pants.

"Give me that," he says, taking my soapy white paper to toss it away. "If you're not going to go straight to the dry cleaner, just dab it with cold water. This would only make a bigger mess." He pulls me in. "Come 'ere."

Peter lifts my left leg, leaning it up against his right thigh. My back rests against the side of the stall. He reaches over me and pulls a brown paper towel out of the metallic dispenser. A lock of his blond hair brushes past my forehead. Holding my leg, he uses his other hand to run cold water onto the towel.

"Now all you want to do," he says, "is dab. Very. Very. Gently."

He does. Peter dabs, and the wetness grows. The wet circle on my pants expands. The fullness of the expansion not completely seen. Well . . . not on *these* pants anyway.

"What about you?" I ask, indicating Peter's.

"Was just your water. Let's take care of you right now."

The familiar words bring back familiar feelings. Forcing me to compare them to my feelings of last night.

"See how it's coming?" Peter asks, holding my leg oh so carefully as he dabs, dabs, dabs.

With each dab I can taste the missing ingredients of Josh. But last night was on a better track, evidence that these things do grow. There was more abandon, more intimacy. And besides, how can I expect those qualities with Josh when they are the very ones I am withholding? Time will take care of everything with us. Just because I may still have feelings for Peter doesn't mean I can have a life with him.

"Thank you." He has finished the job, though he has yet to release my leg. "We should get back."

"What's the rush?" he asks, moving closer, testing the water.

"Hello." I put up my hand to stop him. "But aren't you in a relationship?"

"With Court?" Peter laughs. "We're just having fun. I think she might be a little too young."

"Actually I think she might be a little too dumb."

"Hey, Aimee. That wasn't nice. Whatever weird thing's going on with you and the bread dude, don't take it out on her."

"Nothing weird is going on."

"Good. So let's get out of here before Josh boy asks her out."

"Josh is with me," I say sharply. "In case you haven't noticed."

"Josh is with someone," says Peter. "But believe me, it isn't *you*."

I try to pull my leg away, but Peter won't let me go. "Come on, P. Cut it out."

"When you tell me what's going on." He extends my left leg and places it across the edge of the sink, holding it tight. Thank goodness for those years of ballet. "You know I'm not letting you go till you tell. Fess up."

"There's nothing to tell." I try to move, but he's got me cornered. "Let me go." I try to move again. "Come on."

"I've got nothing to lose here, so the ball's in your court," says Peter, holding on to my leg.

"Stop."

He doesn't. Like a boy in a schoolyard who beats up girls on whom he has crushes, Peter holds firm.

"Ready to spill?" he asks.

I try to remove his hand, but he's stronger and doesn't budge.

"Peter, I said stop it."

"What was that?" Peter doesn't hurt me but presses down hard enough to show just who's in control. "You mind repeating that?"

"Stop."

"Say uncle?"

"No."

He tightens his grip.

"Do I hear uncle?"

"Peter—!"

"Uh-oh. Now look what's going to happen." Peter makes a play to reach for the other leg. As if he might pick me up and sling me over his shoulder like a caveman.

"Okay! Stop! You win!" I say, putting an end to this. "Josh likes shiksas. Happy?"

"So why's he dating you?"

I try to move before he gets it, but Peter gets it in a flash. In fact, he lets go of my leg so suddenly, I practically fall.

"Oh, no. Don't tell me. Oh, man, you've got to be kidding me." Peter howls. I shove my hand over his mouth to keep him quiet.

"I figured you were just playing this guy. Someone maybe you met online and you didn't want him to know too much about you. But you're . . ." He puts his hand on his forehead. He can't quite believe it. "Yeah, you're playing him, all right."

I don't answer.

"He doesn't know you're Jewish? That's it, right? That was the farce in there? He thinks you're a *shiksa*?" Peter knows the word and hits the syllables so they hit me on my head.

"Yes," I say. Quietly.

"Why?"

I can't answer him. Krista is one thing. And Daphne is another. Jon really doesn't bother me. And Tova. Well, that just makes me feel foolish. But Peter. I have never felt so ashamed, and I have never wanted him more.

"When we met, I could tell Josh liked non-Jewish women. I was with Krista, and he thought we were the same, so I kept it that way. It's not such a big deal."

"Of course it isn't," says Peter. "We broke up partly so you could be with a Jewish man, and now you're pretending not to be Jewish. Makes sense to me." He quickly grows beyond disappointment, past betrayal, and well into anger.

"It's just till I get him. Which is working very well, by the way."

"I can see. And once you get him, then who are you going to be? How far do you think you're going with a relationship built on a lie?"

"God. You're turning it into such a *thing*." I see myself in the tarnished bathroom mirror. Unrecognizable. No longer feeling tempted or sexy. Only silly. And a little sick.

"It was a big enough *thing* for you to leave me," Peter says. Turning on the water. Washing his hands. I believe of me.

He unlatches the door.

"Wait!"

I don't know what Peter will do if he walks out now. And I don't want him to be the one to blow my cover.

"Look, Peter. We had our chance. We don't want the same things. But Josh and I do. We're just getting there in a slightly unconventional way. Okay?"

With his hand on the door knob to show he's on his way out, Peter's eyes also show he is hurt. But like Krista and Daphne, Tova and Jon, he will allow himself to be woven into my tangled web.

"Just get this," Peter says in a commanding voice I never have heard. "You are deceiving him that you're his—oh, what do you always call it?—oh, yeah . . . his Shiksa Goddess. And you think he'll fall so in love with you he won't care you betrayed him?"

"Something like that."

"Go back to the table. I'll be there in a minute." Peter opens the door and lets me out. "You know, Aim, if you tried this hard with me, you could have been my goddess and gotten to still be you in the bargain."

I must have fallen down the rabbit's hole, because I walk back to the table smaller than ever. I take my seat and smile at Josh. Shrinking. The food has arrived, and Courtney's pretty happy. I grab a bagel for comfort, put a wad of cream cheese on my knife and give the bagel a big smear. Peter comes back to the table.

"Happy, babe?" he asks.

So out of it, I must be on automatic pilot because I face Peter as if his question is directed to me. Of all the embarrassments of the day, gratefully only I am aware of this one. In some ways, though, it is the worst one yet.

"De-lish," Courtney happily replies, munching. "I'm glad you brought me here, after all. Did you know this place from your ex?"

Josh looks at Peter.

"I dated a Jewish chick for a while," Peter tells him with a subliminal dismissiveness I know is meant for me.

"Things end," says Josh. "Better ones begin."

"You got that right," says Peter. Then he takes his fork and stabs it straight into a chub.

Matzos, Mothers, and the Real Messiah

WE'RE NINETEEN here for the first night," says my mom, busy at work in her kitchen, giving me the platter to dry.

Whenever it's nearing Passover, she breaks out Grandma Frieda's dishes, hand-washing the set to use for the seder. Arriving into the world before dishwasher safe was even a concept, my mother will not risk them in anything other than the kitchen sink. Over the years, the white background has become discolored, but the bright green and yellow floral design remains vibrant. The very sight of the dishes announces both the holiday and spring.

"Hand me that?" I point to the cover that fits right over the large, round serving bowl. Maddie uses her mother's recipe and always fills it to the brim with tzimmes. The aroma of sweet potatoes, carrots, and prunes melding into one will fill the apartment. Requiring a head start, the side dish gets time to slow-cook the day before.

"Your father wants to use a different Haggadah this year," she

tells me, soaping up several dinner plates at a time before placing them all in the dish drainer.

"Which one?"

My father, somewhat of a raconteur, enjoys finding new ways
to tell the Passover story. He will liken the Jewish people's strug-
gle for freedom to modern times, asking all the guests to relate
a personal story. Last year when Hannah's turn came, my niece
told everyone she was still a slave. Forced to wear a dress she
didn't like for a class picture and unable to decide her own bed-
time were her examples of torture.

"Something he read about in the *Times*. I don't care what it
is," says my mother. "So long as he likes it. I have enough to
think about. We're a lot of people. I invited Daphne's in-laws, so
I'll need you to help me serve and clear."

Assuming Josh would be with his family, I figured I'd go to
mine and tell him I was having dinner that night with friends.
We've been spending a lot of time together these last weeks and
most weekends. Divine dinners, driving lessons (I'm definitely
improving), and debauchery—though to a much lesser degree.
But the absolute best happened when, last night, he asked me to
go with him to Passover at his parents.

Finally.

Josh, finally, is including me in a Jewish ritual. It is a start. An
opportunity. And one I do not plan to miss.

"Sure," I tell my mom. "I'll help." I feel horrid lying, but I
don't want to bring up Josh. Not yet. She'll be okay without me.
Daphne will help her, and so will my cousins Marni and Shawn.

"Good. You'll come over early?"

I nod as I open the stepladder. Placing it on the floor in front
of the bold blue cupboard, I climb up and put the clean dishes
back whence they came.

"And the next night we'll go to Daphne in Jersey. I'm so glad this year the holiday falls at the beginning of the week. This way, I can prepare all weekend."

"What weekend?" I ask. "Beginning of what week?" I know I know this, but suddenly I'm aware I'm not cognizant of the dates. "You mean a Monday night and a *Tuesday*?"

"Yes," says Maddie. "That's usually the beginning of the week. The second and the third."

The third? Tuesday, the third?

"Second seder on Tuesday is the third?" I confirm.

"Yes," my mother says, having stacked the last of the dried dishes on the counter, making it easy for me to put the rest of them away. "What's the difference?"

Almost every day for the last few weeks Josh has told me to save the first week of April. Tuesday, the third. He's been on cloud nine ever since receiving the invitation to the grand opening of Copioso. The Mexican restaurant is from the same people who own the elegant Tocqueville and 15 EAST off Union Square. Josh's bread is such a hit, he developed a personal relationship with owners Marco and Jo-Ann, scoring an invite.

In all the nonstop talk about the event, Josh never said a word about it being the same night as the second seder. I suppose his family doesn't do two. I believe in Israel it is the custom to do only one. At any rate, from his point of view, I do none. This opening is very important to him. And I don't see any way I can't go.

"I can't go," I muster the guts to tell my mom, regretting the words as soon as they're out.

"You can't go where?"

"To Daphne's. For the second seder."

The words quite clear about the second night, I am even

more uncertain how I will get out of the first. Not to mention I always keep Passover to the extent I don't eat bread. Since I'm not kosher to begin with, I don't strictly adhere to eating only foods labeled KOSHER FOR PASSOVER. But since unleavened bread is symbolic of the Jews fleeing slavery in Egypt, I eat matzo during the eight-day holiday. And *never* eat bread or flour products. How will I navigate my way around that at a Mexican restaurant? Is it too late for me to give up bread for Lent? Does my religion even do that?

"What do you mean you can't go?" asks my mom. "Why not? What are you doing?"

"I . . ." What have I done? "I . . . uh, made other plans." The business of stepping up and down with the dishes keeps me busy, enabling me to avoid my mother's eyes. "I'm going to Krista's," I blurt into the gravy bowl. "She and Matt are having a seder at her place the second night."

"I always liked Krista. I'm happy she found someone. I'd like to see it happen for you."

But it is, Mommy. It *is* happening for me, and I wish I could tell you. I so want to share my news, but I can't just yet. I know my mother would somehow find out and ruin my plan, so I plan to wait.

"Well, I kind of promised her I'd go. But I'll be with everyone here the first night." There is a decidedly uncomfortable silence. "You understand?"

My mother, surprisingly, does not react. Remaining quiet, she helps steady the stepladder as I make my way down. When my feet safely touch the floor, she looks me in the eyes. "I understand a lot more than you give me credit for," she says. "So if you want to talk to me, Aimee, I'll understand. We all notice you're not yourself since you and Peter broke up. Do you ever hear from him?"

"Uh, yeah," I say, walking out of the kitchen into the dining room. I can picture my family gathered around this table and am sorry I can't join them. Plus now I realize I have to figure out what to do about Easter.

"We ran into each other," I tell my mom. "It was cordial. We were both with other people. On dates."

This raises an eyebrow high enough to almost let me off the hook.

"Anyone nice?" she asks.

"Could be," I say, "but I don't want to jinx it so I don't really want to talk."

"Okay," says Maddie, allowing this mystery date to explain everything away. "Will he be going with you to Krista's?" she asks. Hopeful.

"He'll certainly be invited," I say, making a mental note to ask her if Protestants are the same as Catholics in observing Lent.

But come the afternoon of the first seder, I'm not quite so la-di-da. Josh calls to say he will pick me up at four o'clock to avoid the traffic out to Long Island. He is excited for me to meet his family. I am too, but I am already missing mine.

My mother expects me after three. Around two, I return to my apartment. I've been manicured and pedicured; my hair, too, is fresh from another cut, color, wash, blow-dry, and flat iron. (The money I've spent on my hair since February would certainly have bought me a week's vacation in Jamaica.) A dozen white roses and a good California merlot seem appropriate hostess gifts. I was going to buy a bottle of Manischewitz or a bakery cake labeled KOSHER FOR PASSOVER. But I was afraid it might appear too eager and a bit too in-the-know.

Opening my closet, I unveil the silky new babydoll dress. Yellow with tiny green dots, it has a ruffled cap sleeve, and in a

V between the breasts a dark green satin bow. Suede bag and shoes, that green cashmere cardigan, and, in honor of today, a headband. Brushing my red hair back, I stretch the thick green-and-yellow-striped band tightly over my head. Mascara, then blush. And after the finishing touch—pale pink gloss on my lips—I only wish I had looked like this all my life. Speaking of all my life . . .

1–212–555–0421.

"Are you on your way?" my mother says instead of hello. "I'm ready for you."

"Aaaaaa—*choo.*" There is no response from Maddie, so I do it again. "Aaaaaa—*choo.*" I fake-sneeze. "Aaaaaa—*choo.* Aaaaaa—*choo. Aaaaaa—choo!*" I repeat into the phone, thinking I might have made a pretty decent actress.

"What happened to you? You sound terrible."

I sound terrible? Good. Now I have to really sound terrible.

"I'm very, very sick," I say, sounding as terrible as I possibly can. "I can't move. I'm so sorry. I never missed Passover, ever. But . . . I just can't come."

"Do you have fever? Did you take your temperature?"

Shit. My mother sounds worried.

"I think I just need to rest. Working. So hard."

"What's the matter?" I hear my father's voice in the background. "Who is it?"

"Aimee," my mother calls to him. "She's sick."

"What's the matter?" He's closer to the phone now, so I also hear his concern.

"She's overworked. I've been telling you something's wrong for weeks."

My parents carry on a whole conversation, despite the fact I'm on the line. Too busy talking about me to talk to me. I sit down on my bed and pick up the remote for my flat, little TV. After a few clicks, I get lucky with HBO. I watch *Tootsie* while holding the phone to my ear.

"You still there?" Maddie finally asks. Click. My father picks up, too.

"Yes."

"I'm coming to get you," says Sid.

"No!"

"We'll take a cab, and you can stay in your room and sleep if you're still not feeling well."

"Don't come here, Daddy. You can't." He really, really can't.

"Aimee, you're not going to be with us for seder tonight or tomorrow? I won't accept that."

"Please don't come," I plead. Real emotion, emanating from real fear, helps fuel a nasal, hacking, sick, and exhausted me. "I don't want to get the kids sick. Aaaaaa—*choo.* Just need sleep." Cough, cough. "Tell everyone I'm sorry."

"All right. Call us later."

Call-waiting. Josh is ringing through. In minutes he will arrive.

"Okay. Love you both. Aaaaaa—*choo.* Happy Pesach."

Click. Click. Shift. Shift.

"Well, hello there," I chirp for Josh.

My perky voice back on command, I practically give myself an Oscar. Grabbing the wine, the flowers, and an all-weather trench, I exit my building, ready for the performance of my life.

"Hello, gorgeous," says Josh as I slip next to him into the very wonderfully familiar car. Falling in love with the BMW, I often fantasize a tremendous success with KISS might possibly allow me to consider one.

Placing the flowers and the wine in the back, I lean over and give him a big kiss hello. I am going to meet Josh's family and celebrate a Jewish holiday. Yes, I am nervous, but I can hardly wait.

Once we are safely out of the city, I will question him about the seder. I will ask Josh to tell me about the ritual and prepare me for what's to come. My interest will be acute, my questions on the mark, and when he wants to know why, I will tell him Judaism is beginning to fascinate me. And wanting to fit in with his family, I did, oh, just a wee bit of Internet research in honor of this most important event.

But, as always, Josh surprises first. When we exit the Long Island Expressway, I think we have arrived. But once we're on the Cross Island, he pulls over and has me take the wheel.

"Stay to the right," Josh coaches, but believe me, I'm not changing lanes. To simply stay in mine and drive requires all my concentration.

I go the speed limit and stay steady. The exhilaration of driving on a parkway is tempered by my ability. Still rusty, I'm still tentative. But even I can't deny my obvious improvement each and every week. Now I see I'm truly learning. I have Josh, totally, to thank. Though he is the force beside me, I confess, it feels powerful to steer. And does this baby glide. When I actually merge, exit, and get us onto the Southern State Parkway, I see what all the fuss is about.

"Since you've got the paperwork in place, it's time we think about scheduling a road test," says Josh.

I spent five hours last Saturday completing a safety class at New York Drives, a private driving school in the city. When I showed Josh my MV285 certificate, he *cvelled* as if he was looking at a real diploma. The class was even fun. But now he mentions a road test, and the wheel swirls out of my hand.

"Whoa," says Josh, his reflex fast as he grabs the wheel with his left hand. (Fortunately, he's a lefty.)

"I can't take the test," I say. "There's no good day to take the test. Something tragic always happens, okay? I told you, I can never take the test."

"Calm down, eMay, stay cool," says Josh, his left hand now massaging my shoulders. "How about this? Let me schedule a road test and not tell you when. One day you may think we're out for brunch, but instead we'll show up at a DMV. If you're feeling good, go for it. Otherwise, we'll cancel."

"Perfect," I agree. Permanent or temporary, it's a solution. And the end of that conversation. Now it's time to talk about the seder, and closer to our exit it will soon run out. Our four eyes on the road, I thank Josh for his efforts on behalf of my driving dilemma before telling him how I'm looking forward to tonight, sweetly asking what to expect.

But I practically smack into the Lexus in front of us because Josh happily tells me his family only has Passover dinner and doesn't deal with a seder. Or, as he explains, they feel there's no point to go through a whole boring rigmarole that has no actual relevance when the only thing people really care about is when they are going to eat.

So distressed to hear this, I completely shut down. (I'm sure Josh attributes my silence to my total focus on the road.) No seder? It can't be. Please don't tell me I've gone through all this only to wind up celebrating Passover without a seder.

Josh allows me to finish the drive. He directs, and I follow. My mind can't help but jump ahead to how he would want to raise children. Would they be Jewish in name only, without rituals? Even if one struggles personally with the concept of God, must it interfere with tradition?

I know many people float from holiday to holiday, celebrating with gifts and festive meals, eliminating any religious content. Christmas and Easter, Rosh Hashanah and Passover are all examples. But the exposure to what's behind a holiday makes it more meaningful.

It's hard to imagine Passover without a child asking the Four Questions at the seder table. But the best thing about the questions are the answers. They tell a story: of the Exodus out of Egypt from slavery to freedom. We have the freedom to tell that story however we choose. Every family can create its own traditions. Isn't that something to celebrate? Am I naive to believe we can find ways to make religion work for us?

Put a gun to my head and ask if I can swear Moses parted the Red Sea, and I'll tell you I don't know. If I also tell you I don't care, will you shoot me? Be it fact, folklore, bells, or whistles, at the end of the day—or the end of the seder—it should drive home the appreciation that we are free to create, and re-create, our lives. Something I'm well familiar with since I've met Josh.

The suburban streets are peaceful. The Five Towns have a big Jewish population. One can feel the holiday buzz in the air. I turn off a main boulevard to side streets, affluent and showy, with expensive homes. Is there any correlation between financial comfort and the assimilated Jewish person's sense of religious acceptance?

"We're here," says Josh, indicating with the directional we are headed right. I turn up a long gravel driveway to a somewhat magnificent house. With a big grassy front yard, it's set back from the road. Stately. Beautiful. Brick colonial. White columns. Windows trimmed in white; each adorned with big, black shutters. Front and center is an imposing red door.

I am speechless.

Josh indicates we follow the gravel, circling past the front of the house to park the car with several others off to the side. Upon getting out, I notice part of a swimming pool around the back to my right and a small duck pond under a weeping willow to my left. Tulips of all colors bloom in front of the house. I had no idea he came from this.

Josh beams. Of this, my boyfriend is proud. Why shouldn't he be?

"How's my boy?" is heard when the door opens. A woman steps out and gives Josh a great big hug. But it's not his mother.

"Meet Rosita," he says after he breaks away. "*This* is Aimee."

We shake hello. She is actually dressed in a gray maid's uniform. White cuffs, white collar. White trim.

"I know this fella since he was three years old," she brags. "Mrs. Sandy," she calls behind her, "they're here."

Josh's mother arrives at the door with a brisk and bustling hello. Josh, the elder of two boys, is Daphne's age. His mom is evidently younger than mine. Sandy's short blonde hair is picture perfect. So is her figure. She's bedecked in diamonds—earrings, bracelets, and rings—they shine in the sunlight when she steps outside the door, graciously accepting my bouquet. Josh shows her the bottle and holds up the wine. I smooth over my dress. I hope I look okay.

"So this is the Aimee we've heard so much about."

I step into the marble entryway and notice a staircase that winds at least two more stories high. Rosita takes my coat as someone takes my hand.

"I'm Lee, Josh's dad." Athletic and trim, he's clearly a man who enjoys the good life.

Josh heads off with his mom, presumably to the kitchen. My hand still in Lee's, I follow his lead.

Whose Lie Is This Anyway?

Dressed in black and white, two actor-type cater-waiters circulate with hors d'oeuvres. When Lee directs me to the bar to get myself a drink, I only pray I won't find Peter behind it.

My California merlot fits in better than I do. Once I'm back in the great room with a glass, Josh takes me around and proudly makes introductions.

"You'll have to come to Boston to visit one weekend," says Elizabeth, his brother Zachary's wife. She holds their fourteen-month-old baby, Ava, while five-year-old Benjy plays with the family dog, a Wheaten Terrier of the same name.

"Benjy is just Benjy," Zach says of the pet. A few years younger than Josh, fair-skinned and light-haired, he favors his mother, while Josh has his dad's darker, ethnic looks. "But our Benjy is technically Benjamin."

"And he'll grow into Ben," says Elizabeth. Choosing to name

their firstborn after his grandparents' dog, they have their defense down pat.

Among Ashkenazi Jews, it's the custom to name a new baby after a relative who has passed away. It keeps the name and memory alive, and abstractly forms a bond between the baby's soul and the deceased relative. Though I wonder now if the *B* was specifically for someone, I know I can't ask.

"We just liked it," says Josh's brother of the name, most likely answering my unspoken question.

"Are you Cousin Josh's girlfriend?" A girl of about six yanks twice on my dress before asking. Straight black hair, her bangs falling just above her green oval eyes, she looks as if she stepped out of a catalog for GapKids.

"And who are you?" I ask.

"Hey, Robby," Josh calls to the girl's dad. "Come 'ere and meet Aimee. My first cousin," Josh says of Robby, when a shortish guy a little older than Josh approaches. "My aunt Renee's son."

"You always get the pretty girls," he says, and slaps Josh on the back. "You'll be bringing her, right?"

"Ever been to a bar mitzvah?" asks Josh. Now on his second marriage, Robby has a thirteen-year-old son, Evan, from his first.

So elated about the bar mitzvah, I gush when introduced to Renee, Lee's sister, who is talking with her husband, Josh's Uncle Mickey, and Cousin Robby's wife, Hope. The little girl, Madison, belongs to them. But before I get through the meet-and-greets, we're intercepted by another aunt, uncle, and set of cousins on Sandy's side.

"We're in business together," this uncle explains, somehow engaging me in conversation alone. "But my brother-in-law's the big shot." The sweep of his hand across the upscale room proves his point. "I'm a district sales manager," he says of himself. "Josh tell you he's a big shot now at LoveLoaves?"

"She knows the whole deal, Uncle Phil." Josh steps in and out of the conversation as kids and cousins surround him. Phil, I learn, is Sandy's brother.

"The kid is sharp," he says of Josh. "Good for the *dough*." He emphasizes the last word to push the pun.

As Josh tells it, Uncle Phil believes he was derailed from his promotion when Josh quit lawyering and joined the family business. But Lee never felt his brother-in-law really qualified. Josh's arrival turned out to be not only better for business, but the better way to let Phil down.

"We live in Riverdale," says Phil, pointing to his wife, Marlene. She sits in a small circle with a single daughter, married son, and his pregnant wife. "That's in the Bronx," he says. Unlike the others I've met, his family appears to be more like mine. And I bet they'd be more comfortable at the Albert seder table than here with the Hirsches.

"That's a nice place," I say, and think of Krista's Matt.

"Nice, yes. But not nice like this."

I want to excuse myself from this conversation, but Sandy has just requested that everyone take their seats. Josh, assuming I'm taken care of, is elsewhere, so Phil walks me across the room and up the few steps to the dining room.

My white roses have been arranged in small, matching cut-glass vases at opposite ends of the table. Set in the center, the floral arrangement is classic, like the room. Light from the crystal chandelier reflects off the crystal goblets; tall white tapers perched in glass candlesticks flicker. A bay window looks out on an exquisitely sculpted backyard. Perfect table settings with place cards invite each guest to sit. The room is tasteful, bright, and airy; everything is elegant and chic.

"Oh my," I exclaim when we enter.

Phil grabs my arm when I turn to find my seat. "Be a smart girl," he whispers into my ear. "And play your cards right." I can only wonder what my parents will think of all this.

"Hello, everyone, and welcome," says Lee, taking his place at the head of the table as we assemble. "While we all get settled, let us welcome Josh's new friend, Aimee." People smile and say hello, while the waiters come around and pour wine. Josh presses on my knee under the table.

"Now I don't know what you know about Passover, Aimee," continues Lee, when everyone is seated. "But you're not going to learn much about it here tonight."

All the guests laugh, I notice, except Phil. "I just assumed you were Jewish," he says, quietly, seated to my left.

"Uh, no," I answer. But it seems to me that, like an animal from a similar breed, he sniffs otherwise. "I'm originally from Scranton," I feel obligated to out-and-out lie, as if that will account for being Not.

He looks at me with bemusement, then instantly makes a face that says, *Who am I to argue?* I see Phil's inability to follow his first good instincts have landed him in his frustrated position in life.

"My brother-in-law was hopeful," jokes Lee, who overheard. "He wanted to get some new Jewish blood into this family."

On cue, everyone laughs.

"So for Phil, this year we're going to have a very mini seder."

Good news for both of us, I think.

Phil stands, I know, to say kiddush. Seder, meaning "order," always begins with the blessing over the wine. But instead, out of order, the small cousins, coached by Elizabeth, share in asking the Four Questions in English. Answers not forthcoming, when they finish, Phil takes the Haggadah from her. Pulling a yarmulke out of his jacket pocket, he places it on his head and lifts his crystal wine goblet before reciting the elaborate blessing. As Phil chants, he hangs on to each word, seemingly unwilling to go on to the next. Fondling each one, every word a memory. Of a world he wishes he had not let go. I know the feeling.

"Do you know how to do that?" I ask Josh.

What would happen if I stood now and recited the kiddush? I fantasize standing up in this beautiful room. Not even taking the book, and reciting the entire kiddush by heart.

"I knew once," he says. "But I don't need to anymore."

But I do. Homesick, I need to call my family. The seder appears to be over as the waiters now come from the kitchen, serving bowls of hot chicken soup. The food will be a comfort. About to excuse myself for a minute, I stop when Lee speaks.

"One more thing," he says. Like Houdini, he pulls the embroidered matzo cover off and reveals not the three boards of matzo traditional to a seder table, but bread. A braided, golden brown, made with flour, challah bread.

"The bread brings in the bread," says Lee, "so we're going to bless this too. Phil?"

Phil looks down in embarrassment. Marlene reaches out and touches his hand. I can't believe the Hirsches would actually serve bread on Passover. Even if you don't have a seder, must it be on the table?

Lee, unaware of Phil, does a nice job with the blessing in Hebrew. Then, as is customary on Shabbat, he tears off pieces and passes them around the table for people to eat.

"Aimee?" he asks, making sure Josh has a piece of challah for me.

Oh, no. I figured I could finagle my way out of eating tortillas tomorrow, but I didn't think it was something that would come up tonight.

"Um. I've had this bread before. It's delicious," I say, putting up my hand and waving my piece away.

"Just for my dad, eMay," says Josh, holding up the bread.

"I . . . uh . . . I don't want to get too full."

"She eats like a bird," defends Josh.

"So don't have the whole piece," says Lee. "But I insist you take a bite. You have to taste this. Come on."

All eyes upon me, I don't know what else to do. Josh puts the bread to my mouth. I open it as if I am Juliet, about to drink the poison. Passover has us remember what it was like to be a slave, and how difficult the journey was to freedom. Putting the soft bread to my lips, I bite hard enough to bite back my tears. As a slave to this lie, I am surely not free.

The next night is only better because I am better prepared. In the late morning I call my mother, telling her I'm feeling okay but will still be going to Krista's. She doesn't comment on that but instead proceeds to tell me stories about last night's fun at their seder. Seems, with a little help from Grandpa Sid, Holdenn found the *afikoman*. Of course, Sid gave all the kids a dollar. And Jon. No matter how old he is, when it comes to the *afikoman*, my brother must always collect.

Then I call Krista to see how she's doing. Last night was spent with Matt's family, his older sister, Ilene, hosting. Krista sounds excited about having her own seder tonight. However, Copioso is where Josh and I head. Tony and trendy, it's a definite hot spot, but surely the wrong spot for me.

Quiet, I barely eat, but Josh barely notices. Being here means the world to him, and I'm by his side. He has a blast. Besides, he feels pleased because last night went so well.

"Everyone loved you," he says of his family.

After eating the bread, I hardly spoke. It took all my energy to maintain my front. I wanted to spill so many times, especially in the car ride home. When we got back on the Long Island Expressway, all I could see was LIE. I thought it was a sign. I even came close to knowing what I would say. Once said, however, I had no idea what I'd say next.

Tonight I happily take the backseat to Josh. He tastes and talks and networks away. Marco and Jo-Ann introduce him to people. He gets a tennis game, a meeting, and a new order.

"I'm a little under," I finally say when the party gets to the point where it feels safe to break away.

While Josh waxes poetic to Marco and Jo-Ann, I stand by, knowing we will soon be in a cab and my duplicitous holiday will end. For the rest of the week, I vow, I'll stay away from bread and the like, imagining the small symbolic act might help to cleanse me. All things considered, I think I would have been better off had I chosen to be Catholic. Confession is good for the soul. As a Protestant, I wonder if I can still go, and give serious thought to consulting a priest.

Don't ask, don't tell; my cell has been turned off all night. Now all I want is to be in my apartment, call my parents, sink into a hot tub, and slink away. I need to be alone, and I need some time to think.

"I'll come up, okay?" says Josh, before paying the driver. Regardless of whether or not he stays, he is always so chivalrous to take me to my door. Josh will go all the way uptown in a cab, even if he only turns around to go back down.

"You know, honey, I have a bad headache," I say. "And we have a big KISS powwow in the morning. Would you mind?"

He looks disappointed but is too polite to say. Poor Josh. What am I doing to him?

"Let me just take you upstairs, and then I'll go."

Josh offers his hand to help me out before closing the cab door behind me. The gesture is so kind, I feel even guiltier knowing what he has gotten himself into.

Somehow I will make this right. When I finally tell him, I will make him understand and then make it up to him. But not tonight. I may be a fake, but the headache is real. And I need some peace. Moving through the revolving doors, I look behind to the next partition and see I lost Josh. Outside the door, he holds up a finger to tell me he will be a minute. Indicating gum is stuck to the bottom of his shoe, he moves away from the building toward the curb to remove it.

I deliberately pass the lobby entrance and continue revolving. I might as well go outside and keep him company.

"There she is!"

I could swear I hear a familiar voice as I step out of the partition to the street. Fast as lightning, a woman has run across the lobby and slips into the revolving door shouting, *"Aimee?"*

About to walk to Josh, I turn and, sure enough, I see *my mother* fly through the revolving door. When she hits the walk outside, I push both of us into the small partition, enduring the close proximity for several seconds as she screams at me until we enter my lobby.

"What are you doing here?" I accuse. Heat flashes over my face as I now shamefully face her. She looks very, very relieved and very, very angry.

"Why weren't you at Krista's?"

Behind the black marble reception desk, Willie minds his business. Seeing both of us, my father jumps out of the black leather club chair by the elevator and hurries over.

"We were worried sick, Aimee," he screams as he nears me. "What the hell is going on?"

"I can't believe you two are sitting here waiting for me like I'm in high school."

I am mortified. I look outside the glass window and can see Josh, thankfully, near the curb. Perfectionist that he is, he's still fiddling with his shoe. But I've got to hurry because it can't take very long.

"I called Krista from Daphne's to see how her *knaidlach* came out, she asked for my recipe, and when I wanted to say hello to you, she said you weren't there. And that you *never* planned on coming."

"So what?" Thanks a lot, Krista, I think. I don't know why she couldn't have covered for me. Suddenly she's so high-and-mighty.

"Then we called your cell to see where you were and got no answer all night, no answer at home. We never heard from you, and after a while we thought something happened. Everyone's beside themselves."

"Well, you see I'm fine, so you can go home," I say, trying to usher them out the door.

"Wait a minute, here," says my father. "This isn't like you. Your mother is right. Something is going on, and we want to know." He pauses a second. *"Now."*

I turn and see Josh approach the revolving door. Even if I made up some crazy convoluted story about a surprise visit from my parents, before they even open their mouths there is no way

Maddie and Sid will pass for a Protestant couple from Scranton. Especially to a guy who's New York Jewish, born and bred.

"Look, I can't go into it, but this, uh, this Josh, coming through the revolving door right now, is, uh, my boyfriend, and *just don't let him know you're my parents!*"

"*What?* What's wrong with you, Aimee?" My mother is going to burst a blood vessel.

"*PLEASE.* I'm begging you. Do this for me. I'll explain later."

"Sorry about that," says Josh, ignoring the couple behind me when he gives me a kiss on the cheek, before taking my hand.

My parents observe his proprieties. Regardless of our deal, they stand there waiting for an introduction as if, at the very least, they are acquaintances from the building. It is not forthcoming.

"No problem," I say. "On second thought, why don't you come up for a few minutes?"

"Cool," Josh says, and walks across the lobby to the elevator.

My parents stand, huddled together, bewildered and lost. It is a tribute to me they don't say anything, and I will have to thank them for that. When I catch Willie's eye, he looks away, no idea what scene he is watching and not wanting any part of it.

"It's almost here," calls Josh as the numbers above the elevator flash down.

"Right behind you," I call back, looking at my parents over at my shoulder, taking my left hand and shooing them out the door.

My mother shakes her head back and forth, as my father grabs her to push her into the partition, revolving both of them out of this mess. But before they get inside that door, another one opens.

"eMay, come on. It's here."

The elevator door opens, and out walks Tova. Still dressed up, she wears slippers, keys jangling in her hand. Away for the holiday at her son's in Scarsdale, she must have just gotten home and has come downstairs to retrieve her mail.

"Well, hello."

"Hi, Tova," says Josh. "How are you?"

Upon hearing her name, my parents both quickly turn their heads.

"I am very well, Josh," says Tova. "Thank you. We had a lovely Pes—"

"Tova." Maddie scurries across the lobby. "I'm so glad to see you." My mother approaches my neighbor; my father glares as he trails behind.

"Ah," says Tova, delighted. "Aimee"—she turns to me—"you told!"

"Told *what?*" my parents ask in unison.

I run to Josh, push the elevator button, and just catch it. The doors that had closed instantly reopen. I take his hand and rush us inside.

"Yes, I told them about the leak," I yell as the elevator doors close and whisk Josh and me up and away.

"What leak?" he asks, the elevator taking us higher and higher, elevating us over the problem below.

"New neighbors. Tova's line. Water damage. She didn't know who they were."

And they didn't know what I was pretending to be. But Tova, with them now in the lobby, is certainly filling them in.

If at First You Don't Succeed, Lie, Lie Again

1 REMINDER

Start Time: 2:15 PM

Subject: KISS in Color Launch: Emergency Brainstorm—Round Room 32nd fl

Due In: Five Minutes Overdue

Dismiss   *Dismiss All*

Click to be reminded again in: Two Minutes

Snooze

The Microsoft Outlook reminder has popped up on my computer screen constantly over the last hour. I click Dismiss All and, grabbing my notebook and KISS folder, dash down the hall to the Round Room. This corner conference room with the big round table is where we hold brainstorms. This morning Jay e-mailed the invitation to the PRWAP-NY KISS team for this meeting. He asked that I arrive a few minutes early to talk. I didn't.

The room is already prepared, and, though late, so am I. Drinks and snacks (healthy and un) are in the center of the table. A small chest on the side is filled with squeeze toys, balls, whistles, magic markers, paper . . . in case anyone needs to let off steam, doodle, get inspired, or gets bored.

"Well, well," says Jay. "Look what the wind just blew in."

Krista doesn't look up, reading her notebook and sipping from a bottle of VOSS sparkling water. Seated around the table are the two men on the team, Sean Borrelli and Todd Lonoff, Nancy Cheng, and a new assistant whose name I don't yet know. Her first brainstorm, the AAE, just out of college, looks like a deer in headlights. I make a mental note to drop by her desk, later, and make her feel welcome. Tap, tap on the table. We're about to begin.

"And what level is Gina?" asks Krista.

Oops, they have already begun.

"Same as you and Aimee."

"Gina who?" I ask.

"Gina Jones-Levine," offers Sean. "How's that for a name?"

"A rose by any other would smell as sweet," says Nancy.

"Or certainly a little less shiksa syndrome," I say to Krista, who hardly looks at me, let alone laughs. Everyone else makes up for it.

"She's from our L.A. office. We have so many overlapping events going on, everyone here's booked. The client wants her on hand for backup support," explains Jay. "Plus she's good."

"Good."

"Good you feel that way. She might be taking over, Aimee," says Jay.

The heat of what's really going on suddenly registers. I feel my face turn red.

"As of now, the client is not happy with how you're handling things. Your lack of any viable celebrities these last weeks and your insistence on pushing the unknown Laura Lou Bell."

"Laura Bell Bundy," I correct. "Even if she's wrong, let's get her name right."

"She was fabulous in *Legally Blonde* and terrific in *Hairspray*," says Todd, who saw each show three times.

"Who was she in *Hairspray*?" asks Sean.

"Why do they keep making musicals of movies?" Krista asks Todd like he knows.

"Would you like to go to the theater?" Nancy asks the new girl.

"So now you get her, Jay?" I ask, though I confess I still don't. If he says yes, I still can't come up with a concept to back her. My work has been slipping, I know. But let him table her; I've got a new plan. One, I believe, will make up for everything.

"Laura Lee is history, Aimee. Moving on. Who has an idea to save this launch?"

I wait it out as Jay rejects idea after idea, celeb after celeb. Grunting a unanimous no to all the affordable Broadway stars, the unaffordable celebrities, and all the venues that have nothing to do with New York, kisses, or copiers.

"There's no theme. The reason KISS liked the contest in the first place was because there was a theme." He turns to me. "Aimee. Dahling. You've not said a word. Tell me. Were you tardy, perchance, because you were working?"

I smirk. "You know me too well. But yes. So tell me what you think." I open my notebook to refer to my notes. "Picture this. A New York City street. Roped off. Like one of those street fairs.

Booths of Ramy lipsticks, people collecting money for the kisses ... a huge clothesline with KISS-branded clothespins to hang the kisses after they've been color-copied. In the middle of the street a little stage. In front of it a small platform with ... the KISS copier.

"Music plays. It's sexy and exciting, just like the celebrity judge. Because ..." I pause. "How great will it be to have ... Kim Cattrall? *Sex and the City* meets Kiss in the City: Where You KISS in Color!"

Everyone talks at once, loving the concept and firing out all the hard questions. Scribbling notes, I answer in order.

"Ramy is in. I'm working on a permit from the city, and many New York streets are within budget. Kim Cattrall is in." I pause. "Well ..." I have to tell the truth. "For *fifty* grand she is."

"But I told you—"

"I know, Jay, but if Kim's in, *People* is in, I spoke to them. And TV will come down. Especially since one of the prizes is a color copy of her lips." I wait a sec before I continue. "Look, she's totally cool. I've been crunching the numbers, and what we save with the street—no fancy venue and no big-deal event designer—makes up the difference for Kim. I'm not worried." (Seriously, I'm not.) "Oh. No live music either. Our in-house audio will loop a music CD. I talked to Tony Z. Only songs with the word *kiss*. What else?"

"Maybe Hershey's would partner?" asks Nancy.

"Check into it," instructs Jay. "Well, well, Ms. A. I think you've got it covered."

The room alive, everyone can't wait to get back to work. Yes, it will make a great photo op ... Kim's fabulous legs crossed atop the copier; the winning couple leaning against it in a big embrace. In front of the fabulous signage against the fabulous backdrop of this fabulously romantic city.

"So Borrelli coordinates on the venue and permit with Nancy—schedule a meeting with Aimee to bring you up to speed. Todd, work with Allison to create media lists." Jay looks at the new girl. "Make sure to target national and local—broadcast, radio, print, and online," he says before taking the last swig of Diet Coke, signaling the meeting is officially over. They never last more than one can of soda.

"Krista, work up a production schedule." Jay gets up from the table so his closing comments finish as he walks out the door. "E-mail a first draft by end of day Friday. Coordinate timing with Aimee."

Then Jay looks at me. "You . . . get the fifty, get Kim, and get me a press release and media alert as soon as you confirm. Any questions, e-mail." He stops at the door. "By the way. Who got you to Kim C.?"

"Who else? Glenn Rosenblum, Celebrity Access. You know . . ." I pause. "My best friend," I say, disclosing our in-joke, feeling it's part of the magic.

"Well, good work," Jay says, and is gone.

"Praise the Lord," I shout to Krista as soon as he's out of earshot. "It just came to me, and all the pieces kind of came together. Can you believe it?"

"That was amazing, and I'm proud of you as a colleague." She turns to throw out the remnants of a half-eaten apple. I realize she didn't nosh on any of the junk, observing her waist or Passover.

"But to tell you the truth, Aimee, lately it's hard to believe anything," says Krista. "Especially if it comes out of your mouth," she states, then leaves the room, leaving me in the dust.

Having stayed behind to compare notes, the others can't help but look up when they hear this. You know, before they can pretend that they didn't. But I don't care and chase Krista down the hall, catching up to her by reception.

"I think you're being a little unfair," I say, cornering her near a table that holds all the daily newspapers, my peripheral vision catching a headline. By the looks of things, my approval rating is dropping faster than George W. Bush's in the latest polls.

"Oh, you do, do you?" says Krista, more agitated than I've ever seen her. "Matt picked up when your mother called last night," she says, pulling the black velveteen headband out of her blonde head before shaking out her hair and putting it back. "When I took the phone, he heard the whole conversation. I felt horrible for your mother. *Oy vey iz mir* your poor mother was a total wreck," says Krista, sounding like a total neurotic, a worried Jew.

"Well, you didn't have to let that happen," I say when I open the main door to take us, and our fight, into the hall. "It's all your fault she was upset," I blame. If Krista wants to be Jewish so badly, she'll need to learn about that.

"Oh really?"

"Yes," I say. The blame in position, I now go for the guilt. "You could have told her I stopped to get you like . . . horseradish or something, and I was running late, and then you could have told Matt you just heard from me and, as it turns out, I wasn't coming."

"And when you never got to my house to call back your mother, then what?"

"Well . . . you could have said we were starting the seder and I would just call her when I got home. And then you could have left me messages on—"

"She called after it was over."

"So then you could have said—"

"Sorry, Aimee. I'm not that fast on my feet. Guess I'm just not as good at lies as you. But you're living proof that practice makes perfect."

At a momentary loss for words, we each burn. We catch our breaths and cool down. Backs to the elevator bank, we're unaware the door of Layton Real Estate has opened and Andrew Zeman has joined us in the hall.

"So . . . uh, Matt knows?" I ask, tallying the ever-growing list. "Was he mad?"

"At you?"

"No. At *you*. For keeping my secret."

Krista shifts her eyes and looks down. Ah. I see. She didn't keep my secret. Well. I can't say I blame her.

"When?"

"When we left China Grill." Krista pauses. "Like over *two* months ago, *eMay*."

"Really? I can't believe I've been pretending to be a shiksa for over two months."

Zeman's laugh is so loud and so unexpected, we jump as if someone has just come upon us in a dark alley. "You're pretending to be a shiksa!" He slaps his hand on his thigh, laughing so hard he practically wipes away a tear. "You're scamming Bread Guy?"

I sadly nod.

"That is the coolest thing I ever heard. You sly devil, I thought something was up." He waves his hand up and down, referencing my look.

"Anyway, now that it's all out in the open, I have something to ask you." I speak to Krista, ignoring Andrew, hoping he'll go away. He doesn't, but as Krista (who's since met and disliked him) ignores him, too, I continue.

"This Sunday is Easter. I'm thinking we should celebrate. So what do I do? Go to church? Hey. Want to come? Then we can do a dinner. Yeah, I can make a ham. Since Matt knows, do you think he can be cool? What do you say, Kris? My place?"

"We can do it at mine," says Andrew. "Selina wants to give our relationship a year before she takes on all the Jewish stuff, so we're in for Easter."

"This will be fun." I look at Krista and smile.

"Three Jewish guys and their shiksas," says Andrew.

"Sounds like a sitcom."

"Gotta tell ya, A. You're *much* better as a shiksa. And definitely sexier."

"See," I shout to Krista. "Now don't you see?"

I don't want to lose her friendship. I'm also desperate for her to see my point. She knows Andrew never dated me when there was a viable chance. It's apparent, now, if he met eMay, he'd call her in a flash.

Can't she see we are all sold as a package? And that part of hers will always be that she's the woman who got serious about Judaism after she met Matt? Can't she understand that's part of what she sells; part of what Matt's chosen to buy? True, her goods are real while mine are just—

"So . . ." Andrew now leans into me. Continuing sotto voce, he says, "The guy's all hot for you, right? Bet it works like a charm. Huh, Kris?"

But she only spits out "Thou shalt not lie!" before flouncing back to the office.

"What's her problem? Jeez," says Andrew. "I hope she doesn't turn into one of those uptight Jewish chicks."

"Zeman." No matter what side of the fence I'm on, this comment offends. "Shut up."

"Huh?"

I storm after Krista, arriving at the door in time for it to slam in my face. If that's not enough, when I swipe my card to get in, it won't work. No one hears my banging, Tanisha apparently away from her desk. I stand alone in the hallway, waiting for someone to exit and let me in.

Now I have to get Office Services to check out the activation strip on the card. Maybe I'll have to get a new photo and a whole new ID. I had to redo this one after the hair because the new guy in security didn't take me for a match. And now it doesn't work. Even my ID won't recognize me anymore.

Will the Real Shiksa
Please Stand Up?

THE END OF ANY LIFE has the tendency to put one's own in perspective, even if only briefly. Though it's often at random, we constantly hear about death. A sound bite on the radio. A photo with dates will flash across the TV screen. News anchors tally daily how many have died in Iraq. We hear the news of the one who has stopped, but those of us here keep going just as we had the moment before. Whether it be watering our plants, hopping into the shower, talking on the phone, dashing out the door. We are busy. Living.

But death takes no prisoners. That's the one sure thing everyone does have in common. Every ending will be different. And every loss, depending upon the relationship, will be experienced differently for those who do remain.

Josh holds my hand in the cavernous and ornately decorated living room of the recently deceased Long Island deli king, Saul Greenblatt. A longtime LoveLoaves customer, Saul was also a neighbor and family friend of the Hirsches.

The kids and grandkids in from out-of-town for the holiday, Saul was surrounded by his nearest and dearest when, sadly and unexpectedly, he had a heart attack at the end of the second seder the night before last. Sissy Greenblatt, his wife of fifty-two years, had just served dessert. Saul expounded on the merits of the flourless chocolate cake—deliciously first-rate and still kosher for Pesach—collapsing just moments after taking his very last bite.

"He died surrounded by everything he loved," cries Sissy on the gold crushed-velvet sofa, dabbing her eyes with a tissue while talking to those around her. "His family, his fortress . . . his favorite food. Death by chocolate," she says, still in shock, choking on her small sobs, trying to rally.

In accordance with the Jewish custom, Saul was buried within twenty-four hours of his death. Today is the first full day the family sits shivah, the seven-day period of mourning. Extended family, neighbors, and friends drop by to comfort the mourners and honor the deceased.

"My parents left for Hong Kong this morning, and someone from my family has to pay a shivah call," Josh said when he called me this morning. "I can pick you up at work. Will you come with me tonight to Long Island?"

Sending or bringing food and making donations to a charity are part of Jewish mourning customs. Without knowing why, I know flowers are not. And for this reason I bring them. Shiksa written all over me, arriving with a big bouquet.

"Thank you," says Sissy when Josh introduces us. "How very kind," she says of the flowers, though I see her register that Josh is dating a girl who's Not.

But as with most Jewish stuff, Josh knows. He brings bread. And lots of it: sourdough, ciabatta, and focaccias; bagels, baguettes, and a plain old seeded rye. "Oh, Joshy." Sissy's awed when she looks into the shopping bag.

"Freeze it."

"Saul loved everything baked from your factory." She hands the bread and the flowers to someone nearby, who's eager and ready to help. "You were always on time; he loved that. 'I can count on Hirsch,' he always said. 'I never have to worry with an order from them.'"

Josh pays his respects to Saul and Sissy's kids, who are older than him. He gets a kick when he introduces me to Randy and her son; especially when Josh tells the boy his mother was his age when she babysat him.

Always tons of food at a shivah, the death of a deli king is nothing short of a full-blown smorgasbord. Josh makes me a plate, taking delight in explaining every item on the table. If not a cultural Jew, my boyfriend is most certainly a culinary one.

Their rabbi arrives to conduct the short service. When Sam died, I was not his wife, so was not in the inner circle of mourners. But I sat shivah with his family as if I were. Every night someone else from the synagogue came to lead the prayers. A minyan of ten, the minimum needed to form a congregation, was brought together so the mourners could say Kaddish. The ritual a comfort.

Now it's still early. People are just coming home from work. When we leave here, I will have to go back and burn the midnight oil. At this hour, though, the main visitors are Sissy's friends. Mainly women. Women, most likely, never bat mitzvahed. Looking around, I see hardly any men.

The rabbi smiles as he hands out the small prayer books. He's hip, in his late forties; his hair is kind of long. He has an upbeat spirit. I bet he plays guitar. He stops a moment and counts to see if he has enough people for a minyan. It's close. A few neighbors, Saul's sons and sons-in-laws. Two grandsons bar mitzvahed and over the age of thirteen. All together there are nine.

"Go get Randy or Lynn," someone calls.

"But they weren't bat mitzvahed."

Sissy searches the room. She comes to Josh.

"I was at your bar mitzvah," she says, and hands him a yarmulke. "Get up there."

He won't. "Not me. Get someone who knows the prayers. I don't remember any Hebrew." His participation, he tells me, would be a waste.

"A waste?" I ask. "I don't understand."

He needn't pray; he only needs to stand. To form the minyan. To honor Saul. Doesn't he know how important that is for the Greenblatts? Why must this be about him? For God's sake, what's his problem? But he is his own keeper, and I am mine.

"What about you?" asks the rabbi, to find out whether or not I can count as the tenth?

"Me?" And now we will see how I run my store.

"Yes." His warm brown eyes sear my scorched soul. "Were you bat mitzvahed? Because we're basically Reform here, so it does not have to be all men," he says, and smiles. "You count."

And I want to. Oh, in this moment I so desperately want to count. For I no longer do. I want to claim and reclaim my place. My rightful place, the one I earned. The one I so foolishly abandoned.

I feel Sissy's eyes upon me. She is silent. Perhaps she had sized me up wrong? But it is not me that's important. It is this minyan. Once it is assembled, she will join the congregants to say this prayer to praise God and honor her husband. While in mourning, you say it every day. Depending on how observant you are, you say it for a week, a month, or a year. I know from experience it can help to provide some solace. For the sounds of the words are magical. I so want to recite them.

"Yit-ga-dal ve-yit-kadash she-mei ra-ba." The plaintive quality can touch your essence at critical points in your life; especially now, when one link has come full circle and the next link, one you cannot imagine you even have, must take over. Within all this sadness, that prayer is a motto of life.

"What is your name?" asks the rabbi.

"Aimee," I answer when I stand. Because I do, I stand up. I hold out my hand. I take the book.

"Uh, Rabbi," Josh calls out after I take a step into the circle. "I don't think she gets what's going on. She's not Jewish."

The rabbi stops in his tracks. He looks at me. I search his eyes, and he gets it. He gets what's going on. Without details, he sees. If only I could see me through his eyes, maybe I would understand why I've been doing this. I turn around to see Josh beckoning me to step back. Only now I can't. It's time to move forward.

"Wait!"

But that voice isn't mine. Steve, a high-school friend of Randy's who lives a few towns away, dropped by his parents' before visiting the Greenblatts. Her phone call got him here in the knick of time.

"I'm going to have to put you down for a few minutes, Lili," he says of the strawberry-blonde little girl he carries in on his shoulders. "Can you watch her?" he asks, before standing with the other men in the minyan. When she sits on my lap, Josh protectively puts his arm around my shoulders.

"That was sweet of you to try to help," he whispers. "And look at this." Josh looks from little Lili on my lap to me. He grins. "You're going to be a great mom. Think it's too soon to talk about that?"

So near to getting what I want, I find myself pulling away from Josh in the car ride home, which crazily only makes me more desirable. Somehow the male-female push and pull has the remarkable ability to transcend age, race, and religion.

"So that was pretty weird in there for a second," Josh says, and turns on the CD player, searching for something to listen to. "With that rabbi."

"The longer I'm in New York, the more people mistake me for Jewish," I boldly answer.

"How?" he says, and turns up the volume. The soundtrack of *Garden State* blasts through the speakers. "Look at you."

Yeah, Josh. Look at me. Really look. Then tell me what you really see.

The drive home is mostly silent, but for Josh singing along to Coldplay's "Don't Panic." *"We live in a beautiful world. Yeah we do, yeah we do."*

We finally reach Lexington Avenue, where Josh drops me so I can go back to work. I've been working late these last weeks, and, considering his gripes about Lauren, I've been pleasantly surprised he hasn't said a word. Except all that is about to change.

"I haven't been seeing enough of you," he says when we pull up in front of my office building near Grand Central. As he leans over to kiss me, I notice, again, that Josh is more amorous in public than in private. He creates great expectations on dates, but then I'm disappointed once we arrive home. "Can I pick you up later and you'll stay at my place?"

How far am I willing to let all this go? How much am I giving up so I can get? I keep making myself less in order to get more. In the end I'm afraid it won't be. But what if I'm wrong? Or do I mean right? Once I straighten this all out, could Josh make me happy? For now I'm unsure where we stand on issues I never even thought we would have.

"Look, Josh, we've been going out for a few months and . . ."

"I know, I know," he says. "You don't want to keep going back and forth from one apartment to the next, especially with everything going on at work."

"No, well yes, but it's just that . . ." That happens to be true, but unbeknownst to Josh, that's the least of it. "See . . . I've been thinking about us. And why we never discuss certain things."

"I know," he says. "That's what's so beautiful about this. You're so unlike anyone I've ever dated before. You're so unlike Lauren. Everything with us is so easy. Because you and me, eMay, we're really the same. We have no differences."

Josh lives in a beautiful world because that's all he wants to see. In our case, however, that's also the only color I choose to show.

"Well, I doubt that's true," I say when it hits me. Aren't I the one always saying to embrace the differences? "But I do think that now it's time."

"So do I," says Josh. "Definitely."

Good. Finally we are on the same page. We look at each other with similar intent, except who's to know it's so disparate.

"This weekend," we both say at the same time.

"You go first—"

"No you—"

"How about"—we both begin again.

"Okay."

Together and separate we each stake our claim.

"This Sunday I want you to come with me to church" would probably have been dramatic enough, except Josh says, "I think it's time we move in together."

The die now cast on our respective agendas, all I can say is this is sure going to be one hell of an Easter egg hunt.

The Ether Bunny

EASTER BUNNY CAKE

Remember old-fashioned cutout cakes? This cute bunny is easily made from carrot cake mix, frosted, and covered with mouthwatering coconut.

Prep Time: 30 min
Start to Finish: 2 hr 10 min

MAKES 12 SERVINGS

1 Box Betty Crocker SuperMoist carrot cake mix
Water, vegetable oil, and eggs called for on cake mix box
Tray or cardboard covered with foil
1 Container Betty Crocker whipped fluffy white frosting
1 Cup shredded coconut
Construction paper
Jelly beans or small gumdrops
Green food color

"Ma, it's me," I say after the beep. "Can I borrow some of your baking tins and trays? If you leave them in a shopping bag in the foyer, I can just come by and pick it up. You won't even know I'm there. I have to be on the West Side later anyway. I have to meet my pastor. At my new church."

"Okay, that does it," my mother says, and finally picks up the phone. "It's enough."

Ever since she and my dad found out, no one has returned my calls or my e-mails. Not my brother or sister, not Krista or my parents. Peter had clearly stopped, and for the first time ever Tova didn't stop to talk to me in the hall. However, I do know my mother. I know how to get her attention. And I had to go this far.

"Can I also borrow something you'd use to cook a ham?" My kitchen is small, and I usually buy kitchen paraphernalia on an as-needed basis. But today I don't have time.

"I'm not letting you use the roasting pan I use for brisket to bake a ham."

"Oh, you *bake* it?" I haven't yet researched a recipe, and frankly I was unsure what you're supposed to do with it. I was tempted to just buy an Easter dinner at Dean & DeLuca, but I have to pull out the stops. Tomorrow has to be perfect.

"What do you care what goes in the pan? It's not like your meat's always kosher or anything."

"That's not the point," says my mother. "My heart is. Which is more than I can say for yours. I'm very disappointed in you, Aimee. We all are."

As horrible as it is to hear what my mother has to say, I'm happy we're at least talking. First part of this mission halfway accomplished, I hop in a cab to go cross-town to my church, conveniently located just two blocks from Fairway, where after my meeting I can food-shop.

The West Side, especially on a Saturday, is nothing if not Jewish. As theatrical as the neighborhood was, that's how Jewish it's become. The taxi drives past one synagogue after the next; groups of people all dressed up for Shabbat walk together after attending Saturday morning services. Because I'm still Jewish, the guilt gives me a good *zetz*. But frankly, I'm pretty excited to see this church.

I searched online for the perfect Protestant church, and when I approach the building on West End Avenue I have surely found it. The West End Collegiate Church was originally formed downtown by Dutch colonists in 1628. I read on the plaque that this building, designed in a Flemish style, was completed in 1892 for the Collegiate Reformed Protestant Dutch Church.

One of those people who would be more curious to travel back in time instead of forward, I wish I could snap my fingers and be on this block then. That's impossible, but I do enter a new world when I open the door and take a seat on the wood bench inside.

"Can I help you?"

"Yes, I'm here to see the pastor."

Jim, as he prefers to be called, got back to me immediately when I left a message for him yesterday asking about the possibility of a meeting.

"It's so kind of you to take this time," I say, following behind him on the stairs before entering his cozy study. Yellow daffodils abound in window boxes perched outside. I immediately recognize the chairs as Mission furniture. Two face each other on a diagonal, and I'm invited to take a seat.

I did not feel I could bring Josh here tomorrow without some knowledge of the place first. Honestly, a few minutes ago I didn't even know where to find the entrance to *my church*. Logistics aside, I realized that when it comes to being any kind of a Protestant, I'm pretty much not in-the-know.

Jim wears a suit and has welcoming eyes. He tells me he will baptize his granddaughter at the Easter service tomorrow. He gives the background of the church. Then he asks why I've come.

For the first time since becoming a shiksa, I allow authentic feelings to flow, and my eyes fill with tears. Boy, do I need counsel. It never occurred to me to consult clergy. A shrink, maybe. Or even a rabbi. Truth be told, I'd feel embarrassed to talk to one. But here I feel separate. And safe.

Jim says when it comes to reverence, the Torah is to Jews as Jesus is to Christians. I never thought of it like that but find it more than interesting to contemplate. I mean, Jewish people are known to stress learning. The focus on interpretation and discussion, the openness to debate. Or in the words of Tevye, "On the one hand . . . on the other hand . . . on the *other* hand . . ."

I wonder if all that study gave birth to the stereotype of the overly analytical Jew. I've been accused of that myself. If you're one to think the constant back-and-forth over the same thing a little analytical. Maybe more like a little neurotic. But in kindness it is just the ability to see, yet, another hand. There's always more than one way to look at something, and how you do informs your behavior. I only have to look as far as myself to know this is true.

He talks of the many denominations, and it's analogous to the varying ways Jewish sects observe. That makes me even more curious to understand the similarities between Easter and Passover, and the differences between being Jewish and Not. Not, of course, is built on a huge belief system, but in another way it is simple. Judaism stops at the Old Testament, and Christianity continues with the New. Since the first book *is* the foundation, in that respect I don't feel I stray *that* far from home. I bet, to an extent, that familiarity helps when a real shiksa is open to Judaism. So I tell him about me and my family, about Sam and Peter. About Josh.

"Let's say I told you I really am a Protestant. And that I'm dating a Jewish guy . . ." (One I'm beginning to feel I'd have an interfaith marriage with whether I was Jewish or Not.) "Well, if I told you that, what would you say?"

Jim takes a moment to compose his thoughts. Though I may only fleetingly belong to his parish, we are all God's children and he cares.

"I would say that you live in a terribly important bridge place," he says, "and that you are knitting together two terribly important cultures and traditions."

When we are done, he shows me out, lightness guiding me up to my mom on Ninety-sixth Street.

"Wasn't that brilliant?" I ask when she makes me walk the reservoir with her.

Maddie was waiting for me in the foyer with two shopping bags of baking supplies and two bottles of water. Ready to take me to the park to walk and talk. Surrounded by tall buildings and trees, the water glistens. I love being near water in a city. It's unseasonably cold, but the sun shines and I feel somehow after tomorrow things will get brighter.

"It was," says Maddie. "And I wonder why you didn't go talk to him about this all that time you were dating Peter?"

Peter? "Why are we always talking about Peter?"

"We're not," says my mother, pausing to take a sip of her water. We walk on the dirt path and keep to the right, allowing two joggers to pass. "But we should be."

"Ma, stop. You saw him. The night in the lobby. You saw Josh. You see he's cute, nice, that he's good to me. And he comes from . . . well, wait till you see what he comes from."

"I don't have to see Josh, and I don't have to see what he comes from. I see you. And you don't seem happy with him."

"Of course I'm happy with him. I just always have this lie on my mind. Besides, how do you know how I feel? I never talk to you about it. Why would you even say a thing like that?" While my mom and I are now really talking, this is not my conversation of choice.

"You eat tortillas, *traif*, on Passover? You never had to do that with Peter. From what I hear about this young man, if you do have a family, he'll be on a golf course while you take the kids to temple alone."

"Isn't it like that with *everybody*?" I accuse. "Daddy was always working. He wasn't in there like you were. Doesn't that stuff always fall on the woman? Whether or not she works like a man?" We neared the East Side, and I decide not to walk the full circle. I stop by the benches next to the steps. It's obvious I will get off the reservoir path and exit the park to head home. "Besides, Peter isn't ready like Josh. It makes a big difference, and *that's* something you very well know."

"And just so *you* know," says my mother, pointing her manicured finger to put me in my place. "Peter has been in touch. And his situation will change."

"His situation will . . . what? Why are you being so cryptic?"

But my mother will not answer. She has several more points to make. I could say I should have known better. Except no matter how distressing, after being so alone in this I want to hear.

"If you are in touch with Peter, I'm sure he'll tell you. As for relationships, I'm not from the women's movement, okay? I don't believe any partnership between a woman and man is so equal; I don't even want it to be. But within every twosome there has to be the proper give and take. People need to share. And people need to know how. Peter knows. In *every* way." My mother's look almost scares me. It is so intense; it's as if she has seen beyond my words and into my bed. "Does Josh? And . . ." She looks at me. "I wonder about this, Aimee. Do you?"

"I think that's kind of mean."

"Happy Easter," Maddie says, then makes a 180 in her new Reeboks and walks away.

But it feels more like I've come full circle when Josh and I are seated in the pew the next morning. The sanctuary is so pretty, Victorian and charming. Lilies and azaleas, bright red carpet, stained-glass windows, mustard and burnt-orange walls. The ceiling forms an apex in the center, the dark wood beams matching the pews. The choir sings, and on the pulpit is the word GOD . . . carved in Hebrew!

"What do I do?" whispers Josh. I look to the woman next to me, who smiles.

"Welcome," she says when I ask if she can pass us a few books.

As Hebrew is read right to left, I immediately open the book backward. I wonder if this is why all Jewish holidays start on the night before. Quickly, I flip the book over before Josh might notice. But Josh doesn't, nor has he yet to open his.

"Page 492," I instruct when we stand to sing a hymn preparing us for the baptism. It's sung to the tune of what I know as Cat Stevens's "Morning Has Broken." I am even able to sing along.

Baptized in water
Sealed by the spirit

Today I wear a scooped-neck dress in white, decorated with little daisies. My cherished green cardigan, ballet flats, pearls, and my hair pulled up in a ponytail . . . with a great big bow.

Cleansed by the blood of
Christ our King

Josh stares straight ahead. I reach for his hand, but after a few seconds he pulls his away. When the baptism begins, Jim speaks of Abraham and his talk with God. I give Josh a nudge; his people are represented here too.

"See," I say. "It's just one big pot."

The baby girl is beautiful. And I'm touched when Jim tells the congregation this year Maundy Thursday was during Passover week, two days after the second seder. And what remarkable convergence it is when the holidays coincide. When that happens, this church will conduct a seder. The bridge.

"Isn't this nice?" I ask, enjoying this service.

"It's over at 12:15?" responds Josh, as he looks at his watch to count the minutes.

I ignore him, wishing I could participate and sing full-out. Only I don't know any of the tunes.

"Okay. I'll stop singing," I whisper in Josh's ear when the next song comes. "I don't want you to feel any more uncomfortable."

Suddenly everyone stands and recites: "I believe in God the Father Almighty Maker of Heaven and Earth . . ."

Josh looks at me bewildered. "What do you want me to do here?"

"Sit," I tell him, while I still stand. However, I don't finish the prayer. It's not my belief system, but I'm well aware that if I was raised that way, it would be.

"Let us pray."

I look around to see what that means, then sit and bow my head like everyone else when I see it is a private tête-à-tête with God. When I bend my head, it is the same as when I recite the Shema. In fact, now in my mind I do. I say the Hebrew prayer talking to the same God as always, just in a different locale.

"Now tell him your needs and desires," says the pastor.

Wow. Christians get straight to it, I think. It feels so unencumbered.

In Judaism, we praise and honor God before we ask him for stuff. In fact, for me it has always felt as if we really should skirt around the idea of too much personal asking. Better to ask for help and guidance rather than a direct "Dear God, please let me win that new account." Rewards will be attained through mitzvahs and good deeds. We step back before we step forward. Honor, but know your place.

But what do I know? It's all my interpretation. To me, Jim's words feel like permission to go for it. That said, I'm such a mess I don't have the chutzpah to ask God to hook me up with a husband. My best bet at this point is to ask for help and guidance. Still, I like expressing my needs and desires. I wonder if Christians do it more easily because they have less guilt, or if it's because every week they give.

"We pay up front," says Josh when I open my wallet and add to the basket, making a donation. "High-holiday tickets are big money."

I know. But this way or that, in the end it all comes out in the wash.

As in Judaism, the service ends with a benediction. After the candles are extinguished, two young boys bring the light to the door.

"Isn't this the most wonderful day?" exclaims the woman next to me, who introduces herself as Mary Lou, but I can call her Mary. "Whenever there's a baptism, it just brings tears to my eyes." She invites us into the parlor for lunch. Josh pulls my hand as a way to say no.

"I prepared a big meal at home," I tell her, and did I ever. On our way out I introduce Josh to Jim, who shakes my hand and greets me by name. I am impressed. The familiarity, I see, scares Josh.

"How often do you go there?" he asks back at my apartment.

An EASTER BUNNY sign hangs on my front door. A basket of dyed Easter eggs (that part was so much fun) sits on the doormat below. Once we're inside, I light candles. Vases of tulips are everywhere. The table already set, my Easter Bunny Cake is the perfect centerpiece. I bring the ham to the table alongside a green bean casserole and deviled eggs. Speaking of which, at his place setting is a yellow Easter egg decorated in decals, JOSH written across it in letters of bright orange.

"This is very . . . nice," Josh says when he takes his place at the table.

"I'm so glad you like it," I say. "Now let's join hands and say grace."

"Say what? When'd you start doing that?"

"What do you mean start? You always say grace on a holiday." I look confused. "And this is a very important one. Christ rose from the dead. We need to celebrate." I reach across and take his hand. "Dearest God," I begin. "We thank you for all the abundance we have in our lives. For the gift of life itself, food, shelter, our material things. But most important, God, we want to—"

"Okay, Aimee. Please stop."

"But I was just getting to the good part. The part about love." I smile. I blow him a kiss across the table.

"Well, I'm not into grace," he says, "I'm Jewish; we don't do that. And I'm hungry." He looks disapprovingly at the food.

Oh. So suddenly he's Jewish. How about that? Though I don't see why he would object to my grace. It wasn't religious. There's nothing wrong with being grateful.

"You know, this is really nice and everything, but I wish you would have just let me take you out."

"You shared your holiday with me. I just want to do the same. After all, days like this will be most important when we're a family."

Josh practically spits. When I hand him a knife to slice the ham, he seems tempted to use it on himself. Meanwhile I dip a serving spoon into the green beans and put a portion on his plate with several Dole pineapple rings, a few deviled eggs on the side.

"Do you have any bread?" he asks.

I go into the kitchen and bring back his Breakstone's butter with a loaf of Wonder Bread. What can I tell you? I couldn't resist.

"So what did you think about today?" I ask, diving into my meal. "Tell me everything."

The ham came out pretty good, and Krista is definitely right about casseroles. My favorite part of the bunny cake is the ears. I went through five sheets of construction paper until I got them right, and I spent what felt like a hundred hours in the kitchen. But it was all worth it. This is one authentic goyishe meal, and Josh, for all his secular fanfare, is choking on every bite.

"What's the matter?" I finally ask, having given the awkward silence its appropriate amount of time.

Josh puts down his knife and fork. Walking away from the table, he goes to the window and stares out at the city. His dramatic moment. Poor Josh. Contemplating a future with—

"A woman who's a churchgoer and would want to raise our children Christian," he finishes for me, upset and astonished, fit to be tied.

Hallelujah! Praise the Lord!

"But Josh," I ever so sweetly begin. "You knew this was important to me from the beginning. You said so yourself after our trip to Scranton. Why is it suddenly a problem now? Especially since you always tell me how disinterested you are in Judaism. I mean, children have to be grounded in *some*-thing."

Josh looks pained. Embarrassed. He doesn't know what to say.

"I just figured it would be . . . you know . . . like we'd kind of raise kids to celebrate, uh, holidays."

"And that's what today is," I say. "So what is actually wrong?"

Now I wait. I want to hear this explanation.

"It's the whole Jesus thing," he blurts out. "I'm sorry, but I'm just uncomfortable with it."

Most Jewish people are. He's the big unspoken divide between Jewish and Not. Embracing Jesus is alien to Jews. Perhaps things would be better among us all if we were all more attuned. But no one asked Josh to accept him as his savior. And the church today did not have a crucifix. There is no crucifix in my apartment. Nor was Jesus' name mentioned during my grace.

"So what's your problem with Jesus?" I ask, defensive. "That he exists?"

Josh sits down on the couch. He doesn't know how to articulate his fear. And that's what it is. Of losing the known, taking on the unknown. But I use it to forge on.

"I mean, if you're that uncomfortable with this, we wouldn't *necessarily* have to get married in my church in Scranton," I say, jumping way, way ahead, purposely pushing this to its limit. "But I can't say for sure."

"Married in a *church*? I could never!" he says. "I always thought we'd just do it in a hotel. Or . . . or . . . on a boat!"

He is up now. Pacing. Back and forth and back and forth. I've never seen him so distressed. Good. Let him get in touch with how he really feels about all this. Push comes to shove, let's see how much he really wants to make a life with a shiksa who doesn't want to convert.

"And who would officiate?" I go on. "Because I feel I would have to marry under God. I mean I am Christian. I'm baptized, Josh. For Christ's sake, I made a covenant with Jesus!"

Josh spins around out of control. Grabs, kisses me. Then abruptly breaks away. He pulls his leather jacket out from the front closet and in one swift motion slides, no slams, back the closet door.

"I have to think," he says, jacket thrown over his shoulder, his hand flagellating in the air. Pointing aimlessly to all the things he is walking out on. The Easter Bunny Cake, the conflict . . . the Wonder Bread, the ham. "I'll call you later. I love you, eMay," Josh cries. Then he is out the door.

Oh my goodness. Josh loves me. This is the first time Josh has told me he loves me. He'll be back later to make it all up, apologizing on his hands and knees. The bar mitzvah of his cousin's son, Evan, is only a week away. I will "study up" on the Shabbat service to "surprise" him. By that point, putting a yarmulke on his head will be like putty in my hands.

The Accidental Tsuris

THE DOOR IN THE VESTIBULE is open when I arrive. Its kickstand down, I close it with my foot, securing the door so some nut won't get in. Once inside, I head up the stairs, having to wonder if indeed that is me.

The scent's still familiar, the stairwell the same. With a sense of balance—only because I'm carrying two equally weighted shopping bags—I glide up the stairs. When I hit the second landing, it feels like home.

"Ruff! Ruff!"

Baxter. He still knows me. I wish I had a key so I could go inside and visit. Hearing his bark . . . I miss him so. But I don't have one. Not that I would use it. Anyway, I don't plan to stay. Or even say hello. It being Easter, I'm sure Peter's not home. I will hang the bags on his doorknob and go away.

It seemed a shame to waste a good Easter dinner. Not to mention the Easter Bunny Cake. Peter will love that. He will enjoy the ham and the casserole. The eggs both deviled and dyed. Peter would have loved this entire day. He would have appreciated me going to church. Of course, unlike Josh, Peter is Christian.

But unlike Peter, I realize I never made an attempt to do anything like this for him when we were together.

I place the Easter basket in front of his apartment door, then tape the bunny sign above it. After hanging the shopping bags, I arrange my note so it will stick out of one bag.

Happy Easter!
For You, P
Aim
PS—Homemade Everything ☺

Baxter's going nuts. He's woofing and barking and practically thrashing himself against the door. He smells me. Or certainly the food.

"I'm sorry, buddy. I miss you too."

I'm already on the next level down when he calls. I look up and see Peter standing behind the railing, peering down over the stairs. He holds the basket; Baxter runs ahead and rushes on down.

Whoosh!

"Hey—you're gonna knock me over." Standing on his back legs, Baxter is almost as tall as me. His tongue reaches my face to say a slobbery hello.

"Is there enough for two?" calls Peter.

I walk back up the flight of stairs, unsure of where I'm going. But when I get inside Peter's apartment, it's obvious I'm not the one going anywhere; he is. Boxes are packed; pictures are off the wall. Bulging suitcases sit in the center of the living room.

"So you came to say good-bye," he says, taking the food out of the shopping bag, opening plates wrapped in foil. "Smells good. I'm hungry. Thanks."

Baxter begs. Peter offers to fix me a plate. I've just lost my appetite.

"Where are you going?"

"Didn't your mother tell you? Isn't that why you're here?"

"She indicated you had some opportunity, but she didn't . . . you and my mom in touch a lot?"

They talk about me? About what I'm doing with Josh?

"Enough," he diplomatically answers.

"So tell me your news. What happened? Where are you going?"

"Los Angeles. Casting director came down to the club. Unbelievable when it finally happens. I'm doing a pilot. A variety show with sketch comedy, remember those? They're bringing 'em back. Maybe it'll help get rid of all that reality TV. Anyway, they like me, but they really like my material. May even get a shot writing on it, too."

"That's *fantastic*, P!" I run and throw my arms around him, but after the perfunctory hug we both pull away. Into the other shopping bag, he unwraps the Easter Bunny Cake. Peter looks at it and laughs.

"Very cute. So this is my bon voyage, huh?"

"I guess." I don't know what to do with myself, so I sit on the floor. "It's not like I ever thought you'd be leaving." Next to a pile of books, I peruse titles while we talk. "Not permanently anyway."

I can't imagine Peter not being in the city. Not being downtown. Peter not accessible. Peter not in my life.

"Hey—what's permanent these days?" he rhetorically asks on his way to the kitchen. "I'm doing a legal sublet with the apartment," he says when he returns with a knife. Peter cuts into the bunny's belly to serve himself a piece of cake. "Great," he says after he tastes. "I appreciate you doing all this for me."

"You're welcome. Easter and all."

Stacked on the floor are four Dean Koontz titles, on top of which is *The Abbott & Costello Story: Sixty Years of "Who's on First?"* by Stephen Cox and John Lofflin.

"Didn't think you thought about that," says Peter. A little teasing. A little testy.

"Yeah . . . well." I trail off when the spine of a skinny yellow book at the bottom catches my eye. *Jewish as a Second Language.* I pull off my coat before I pull it out to look.

"But a shiksa *would* be aware of the holiday," he says, not teasing but testy, inviting the elephant into the room. I flip the book over to read the back cover and practically feel him stomp.

Molly Katz is Jewish and her husband is Not.°
°Not; your religion; e.g., "She's Jewish, but her husband's Not."

"I'm aware of a lot of things. I'm sorry for a lot too." When I look up at Peter, it comes over me. "I miss you, P."

Upon hearing that, Peter drops everything and kneels beside me on the floor. He takes me into his arms. It feels good. Every two people are their own entity and make something new. If I could color the feeling of Peter and me, I'd use pastels and earth tones. Patches would bleed into each other, creating new shapes and new colors; wavy lines in black and white, bright reds and purples would streak their way through.

"Come with me, Aimee," he suddenly announces. "To Los Angeles. Yes." He affirms it's now a really good idea. "Come with me to L.A."

"I . . . I . . ." Los Angeles? With Peter. Just leave? Now? "I can't, I can't go. Besides . . ." Shaking my head sideways, I move my hands up and down, and mime a steering wheel.

"I'll help you," he says. "Nothing to it. You just never lived in a driving culture. Whole different ball of wax."

Overjoyed the Easter Bunny has solved all our problems, Peter kisses me. I respond in spite of myself. My head and my heart duel throughout the arousing kiss, until my head wins out, forcing my body away.

"I can't, Peter. Not like this, not L.A. Not now," I say, and change his green light to red. "I have so much going on with this product launch, and I wouldn't be independent there. It takes time to figure out work and the whole thing with the car. I mean I don't even have my license, well, not yet, so I can't just . . ."

"Yet?" He pipes in, seeing a yellow light flashing. "What do you mean by yet?" he asks, slowing down, cautious to heed the warning.

"Nothing. I mean, you know, I'm not *yet* ready to drive."

"No. You mean you've been out. Driving." Peter waits because he knows there are implications to this. I always thought he'd have made a good lawyer.

"Maybe a little. I've been out. Driving. A little. Just a little."

"Where? In Scranton?" he asks almost defiantly, turning his back, opening the flaps of a box, and placing the books inside. I see the copy on the front cover of the Jewish humor book: *How to Worry. How to Interrupt. How to Say the Opposite of What You Mean.*

"Josh took me a couple of times. No big deal."

"He's still in the picture?" he asks before he looks to the food.

"Is Courtney?"

Peter doesn't dignify the question with an answer. When it comes to dating and relationships, he always knows his mind.

"So is he?" he repeats.

Even after what happened today, I think yes. If I was a contestant on the game show *Who Wants to Be a Millionaire,* I would ask the studio audience. My silence, however, serves as an answer.

"I can't believe you. What's happened to you?" Peter abruptly goes to the table and now looks at the Easter feast before him with annoyance.

"What's the difference if I drove with him a few times? We're in his car a lot. It wasn't like with us where you'd have to rent one."

"You two have a fight today or what?" he asks. " 'Cause you obviously didn't come here to make up with me." Baxter starts barking. Peter reaches over the table and quiets the dog with a piece of ham. "I don't think you cooked all this for me either. Did you?"

I can't answer him. I can't out-and-out lie. Well, I guess we know that I actually can, but I can't right now.

"You let him help you drive. For him, you try. You'll even, what? Overcome your fear and take . . . a *road test*?" He says my dirty words. "You roll up your sleeves and get into Easter. For God's sake . . . you *cooked*? Everything you ran away from with me, you do with him. Except he doesn't know who you are. What the hell is it, Aim? And why can't you share it with me?"

"Boy, Peter, suddenly you're so self-aware. A few months ago you were *too young* for all this. You didn't want to talk about anything. Now you get a TV job and you're a whole different person."

"I get a TV job and you are. You only came because now I'm going to make some money, didn't you?"

"That's not true. I had no idea you even got a job."

"Then why did you come here today? And why did you bring this?" His hand motions to indicate the food, but it returns to his chest and leans against his heart. Why did I bring this angst? Why did I bring this confusion?

"I have no idea why I came. But I think I should go." Too humiliated to stay a moment longer, I gather up my coat to put it on in the hall. When I get to the door, I stop.

"I understand a lot better now the concessions you made for me, P." I talk to Peter, but my eyes look down at the floor. "But just know that however this dinner came about, what's important is that I wanted you to have it. You . . . I'm not blaming you, believe me, but I think you've misunderstood."

"Really?" He marches to the door, Baxter leading the way. "You're the one who's misunderstood. By yourself. This might be a good time to go to your synagogue and get some help because—and I never thought I'd say this to you, Aim—you're lost." Peter crosses his arms in front of him. I turn to face him, mirroring his body language; we stand just the same.

"Funny, you were the one person I always thought knew who she was, but now I don't think you know a bagel from a schmear."

Despite my upset, his joke is funny, so I laugh.

"Gee, I made an urban Jewish joke. Think we can build a life on that, or should I just save it for my show?"

I don't know what he read in that Jewish book, but he certainly got good with the guilt.

Out on the street I am overwhelmed, overloaded, and hungry. I stop on Broadway and buy a slice at Sbarro's. The store's filled with tourists eating pizza. No Easter dinner for them. I consider walking over to my office, but without any peace I'm unable to concentrate. Sadly, work is not an escape. Instead, across the street is a movie theater. I go to the box office and buy a ticket to see *The Hoax.*

Meanwhile, if I had eyes in back of my head, here's what I'd have seen.

Tova walks back to her apartment after putting her garbage in the trash room. It is midday, and she is going to a matinee. She stops in her tracks when she hears yelling from an apartment. Inching down the hallway, Tova realizes it is Aimala's. Not to intrude but to be sure all is okay, she stands outside 15J and listens.

"Married in a church? I could never! I always thought we'd just do it in a hotel. Or... or... on a boat!"

"And who would officiate? Because I feel I would have to marry under God. I mean I am Christian. I'm baptized, Josh. For Christ's sake, I made a covenant with Jesus!"

Suddenly, the apartment door swings open. Tova rushes down the hall to 15F, grateful not to be seen by Josh. First thing she does is go to her address book. Under *A*, she locates the Alberts' number, picks up the phone, and dials.

"Hello?" answers Sid.

"My goodness, Sidney," says Tova. "I am so glad you are home. Where is Maddie? You'll get her, and put her on the telephone now?"

"What happened to Aimee?" asks my father.

"Something happened to Aimee?" Hearing the alarm in his voice, Maddie grabs a cordless phone. She sits in a chair across from Sid, who talks on the landline in their bedroom.

"I don't know how to tell you this," says Tova. She, too, has a landline and out of nervousness wraps her fingers inside and out of the long, white squiggly cord.

"Is she safe?" cries Maddie. "Did something terrible happen?"

"Just tell us," cries Sid.

"Well." Tova takes a deep breath. How will she break this news? "I heard them just now when I was taking out the garbage. They were fighting."

"Who was fighting?" Maddie and Sid ask at once.

"Aimee and the boyfriend. Josh. The Jewish one."

"Is she hurt?" asks my mother. "Did he—"

"No! No. Not like that. I am on my way to the ballet, and believe me it was not my intention to eavesdrop. When first I heard the noise, I didn't even know who it was. But I walked down the hall to locate the voices—"

Sid turns his right forefinger in circles, motioning to his wife that Tova needs to hurry up.

"Please cut to the chase," he says when he is no longer able to contain himself. "Tell us already what happened."

"Aimee and Josh are planning to marry," says Tova. "And she wants to do it in a *church*. Our Aimee is a convert. She turned Christian!"

My mother falls on the bed in a heap. My father is prepared to fight.

"Get Aimee on the phone," he says. "We're getting to the bottom of this right now."

When my cell rings, I quickly power down. Later, at the movie, I can't answer. After, I check my voice mail and hear an uproar of such disproportion, I only send back a text message to say I'm okay. The week goes by, I answer e-mails but no questions.

No calls on the phone. I need time. Work, of late, is crazed. And luckily I'm unaware of this:

To: momalbert@yahoo.com
From: k.dowd@prwap.com
Subject: Aimee

Maddie, I see Aimee at work, and she's fine. We're not exactly on great terms, so I can't say for sure. But do think she's still Jewish, even though she's a shiksa.
—Krista

To: daph2@gmail.com, jon@japhotography.com
cc: k.dowd@prwap.com
From: momalbert@yahoo.com
Subject: Fwd: Aimee

Daphne and Jon,
What do you know about what's going on with your sister?
Come to the city this weekend. Family meeting! xxoo

To: momalbert@yahoo.com, sid.albert@ssco.com
From: pmck@gmail.com
Subject: Re: Were you in touch with Aimee?

Maddie and Sid,
I won't be around. Already here. L.A.'s great. Settling in over weekend, work starts Monday. Jazzed.
Saw Aimee in NY last Sunday on Easter. She didn't say anything about converting. But don't think anything else has changed. Hang in there.
—Peter

Josh is back, wining and dining me like never before. We don't talk about what happened, which is fine with me. I have no energy for it. Not to mention I spend most nights this week at the office working. Late. Way, way behind, I am eager to catch up.

"You're still here?" I ask Krista Friday night, running into her in reception, finally on my way out the door. "It's Shabbat; I thought you'd be at services."

"Not tonight," she says, eyes glued to the papers she just retrieved from the copy machine. "Too much going on. That launch."

"Tell me about it."

The silence is awkward. How long has it been like this now?

"What are you up to this weekend?" she asks. Nonchalantly.

"Going to a bar mitzvah tomorrow." I beam. "My *first*." Krista doesn't laugh. "Josh's cousin's son. In Larchmont. Getting my hair done now, and my nails. Got the last appointment of the night."

"Well." Krista lifts her eyes. Just slightly. "Have fun, Aimee."

"Thanks." I hang back a moment to see if there's more to this talk, but there's not. *C'est la vie;* it's a start. I check my watch. I don't want to be late.

To: momalbert@yahoo.com, sid.albert@ssco.com
From: k.dowd@prwap.com
Subject: Aimee and Saturday

Good news. Just found out Aimee will be away all day at a bar mitzvah tomorrow in Larchmont. Imagine she'll be home early evening.

—Krista

"Willie says he will call upstairs and let us know when Aimee comes in," Tova tells my mother when they speak later that night.

"Thank you," says Maddie. "She likes being a shiksa? Let's see how my daughter feels when she finally meets *her* maker."

From: info@evite.com

Subject: The Alberts have sent you an Evite Invitation

evite

You are invited to attend a SHIKSA INTERVENTION by Maddie and Sid Albert.

ARE YOU IN?

Not Is Not Enough

IT'S A PRETTY SYNAGOGUE in the suburbs. Modern architecture, a sanctuary of wood and glass. The ceiling is quite high; soft light shines through a skylight. The Hebrew alphabet, each letter carved in bronze, is arranged around the Ark that holds the Torah. Prayer books in hand, the bar mitzvah boy and his divorced parents, together for this special occasion, sit on blue velvet chairs on the bimah.

"We call to the Torah . . ."

Family members are announced. They come up to the bimah to recite the first blessing before the reading of the Torah.

"Ba-re-khu et . . . ," they begin. Then the congregation answers. The Hebrew words mean "We praise God, who is to be praised, praising him forever and ever." When they are through, they give Evan a handshake or a hug. Proud, and proud to be given this aliyah.

I turn to Josh and smile. It is the first time I see him in a yarmulke. Orange on the outside, dark blue on the inside. EVAN POMERANTZ BAR MITZVAH and the date are embossed in gold.

I reach for Josh's hand and squeeze. He squeezes back. After our day at church, there was much less flack about his sitting through this service today. Besides which, when it's over, there's a big party. But we have only just begun.

Evan seems naturally gregarious, but in today's reverent setting he can't help be a bit subdued. Hebrew, however, comes easy to him. Ready and well rehearsed, he effortlessly chants his haftarah portion. The cacophonies of the words create beautiful harmonious sounds.

With humor and presence, Evan speaks of his mitzvah project during his speech. Of volunteering to help disabled children prepare for their bar mitzvahs.

"Were you like this at yours?" I lean over and quietly ask.

"Me?" Josh cracks up. "We had to get a tutor for me. Could barely get through it. But my party was awesome," he whispers in my ear. "The theme was *E.T.*, and we gave everyone toy phones with my picture to *take* home. Get it?"

Take home, phone home. "Got it."

My bat mitzvah didn't have a theme. After the service, we had a luncheon in a neighborhood restaurant that had a private room for parties. Everyone came up to me to say how amazingly I had done with my haftarah, and I remember feeling proud. Plus Michael Cohen danced practically every dance with me. Looking back, if pressed to come up with one, I would color my theme happy.

The bar mitzvah boy suddenly throws up his hands. Guarding his face and protecting his body. From the attack. By the candy brigade. Earlier, little candies were distributed to Evan's friends, who now throw them at him on the bimah. Customary in wishing him a sweet life.

Josh runs up to some kids and grabs a few wrapped hard candies for us to throw. Everyone hoops and hollers. It's joyful. And fun.

"Zach loves this," says Josh of his younger brother. The first positive thing about any Jewish tradition I've ever heard him say.

Benjy has a temperature, so Zach and Elizabeth were unable to come. Still in Hong Kong, Josh's parents also are not here. I don't imagine my folks would plan a trip abroad if one of their sibling's grandkids were to be honored. Even if divorce had made them somewhat estranged. It's not surprising Josh feels such a disconnect. But by attending this bar mitzvah, like the shivah, Josh shows his heart is in the right place.

Perhaps the takeaway feeling has a lot to do with your early exposure. If the culture is presented to you as unimportant and a bore, it's likely you will grow up feeling that way. If it's presented as the "be all and end all" and shoved down your throat, that too can be a turnoff. Now I'm hopeful that Josh might gain some appreciation seeing it through "an outsider's" eyes.

The Torah is marched around. People touch it with their siddurs and then kiss the prayer book. Seated on the aisle, I lean past Josh as the procession walks by, extending my book out to reach the Torah. I take a look around first, making sure Josh sees I am only copying the other congregants.

In the procession, Robby gives Josh a high-five when he passes, winking at him when he sees me kiss the book.

"You don't have to do that," Josh tells me, at this point the singing so loud and jubilant he needn't whisper.

"When in Rome," I say, and leave it at that.

"Please stand for the Amidah," says the rabbi. Meaning "standing," this prayer of gratitude is repeated during the Musaf service, the additional service said on Shabbat.

I haven't been to synagogue in such a long time, it all feels so good. I must start to go again, I think. Just as soon as things straighten out, I think. And I want to go on Saturday mornings, when I tend to feel an even larger sense of community. How many years did I attend Saturday morning services? The structure and continuity of the prayers are such a part of me. While every synagogue has its own spin, I am at home with every nuance and every word.

"Page 286."

My siddur closed, I open it quickly. The right side of the book, its pages written in Hebrew, I hold close to my nose. I take three small steps backward before taking three forward, approaching God as you might a king. I bend my knees, bow my head, and pray.

"What are you doing?" asks Josh. Stunned.

"Sssshh."

"How'd you know to do that?"

"Huh?"

Oh. Oh, no.

"I, uh, studied up," I whisper. "And didn't they already do this one before?"

"Don't ask me," says Josh. Standing. His prayer book left on the seat. Closed. "Aimee, you don't have to participate. You can just chill."

We stand, we sit; we sit, we stand. The up and down so automatic, I must remember to watch Josh to take my cues from him. Except now in this synagogue I no longer want to. During the Amidah, especially when first said as a personal prayer, I asked God to please guide me out of this mess. In the end, however, what happens will come from me.

People often ask how God can allow murder, disasters and disease, terrorists and war. People often say religion causes war. But religion doesn't. People do. God gives us free will. I don't think God controls all that. He sure doesn't control me. But my intention does.

Connecting to one's intention will create and make change. People call it the power of positive thinking. Of late, many think that's *The Secret.* But it's just our higher self. So is it our higher self that's God? I think that is a part of God. God is an entity I don't quite know how to define. And I believe that's kosher with him.

One Rosh Hashanah, I arrived at the synagogue later than I wanted. Flustered, I grabbed a prayer book, but the moment I opened it, it flew out of my hands. I retrieved it in the aisle by picking it up and kissing the book, showing respect for God's teachings.

"You think this a bad omen?" I asked the man sitting next to me.

"Excuse me?"

"You know, so close to our fates being sealed for the New Year, I go and drop the siddur on the floor."

The man looked at me kindly and then answered, "What kind of punitive God do you pray to that would be so angry because you accidentally dropped a book?"

Overall, I believe the love is what's most encompassing. There is surely something, someone, and it is surely bigger than us. Right here I feel it. Right now I need to connect. And I need to be open, for I need to be led.

I remain quiet during the concluding prayers. My body sways when I sing "Ein Keloheinu" in silence, appropriately honoring the four different ways to say God's name. But when we get to Aleinu, I unconsciously bend at the knee and waist, bowing along with most other congregants. Most others, not Josh. For when I straighten myself back up, his eyes are there waiting, questioningly meeting mine.

"I just followed the crowd," I say.

We sit for the Kaddish while those currently in mourning stand. I look around and study their faces. People deal with loss so individually. The final hymn is sung. I am sad the service will end. "Adon Olam" is vibrant, the congregation impassioned as they sing along: *"V'im ruchi g'viyati."*

Anyplace I've ever been, the ending is the same. Everyone always slows down on the last line for the great, big finish. I belt it out with the rest of them.

"Shabbat Shalom," I say, and turn to Josh. I give him a big kiss, but he is still. "What?"

"Where'd you learn all that?" he demands.

"The last line of that song? There was transliteration on the opposite page; the tune was repeating over and over. Anybody could pick it up. No big deal."

We exit the synagogue, stopping on the receiving line to greet Robby. I meet Evan and see the ex.

"You were great," I tell the kid.

"Thanks."

"Hey, dude, good job," says Josh. "He was into it, Robby."

"So was Aimee," Robby responds. "I was watching her from the bimah. A little conversion action?"

"Not for us, bud," says Josh, patting his cousin on the back before bringing me over to the cocktail hour.

At the bar, Josh gets a beer, and I get a Bloody Mary. Then we check out the food. There are stations all around the room with food from all around the world. Because we're in a synagogue, everything is kosher, but it's all here: pigs in a blanket and chicken on a skewer; a choice of pastas or sushi; made-to-order omelets; salmon and cheeses and bagels and more.

"Well, hello!"

"So glad you could come."

Aunt Renee and Uncle Mickey seem more than happy to see
Josh. They are sitting at a small round table with Robby's wife,
Hope, and . . .

"Do you remember my name?" Josh asks their little girl.

"Ummmm . . ." Adorable in a pink gingham party dress, she
shyly shakes her head.

"This is Cousin Josh," reminds Hope.

"Hi, Madison," he says. "Were you proud of your big
brother?"

Renee looks at me, throws out her hands, and lifts up her
eyes. As everyone's distracted, she takes my hand in hers and
leans in confidentially.

"Such complications," she says quietly of second marriages
and half-siblings. Josh filled me in on Robby's contentious divorce, made better since his ex-wife's remarriage to a wealthy
man. "Try to do it right the first time," she says, as her head nods
in approval of her nephew.

"Saw you davening at the end in there," Uncle Mickey breaks
in. "Impressive. I was confused; I thought you weren't Jewish."

Oh, but I am. How simple it would be to say. Maybe I'll just
do that. Yes. Imagine that. Josh couldn't make a scene. Not here
in public. Especially at a family party. And a Jewish one to boot.

Hmmm . . . maybe I really should. For this very moment the
fall-out almost feels easier than having to stand here and pretend. I search to see if I have the guts, but Josh answers before
I finish.

"She isn't, Uncle Mick. She said she just picked it up."

"Is that so?" asks his uncle.

"Well, it's not like this is the first bar mitzvah I ever went to,"
I answer. "I do live in New York City, you know."

"You never told me you'd been to a bar mitzvah," says Josh.

"You never asked."

"Well, Rob sure is glad you're both here," says Hope, reaching her arm around her husband when he arrives. He tells us the main room is now open. We will all be seated together at the same table.

The synagogue's ballroom is huge, and I'm dazzled by the decor. Evan's theme is baseball, and the party planner definitely hit a home run. *Let's Go, Mets!* Everything is decorated in orange and blue. Stadium sound effects fill the hall, while baseball games loop on a flat screen. The food station for the kids has pizza and frankfurters, French fries and bags of popcorn. Off to the side a miniature batting cage with plastic bats and balls is set up for practice. I reach into Josh's pocket to pull out the yarmulke and we laugh, having figured out the reason for its unusual colors.

Tracking down our seats, we find ourselves at the Jose Reyes table. A photo of the player with a printed card detailing his Selected MLB Statistics creates the centerpiece; irises and bird-of-paradise flowers surround it in a wood vase shaped like a bat.

"We rate," acknowledges Josh, "Reyes one of the top players in the National League. Though he admittedly swings back and forth, he's really a bigger fan of the Yankees."

To be honest, whenever I imagine Josh meeting my family, his baseball persuasion has me more worried than any religious one. Jon is an avid Mets fan. I take that back; when it comes to New York and baseball, my brother believes only one team exists. Don't even say the word *Yankees.* I said *don't.* Jon will have your head. Once Peter brought me to a game at Yankee Stadium; free tickets, I swear that was all. Well, I thought Jon would go through the roof.

"Hat day?" he said with bewilderment, as if the guy had

taken me on a date to a wake. "He brought you to *hat* day?" he despaired, seeing us after the game. Tear-struck at the navy and white baseball cap on my head.

"I don't get it," Robby says of his son's taste in teams. "But hey—that's what makes horse racing, right?"

"The Yankees have a stadium now in my hometown," I pipe up as we seat ourselves. On the table before us is bread and salad, pre-served. Having just eaten, we see it's time, again, to eat.

"Yeah, tell me about that," says Mickey. "Where are you from, Aimee?"

"Scranton," answers Josh. "Nice place."

"The Scranton/Wilkes-Barre Yankees are the Class-AAA Minor League Baseball affiliate of the New York Yankees," I recite by heart.

"You see the stadium?" Robby asks Josh.

"Not yet. Next time. Soon," he says, then looks at me. "Okay?" Josh is pleased about his bonding with Pennsylvania. He turns back to his cousins and continues to talk.

Blah, blah, Syracuse. Blah, blah, Scranton.

He takes my hand and smiles. I return the smile but would rather stick out my tongue. Because Josh not only tells everyone about our last trip but asks Robby and Hope if they'd like to accompany us on our next.

No way. I can't go back there. I don't want to go back to Scranton. I don't want to introduce him to people at my church. The minister didn't get his eggnog from me, nor did herbs ever grow in our garden. Another visit to 1764 McDonough Avenue will make me seriously ill.

Blah, blah. Josh squeezes my hand as the conversation continues. Blah blah blah.

"Of course," I say, adding no more than a postscript that's benign.

For I do not contribute. I sit. Listen. I nod in all the right places. My brain a pinball machine. Josh's words the small metal ball that bings and pings and collides into every part of my real identity so I cannot join in this talk. Each nod of my head flips the ball and scores me more points. I get a free ball and win a free game. Even though I no longer want to play.

"... probably a great field ... head cheerleader ..."

Nod. Smile. Smile. Nod. Don't ask to see my high school because I haven't the foggiest idea where it even is.

"... can show us?" asks Robby.

Hip Hip HooWRONG. I never led a cheer because I'm not really a cheerleader. Hey, I'm not even a redhead. My smile frozen, I laugh in all the right spots. But I don't have anything to say. And it hits me. No one even cares. No one cares if I have something to say, or not. I have no personality. I can never take a stand because I stand for nothing. And Josh actually likes that. He likes that I'm nothing more than an ornament. A shiksa on his arm.

"Of course you can have it," I exclaim, directing my glance to Hope. Only I don't have a recipe because I don't bake pumpkin pies. I don't even like them.

"... her neighbors ..."

If you really want to know, Mrs. Plunkett is a screwball and I can't stand Muffy Steinberg. And if you think Martin is a bore, wait till you meet my parents. You try living on Plantation Island.

I dislike everything of my creation, not the least of it me. So instead I focus on what's right in front of my rhino-plastic nose. Josh. I focus on Josh, and now I don't like him. I don't like Josh.

Not a whit. I look at him holding my hand and smiling at this girl he adores who's not me, and I resent him for it. I resent that, and every other single thing about him.

I resent being here with his family when I can't bring him to mine. I resent seeing his home in Hewlett and then hiding when we're blocks from my folks' apartment. I resent his BMW to my subway, his co-op to my rental, his BlackBerry to my cell, and, believe me, there's more.

I resent Josh's beer to my Bloody Mary and his real nose to my fake. I'm through hearing about his Yankees to my Mets, his brother's wife to my brother's girlfriends, his niece and nephew to my . . . my, God. My *nothing.* I have no niece, no nephew, and no brother-in-law because I have no sister! I've wiped them all out. That is so awful, but that is not all.

I don't want to eat his Passover bread; I didn't even want to eat my Easter ham. I'm soured on singing hymns I don't know in church because I'm unable to sing the ones I do know in shul. I'm sick of every holiday and feel sick every day, because out of every single thing I resent, the biggest resentment is that no matter how he may feel about it, Josh gets to be Jewish while I get to be Not. And it's simply not enough.

"Shall we dance?"

Renee motions for us to all go to the dance floor when the klezmer music begins.

"I want everybody up on their feet and on this dance floor," the deejay energetically announces into his microphone. "Let's join hands and make a big circle for . . . *the hora!*"

Hava nagila, Hava nagila, Hava nagila venis'mecha. The Hebrew folk song plays. I'm careful not to sing along.

"I'm not a big dancer," says Josh, reticent to join the mob scene trying to form a circle that can include fifty people.

"You know I love to dance. Please?"

Reluctantly, Josh takes my left hand in his right hand after his aunt grabs his left. Madison and Mickey are left of Renee. Hope places her hand in my right one; she's left behind as Robby dances in the inner circle with Evan and his mom.

We try circling right, but people are so squished together we're barely moving, let alone dancing. It feels more like trying to find a seat on the subway during rush hour than a dance.

"This is fun," I say to Josh anyway, because crowded as it may be, it is. Especially for me, able to join this circle no questions asked.

"Now circle left," calls the deejay.

Bunches of people pull out and form smaller circles. With room to move, people begin to dance. Renee and Mickey start with the jump. Hope, on my right, also knows the steps. Madison, too young to learn them, just jumps and laughs as she bounces up and down. I look at Josh's two left feet.

Hava nagila, Hava nagila . . . Yes, I've been to bar mitzvahs before, but did I ever learn the hora? I could have, I think, while Josh and I only walk in rhythm, holding the circle back from being able to fly.

"You know I took ballet," I shout to Josh over the loud, loud music.

He nods.

"I'm good with my feet," I say, giving him a heads-up for *I think I shall add the jumps.*

To tell you the truth, the hora is the easiest little dance. After you jump, it's just a little grapevine that you do with your feet. If you're going left, as we are, you place your right foot *behind* your left and then step out on your left. Then put your right foot in *front* of your left and step out on your left before you jump and repeat it all over again. If you're going right, you reverse it.

Jump!

I jump when everyone else does, holding back from doing the grapevine. But truly, after all those years of ballet, I'm sure even if I'd never seen this dance before in my life, I could pick it up one-two-three.

Jump!

"Come on," I urge Josh, not to dance but to jump. Jump. Jump, jump, jump.

"Okay, girls!"

Feeling my enthusiasm, Aunt Renee plucks both me and Hope out of the circle and into the center. The three of us form our own circle. Linked at the elbows, Renee wraps her right arm around mine and spins me. Quite the fancy dancer, she moves on to Hope, linking elbows on their left before they spin. Hope approaches me as the music gains speed. Tempos rising, we rotate and spin before we all join hands and *jump!* The hora is so ingrained in me—body and soul—that without my head giving the say-so, my feet take off and ... *U! ru! U! ru! a! chim!*

We spin in circles at rapid speed. My feet lead the way. I crisscross my arms, like Renee, and we join hands. At arm's length, holding tight, our bodies lean back while we whirl. Twirling and whirling faster than a carousel.

I kick off my high-heeled black satin sandals, losing Renee, Hope, and myself. Now lost to the dance, all I do is feel. The music and the movement. Holding court in the center of the circle, I see nothing and no one. My arms fly up on either side of my body, bent at the elbows. Palms open, my fingers point to the heavens. Alone, I *hora!* Each jump takes me higher and higher.

The grapevine steps grow longer, swiftly traveling me round and around.

Center stage, I continue. Everyone in the outer circle clap-clap-clapping to the music while I dance, I fly, I soar. The grapevine morphs into choreography. Jumps turn to leaps, my kicks worthy of any Rockette at Radio City Music Hall.

A handful of men have joined me in the center. They're setting up chairs for the bar mitzvah boy to take a seat to be raised. Evan sits on the straight-back armless chair. He will be lifted up and paraded around the room to celebrate his Jewish transformation from a boy to a man. Except I'm there dancing and I'm in the way.

"Uru achim b'lev same'ach," I sing as I dance. Knowing *b'lev same'ach* means "with a happy heart," I sing that extraloud because, suddenly, I have one. So much so, I can't stop. I can't stop celebrating. And I can't stop dancing.

Hava nagila...The song repeats, yet again. I dance and keep dancing though Evan's ready and waiting to be lifted in his chair.

"Can you move?" he asks as the big guy giving support on the chair's back end tries to get rid of me by attempting to trip me with his foot.

But I fix him. Stepping back, I do a series of pirouettes so wide and *so* energetic, the force spins me straight into Evan, the momentum causing my hands to push him out of the chair just as the men pick it up. Only when they lift, it's not him in the hot seat. It's *me!*

The kid looks up from the floor stunned that I took his place, but in this altered state I don't know how to care. The men are strong and lift the chair high. From far above, I sing my Jewish heart out.

People look up, wondering who I am. Some find it funny, some others don't, while others even cheer. Yet have no doubt, this is a transformation. And now it is mine. I may have gone up a shiksa, but when this chair comes back down I will be transformed. Back to my Jewish self.

"Your turn," I tell Evan, gliding off the chair as my bare feet touch the floor. Lighter. Unfettered. Finally free.

I find my shoes buried behind a stack of plastic baseballs on the other side of the dance floor. When I kneel to pick them up, I feel a hand touch the back of my neck. I look up and see Josh, looking down at me as if we'd never met. His brown eyes, always so warm, now have different hues. And before he says a word, they talk. They say *bamboozled*, *beguiled*, and *betrayed*.

Close Encounters
of the Unkind

PLEASE. Just let me explain."

The first words out of my mouth, and they sound so cliché. That's what people say when caught cheating. Though not with another man, I have been caught. And to be honest (at this point do I have another choice?), I have been cheating.

"Josh, I'm so sorry. Truthfully, I never thought it'd go this far."

I wait for him to say something. To question me, get angry. Tell me to stay or go away. Josh, in shock, does nothing.

"But now that you know the reason for the behavior, it may even start to make sense," I say, standing up, adjusting my dress, putting on my shoes.

His family, I notice, has gathered. Mickey and Renee, Robby and Hope, Madison and Evan are all there. I think to protect him.

"And despite what you've seen here today, you have to know that underneath it all I really am the same person."

Josh looks at me, hard. Searching hard to see her; he wants

that so much to be true. With everyone watching, we stand for what feels like an eternity. The fallout is not what I expected, but it's too soon to actually know what it is. After much deliberation, Josh turns to his family. Finally, he speaks.

"See, everybody. I was right," he triumphantly announces. "I told you so," he tells them. Then he even smiles.

He *knows*. Oh, my goodness. Josh knows . . . and he smiles.

"You forgot what we just discussed?" Uncle Mickey cries from the sidelines. "Stop fooling yourself already, Joshua."

"Mickey, be quiet," snaps Renee. "Let the kids sort it out."

"I understand, eMay," Josh says, the warm hues back in his eyes. "I really do understand. And it's okay."

"It is?" This is too good to be true. The weight I've been carrying falls off my shoulders and into a helium balloon. I can let it go and be set free. "You mean it's okay? You're not mad I didn't tell you?"

"You could have told me from the very beginning," says Josh, taking my hand in his. "You could have trusted me."

"Oh." I throw my arms around his neck. "I can't believe this. Oh God, I'm so relieved. I read you wrong. I read everything wrong. I'm so sorry. But you'll see. I'll make it up to you, I promise. Now things between us can be even better."

"I'll make sure of that," says Josh.

"Everybody happy now?" asks Renee. She claps her hands, getting everyone's attention, gathering up the crew to go.

"Not so fast," I hear Mickey say. He turns to Josh. "What do you know?"

Josh looks quizzically at his uncle.

"Suddenly it's all patched up? What is it about her you think you finally know?"

"Uncle Mick, cut it out. Don't make me say," says Josh. "I don't want to embarrass Aimee."

"Believe me, Josh, don't worry. It's not exactly something I'm embarrassed about," I say, sad to realize he may really be closed to Judaism after all.

"Good," says Mickey. "So let it all hang out."

Josh, the consummate gentleman, looks uncomfortable, but he needs to appease his uncle. He looks to me first, hopeful I'll understand he does not mean to cause any further dismay.

"The whole time we've been together, Aimee's been totally consistent and never depressed. So if . . ." When he continues, he talks under his breath. "Like maybe she forgot her meds, or just needs new ones, so give her a break. It was the first time she's had a manic episode."

"*Manic?* That's what you think?" My cackle, reminiscent of the Wicked Witch of the West, only furthers Josh's point.

"You're not in manic mode?" he asks, taken aback.

I look first to Uncle Mickey. But his expression tells me if I don't soon, he will. While I naively thought I could escape this moment, surrounded by witnesses I now meet it head on.

"No, Josh, your uncle is right. I'm not manic." Looking directly in his eyes, I am certain to be clear. "And I'm not depressive."

Josh looks confused. "So then what are you?"

"Jewish." I pause to let it sink in, but it doesn't. "I'm not a shiksa. I just pretended. But really, I'm like you. A Jew."

"A . . . ? Oh, no. *Oy gevalt!*" Having just met the devil, Josh greets him with the first Yiddish words I've ever heard to come from his mouth. "I can't believe this. This is awful. *Oy yai yai,* I've got to sit," he says, and without a chair crashes down on the floor. Josh's world has come to an end, and he curls up in a ball like a baby.

"What?" I lean over and talk to this fetus. "Better I should be a manic-depressive than a Jewish girl raised on the Upper West Side?"

"No, no. Stop. *Stop!*" He covers his ears with his hands. "Look. You're already nagging. You already sound so"—Josh suddenly looks up—"wait, you're kidding, right? Upper West?" It's all too painful to accept. "You mean . . ." He takes a breath, barely able to get out the words. "No . . . Scranton?"

I shake my head. "West Ninety-sixth Street. My parents are still there."

"No . . . Plantation Island?" His voice wavers, unsteady.

I shake my head.

"No . . . *Martin and Muffy Steinberg?*" Josh says their names in a great, big wail.

"Muffy Steinberg?" asks Hope.

"Mommy." Madison tugs on her mother's sleeve. "Who's Muffy Steinberg?"

"Well, she didn't fool me," says Mickey.

"I told you all at Passover," says Robby. "I could tell by her nose."

"You guys are whacked," says Evan before he turns away. "I'm going back to my party."

Mystery solved, everyone takes their cue to leave.

"Wait, wait." A small, sad voice emerges from the ball on the floor that is Josh. "What about me? What do I do now?"

"Get up off the floor, wash your hands, and take your date back to the table," says Mickey. "They started serving dinner."

"Are you kidding me? Take my date . . ." He lifts himself from the floor with whatever dignity he can muster. "I never want to see Aimee again."

Well. Okay, then. I'd have to say Josh just let me know we're most certainly through. Mortified, not that I don't deserve to be, I make sure to avoid everyone's eyes, deciding it's best if I leave immediately.

"Aimee." Josh stops me. "Wait. Just tell me this."

I look at him. His look so sad.

"Why did you do it? I mean, how could you do something like that to me?"

The million-dollar question.

"It wasn't against you, Josh. It was for me. But I didn't mean to hurt you. Or play you. I so apologize for that." Seizing this opportunity, I attempt to explain. "See, I saw you, at that event at DOWN. And I tried to meet you, but you ignored me. Then we met again, the night with Krista. And it seemed like you wanted to go out with me because you thought I wasn't Jewish. Like her. And since I really wanted to go out with you, I let you think it. I'm sorry."

"Don't be so sorry," Renee says to me. "It worked. Your mother will be thrilled to have someone in the family with a little *Yiddishkeit*," she tells Josh. "Sandy just goes along with all that crap because of your father, isn't that right, Mickey? I mean, really. Hong Kong. Give me one good reason why my brother's not here today."

Mickey doesn't answer. He's worried about Josh, so humiliated and wounded.

"It took on its own life," I explain to Josh. "I guess you could say I got a little carried away." I pause for the conciliatory laugh. It's not forthcoming. "But you and me, we're still the same people. And it's good we're both Jewish. Better. It's easier for a relationship . . . for kids. It's not like you were so happy when we went to church—"

"You went to *church*?" asks Renee.

"You got this guy to a church," says Robby. "Impressive."

Hope gives him a whack.

"It was Easter," I explain.

"Of course," everyone murmurs as they nod their heads. Easter.

We find ourselves at an impasse. And this juncture contains the inevitable, interminable, and uncomfortable silence. Each person looks to the next to break it. Until everyone looks at me.

"You've all been lovely to me, especially considering my, uh, outlandish behavior. I'm not proud of it, but in the end perhaps there's really no harm done?" I begin my plea. "Josh, could we maybe take a walk and just talk about—"

"Talk about what, Aimee? If that's really even your name. Is it?"

Surprised by his question, I don't readily answer.

"I asked you something, *eMay*." His sarcasm drips to the floor. "What's your real name?"

"Aimee. Spelled like I told you. Aimee Dale Albert," I shamefully say. "Did I ever tell you my middle name?" Though the question is somewhat rhetorical, Josh doesn't step in and save me from my blabber. "My Hebrew name is Ayah. Oh. The English translation of my Hebrew name—you'll appreciate this—is 'vul—' "

"I won't appreciate anything from you, Aimee Albert." He can barely bring himself to look at me. "You and I are done here. I have nothing more to say, okay?"

Madison starts to cry. Robby and Hope look at me sheepishly

as they each take one of their daughter's hands and leave. Renee squeezes mine. "Give him a few days to cool off," she suggests, and motions to Mickey that now it's time to go.

"Meet me at the table," he instructs his wife. "Well," he says, staying behind. "Now I've seen it all." Mickey looks at me with pride and prejudice. "It may have started as a joke, Aimee, but among many other things, it was also unkind."

"I know, I'm sor—"

Mickey puts up his hand. I stop.

"But Renee's right. It worked. This girl got to you, Josh. I understand you feel betrayed. But is it the Judaism . . . or the fraud?" he asks his nephew. "A few minutes ago you were will-ing to accept a manic-depressive Aimee. Was that preferable to a Jewish one?"

"Shiksa syndrome," I volunteer. "Just another disorder, only I didn't know a better cure."

Uncle Mickey laughs. Josh refrains from the feel-good mo-ment.

"You're a smart cookie," Mickey tells me. "See if you two can work it out. And this time, play fair," he advises before he walks away.

If we can make this work, I figure I already have a head start on his family's dynamics. I wonder what it will be like if Josh meets the Alberts. Well, he almost met my folks, and he actually did meet Daphne. My long-lost sister. It's so nice to have her back. It's so nice for me to be back.

Suddenly I feel a new energy about us. I look at Josh, and suddenly we seem possible. For real. No secrets, everything out in the open. I know in my heart it could work. We can really get to know each other. Move forward. Be open. Talk. Dating is easy. A real partnership's a far more serious undertaking than people dating generally consider. But before the thought's even formed, I learn that between us it will not be considered.

"I'll drive you home," says Josh with finality.

"No, it's okay," I instantly respond, being together in the car too uncomfortable to bear. "I'll call a taxi to take me to the train. Metro-North runs all the time."

"You're sure?" Josh asks, relieved.

"It's no problem. I think it's best."

I'm spent on the ride home. It's been hours of waiting between the local taxi and the weekend train service. But alone, I can look out the window and cry.

The ride is fast; we make tracks. Passengers get off and on as we pass different towns. Different houses. Passing suburban homes filled with families. Families that began after two people went on dates. Dates that led to marriage, not disaster. Dates built on trust, instead of deception and lies.

"Eighty-seventh and Second please," I tell the driver when I hail a cab at Grand Central. The city feels so empty. But it's swarming with people. The emptiness, I know, is in me. I wish I could talk this out with someone, but I've alienated everyone who would have listened. The cab turns to go east. When I look west on Forty-second Street, I am overcome with the double loss of knowing Peter's no longer across town. He's been gone just a week, though it feels more like a year. It feels permanent. And it makes me so sad.

"Good evening, Aimee," says Willie when I make my entrance into the lobby through the revolving door. "Did you have a nice day?"

"I sure didn't," I say, crossing the lobby and ringing for the elevator. "I had a rotten one. But thanks for asking and have a nice night," I call to him at the desk when the elevator doors close.

I'll take a bath. I'll pour a glass of wine, light candles in the bathroom, and sit in a hot bath. Then I'll put on my sweats, order in Chinese, and escape into a pay-per-view movie. Something romantic and funny. Okay, something funny.

Tomorrow I'll call Krista and see if I can meet her for dinner. I'll call my parents and see if I can meet them for brunch. Maybe Daphne will come in during the week. And Tova. If I feel better later, maybe I'll go down the hall to see Tova. But when I reach the fifteenth floor, she coincidentally happens to be standing outside the elevator door.

"I was just thinking about you." But something must be terribly wrong because instead of her naturally spirited self, she looks rather serious. "Did something happen? Tell me, Tova, is everything okay?"

"Yes, yes. With me everything is fine." She peeks into the elevator doors as they close.

"You lose something?"

"I was just looking. Your boyfriend. He is not with you?"

"Oy." I shake my head back and forth. I don't know what to say. "Don't ask."

"Then maybe you would like to come into my apartment for a cup of tea?"

"I actually would. But maybe later? All I want to do is go to bed."

"Aimala, no one means to hurt you, but I think you need to come *now*."

"Huh?" No one means to hurt me?

But Tova has already turned on her black Easy Spirit heels to march down the hall. She motions for me to follow. It is not an option; it's an order. When she opens the door to her apartment, I see why. It's a party. But why would she insist I come to a party where I might get hurt? Especially when I'm not in a party mood. The party, however, seems to all but stop when I walk into the living room. Even odder, I conclude from a quick glance at the guests, it appears to be for me.

"Oh, my God!" I shriek. "What are you all doing here?"

Front and center on the big, burgundy chintz sofa are my parents. Kitty-corner on a rosewood side chair is my brother, Jon. Seated on the piano bench is Daphne. She signals to Rich, playing on the floor with Hannah and Holdenn, to take the kids and the Harry Potter puzzle into another room. A guy I don't instantly recognize sits across from the piano on a loveseat. His arm solidly wrapped around a woman. Ohmygod. It's Matt . . . and Krista. Tova, behind me, motions to the latecomer, who came in behind us, to take a seat.

"Wow, Aimee, you look fabulous. You been doing it yourself, or you go somewhere to get it blown dry?"

"Jackie?"

"I'm sorry I'm late," says Jackie, going to sit next to my dad. "But Jon said I had to be here because the makeover got the whole thing started. So what'd I miss?" She pauses to take a breath. "I've never been. What do you do at an intervention?"

"A what?" Starting with Krista, I look from person to person. My eyes make contact with each individual till they finally land on my mother.

"It's a shiksa intervention," announces Maddie. "We're all very concerned. I'm sorry, Aimee, but I didn't know what else to do," she confesses. "Where's Josh?"

"He's not here," reports Tova.

"Is he in your apartment or parking the car?" asks Maddie.

And if he was? Then what? Were they going to embarrass me

shamelessly in front of him? How would that have made both of us feel? Did they think he'd just bless the relationship in its new kosher package, and we'd all have a good laugh and order in? Yet knowing how Josh reacted today upon learning the truth, I realize the bigger question now is, did I?

The thought of Josh potentially walking into this is chilling. Having bypassed this potential disaster, I want to yell at everyone for what they almost did to me. For what they are doing. How dare they? But no one looks angry. The tone in the room is subdued. Everyone is here because they care. And after all I've put everyone through, I'm glad they still do.

I open my mouth to speak, but, instead, all that comes out are tears. Tears of loss and embarrassment, of remorse, reproach. My mother rushes off the sofa and puts her arms around me. She's quickly followed by Krista and Daphne.

"I'm sorry," I say to Krista, repeating it over and over to Daphne, who doesn't even completely know why. "I'm such a mess, but I'm so glad to be back."

"So where is this Josh?" asks Jon. "Forget about what happens with you two. You said he's a Yankee fan, and I'm going to kick his ass."

"Well, you can't now," I blurt, riding a new wave of tears. "It's o-ver."

"He knows?" asks Sid.

I nod.

"How'd it happen?" Everyone asks the big question in different ways all at the very same time. This is the news they've been waiting for. The room buzzes with the expectation of hearing how I actually spilled the beans.

"Wait one moment please." A singer, Tova speaks several octaves above the noise in order to be heard and quiet us all. "I have a delicious dairy meal prepared. So you'll all come to the table, and while Aimee tells her story, we will eat."

I take a seat at the head, grateful to be surrounded, again, by my family and friends. I've never been to an intervention, but I doubt the problem's usually solved before it even begins. I also doubt the hosts generally serve such great food. I reach into the bread basket and grab a bagel. First I slice it in half. Then I begin to talk.

The Red Hairing

HOW STRANGE IT FEELS to sit next to Krista at a Shabbat service. She and Matt hold hands, and I am surprised to see the extent to which she can participate.

The idea of socializing with Matt had me more than a wee bit embarrassed. After all, I did kind of get off on the same foot with him as with Josh. But since he's not emotionally involved with me, it was easy for him to forgive and forget. Especially after the intervention. Should you ever find yourself on the receiving end of one, do try to resolve your problem quickly. Already surrounded by your closest friends and family, it can make for a lovely little get-together.

The rabbi talks about the recent debates featuring the Democratic candidates for president. The obvious front-runner, so far, is the mission. Before any one candidate emerges, all candidates express the overwhelming collective objective to replace the current administration. That prompts the rabbi to talk about lies. How lying affects relationships. While he considers those political, it is the personal that resonate for me.

"To lie is a fragmentation of the soul," he says. "It is fraud." Involuntarily, my face turns red. "And if you are successful.

If you are able to—pull it off—you cheat not only the people you lie to, but yourself. For you are not whole. You are broken."

The rabbi discusses recent history, and my eyes fill with tears. Thoughts of our president, starting with how he got into office, can easily make me cry. But now I feel as if God looks down at me and points.

When the service is over, I want to go home, but Krista and Matt insist I join them and a few friends at Krista's for dinner. Downtown, at her apartment, my friend lights Shabbat candles and puts out a traditional meal.

"Admission," Krista says after the fourth compliment on the chicken. "Dean & DeLuca. What's a working girl to do?"

In her way, she has embraced Friday night rituals. Later in the kitchen, while I help Krista prepare the dessert, she tells me she is sure she will convert.

"Things between you are that solid?" I ask. Impressed she formed a real and lasting relationship in the same time frame I created a holy mess.

"Yes," says Krista, arranging whole strawberries around a sour cream coffee cake. "Matt's younger sister, Leah, is getting married at the beginning of June. And after that . . . well, at some point, I hope he'll pop the question."

"Well"—I'm not sure why I'm so surprised—"they always say when it's right you know."

But they don't tell you what you need to know about yourself first to recognize it. And for each person that's different. If there's anything I have learned about how *It* happens, it's that there are no rules. There's no right way to meet. No best way to date to ensure you will mate. Though I can safely rule out a few things.

"You do this one." Krista hands me a decanter to fill with tea while she handles the one with coffee.

"Boy, while I was playing Shiksa Barbie, you turned into quite the *baleboosteh*."

"You saying I went up a bra size?"

"No." I laugh. "It means 'a terrific housekeeper.' Like . . . you can eat off her floors! She's some *baleboosteh*."

"Oh. For a minute I thought you meant I gained weight," says Krista, patting her stomach.

"Not a pound. But I think I have a little since Josh and I broke up. I may feel like crap, but I'm not anxious anymore," I say, cutting off a piece of coffee cake to pop in my mouth. "My appetite's back."

"Good. You were a little too thin," says Krista, suddenly perfecting my mother's New York accent. "Speaking of Josh. Any word?"

"Nope. I think he's still pretty mad."

"He'll come around. Matt thinks so too," Krista says as she places the cake and some coffee mugs on a big tray. With a nod of her head, she indicates I carry out the two beverages.

"Hey, Kris, how do I ask you something without hurting your feelings?"

"You probably don't. But at least I won't be carrying the hot stuff."

"Don't you feel that maybe it went so fast with Matt because you kind of made yourself into the girl he was looking for? I mean, I know firsthand now what it means to give up a part of who you are. Are you really so okay about all this?"

"All right, Aimee. Here's the truth," she says, placing the tray back on the table to talk. "The truth is I didn't grow up with any sense of who I was in a religious or spiritual way like you or Matt. I didn't even know how much till I met him, but I was looking for something. And Judaism fit for me the same way Matt did."

The words sound familiar. To some extent, it's what Peter had said to me.

"You're lucky, Aimee. You know who you are. Believe in that. Believe in your passions. Believe what *feels* right. Then identify *who* feels right. You love being Jewish. That will always belong to you, no matter who you belong to."

I take Krista's advice into a taxi along with my reclaimed box of JEWISH THINGS: TO BE OPENED WHEN I'M SAFE AND MARRIED. Now, alone in my apartment, I open it. Neither safe, nor married.

As I return each piece to its proper place, I feel another piece of me return home. Finished, I'm ready to dispose of the box when I hear something inside move. I undo the flaps to see what I forgot to unpack. Grateful to find I did not accidentally throw out my siddur, I flip through the pages before putting it back on the shelf. Hebrew words fly by in a blur, but when I close the book I notice—for the first time ever—handwriting in the back.

The note is on the inside cover, written with a black pen. The firm slants and squared-off edges are so memorable, I cannot believe they've been all but forgotten.

> *My dear Aimee, my sweet Ayah,*
> *You never know what a day brings. And today, as a bat mitzvah, you made me especially proud! Whatever you do, you always will. Remember that. Enjoy your life, and no matter what, always stay true to yourself.*
> *Love,*
> *Grandpa Jack*

"So what are we doing?" Nicole asks the next morning, snapping me out of my daydream. I am still stunned I'd never seen my grandfather's inscription before. I called my mother to see if she knew when he wrote it.

"You think I'm going to remember when he wrote it? I don't know what I ate for breakfast, and I'm going to remember what my father wrote the day of your bat mitzvah?"

But what a gift to receive. Especially now. Dropped down from the heavens, it is the icing on Krista's cake of wisdom. All these months I had myself believe my posturing was for a greater good. Now I see it only compensated for something I could not face inside me. Except I'm still not sure exactly what.

"Yeah. The same," I tell my hairdresser now. My mind on everything but my hair. Nicole's professional hands and eyes examine it.

"Your roots are showing," she explains, and pulls up a lock to show me in the mirror. "We'll need to do color. Okay?"

"Okay," I tell her, staring past my Raggedy Ann reflection. My ragged unblown and unkempt hair.

"Have you been sick?" Nicole asks, putting on rubber gloves to mix the color in a small plastic bowl.

"That would be a pretty fair assessment." I look at my watch. I'll have to go into work after this. It may be a Saturday, but KISS is exactly four weeks away.

"Since it's already May," begins Nicole, "would you like me to add a highlight for extra brightness? A lighter red for summer?"

"Why not?" I'd never been anything but a brunette in summer. Gosh. There's always so much prep for summer.

"But you'll need to keep your hair out of the sun," she says, lifting the small brush to the first strands. "Red oxidizes."

"No problem. I doubt I'll be out in the sun this summer."

"No? You and your boyfriend won't be in the Hamptons?" she asks, picking up another clump to paint with her brush.

"Broke up," I say, picturing a summer of Saturdays in the office instead of Sag Harbor.

"You'll meet someone else." Nicole winks. "Someone attracted to redheads."

Redheads? I may have considered myself a shiksa, but I never thought I was a redhead. Well. So what? It's nothing bad. Except . . . I don't want to be a redhead. And I don't want to be careful about my hair.

I love what the beach does to it. The saltwater, the wind, the sun. People buy products just to reproduce tousled waves like the ones you end up with at the beach. It's fun, and when I most love my dark wavy curls.

Ohmygod.

"Stop." I bolt up in the chair. I pull away before Nicole can paint another hair on my head. "I changed my mind. I don't want to do this."

"Okay," she says, and stops. "But I can't leave you like this, Aimee. Do you know what you want?"

"Yes. I do."

Nicole throws a brown rinse over my hair that sorta-kinda matches my real color. It will suffice till the roots all grow out. I make certain she doesn't use a flat iron after she blows it dry.

Munching on a bagel while meandering over to the office, I catch my reflection in a storefront window. I am more than pleased when Aimee smiles back.

Now logged on to my computer, I begin a new e-mail.

To: josh@loveloaves.com

From: a.albert@prwap.com

Subject: Allow Me to Introduce Myself

Finally, I can.

Grown Unaccustomed
to Your Face

P LEASE TELL ME this isn't happening."

When you get an e-mail that makes you unhappy, if you stare at the screen long enough will it go away? I don't understand. How can he do this?

Krista arrives at my office after receiving my frantic call.

"Yikes," she says, hovering over my desk. She shakes her head as she reads each and every abysmal word.

"I sure never planned for this," I say, and know just how bad it is because I can feel panic announce itself in every nerve center of my body.

"So what now?" she asks.

"I don't know. But there has to be a way to fix it. And I think it's up to me to figure it out."

We look at the clock; it's getting late.

"Well, I'm headed uptown now," says Krista. "Meeting Matt. Friday night." She looks at me.

"I'm leaving too," I say, and gather up my stuff. "Just running to the ladies' room first."

"You're going?" Krista sounds concerned enough for both of us.

"Well, I can't change anything tonight staying here." My voice is strong, but worry spreads itself across my face like a makeup base.

"Okay. Meet you out front in five." Krista gets to the doorway and turns to face me. "I'm impressed. I think maybe a little shiksa rubbed off on you, after all. Oy, I'd be a nervous wreck."

Masks off, we still seem to be exchanging traits. Or, perhaps, now we share them, moving in a similar direction. Also true of the subway, we both exit the 1 train at Eighty-sixth Street.

"Do you want me to meet you later?" she asks. Ever since the intervention, Krista has been most protective.

"I hope you won't have to," I say. "I'll call you tomorrow, okay?" Then I leave Krista at the corner and continue north for a few blocks.

It's above a boutique and a knitting store, the entrance on Broadway. I was never here, and it's awkward to come now. But before I know it, I am in the small building, riding up in the elevator that opens onto the fourth floor, a big open space devoted only to this company.

The front desk is empty, everyone gone for the day. I suddenly wonder if so is he, and the joke is on me. I feel like a fool standing here. But with the sound of approaching footsteps, my fears, or some of them, are soon allayed.

"Can I help you?"

"Hi." My heart beats fast. I'm taken by surprise to find how much I've missed him the past month and just how good he looks.

He stands with uncertainty at the entranceway of the reception area, not venturing toward me. "Aimee?"

"You were expecting someone else?"

"Uh . . . kind of," says Josh. He walks with caution; his eyes narrow as if to be sure. "It is you."

I don't understand what he doesn't.

"Your hair," his words explain. "And . . ." He looks closely. "Your eyes," he says, seeing me for the first time in glasses. "And . . ." Josh peers in even closer and looks at my waist. But gentleman that he is, he doesn't utter a word.

"Yeah, well . . . this is the real me," I say, unprepared that he would be upon seeing a curly haired, brown-eyed, slightly (only *slightly*) plumper brunette.

"Well, you look great," Josh says, recovering.

"So do you," I say, no lie.

"Thanks for meeting me here. I appreciate it. A bread emergency," he quips. "We just have to make a quick pit stop before dinner."

"No problem. Right after I got your e-mail, I got another one, and . . ." I shake my head.

"What happened?"

"The KISS launch. It's a disaster. I'll tell you later. First show me around LoveLoaves headquarters." It's quite an operation, and these are just the offices.

"I'd love to go with you sometime to the factory," I offer. "When I was a kid, we went on a class trip once to a bread factory. Silvercup. Now it's a movie studio. You know, in Long Island City."

"Oh, yeah?" asks Josh.

"You know it, right?" I trail behind Josh as he makes sure all the lights and computers are off for the weekend, then rings for the elevator. "What's the matter?"

Josh carries a shopping bag filled with a bunch of challahs fresh from the factory. A delivery truck behind schedule, he offered to walk them over to the synagogue that needs them for tonight's *kiddish*.

"It's strange to hear you talk about your childhood in New York," he says once we're outside. "Although this Aimee looks more like she's from here."

In regard to my looks, the statement does not feel like a ringing endorsement. But, instead, I explain how my shiksa look had come and gone.

"This Aimee feels the same though, right?" I take his free hand in mine.

Josh takes my hand but smiles uncomfortably. I try not to push for too much too soon and so walk with him in silence. A few blocks later, I can only laugh out loud when we arrive.

"Temple Shalom?" I shriek. "This is wild. This is my parents' synagogue. I was bat mitzvahed here," I say, happy this info is not a secret.

"All right," says Josh, uncertain how to negotiate this new version of me.

We walk up the entrance steps into the austere lobby. I point ahead to the staircase that leads downstairs.

"The kitchen is down here," I say as we make our way. "Between Hebrew school, the bar mitzvah circuit, and the Teen Center, I can't tell you how many millions of hours I spent in this room." My hand references the banquet hall we enter.

Josh reaches into his pocket and retrieves a slip of paper with the name of the person who is to receive the bread. But a blonde woman exits the kitchen to greet us.

"Just in the knick of time," she says, eyeing the beautiful challahs that stick out of the brown paper shopping bag. "You're Josh, right? I'm Janis. Thanks a million. Let's put them on this table over here."

We follow behind the woman, who I now am certain is . . .

"Aimee Albert?" she says when she turns to take the bag.

"Janis Greenberg? Is that you?" She nods, and we give each other a big hug. "How funny. Her daughter, Meryl, was in my class at Hebrew school," I tell Josh. "Does she still live in D.C.? Oh. Janis, meet Josh Hirsch."

"Hel-lo," says Janis, as if she's just answered the telephone. "Sound familiar? We never met in person, but we speak often enough on the phone."

"Nice to meet you," Josh says, and extends his hand. "Officially."

"Your mother didn't tell me you were with the guy from Love-Loaves," says Janis. She looks back to Josh and gives an approving smile.

"Oh . . ." I look to Josh. I'm not about to explain. "I didn't realize you and my mom were in touch."

"Sure," says Janis, arranging the breads in baskets. "In fact, she's upstairs. We're honoring our Hadassah group tonight. And services should be over right about—"

The empty hall is suddenly swarming with the patter of feet and voices several decibels high and climbing higher. But the voice that emerges as the highest is of such intensity, it shoots across the room and knocks me for a loop.

"Look who's here! Is that Aimee?"

"Hi, Ma," I say, glancing over to Josh as Maddie comes rushing toward me. Dressed in black pants and a hot pink sweater, she looks very nice. I'm glad as I will now, finally—

"I'm Aimee's mother," she says, reaching to shake his hand. I knew it was a mistake telling her today I was seeing him tonight.

"Hello, Mrs. Albert."

"Call me Maddie."

"Okay, Mom, chill out." Her eyes are already lit up with hope. "This is Josh."

"I remember you. From Passover. That night in Aimee's lobby."

Josh quizzically looks at me. How did I think we could pick up where we left off when practically everything about me is new to him? And most of what he does know he'll need to forget.

"I've heard such nice things about you, Josh," Maddie says, as if this is a normal introduction at a cocktail party. "Tell me. Are we going to break *your* bread?" She laughs at her joke along with Janis, who holds the challahs up as trophies for her to see.

"Thanks, Maddie. And I heard nice things about . . . though I'm not sure if what I heard is actually tr . . ."

It's a beautiful night, and we walk east through the park. Hoping to reacquaint ourselves and find some kind of comfort level before we eat.

"So," says Josh. "Your mom. That was a trip. I'd never say she was from Plantation Island."

We are able to laugh. It's encouraging.

"Wait till you meet my dad."

"Now your dad *is* in advertising, right? And that *was* your sister?"

The baby naming for Adam and Stacy's newborn girl was last Sunday. I knew about it from Daphne, who was invited, but said she did not discuss me when she briefly spoke with Josh.

The small talk takes us only about as far as the restaurant.

After we order, we stare at each other across the table. Both wishing the other person would do or say the magic something to dissolve our discomfort into a puff of smoke that would float away.

"How's your uncle Mickey?" I finally ask. "I really liked him," I tell Josh. I pause. "After what happened, does your family hate me?"

"No, I think they hate me," says Josh.

"Do you?" I ask, the elephant now on the dinner table along with the edamame.

Josh reaches across the table and takes my hand. "Nobody hates anybody."

"I know, I know. I use the word like hyperbole. I really don't mean *hate*, you know. Not literally anyway, I mean—"

"Calm down," says Josh. "Boy, you're wound tight as a top. When did this happen?"

"Happen? This is me. Kind of."

It almost feels like a blind date where you each show up with an expectation that's not met, but you don't let go because you expect it soon will be. Josh apologized for his behavior at the bar mitzvah, but under the circumstances it was hardly necessary. I am so ashamed of what I have done. I feel so dishonorable, my only goal is to get us on an equal footing so we may begin again.

"Well, the Aimee I knew was, I don't know, more self-contained," says Josh. "You were always . . ."

"Hard to read? Yes, eMay kept you wondering." I wait a few seconds before . . . "Do you think that's better, Josh? Because I think we only fill in what we want to hear in those silences. It doesn't mean it's real, you know."

"Yeah, I know," says Josh. "But even though I know, I don't get it. I guess that's why I'm here tonight. To see . . . to try to . . ." Josh pauses. "So what had you so bent out of shape at work?"

And just like that, the conversation turns to work. Well, I've been holding all that in, too, and feel like I'm going to bust.

"You got Kim Cattrall. Awesome. She was my favorite when the show was on," he confesses.

"Well, Glenn wrote today—I told you about that booker at Celebrity Access, right? Well, Glenn sent an e-mail just as I was heading out to meet you that, listen to this: *Kim might not be able to do it!* They were supposed to be finished with *More Sex and the City*. I can't believe they talked about doing a movie for years. And when it finally happens, it's the same time as KISS! So they've been shooting in New York, obviously, and Kim was going to be free for the launch.

"Only now there's some film problem, technical glitch, I don't know what he was talking about, but some of her scenes need to be reshot. And the other actor in them is a big TV star in L.A., and he's doing a series and doesn't know when he can get back here. So she may have to go out there. And it might be exactly the day of the launch. But wouldn't that only work if it's interior scenes? Not that that's my problem. Believe me, I've got plenty of my own, because listen to this . . . he told me to start thinking about other people who might work. But it's *got* to be Kim. I can't look for a backup.

"Backup? I mean I can't get someone else. The whole concept's based around *her.* We have a contract; I *think* she already signed. I'll have to check with legal and see what's up with that. Maybe someone can, you know, put the screws to someone. I mean, there's a lot riding on this. Especially for me."

I take a breath before taking a sip of sake. That might be the most I've talked at once since I've known Josh. It's also the most upset I've been about anything, aside from lying to him of course. But Josh is cool. He's smiling. Or is that a smirk?

"What's funny?" I put down my glass.

"You remind me of Lauren. Jewish girls can get really intense about work."

Oh, how I wish I had the opportunity to replay this scene as eMay. I can't help but wonder how he'd have reacted if we had this identical conversation prior to my coming out. Yes, I spoke less before, and yes, I feel different with Josh now, but I'm no actress. So am I really acting that different? Is how we relate to others based on real interactions or on our perceptions of what we need them to be?

"Gosh, Josh, I don't know how to say this. But, uh, you're making sweeping generalizations."

"Excuse me?"

"Like when we were together, you made assumptions. I understand; so did I. I assumed you wouldn't like me if you knew I was Jewish. I didn't give you a chance. Who can say if that was even true?

"But you also assumed things about my sexuality, my drinking. My work habits. All based on me being a Protestant. But they weren't true, and I wasn't even a Protestant. And now you're making them based on me being Jewish. And I'm the same girl. I'm just me. You see?"

Silent, Josh looks down at his uneaten sushi.

"I'm sorry. Have I hurt your feelings?" I ask. "I don't mean to. I'm confused by my own behavior as much as anything else. I want to understand and make it better. I just want to talk."

"I'm happy to talk, Aimee. I know all about *wanting to talk,*" says Josh. He drops his chopsticks to use his forefingers and middle fingers to mime quotes around the words. "But you're not talking to me; you're challenging me. It feels way too familiar." He shakes off the negative memory. "And you never did that before. So why now?"

This new Japanese place is off the beaten track, and I'm grateful for our quiet table in the dark corner. I am hopeful it is so dark that Josh cannot see I have started to cry.

"Oh come on, A," he says, shocking me with this new shorthand of my name. "I didn't mean to make you cry. I'm sorry."

"I'm sorry, too. I don't want to hurt you anymore, Josh. I . . . I . . . just . . ."

"Just tell me." He takes a napkin and reaches over to dry my eyes. "Let's put it all out on the table, okay?"

"Okay." I touch his hand before he takes it back. "I gave this a lot of thought, you know. I mean, I had to live with the lie, and, believe me, it wasn't easy. And . . ."

My shiksa was a jigsaw puzzle. Its pieces, small and oddly shaped. Two of them might fit together but did not link with a third. They could not latch on to a fourth. They would not hinge together to form a complete picture.

With red hair and green eyes, some pieces were bright enough to find, colorful enough to stand on their own. But others, the pieces with omissions taken for admissions, got lost in the pile. The mismatched pile only grew, making it harder to interlock with the existing pieces that were in place. As a limited edition, I offered limited pieces. My internal ones remained unavailable.

"You never gave me a hard time about anything," he says. And that is how Josh saw it. Nothing really mattered because he was pleased enough with the fit of the pieces he did have. "It only made me want to give you more," he confirms.

"I didn't feel I deserved it because I was lying. You were really good to me. About so many things, like, oh my God, the driving."

"I haven't forgotten about the road test," Josh warns.

"The road test." I shudder. "Yeah . . ." I don't want to think about the road test, so I don't. "Well, I always held myself back. I didn't like it. I didn't like me. So how come now, us really talking, me expressing myself, how come that feels challenging? Why isn't it stimulating? Tell me, because I don't understand."

Does he?

"It's like whatever you say, Aimee, is the bottom line."

"Bottom li . . . huh? A minute ago? I was just going on and on about what happened at work." I try to ask gently, "Did you think I took my work less seriously before than now?"

"I thought you sounded a little tough now when you talked about work. eMay was sweet."

"Was she? Was eMay really sweeter than Aimee, or was she sweeter because of how she was seen? Why was she allowed to be herself?"

"Jesus." Josh's hand rests against his forehead as he allows his head to drop down. "You're so . . . analytical."

"Please, Josh." Analytical, in this case, hardly a compliment. "Look in my eyes. I'm the same person."

Slowly, he lifts his head to see. Our eyes lock; we study each other. Searching out all that was lost, all we never found.

"I see you now, Aimee, and I feel . . ."

Josh stops talking. But I do not chime in. If I have learned anything from eMay, it is how my silence will separate the wheat from the chaff.

"I don't want to be mean," he says. "I just . . ." Josh knows what he wants to say, and I want to hear it.

"More sake?" The waiter inadvertently interrupts two people eager for any interruption. We sip in silence until Josh blurts out, "I'm afraid you would try to tell me what to do."

"What?"

"You know, like my mother."

"Your *mother*? *What*?"

"I didn't mean *my* mother," Josh tries to joke, but I see we hit a nerve.

"Are you afraid if you married someone Jewish, she'd eventually become more like your mother than your wife?"

"I never thought of it like that, but maybe. Sounds plausible."

What is it about the Jewish Mother? What in the world has she done to make so many boys want to run? How does it happen that if a woman is Jewish and has an opinion and a responsible job, her self-expression, instead of being applauded, is interpreted as abrasive and reminiscent of someone's mother?

"So what happens to you? Do you get more like your father?"

"My dad's cool, but I don't want his life. I don't want all that responsibility."

"What responsibility?"

"Wife, kids, house, business . . . you know."

"But you talked about having those very things with eMay. What's the difference if it's with someone Jewish? I don't get it."

Josh goes to speak and then changes his mind.

"What?"

"Never mind."

"No. I told you stuff. Now you tell me."

"Well, just remember, you asked. I think a woman who's Jewish wants to be in control," admits Josh, causing me to wonder if that's why a natural Jewish wife raising Jewish kids hits the nail on the *too Jewish, too maternal* head.

"So if I'm not Jewish, if I'm your sweet shiksa, then you feel in control?"

Josh nods.

"I got to tell ya. If you try to keep me from my power, and what I mean is my strength, just because I'm Jewish, that's controlling." I laugh to sound light, though it's not exactly funny.

"Yeah, well, it may come out like that, but I don't think of it like that when it's happening," says Josh. "It's more like a little of this, a little of that." He ends the conversation when he pays the check.

My mind is racing when we leave the restaurant. There are more components to this, I know. But already round and round the track, I cannot catch up to them tonight. Meanwhile, I don't blame Josh for how he feels. I only want to better understand. And still try to make it right.

"Do you want to come up?" I ask Josh in front of my building.

"And make love to a controlling Jewish woman?" he teases.

"You can always pretend I'm your sweet shiksa. Your choice."

Talked out, we head straight to bed. A bed made with disillusion and puffed with pillows of disappointment. We quickly undress, pull down the covers, and lie in it.

Talking Heads

W E ARE NOT GOING to let you down," Jay promises in earnest, though he looks at me and rolls his eyes. "Right, Aimee?"

I give him a fake punch before I tell Alex, "We're in excellent shape, so do not worry. Just let me dial up all the coordinates before I bring you back on board." Jay's eyes say, *Who do you think you are, missy?* but my hand waves the worry away.

It's so much easier to have meetings on a Soundstation than face-to-face. The black plastic box, shaped like a starfish with a keypad, is an amazing conference call device. Mechanical voices announce each attendee, and the sound through the speakerphone is practically as good as in person. What's more, you can shoot notes and looks to your team that will help you play against the other one. Especially if it's your client.

"KISS is counting on you," reminds Alex, and then he clicks off.

"Whew." I grab a handful of M&Ms from a dish in the center of the table in the Round Room. Krista, Todd, and Sean are there for support, but the client spoke only with Jay and me. "So you think we bought some time? I think we bought some,"

I say, swooping up a handful of Milk Duds and quickly gobbling those.

"Stop eating all that junk," says Sean, swatting my hand hard with his fingers.

"What's it to you?"

"You'll ruin your new figure."

"Everything else is ruined, why not go for broke?"

"Boys and girls, pay attention," says Jay, downing his *second* Diet Coke. "News flash. Aimee has not come up with a backup for Kim Cattrall. Next. What happened with the signage?"

"It's here," says Krista. "It was too late to issue a stop."

Scheduling the TV actor (whoever he is, because no one will tell) is the problem. One minute he's clear to fly east for the re-shoot; an hour later he isn't. Not that the production company has been able to choose a date for Kim to film out there. Talk of an impending writers' strike has everyone scurrying, trying to get as many shows as possible in the can. Kim's people think if we can sit tight, it'll work out. It's just that no one can give a guarantee.

"We never had this happen before, but what if day-of a celebrity got sick?" Krista poses the question. "We'd have to do something."

"You're right," agrees Sean. "What would we do?"

"I know," says Todd. "We hire a Kim Cattrall impersonator as the backup," he says, joking.

"Oh my God, that's hysterical," I say. "It's so ludicrous, it's perfect."

"Sheer insanity," says Jay.

"So much so, it could actually work," I blurt before I even know what to say next. But suddenly everyone gets excited. I feel I owe them something. With their expectant eyes upon me, I have no choice but to improvise.

"Yes. And, ummm . . . we're selling a *copier,* right?" I say, free-associating as fast as my mind will allow.

"And we're promoting the latest in innovative imaging capabilities, right? So . . . if all else fails and she can't come . . . we'll have an impersonator." And it hits me. "We'll have *an innovative copy.*"

Making my pitch with all the blunder of Darrin Stephens bailing himself out of a situation on *Bewitched,* I'm too embarrassed to face Jay. But when I hear applause, I find the courage. And much like Larry Tate, Jay embraces the idea.

"Right. An innovative copy. Right! Because if all else fails, that won't."

Huh? I think this idea is beyond ridiculous. After decades of PR, I think Jay has finally lost it. Now looking about the happy table, I wonder if we all have.

"By far, that's the craziest thing I've ever heard from you yet," Sid tells me at brunch that weekend. "Cattrall's name's all over the signage. You'll be sued for false advertising if you don't watch out," he broadcasts between bites of his bagel. I'm back in Barney Greengrass, splitting the lox platter. "So tell me, have you found anybody?"

I shake my head. We held an audition yesterday at the office. Talk about scary. Not only the worst Kim Cattrall impersonators but also the most embarrassing Joan Rivers, shameful Barbra Streisands, and god-awful Judge Judys.

"Why were the performers doing women you don't need?" asks my father, his fork reaching across to my plate for a taste of fried eggs.

"Who knows? As of yesterday, Kim's publicist still had no definitive news, and we were still unsuccessfully pushing the client into the backup idea."

"Do you remember . . . ?" Sid puts down his utensils to lean back against his chair so his thought takes center stage, "that April Fool's show at the LaughTrack Peter emceed? And there was that terrific female impersonator. Your mother thought she really was Judy Garland."

I give Sid a look. "Your point?"

"Can you find out who that was? She could do it. Kind of looks like her too. Maybe . . . ask Peter?" Mission accomplished, Sid goes back to his bagel.

I thought of that. And turns out the impersonator, Dee Rose, is out of town till the end of June. But I got all my information through the booker at the comedy club, not Peter.

Since the intervention I've sent him e-mail, left voice mail. I want to make amends. So I was almost happy when this situation arose. It was not about *us*, so I thought Peter would definitely address my frantic but professional text message and write back. Hopeful to hear from him, I was hoping his response might be a crack in an unlocked door. But he has only ignored me.

"I'm two for two," I tell my father now, who, in regard to Josh, has been brought up to date by my mother.

"She says he was a lovely boy."

"They're all lovely boys. Once, Dad, even you were a lovely boy."

My father's response is to catch the attention of a waiter. With the swirling motion of his finger hovering over our cups, he indicates we'd both like a refill on coffee.

"Aimee, I don't know Josh, and with all the subterfuge it's hard to understand what even went on between the two of you.

Beneath the surface," he diplomatically adds. "But I do know about you and Peter. And Peter's a fine young man. Maybe a bit of a late bloomer, but that's not the worst thing, you know."

After she found out things with Josh and me were totally kaput, my mother alerted me that Peter was "doing very well." However, beyond that she offered no info—no contact or other details. Obviously in touch to some extent with my parents, he is totally off-limits to me. And for once in her life, my mother is butting out.

"If he wants you to find him, I'm sure he'll make himself known," she told me on the phone. Disconcerting as it was that she kept Peter's business separate, my mother still stuck her nose into mine.

"It ended with Josh?" she asked. "You two seemed fine when I saw you. I thought you said you had a good night?"

"We did." We had. It had seemed we were starting anew.

"So. What happened? What did he say?"

It reminded me of a bad breakup during my junior year at college. Painfully confused, I went to see a therapist.

"Sometimes things do end that way," she explained, helping me to learn that lesson early on.

Drew was premed, and our rapturous semester came to an abrupt fork in the road when he said he'd want me to quit work and be a doctor's wife once we had kids. That was so retro, I thought he was joking. Besides, it was so far off in the future. But then the issue came up again, in a heart-to-heart that left us shaken to discover how threatening it was to our otherwise blissful relationship.

That night we clung to each other, holding on tight. Lovers latched on to a piece of driftwood, keeping their relationship afloat. And we believed we would make it, for wasn't our talk really the first step to resolution? However, unbeknownst to both of us, it was the last.

After all the spoken words, it is only the feelings that remain behind, the only things that count. Used and used up, words often juxtapose them. But in the light of day, it is the feelings that prevail. And, soundlessly, they say it's time to move on.

I comforted my mother, who genuinely liked Josh once they actually met, by explaining Josh's acute shiksa syndrome.

"Everything's always the mother's fault," my mother synopsized as a way of trying to fit this half-baked breakup into its bread box. "What did we do that was so bad?"

"Do you know what that's all about, Daddy?" I ask my father now. He might have some insight, having the advantage of being a Jewish husband, father, and son. I confide in my dad and tell him about the other night. A captive audience, I tell him a lot more.

"I love your Absolut Shiksa," says Sid. In fact, I think we'd have a much more open conversation if he had a shot of that. But if I think my father knows best, my best bet to get him talking is to advertise.

"Yeah, you like that? Then you'll love this. You know what I called myself?" I pause. "Shiksa Barbie."

"Shiksa Barbie." Sid's eyes light up. "I like that. There's definitely something to that." He scratches his head and thinks. "You know, A, there truly is."

Sid eats in silence, though his mind, I know, is talking. Tossing out ideas, saying yay or nay. As my father does get shiksappeal, he is careful not to hurt my feelings.

"Barbie is a doll," he finally says. "And you play with a doll."

"So?"

"So, if you're Shiksa Barbie, then you're a doll a Jewish man can play with."

"How do you mean?"

"Take your friend, Krista. Now first let me say that I know she and Matt are in love, and I know she legitimately expressed interest in Judaism prior . . ."

Oy; enough with the political correctness. I appreciate Sid feels he should tread carefully; but if he's on to something I wish he'd stop mincing words and get to the punch. "You're talking to me, Dad. Just say it."

"Okay. Jewish men will marry women who aren't Jewish, but often those women take on Judaism, especially to raise a family. You see a lot of that, but not so much the other way around. Not so many Jewish men converting for non-Jewish women."

Sid continues when he sees I agree. "You might say the Jewish men are playing a game. Like you play with a doll. I remember how you and Daphne played with those Barbies. I was fascinated with them."

TMI! The waiter comes to pour more coffee, and I only wish there was something stronger.

"You girls had a ton of them. Ski Barbie and Flight Attendant Barbie. A skater, a gymnast . . . I'll never forget because it was the seventies and I used it in a pitch. Nurse Barbie *and* Doctor Barbie. See?"

"That you were obsessed with our dolls? You're scaring me, Dad."

"Aimee. You girls learned you could grow up to do anything. When you made up games, the dolls could be everything. Their legs and arms were bendable; you even shaped them. Shiksa Barbie. Play the game. Let the Jewish man shape you into the kind of Jewish woman he wants."

He is on to something, but this last part leaves me disappointed. As if the Jewish man still needs to feel in control. And let's say he succeeds in not marrying his Jewish mother. Does that guarantee he will not turn into his Jewish father? To me the issues have less to do with accepting religion and more about accepting responsibility for others, and that we all have to grow up.

"Just wait till the Jewish guy winds up turning the shiksa girl into his Jewish mother. Then what?"

Sid only laughs. "But didn't Josh want to shape you? I mean shiksa you?"

"I suppose in his way," I say. "He sure wouldn't have converted for eMay, but he also wouldn't have shaped her into much of a Jew. To tell you the truth, when it came to Judaism, Peter was way more open."

"To what? Shaping?" my father asks. "Or," he pauses, "being shaped?"

Thoughts percolate as soon as I hear those words. But the ring of my father's cell concludes the conversation. My mother, out to a ladies' lunch, calls to make sure that before I head east I pick up the shopping bag of food she left for me at the apartment.

"Onward?" asks Sid.

I nod my head, as that direction sounds good to me.

Promises, Promises

THE LETTERS HAVE NOT BEEN RETURNED. Unless he has burned them, I assume that they've been read.

In the beginning, it was just to apologize. Just. That alone could fill volumes. But while writing a letter is certainly one-sided, it opened a channel to communicate. So I continued to write, then wrote some more. And the more I wrote, the more it became apparent. The extent to which I had been unfair.

I see why people pretend. It takes you away from being yourself. It gives the opportunity to experience life walking in someone else's shoes. Being a shiksa opened a real window of opportunity.

Ironically, in regard to Jewish tradition, I made allowances for Josh I did not for Peter. But, ultimately, I'd have been hard-pressed to accept that Josh would reject it. It's hard to say, now, where he'll go from here. But his rejection of what's Jewish, aka me, opened my eyes to how I reject what's Not. And now I must see how that rejection affected Peter and me.

Every two people create something new. Every twosome can't

work, but you have to know when you have one that can. One worth working on. Every person offers something different. Different might not be better, but it might be just as good.

Sam was a fit that came ready-made, one that did not need adjustments. I tried to find another like that, but I couldn't. In time, I understood that I wouldn't. That's when I stopped looking and, instead, I found me.

Each day I'm grateful when envelopes marked RETURN TO SENDER do not flood my mailbox. But in the two weeks I've written, I've yet to receive a reply.

Still, I keep writing. Once, sometimes twice, a day I write. I ask questions, share stories. I might cut out a cartoon from the *New Yorker* or send along the sports pages from the *Daily News*. Finally unencumbered, I write from my heart. And while my heart has long been punctured, it is only now I feel it's truly beginning to heal.

Being a shiksa taught me a lot. But among the things I discovered, Peter, was that when it came to the idea of us being a family, I did not give you a fair chance to design your half of what that could look like.

Krista shows me, by example. KISS's corporate office so close to Saks, after the meeting we stop in the dress department. Waiting to pick up hers, she fills me in on the details for the wedding this weekend. My friend is honored to be one of two witnesses to sign the *ketubah* along with the groom.

"What an awesome religion to have the man put his marriage responsibilities to the woman in a contract," she exclaims. "Leah says the *ketubah* protects the woman's rights during the marriage, or if something happens and it doesn't work out. She's been great," Krista speaks warmly of Matt's sister.

"It's so nice she asked you. You know, Peter was once a witness." I laugh as I recall the shotgun wedding for an interfaith couple held at the club. "He joked he reviewed every clause, and his only request was that they don't remove Santa."

Krista laughs too. Always a good audience for Peter.

"So have you seen his John Hancock?"

I shake my head.

"I guess that's that. But at least I got to say my peace," my response in line with the wedding-themed talk.

"Did you tell your mom about the letters?"

"No, but in the letters I did tell Peter how I got his address."

When I picked up that food at my mom's after the brunch at Barney Greengrass, I couldn't help but notice the bag was strategically placed on the entry table alongside a postcard of the Hollywood sign. Well, of course it caught my eye. Of course I picked it up. And, of course, after I read it I copied Peter's address in California onto the shopping bag.

"If I know your mother, your mother already knows," says Krista.

"I think so too," I say, pretty certain my mother probably cooked the night before to have the leftover stuffed cabbage to put in a shopping bag to place next to that postcard just so I would see.

"How'd Peter sound?" Krista fishes. "In the postcard?"

"He didn't say anything about me, if that's what you're asking. Likes work, said he likes driving around. Oh, speaking of—listen to this. Remember that whole thing with Josh and . . . the road test?"

Krista nods.

"Well, he sent me an e-mail this morning. We're definitely still history, nothing changed there, but apparently he made an appointment for me a while back to take the test. Turns out it's for three o'clock today." Josh. He was a real *mensch* to follow through. "Anyway, he wanted me to know. Like I'm really going to take it." I look to Krista to concur that this is a certifiably crazy idea.

"Why not?" she asks, pointing to her watch to show there's time. "That was kind of him, and it would be good for you to—"

The saleswoman interrupts when she unzips the plastic covering to show Krista the finished alterations.

"Ooooh, this is so beautiful," I say, checking my hands are clean before fingering the soft panels of pale peach chiffon. "You'll look stunning."

"Believe it or not, it's my first Jewish wedding."

"But hardly your last," I say, and wink at my friend.

"*Halevai,*" says Krista, surprising me first with the Yiddish word that means "if only," and again when she spits twice between her two forefingers. "I want it so much, I don't want to give myself some cane-hurrah."

"A *kaynahorah,*" I say, spitting, too, between my fingers to ward away the evil eye. "Don't worry. God's sure to protect anyone who can learn that much Yiddish so fast."

But our mood quickly changes when Krista checks her Black-Berry and finds a message from Jay ordering us back to the office for an emergency meeting regarding the newest development on the launch.

"What could have happened?" I ask Krista. "We just left there." And we left KISS happily backed up with an impersonator, and foolish enough to think we could sneak in an early lunch.

"Whatever it is should be showing up on *your* BlackBerry," Krista says, back at work, marching down the corridor to Jay.

"But I don't have a BlackBerry," I say, my stomach in knots having just read the e-mail sent to us all.

"Exactly," she says as we sit down at the small round table in Jay's big corner office.

"Decisions need to be made," says Jay. "Now."

Both bewildered, we note there are no boys and no candy; just the facts, Jay, Krista, and me. Breaking news. Bound by a contract, my best bud Glenn from Celebrity Access worked with Cattrall's people and came up with a new solution. He did promise. And since KISS loves it, so will we.

She can't do it here. Kim Cattrall is being flown out for the reshoot and will not be available for the launch Monday in New York. However, the production company has made it possible for the whole thing to happen on Sunday. In Los Angeles.

"What?" Today's Friday. Is everyone out of their minds?

To film the exterior shot, a New York City street is being built on a Hollywood lot. The KISS launch will take place on the *More Sex and the City* set, on a street that will look just like a street in New York. Just like our original concept.

"Ramy is ready to overnight all the product; no problem there. The L.A. office is pitching the alert as we speak." Jay looks at me. "So sure of media, KISS has their advertising people pushing some last-minute ads." A fact I already think I shall keep from my dad. "Attendance for the contest will be huge. Listen to this." Jay practically hugs his heart. "Patrick Dempsey is the TV star, and since his schedule contributed to the change, he's offered to *stop by on Sunday* . . ." Jay pauses for a very McDreamy moment, and as much as I'd like to, I'm too panicked to join.

"So . . . looks like this launch will be a winner. Your stalling worked," Jay says to me. Pleased. "Pay off the impersonator, have the team pull everything in New York. Then pack your bags for at least a week, because tomorrow, Ms. A., you're headed for L.A."

Krista jumps up and down, thrilled to hear she's not going. She was never supposed to attend the launch on Monday anyway, hard at work on a new business account. Grabbing her Black-Berry and her Saks bag, she heads toward the door.

"Have fun, you guys. Since I'm not needed, I'm out of here," she says. "Thank God," I hear her murmur under her breath as she brushes past.

"Thanks, Kris," calls Jay before he turns to me. "Aimee, I'm proud you did it. And see how important it was? This came up unexpectedly, but now you're prepared. You got your license."

Jay claps his hands together. The sound and the words bring Krista, who is almost out the door, to a complete stop. She turns and looks at me, her face gone white. But the red of embarrass-ment shines on me.

"Don't tell me," says Jay, observing the interaction and sink-ing into his chair. "Oh no, that's impossible. We made an agree-ment." Shaking his head back and forth, he waves his hand to beckon Krista back into the room.

"I know, Jay. I was on track. I thought, for sure, I'd have it but . . ." I stop talking. What can I tell him? I forgot because I was too busy pretending to be a shiksa to remember? Not to mention too scared.

Krista slowly walks back into the office and places her Saks bag on top of the table. The three of us stand around it. No one makes the next move. Krista and I defer to Jay.

"In other words, Aimee, you still don't have a license to drive a car."

"Correct. But I don't see what that has to do with—"

"There's *nothing* extra now." Jay rubs his fingers together to indicate money. "Not after the location change. Plus hotel and per diem for you. We can have someone pick you up at the airport tomorrow, but after that it's a rental car."

"Who needs car service? I'll just pay for my own cabs."

"You think you're in New York? We even rent cars here for events. With all the setup and transporting product and signage and who knows what else, you think we can depend on taxis? And in Los Angeles?" Jay glares. "Krista, you're going to have to sub for Aimee. You go tomorrow."

Jay shoots me a look of profound disappointment before he walks away from the table and back to his desk. Krista spins around and goes after him.

"I can't. It's my boyfriend's sister's wedding this Sunday. Rehearsal dinner's tomorrow night. I can't go, I can't. Aimee"—she turns to me—"fix this."

I think I know what she means, but it's so daunting I try another way.

"What about what's her name? From our office in L.A.? You said yourself she's great. I'll brief her, and she'll take over, you know . . ." My eyes appeal to Krista to show her I'm trying. "Gina Jones-Shapiro?"

"Jones-Levine," snaps Jay. "She'll be there as support, but it's a New York–generated launch and the New York office must be present."

Krista and I name everyone on the consumer team, but anyone who has the expertise to work the event is already spoken for.

"I'm sorry, honey," Jay tells Krista. "We'll make it up to you. Now if you ladies will excuse me . . ."

"No," says Krista. "Aimee *can* do it, right, Aimee? Tell Jay."

"Are you holding out on me? You have a license?"

"I'm not holding out on any—"

"Yes you are, Aimee," announces Krista. "You are. You can get it today."

Jay's brown eyes bulge. "Is this true?"

Is it? Ohmygod, I never thought about it like that but . . .

"Aimee, we have no time to waste. Regarding L.A., are you in or out?"

Krista waits, breathing hard, clutching the Saks bag to her body that shakes behind it. Jay taps his middle finger on the desk. Next door a Mozart Sonatina ring tone plays over and over as someone does not answer their cell.

"I'm out." No sooner do I say the words than Krista and I are both out in the hall.

The SAKS bag held close to her chest, Krista runs down the corridor. She cries so hard, I fear her tears will drop down through the tissue paper and damage the dress. But damage has already been done. Damage, I fear, that's irreparable. I chase Krista, wanting, begging her forgiveness.

"Krista, wait! Don't you see? It's not my fault."

Stopping outside her office, Krista turns to face me. While she does not speak, her heaving body and tear-struck face would hardly agree. But how can I unravel my fear? What horrible thing will happen now if I do take this test?

"I . . ." Are there even words to explain? "I would go . . . if I could . . . but . . ." Are there words to give this weekend back to my friend? Hyperventilating, I can barely get out the only ones that might matter. "I'm sorry, I'm so, so sorry, Kris, but . . . I just"—it comes out in a whisper—"can't."

"Aimee, you *can*." Krista's words are measured along with the weight of a look I don't want to remember but will never forget.

It's so haunting, I only sob and sob when, back at my desk, I stare at my screen reading Josh's e-mail again and again.

To: a.albert@prwap.com
From: josh@loveloaves.com
Subject: Road Test 3 PM Today—20th Avenue in Queens

Hey Aimee . . .
Remember when I told you I'd surprise you with an appointment for a road test?
Well . . .

Cut to the Chase

I LOOK UP, and instead of skyscrapers I see mountains. It seems as strange to me to see a mountain in this city as it probably strikes others to see a lake in Central Park at home. But I am not home. I am here. In Los Angeles.

"Where do you want this?"

Summer interns who have just begun working at PR With A Point in L.A. serve as the support staff, eager to help. On schedule, we still feel like we're running behind, praying the last-minute details won't turn into potential pitfalls. Murphy must have been in PR when he created his law.

"How about the two of you run this banner from lamppost to lamppost." I point to the fake New York street on the *More Sex and the City* set that appears more authentic than the real New York street we would have used tomorrow.

"The platform and the copier should be delivered any minute, and they'll be setting up a little stage . . ." I glance down at my clipboard and catch a look at the stellar production schedule Krista whipped up. "Starting in about fifteen minutes."

A car service picked me up yesterday at the airport and brought me to a Hyatt on Sunset Boulevard. It is in walking distance of many shops and eateries, and through the concierge I discovered it is also on a bus route. Although slow and unreliable, the bus is definitely an option. If I wake up superearly and bring along a good pair of walking shoes, I can take it back and forth to the PR With A Point office starting tomorrow. Meanwhile, there is this rental car . . .

Per Jay's instructions, I got the car. Parked on the lot, a shiny red Dodge Neon sits in a VIP spot. Enterprise drove it over. I took a cab and asked the rental company to meet me here. One of the interns can drive it back to the Hyatt later; the car will stay parked in the hotel's garage for the duration of this trip.

But we did all the paperwork, and upon showing my corporate AMEX card, I also produced my learner's permit *and* my temporary license. I passed! This license is good until the real one arrives in the mail.

I wasn't going to go. I had no intention, whatsoever, of going. But when Krista said "you *can*," I heard her telling me I was able. A fact I could not dispute. I did not know if I'd pass, but I was able to find out.

Asking one of my family members to accompany me felt as scary as playing Russian roulette with their lives. Daphne, probably out carpooling, didn't pick up her phone. Jon, up in Nyack on a shoot, said it was impossible for him to walk out. Maddie was free, and delighted by the way, but didn't have the car. Sid took it to work because of a business lunch with a client in Yonkers. I caught him on his cell right in the middle.

"We're not nearly finished," said my dad, afraid with traffic he might not even make it back in time. "Can you schedule something for another date in the city, and I promise I'll take you?"

"They don't give road tests in Manhattan," I told him, my eyes suddenly welled up with tears. To help make the decision,

I prayed to God for a sign, and staring me in the face was one so big you'd have to have been blind not to see it.

"You need to take the test in the boroughs. Josh picked Queens." I was shaken. I knew I had to go through with it, but was terrified to do so.

When I looked up the location of Twentieth Avenue in Queens, it turned out to be only a stone's throw from the Silvercup Studios in Long Island City. The primary shooting location for *More Sex and the City*, starring none other than . . . Kim Cattrall.

"Oh. I thought you'd be relieved to postpone," said my dad, only to hear me bawl when I finally explained all that was riding on this. And before I finished, Sid excused himself from the lunch, explaining he'd take the FDR Drive to the Fifty-ninth Street Bridge and to meet him in Queens. My heart in my mouth, I ran out of the office and leaped into a cab, taking my biggest ever leap of faith.

My father held me as I cried the fear away. Then with a strength I did not know I possessed, I composed myself, climbed into his car with the instructor, turned on the ignition, and drove away.

And hey. So far so good. I got my license, flew out here, and no one has died. Though driving home, after the test, we heard on the radio that Jack Kevorkian had been released from prison. Sid was quick to assure that if anything were to happen that day, it would not be traced to me.

"Are you Aimee?" Of course, I recognize the voice. It belongs to none other than Kim Cattrall, who is standing right beside me. In a blue silk wrap dress. Her blonde hair shimmers in the California light; her smile is sunny.

"Hello, there." I shake her hand. Media savvy, I don't go gaga over celebs as a rule. But my heart pumps a few extra beats upon meeting this star. In person she's even more of a knockout. "Thanks so much for helping to make this happen," I say, and gesture to everything going on around us.

"Honey, it was no problem," says Kim. "Well, actually it was, but it was fun to solve. You know, I may not be a publicist, but I played one on TV."

"Ohmygod, that's right," I remember, amazed how it all comes together.

Soon the media circus will begin. We have pre-event interviews scheduled, and expect several camera crews to drop by throughout the day. Photographers will be on-site for the photo-op with the winners, and we will e-mail pictures to every publication—online and off—before we leave the venue. Our list of confirmed media includes *Extra*, *Access Hollywood*, *Entertainment Tonight*, all the local television affiliates, local TV, the *Los Angeles Times*, *People* (yes), and more. You never know who'll be a no-show, and some certainly will, but I think our hits will be pretty high.

"Do I look okay?" asks Kim, grabbing a bottled water out of the cooler and fluffing up her hair. "Maybe a little lipstick?"

"We've got plenty of that," I say, and lead her over to the Ramy booth that's all set with the colors that will be used for the kissing contest.

There is something so exciting to me about seeing anything in bulk. An office supply store once created a window display using several thousand unsharpened pencils that blew me away. Now, in front of us, are rows and rows of Ramy lipsticks. And I suddenly can't wait to try them on.

Behind the table sits Tara, the Ramy rep, and another woman who, by the looks of it, has just slipped in.

"Sorry to be a bit late. You know this all came up so quickly, and this morning was my nephew's bris. I'm from the agency and supervising the contest with Tara," says the woman, who introduces herself as Gina Jones-Levine. Her dark hair is swept up into a ponytail, and her confidence is tucked into her charm. She is tall, black, and beautiful. Talk about shiksa syndrome.

"I'm so glad to meet you," I tell Gina. "Everyone in the New York office sings your praises."

"Let's hope that's still the case after today," she says.

"I know what you mean," I agree. "We'll see how it shakes out tomorrow."

"We've got a desk all ready for you in the office next to mine."

"Ladies, I don't mean to interrupt," says Kim, "but get a load of these lipsticks."

We pick up the different lipsticks, to try the different colors. The colors are too cool. And the names are too much. So descriptive, each one tells another story.

"How does this look?" asks Kim, pulling off the top of *Too Good For Him Berry*. She puts a coat on her bottom lip and picks up a hand mirror.

"I think you should try this one," says Tara, handing her *All His Fault.*

"I like you in that one," I say.

"Which do you think for me?" Gina shows us *Smile! Laugh!* and *Happy!*

"Happy! becomes you," I tell her, and it does. I certainly don't know the ins and outs of Gina and Mr. Levine, only to guess that there had to have been obstacles to overcome. By the looks of things, they did. Though my mother makes sure to always remind me you never know what goes on behind closed doors.

We are all so impressed by presentation. Josh loved how he

looked with eMay; my mother loved how Aimee looked with Josh. I loved how I looked with Josh . . . on paper. If I had to write a shopping list of what I was looking for in a mate, Josh would match my list. But the reality of me and Josh was not a fit. Whereas I would say the opposite of me and Peter.

"Hey, this looks like a good color for you," says Gina, handing over a pale pink I like so much I try it. Except when I look in the mirror I look all washed out, and it doesn't suit me at all.

"Let me see," says Kim, wiping her mouth with a tissue before applying the lipstick to look pretty in pink.

"Excellent," says Tara. "That is so your color."

Kim flips it over to see the name on the bottom. *"Shiksa Goddess!"* she reads. "Well, if the shoe fits."

I laugh along with the women. Yep, it sure fits Kim, but it sure doesn't fit me. I look for a color named for a non-Jewish man. If there's one called *My Shagetz!* I will take it as a sign. But there isn't, and Peter is clearly finished with me. Just here for business, I do not plan to call him. Sadly, I must leave well enough alone.

"What else you got here that would work for me?" I ask about the lipsticks, hoping for a color that will brighten in more ways than one.

The crew from *Extra* arrives early for their appointment with Kim. They need set-up time, allowing us to review the talking points for the product.

"I'm very good at this, and I will find you the perfect color," says Kim, rummaging through lipsticks while I put the product fact sheets out on the table with the makeup.

Yet I can't stop thinking of P and wonder if I'm making the wrong decision. After all, I'm not a stalker. I am here for legitimate reasons. How would I feel if positions were reversed and he didn't contact me? And what if he has a new California girl? But what if he hasn't.

"Now, *this* is you," Kim says, and hands me a lipstick just as my phone beeps and signals a text message. My mouth open as she applies the new color; it only opens wider when I look sideways at my cell and see . . . Peter's number! And that he's finally responding to the message I sent him that week.

wk nuts, sorry if late. # Dee—212–555–8976. on hiatus
now & headed LAX w/in the hr 4 new horizons! P

I read it a few times to comprehend, but it comes together in a flash when Kim tells me *this* one's my color. Once she announces the name, there is no doubt. *"Epiphany!"*

"We're ready for Ms. Cattrall," a production assistant rushes by to relay.

"Come on," says Kim, waving her hand in front of the hand mirror, alerting me it's time to go. Because I don't move. The media are arriving, the event is beginning, the contest is starting, and Peter is leaving. And all I know is I must get to him before he takes off.

"How far is . . ." From my wallet, I pull out the scrap torn from a piece of that shopping bag I've been carrying around. "North Hollywood?" I read off his address, as Gina leans over my shoulder to look.

"And Magnolia Boulevard," she says, the street names Greek to me. "Twenty minutes from here, no traffic. Why?"

The story comes pouring out. "But how can I leave?"

"I'm here," says Gina. "Just go."

"Well," I hedge. "How soon can I get a cab?"

"Not soon enough." Gina laughs. "You're not in Kansas anymore. Didn't they rent you a car? The only way to catch him in time is to drive."

"Oh no," I wail, and tell them all the rest of my saga. I look up at the heavens to stick out my tongue at the guys playing the joke on me. I can't believe this. So far from the New York City subway, this moment is now offered to me to face. Head-on. Though I confess I'm afraid of a collision. Still, I want to do it. Maybe I even can, but . . . but . . .

But . . . I finally see the thing I could not face inside me.

Many things have come easy to me, but all fairly traditional and by-the-book, they've all fit in my box. However, for all my faith, perhaps it is lacking when it comes to trusting my own ability to do the harder work for something that appears to be out of it. Yet have I not learned that so much of the fit is illusion?

"You have to go," says Kim.

"It sounds so romantic," says Tara, while Gina writes directions on the back of the press release and Kim runs a comb through my hair.

"Ms. Cattrall, we're ready for you now," calls the production assistant.

"We have to go." Gina indicates she and Kim are walking over.

"Do you all really think—?" I begin, and am interrupted by Kim.

"Honey, if Mr. Big can fly to Paris to claim Carrie, you can certainly drive to the Valley."

I don't know if that's true, but there's only one way to find out. Trying to leave the parking lot, I feel like a character doing a bit in a movie. I step so hard on the gas pedal I fly forward—until I fall backward, having stepped too hard on the brakes. Regrouping, at twenty-five miles per hour I exit the lot and turn onto Hollywood Boulevard. At a red light, a homeless man begs on the corner behind another who pees into a palm tree. So shocked to see this in the glamorous city of Hollywood, not to mention petrified behind the wheel, I don't go when the light turns green. Crazy drivers curse me and drive past.

Finally, I just pull over. I can't. I want to. I really, really want to, but I can't do this. I'll just call Peter, I think, as I rummage in my purse for my cell. No. His new horizons probably don't include me anyway. Never mind. But instead of my cell, my hand touches something else. My prayer book. My siddur. I have it with me, my way of bringing Grandpa Jack along on this trip.

"Always stay true to yourself," I read his inscription. Yes. Yes, Grandpa. That would mean facing Peter. Driving there, proving I am ready for him. But if I can, please show me how.

I flip through the pages for inspiration and come across a bunch of prayers. There are prayers for everything. Eating bread and drinking wine. Upon seeing a rainbow, or the ocean, or a tree blossom in spring. A prayer for bad tidings, another for good, and then I see a prayer that's said when embarking on a journey.

"Y'hi ratzon milfanecha..." May it be Thy will, Lord our God, to lead us in safety . . . bring us to our destination in life . . . deliver us from every lurking enemy and danger on the road . . .

I almost close my eyes as I speed up enough to merge onto the 101. I stay to the right. At forty-five miles per hour I feel like I'm practically speeding, but everyone's out for my blood. Cars zoom by, honking their horns, one coming so close as to almost hit me, to give me a good *what for.* So this is the Los Angeles Freeway. God help me. Only I know that he is.

My drive exposes me to a less glittery Tinseltown; people hold WILL WORK FOR FOOD signs at the exit ramp. I read others to

Universal City, driving past on a street called Cahuenga—please don't ask me to pronounce it. But my quaking during the car ride escalates off the Richter scale when I make the right on Magnolia. Searching the four-digit house numbers, curiously painted onto the street, I drive slowly until I arrive at an apartment complex I know is his.

For no sooner do I pull up than Peter, in a white two-door Toyota Corolla—I know that because I read it in his postcard—pulls out of the driveway. Overcome with emotions ranging from absolute victory to very acute fear, I hit the accelerator and the car lurches. I jam on the brakes so fast, we almost collide. Baxter barks when Peter, stupefied as I've ever seen him, slams out of his car. Putting his hand through the open window, he reaches inside, unlocks my door, and pulls me out of mine.

"As I live and breathe. Aimee Albert. In L.A. Driving!"

"I drove to you!" I say. "I'm here."

Sealed with a KISS

EVERYTHING WENT FINE without me. Or let's put it this way. If a crisis came up, they handled it fine without me. Most media showed and two canceled, but the best is yet to come. Patrick Dempsey's cameo coincided with the arrival of *Access Hollywood,* bringing KISS a major coup.

Couples upon couples line up to kiss, while Kim gets ready to judge. Along with Gina and Tara she waves, as Peter, Baxter, and I walk by.

"Impressive," says Peter, holding my hand as I show him around. But if you ask me, impressive belongs to him.

Almost done taping, Peter's show has a very uncertain future. So Peter made plans of his own. Signed to an agent, he's being tried out for several jobs. His best bet, a staff writer on *Letterman.* I caught him heading back east for a meeting. Because it's not scheduled until next week, he will now wait to fly home with me.

"I was more than nervous about your *new horizons,*" I confess, walking with Peter and Baxter on this New York set that feels more like home than home.

"It was part work, but more about you," says Peter. "I knew from your letters things would be different. You were ready for me, and I got ready for you."

Peter's hair has golden streaks from the sun. He's in wonderful shape. Clearly happy, he carries himself with a humble pride that's most appealing. Coming into his own makes him feel proud. And I am proud of him.

The clothesline of photocopied kisses extends to the end of the street. We'll have time alone later, and I need to get back and work the event. But Baxter pulls himself away from Peter and runs off. Woofing and howling like he saw an old friend. Chasing him, we turn a corner and discover that he has. Still on the set, we are now on a block that looks so much like Peter's in Hell's Kitchen, I practically smell the aroma from the pizza place over on Ninth.

"Oh . . . will you look at this," I say, seeing a walk-up I'd swear was Peter's. "Let's check out 4G," I tease, and climb the stoop as Baxter leads the way.

"I won't miss leaving this behind," says Peter, already spending his hoped-to-be-earned income on a new apartment. Once at the top, we open the door, but all that's behind it is a platform.

"Of course. It's a set. It's just pretend," Peter says, and rests his hands on my shoulders. "I don't want to pretend anymore."

"Don't look at me, 'cause I'm through," and am I ever. "But I'd do it again in a heartbeat if I knew it would bring me here." I look up at Peter. I must tell him, and it must be now. "It won't happen again. I won't ask you to give up what's meaningful to you, P. I don't know yet how, but we'll find the way. A way that—"

"Ssshhhh." He gently puts his hand over my mouth. He combs his fingers through my scalp and, by gathering up my hair, pulls me toward him and holds me close. He leans over and whispers in my ear, "I love you, Aimee."

"Peter." Oh, thank God. "I love you, too. So very much."

"And . . . because I do . . . and because there was . . . a lot to sort out"—he raises his eyebrows—"I did something. I took a class. Intro to Judaism. I was the only *shagetz* in a room full of shiksas willing to convert."

"Waiting first for you, so they'd at least be doing it for a Jewish guy."

We laugh.

"But . . . well, you know that's a very big step," I say. "And please don't feel like you have to convert." I look at the steps this man is taking. And not just for me but him. He has stepped up and grown in ways I could not have imagined. And now, that he is so willing, I want him to be sure he only does what feels right for himself. "Because I can bend, too," I say, knowing I mean it. "I can."

Peter smiles. "I appreciate that. And we'll see; one step at a time. But it's funny. It's a pretty Jewish industry out here, and another writer and I went to the class on a lark, for a sketch. Then I got hooked; the teachings are amazing. In Judaism there's always a reason, an explanation. And if you don't like that one, there's another."

On the one hand . . . on the other hand . . . and on the *other* hand . . .

"It's all about family. Food." He winks. "But I get what you love about it, and I love you. I want that, all of that, with you. So we move in that direction. Yes?"

"YES."

I look at Peter and see our future. Though I arrived at this place via pretend, it's more real than anything I've known. We tell our truths on a make-believe Hollywood set; Peter and I end this act as a new one now begins.

It is the magic hour when the soft light glows just right. It is the perfect light. My lips melt into Peter's. On this empty platform behind a New York City door, his lips melt into mine. Near palm trees beneath mountains, illuminated under the California sky.

Suddenly, Peter picks me up. Opening the door, he carries me across its threshold. We kiss. We are in Hollywood and can walk off into the sunset. But since I have the rental car, we drive.

Glossary

"Adon Olam." Hymn sung at the close of the Sabbath and festival morning services.

afikoman. A piece of matzo that's hidden at the start of the seder and later eaten as dessert. Whichever child finds it is generally rewarded with money.

Aleinu. The closing prayer on Sabbath services.

aliyah. An honor; literally an ascension.

Amidah. Means "standing"; it is the central prayer of the Jewish liturgy.

appetizing. Refers to "the foods one eats with bagels," such as smoked salmon and whitefish.

Ashkenazi Jews. Coming from eastern European communities, this group, which makes up most of the Jewish population, speaks Yiddish and has a distinct culture and liturgy.

baleboosteh. A terrific housekeeper, mistress of the house.

bar mitzvah. An initiation ceremony that takes place when a Jewish boy turns thirteen that proclaims him an adult, responsible for his moral and religious duties; also an important social event.

bashert. Meant to be.

bat mitzvah. The same ceremony as the bar mitzvah, but for a girl.

beracha. A blessing or prayer.

bimah. The elevated area or platform in a synagogue intended to serve as the place where people read aloud from the Torah.

bisel. Little.

blintze. A crepelike pancake that is folded around a filling of potato, cheese, or preserves.

borscht. A cold soup made of sliced beets.

bris. Circumcision performed on a male Jewish baby at the age of eight days. A baby naming is the ceremony for a girl.

challah. A rich bread made with many eggs, eaten on the Sabbath and on all Jewish holidays except Passover.

chub. A small whitefish.

chutzpah. Nerve, audacity.

cvell. To gush with pride.

daven. To recite the prayers in a Jewish liturgy.

dreidel. A four-sided spinning top with a different Hebrew letter on each side, used to play the Hanukkah gambling game.

"Ein Keloheinu." A hymn proclaiming God's uniqueness.

erev. Evening.

farkakte. Derogatory adjective to describe something that's worthless or useless.

fermished. Mixed up.

gefilte fish. A ground fish mixed with crumbs, eggs, and seasonings, cooked in an oval-shaped ball, and served chilled in its own jellied stock.

gentile. Not Jewish.

goy. Yiddish word for someone who is not Jewish.

goyishe. Of things not Jewish.

Hadassah. The Women's Zionist Organization.

haftarah. A selection from the Prophets that a bar (bat) mitzvah reads in synagogue on the Sabbath.

Haggadah. Means "the telling"; this book contains the story of the Exodus, which is read at the Passover seder.

halevai. If only.

hamentaschen. Traditional treat for Purim, the three-cornered pastry is filled with poppy seed or other sweet preserve fillings.

Hanukkah. An eight-day Jewish festival, held annually in December, commemorating the rededication of the temple at Jerusalem in 165 BC.

Hillel. The largest Jewish campus organization, providing opportunities for Jewish students to explore and celebrate their Jewish identity.

hora. A festive circle dance, a "must" at Jewish weddings and bar and bat mitzvahs.

JAP. Jewish American Princess; implies a Jewish woman who's materialistic, selfish, and spoiled.

Kaddish. A Hebrew prayer said in remembrance of the dead.

kaynahorah. The evil eye.

ketubah. The Jewish marriage contract.

kiddish. A celebratory meal after synagogue services.

kiddush. A blessing recited over wine.

kiddush cup. Goblet used to say the blessing over wine.

klezmer. A type of music from Ashkenazi Jews.

knaidlach. Jewish word for matzo balls.

kosher. Dietary laws that indicate what foods an observant Jew can and cannot eat, and how those foods must be prepared and eaten.

kugel. A noodle pudding.

latkes. Made of grated potatoes and fried in oil, these potato pancakes are a traditional food served during Hanukkah.

L'chayim. To life. Often said as a toast.

Lox. Salmon, known for being eaten on a bagel with cream cheese.

Manischewitz. A leading brand of kosher products that is well-known for a wine that is very sweet.

matzo. A brittle, flat piece of unleavened bread, eaten especially during Passover.

matzo ball. A small fluffy dumpling made of crushed matzo and served in soup.

megillah. The Purim story.

menorah. A nine-branched candelabra used for Hanukkah, with one branch for each of the eight days, plus one central light used to light the others.

mensch. A good man of honor and integrity.

mezuzah. A small case of wood, plastic, or metal that contains a piece of parchment with important words from the Jewish Torah and that is attached to the doorpost of a Jewish home.

mikvah. A ritual bath for women used for attaining purity. Immersion is used in connection with conversion.

minyan. Quorum of ten or more adult (bar mitzvahed) male Jews that form a congregation for public worship. Reform Judaism includes women who've been bat mitzvahed.

mishegas. Craziness.

mishpacha. Family.

mitzvah. Any act of human kindness.

Musaf. The additional service added on the Sabbath.

nosh. A nibble, a snack food.

nova. A mild, unsalty, cold salmon that is served sliced.

oy. A sigh of woe.

oy gevalt. An interjection of grief or woe.

oy vey. An interim sigh of woe. Oh, no!

Oy vey iz mir. Woe is me.

oy yai yai. Oh, no no!

Passover. A Jewish holiday that commemorates the Exodus, the liberation of the Israelites from Egyptian slavery.

Pesach. Hebrew word for Passover.

pierogi. A dumpling stuffed with cheese or potato, shaped like a half moon, and cooked boiled or fried.

Purim. A fun holiday that commemorates when the Jewish people living in Persia were saved from extermination.

rabbi. A person trained in Jewish law and ordained to lead a congregation.

rebbetzin. Wife of a rabbi.

Rosh Hashanah. Jewish New Year.

rugelach. A cookie of cream cheese dough spread with filling, such as jam, nuts, or chocolate, and then rolled up.

schlep. To carry.

seder. Means "order"; refers to a Jewish feast and service, held on the first (and second) night of Passover, that commemorates the Exodus through a structured order of symbols, stories, and prayer.

Shabbat. The Sabbath.

shagetz. A non-Jewish man.

Shema. A centerpiece of all morning and evening Jewish prayer services, it is considered the most important prayer in Judaism.

shidduch. A romantic match.

shiksa. A non-Jewish woman.

shivah. Judaism's weeklong period of grief and mourning.

shul. Yiddish word for synagogue.

siddur. A Jewish prayer book.

Torah. The holy book of written Jewish laws.

traif. Not kosher.

tsuris. Yiddish word for trouble or aggravation.

tzimmes. A Jewish casserole of sweet potatoes, carrots, honey, and prunes that is cooked slowly over very low heat.

Unkosher. Not kosher.

whitefish. A flaky freshwater fish served whole, so the head and eyes are visible.

yarmulke. A skullcap worn by Jewish males during prayer and religious study.

yenta. A gossip; a woman who can't keep a secret.

Yiddish. A dialect of High German including some Hebrew and other words.

Yiddishkeit. Means "Jewishness"; suggests more emotional attachment and identification with the Jewish people than a religiously observant lifestyle.

Yom Kippur. Day of Atonement. This high holiday is observed by fasting and prayer for the atonement of sins.

zetz. A smack or a punch.

1. What were your expectations of this novel, based on the title and cover? Now that you've read it, were your expectations fulfilled?

2. Which character did you identify with more closely, Aimee or Krista? In your opinion, which one stayed more true to herself? Who was the better friend? Why?

3. Discuss the metaphor of driving. In what ways was Aimee's reluctance to learn to drive a reflection of her life in general? And what did it signify when she did get her license?

4. Dating outside your faith is a highly personal decision. Have you ever done it? Why do you think Aimee was willing to date Peter in the first place, considering her beliefs?

5. What role did Peter play in Aimee's predicament? Did they break up because of her assumptions, or because of his behavior? Discuss his Christmas gift to her, and especially its packaging. How would you have responded?

6. Have you ever pretended to be something or someone you're not in the name of love? How did your results resemble Aimee's?

7. What role did Aimee's parents play in her decisions? Was she correct in her assumptions about what they really wanted for her? Why was Aimee so set on marrying a Jewish man, when her parents didn't seem to mind either way?

8. Discuss the concept of *shiksa* as a brand, especially Aimee's assertion that "Your brand stands for something to your customers. They can relate to who you are because somehow you've created a connection with their soul. And you can control that perception" (page 48). In her relationship with Josh, how did this work in Aimee's favor, and how did it work against her?

9. Throughout the book, characters buy into stereotypes: Josh thinks Aimee will order a cocktail because she's a shiksa; Krista thinks a Jewish man won't ever cheat; and so on. How does it harm them to make these assumptions, and how does it help them navigate life? Does it matter if they're right or wrong?

10. On page 59, Aimee tells Krista "I don't feel I'm doing anything to Josh he doesn't want done." Does she really believe this? In what ways was she right, and how was she wrong?

11. Re-read the section on page 153 in which Aimee compares herself to Esther. Is her comparison apt? Why?

12. At the Shabbat service, the rabbi says (page 263–4): "To lie is a fragmentation of the soul. It is fraud. And if you are successful,

if you are able to—pull it off—you cheat not only the people you lie to, but yourself. For you are not whole. You are broken." At what point does Aimee realize she is broken? Why does it take her so long? What does she do about it?

13. What about Josh? How did his treatment of eMay differ from the way he would've treated Aimee? Re-read the conversation they have in the Japanese restaurant, starting on page 280. Whose behavior was worse, ultimately?

14. Of all the many lies and betrayals Aimee commits during her shiksa period, in your opinion, which is the worst, and why? How did you feel about Aimee when she did that? Would you have forgiven her, if it were your life?

15. How does pretending to be a shiksa expand Aimee's worldview? Her personality? Her life experience? In the end, was it good for her? Would you ever want to try such an experiment?